A Different World

a&b

A Different World

MARY NICHOLS

Allison & Busby Limited
12 Fitzroy Mews
London W1T 6DW
www.allisonandbusby.com

First published in Great Britain by Allison & Busby in 2014.

A CIP catalogue record for this book is available from
the British Library.

First Edition

ISBN 978-0-7490-1553-4

Typeset in 11/16 pt Adobe Garamond Pro by
Allison & Busby Ltd.

The paper used for this Allison & Busby publication
has been produced from trees that have been legally sourced
from well-managed and credibly certified forests.

Printed and bound by
CPI Group (UK) Ltd, Croydon, CR0 4YY

Dedicated to all the brave Polish men and women who came to Britain in 1940 to fight, many of them to die, in the cause of freedom. And to those in Poland, who struggled on alone

Chapter One

1st September 1939

It was pandemonium in the playground. Some of the children were using up their excess energy chasing each other, laughing and shouting; others were subdued, standing about looking bewildered. Heaped up against the school wall were their abandoned cases and bags. The summer holidays had ended a few days earlier than usual and though they had rehearsed this exodus several times in the previous term, Louise doubted they really understood what was to happen. How could they, when she hardly knew herself? The authorities must be very sure there was going to be a war and the cities would be bombed to have organised such a mass evacuation of the capital's children.

Miss Hereward, the deputy head, had the school bell in her hand and rang it vigorously, as five charabancs pulled up at the kerb outside the school gates. The children subsided into silence. 'Find your cases, children, and get into your class lines,' she called out. 'You should know the drill by now.'

Louise grabbed two of her class by their coat collars. 'Lead the way, Frederick Jones, and you, too, Margaret Gordon. The rest of you fall in behind.'

The other teachers were doing the same and slowly order came out of chaos and eventually five double lines of children faced the school gates, ready to move off. Their cases had already been opened and examined to make sure they had everything on the list which had been sent home to the mothers. The boys were supposed to have spare pants, socks and a clean shirt, the girls knickers, socks and a second gingham dress or a skirt and blouse. Both should have pyjamas, a hairbrush, flannel, toothbrush and toothpaste. In spite of the heat of the day, they were dressed in an assortment of coats which were easier to wear than to pack. Each child had a packet of sandwiches and an apple to be consumed on the journey and a tin of corned beef and another of sliced peaches to be given to their foster mothers. Labels were pinned to their clothes inscribed with their names, addresses and the name of the school from which they had come. Similar labels were attached to their baggage. They also had small cardboard boxes containing their gas masks hung round their necks with their names on those too. It was easy to write lists, Louise thought, but although Edgware was by no means a deprived area, it was not so easy for some mothers to comply. And had anyone thought how heavy that lot would be for small children?

She called the register of her class of eight-year-olds and found two were missing.

'They ain't coming,' Freddie Jones told her. 'Their mum changed her mind. She said to tell you if they're going to die, they'll die together.'

'The Bright twins haven't come,' she told Miss Hereward, who was ushering her own class into the first of the charabancs.

'They're not the only ones. We'll have to go without them.'

Louise turned back to her crocodile of children and realised that Tommy Carter had firm hold of a very small child with every intention of boarding the bus with her.

'Thomas, who is this?'

'My little sister. Mum says I'm to take 'er wiv me and look after 'er.'

'But you can't do that. There's no provision . . .'

'But I gotta.'

Louise looked about her, wondering what to do. On the opposite side of the road, lined up along the kerb, were a crowd of mothers and a few fathers waiting to see their children off. Some were in tears, some stoically smiling, some stood in dumb misery. 'Is your mother over there?'

'No, she's gone to work. That's why I've gotta take Beattie wiv me. Me Auntie Gladys always looks after her when Mum's at work, but she's took her kids to the country and there's no one to see to Beattie. She ain't really me auntie,' he added as an afterthought.

'What about your father?'

'He's in the merchant navy, miss.'

The bus containing Miss Hereward and the top class had already moved off; Louise could not ask her advice. She looked down at the little girl who was sucking her thumb. 'How old is Beatrice?' she asked.

'It's Beattie, miss, and she's four. She's a good girl. She won't be no trouble, honest. I'll look after 'er.'

Louise could not see how he could be expected to do that. There was no telling what faced them at the end of the journey, but she could not possibly abandon the child. 'In that case you had better get on the bus,' she said. 'And mind you do look after her.' Perhaps, when they arrived at their destination, she could ask Miss Evans, who taught the five-year-olds, if she would have the little one in her class. And she would write to the child's mother.

The children had all been given stamped addressed postcards to send to their parents to tell them they had arrived safely and to pass on their addresses, but she ought to write to them herself to reassure them.

Theirs was the last bus to leave, the others were already out of sight. Louise climbed in behind the children and told the driver they were ready to go. They moved off with the children pressed against the windows waving to the watchers on the other side of the road. Looking back, Louise could see some of the parents had run into the middle of the road and were waving their handkerchiefs. She subsided into her seat beside Tommy and his sister. What lay ahead, no one knew. What lay behind her was her own parting with her parents.

Her father had been furious at her insistence on accompanying the children when the subject was first brought up earlier that summer. 'There is no need whatsoever for you to go with them,' he had said. 'There will be teachers where they are going. Your mother needs you here. You know she is not strong . . .'

'I'm all right,' her mother had put in feebly. She was so browbeaten by her domineering husband that she rarely ventured an opinion about anything without consulting him first. 'If Louise feels—'

'No, you are not all right,' he had snapped. 'And Louise will do as she's told.'

'I have been instructed to report with my class,' Louise said, being assertive for once in her life, though she worried about her mother. 'It's my job. It's what I'm paid to do.'

'You are paid to teach at Stag Lane Primary School, nowhere else. Goodness, I pulled enough strings with the local education authority to get you a post near home on account of your mother's ill health and I won't have that thrown in my face.'

'But I think the school is going to be shut down. I wouldn't have a job if I stayed behind.'

'Then you can stay at home and help your mother. She is finding the duties of a vicar's wife too onerous.'

'I'm sorry, Father, but I have duties too.'

'It is your duty to obey your father and mother. It is one of the ten commandments.'

'Honour, not obey,' Louise put in with a half smile. Her father was a stickler for exactitude and it gave her a tiny sense of triumph to correct him. She would not have dared to do it if she wasn't going away.

'Same thing,' he said. 'We won't split hairs. You will tell the school you cannot go.'

As far as he was concerned that was his last word, but for once in her life she had disobeyed him. She was twenty-three years old and the only time she had ever spent away from home was her three years at Homerton qualifying to be a teacher, and even then she returned home for every vacation and most weekends. But college had been her first taste of freedom. She had been nervous of going and it took her a long time to become used to the free and easy way the students behaved, the way they drank and smoked and talked about boys. It had given her an insight to a world outside the repressive atmosphere of the vicarage. Now she had been given the opportunity to cut the apron strings and she meant to take it.

The scene at the vicarage two hours before when she had said goodbye had been one of anger on her father's part, fear on her mother's and determination on hers. Father had shouted until he was red in the face, Mother had wept and so had she, but she would not change her mind. 'I am an adult,' she had said. 'I make my own decisions.'

'Adult, pah!' her father had said. 'If you go and find yourself in trouble, don't come whining back to me. I wash my hands of you.' With that he had stomped off into his study and slammed the door.

'What does he mean, find myself in trouble?' she asked her mother.

'I think he meant – you know – young men.'

'That's ridiculous. As if I would. I am a grown woman and I do know how to behave. It's been drummed into me enough.'

'I know, dear, I know.'

Louise hugged her mother. 'You do understand why I have to go, don't you?'

'Oh yes, I understand.' She had kissed her daughter's cheek. 'Don't worry, I'll be all right. Your father will calm down after you've gone. Let us have your address as soon as you know it.'

Louise looked round at the bus-load of children, wondering what their goodbyes had been like. It must have been heart-rending for their mothers to let them go. She wondered if she could have sent a child of hers to live with strangers, not even knowing where they were going to end up. It must have been a terrible decision to make, to weigh up the pros and cons of sending them to safety or keeping them at home to face whatever was to come. And how had Mrs Carter felt about giving little Beattie into the care of a eight-year-old boy? Louise looked down at the child still sucking her thumb, but apparently content, and could almost feel the pain of it herself.

'How long has your father been in the merchant navy?' she asked Tommy.

'Always,' he said. 'He's a stoker.'

'You said your mother had gone to work. What does she do?'

'She works at the Oaklands laundry.'

'Perhaps she will come and see you when you're settled.'

'Perhaps,' he said, but he didn't sound as if he believed it.

'When is Beattie due to start school?'

'When she's five.'

'When will that be?'

'Next June.'

'Oh, so there's a whole school year to go.'

'S'pose so.' He fetched a grubby handkerchief from his pocket and held it to Beattie's nose. 'Blow,' he commanded.

She obeyed and he wiped her nose and returned the handkerchief to his pocket.

'Do you often have to look after your sister?' Louise asked.

'Yes, after school and on Saturday mornings.'

'Do you mind?

'No, miss, she ain't no trouble. And Dad said I was to be the man of the house when he's away.'

'I'm sure you do it very well but you must wish sometimes you could go out and play with your friends.'

'I can do that when the jobs are done, but then Beattie comes too.'

Louise smiled, realising how restricting that must be, but apparently Tommy accepted his lot as something that couldn't be helped. The poor boy had had to grow up too fast. And now he was being given even more responsibility. If she could ease his burden a little, then she would do so.

The bus drew up outside Liverpool Street station and the children tumbled out to be organised into their crocodile again. When they had rehearsed it, they had simply reboarded the bus and been taken back to school. But today was different, today was the real thing. Louise marched them onto the station.

If it had been pandemonium at the school, the scene on the station was much more so. An engine with steam up and a string of carriages stood at every platform and hundreds, no thousands, of children were being herded into them by teachers, officials and station staff. And milling about in the concourse were hundreds of mothers, deterred from actually going onto the platforms to see the children off. It was bordering on panic as more and more children arrived and trains full to bursting were sent on their way. Louise supposed the scene was being duplicated at every main-line station in London. It had taken monumental organisation.

Louise halted her line of children and went to ask a man with a clipboard where the rest of the Stag Lane infants were. He consulted his list. 'They've gone. Went a few minutes ago. I suggest you get your children onto that one.' He indicated a train with the pencil he had in his hand. 'You'll catch up with them I expect.'

Louise returned to her group and ushered them into three adjacent rear carriages. Many of them had begun to realise that this adventure was not what they had expected. They didn't like the noise and the crowds and the absence of their mums. Some were crying, others, though dry-eyed, were feeling the tension that was all around them, even among the adults. A few were laughing or squabbling loudly about what they thought was going to happen. She settled them all into seats and stowed their small cases in the racks above their heads, then taking Beattie by the hand, found a seat for herself. The carriage doors were slammed shut by the guard, he blew his whistle and waved his green flag then hopped aboard as they began to move.

The station, the sidings, the dilapidated buildings beside the line were left behind as the train carried the children northwards away from the city and into the countryside. Where they were going, only the driver knew.

* * *

'They're late,' Mrs Wayne remarked to Mr Helliwell, the billeting officer. 'You don't suppose they're not coming, do you? We might as well send all these people home, they are getting decidedly restless.' Edith Wayne was the wife of the most prominent farmer in the village and a founder member of the local Women's Voluntary Service whose task it was to coordinate the homing of the evacuees. The village hall was the venue for prospective foster parents to meet the children they had agreed to take, some willingly, some reluctantly, but though the village women had turned up there was no sign of the London children.

'Wait a bit longer,' he said. 'It took heaven knows what to persuade some of them to come; if I send them away, I'll never get them back again. I'll ask Mrs Johns to make some more tea.'

They had already drunk two lots of tea and eaten all the biscuits and were grumbling. 'I ought to go home and get my old man's tea,' Mrs Sadler said. 'He'll have done the milking and cleaned up ages ago.'

'And mine has to go to a meeting of the Farmer's Union,' Mrs Barker said, accepting a cup of tea from Mrs Johns. 'If they don't turn up in the next ten minutes, I'm off.'

But ten minutes stretched to twenty and then forty and Mr Helliwell was on the point of telling them to go home when they heard a bus draw up in the school playground. A few minutes later the door opened and a bedraggled, filthy, smelly collection of urchins trooped into the room, blinking like owls in the light, for it was pitch-dark outside. They were followed by an adult carrying a small, sleeping girl.

'Oh, my God!' exclaimed Greta Sadler on behalf of all of them.

'I am sorry they are in such a state,' Louise said. 'But we have been travelling all day and some of them have been sick.'

'And some have messed their pants,' Honor Barker added,

15

wrinkling her nose. 'Hasn't anyone told them about lavatories?'

'Of course they have,' Louise said sharply, moving Beattie from one arm to the other. 'They are normally very clean, and are as unhappy about it as you are. It's been a trying and upsetting day for them. We left quite early this morning and they are all very tired.' She did not say she was exhausted too, that she had spent most of the journey holding children over the open window so they could be sick outside the carriage, taking some to the WC and trying to prevent the bigger boys peeing out of the windows, but if the toilets were in use and they were desperate, what else could they do? It was a pity they had to make a game of it.

Mr Helliwell came forward with his clipboard. 'Walthamstow Juniors?' he queried.

'No, Stag Lane Infants.'

'Where's that?'

'Edgware.'

'What happened to the Walthamstow lot?'

'I have no idea.' Beattie was heavy in her arms. She sank onto a wooden chair with the child on her lap. 'I don't even know where we are. It was dark by the time we reached Ely. We stopped there for ages while they shunted another engine onto our half of the train. I could not see where we were going after that. When we stopped again, we were told to leave the train and board the bus.'

'Where were you supposed to go?'

'I don't know that either. We were separated from the rest of the school.'

'No matter,' Edith said briskly. 'One place is as good as another and I reckon Cottlesham is as good as any. It's clear you can't go anywhere else tonight, so let's get these children into digs and cleaned up. Honor, you said two boys, didn't you? And Greta two

16

girls. Pauline, a girl. I don't mind which I have myself. I've got room for a family.'

Gradually the children were paired with their new foster mothers and were taken away. Louise watched them go with some trepidation; they looked lost and bewildered, so tired they were past crying. One or two who had siblings in the other classes were worried about what had happened to them and what their mothers would say when they heard they had been separated. Someone had offered to take Tommy Carter, but he had steadfastly refused to go without his sister. Beattie had woken and was grizzling. 'Hush, sweetheart,' she said. 'We'll soon have you comfy and in bed.' But she wasn't too sure of that. Mrs Wayne had said something about driving them round the village knocking on doors. How humiliating to have to beg like that.

She was drinking a cup of tea when a very large man entered the room. He was in his early forties with a mop of pure-white hair and the bluest eyes Louise had ever seen. 'I'm not too late, am I? Couldn't get here before. Some of those RAF chaps are a bit boisterous and I didn't like to leave Jenny on her own.' He eyed Tommy and Beattie. 'This all that's left?'

Louise gave him a tired smile. 'I'm afraid so.'

'You their mother?'

'No, I'm Louise Fairhurst, their teacher.'

'Poor you.'

'It's not me who needs sympathy, but the children,' she said. 'Are you going to take these two? I must find digs for myself when I know everyone has been homed.'

'I'm not sure about the little girl.'

'I'm afraid it's both or neither. Thomas has strict orders from his mother to look after his sister.'

The man grinned. 'Right you are, then. Come along.' He took

Beattie from her. The child squirmed and tried to reach back to Louise. 'Don't worry, little one,' he said. 'Your teacher is coming too.'

'Go along,' Mrs Wayne told Louise, as she hesitated. 'The other children will be all right tonight. I'll come and see you in the morning and we can check on them together.'

Thomas, determined not to lose sight of his sister, was disappearing through the door behind the big man. Louise retrieved her suitcase from the doorstep where she had left it and went after them.

Her billet, she discovered after a short ride in a pony and trap, was a public house called The Pheasant. She had never set foot in a public house in her life and smiled to herself as she followed their host round the side of the building and in at the back door; her father would be horrified if he could see her. In his eyes, public houses were dens of iniquity.

She found herself in a large kitchen. A woman in her late thirties was washing glasses at the sink. She turned when they came in, dried her hands and gave them a smile of welcome. 'You must be exhausted,' she said to Louise, while taking Beattie from the man.

'This is my wife, Jenny,' he said. 'I'm Stan Gosport, by the way. We run the pub.'

Louise said 'How do you do,' and offered her hand which was taken in a huge clasp and pumped up and down.

Jenny laughed as Louise winced. 'Stan don't know his own strength.'

'I'm Louise Fairhurst, the children's teacher.' She put her hand on Thomas's shoulder. 'This is Thomas Carter and his sister Beatrice.'

'I'm Tommy, not Thomas,' the boy insisted. 'And that's Beattie. She's four.'

'Let's get you to bed,' Jenny said. 'Time enough tomorrow to learn your way around. Come along, young man.'

Jenny set off along a hall and up a flight of stairs, with Tommy at her heels. 'Have you heard the news?' she asked over her shoulder, as Louise followed.

'No. We've been on the move all day.' The strange smell coming from the front of the building was beer, she concluded, though she could no longer smell it by the time they reached the landing.

'Hitler has invaded Poland. I reckon that's put the lid on it. There'll be a war now, for sure.'

'Oh dear, I'm afraid you are right.'

The pub was a large one if the number of doors leading off the upper landing were anything to go by. In no time at all the children had been washed and put into night clothes and tucked into bed, and Louise found herself in a comfortable bedroom next door to them. For the first time that day she was alone and quiet and able to contemplate a day that had been like no other.

She was exhausted, but though she went to bed, she could not sleep; there was too much going on in her head. She could still feel the movement of the train, the rattle as it went over points, the whistle as it approached a station and ran through without stopping, the sudden silence as they sat motionless in a siding while a freight train rumbled past. She could still hear the children: 'Miss, I feel sick. Miss, Johnny's eaten my sandwich. Miss, I want to go to the toilet. Miss, where are we? Where are we going?'

Where were they? The name Cottlesham meant nothing to her, but she supposed they were in Cambridgeshire or Norfolk; name boards had been taken down from the railway stations and, being unfamiliar with the line, she could only guess where they were.

19

What had happened to the rest of the school? There had obviously been a mix-up, but would it be put right? The thought of taking the children on yet another train and having them looked over like so much cattle all over again was daunting. If they stayed where they were, she would have to make some arrangements about the children's schooling.

Added to that the news was grim. Mr Chamberlain had tried appeasement the year before and had given way to Hitler over Czechoslovakia, but the previous March the dictator had broken his promise not to try to extend his territory and had occupied the whole of Czechoslovakia, not just the Sudetenland. His next demand had been for the Danzig Corridor, part of Poland. Britain and France had promised to help the Poles if Poland was attacked and they could not go back on that. War looked inevitable, which was why the children had been evacuated and why the territorial army had been mobilised. She wondered what war would mean to the ordinary man and woman. The last conflict had been horrific: so many young men dead, wives left without husbands, children without fathers, parents without sons. Others had been so badly wounded or their lungs so irrevocably damaged by mustard gas they could not work again. Was that what they had to look forward to this time?

She slept at last and woke when Jenny knocked and came in with a cup of tea. 'The children are having their breakfast. He's a funny one, that Tommy. He's looking after his little sister like a mother hen with a chick.'

Louise sipped the tea, which was hot and strong. 'I think he's had to do a lot of that. His mother works in a laundry and his father is in the merchant navy.'

'Poor kid. What are you planning to do today?'

'I must try and locate the rest of my school and I must check on the children and find somewhere to use as a classroom, if we are to stay here. Where is here, by the way?'

Jenny laughed. 'Don't you know?'

'I believe the village is called Cottlesham but where it is and how big it is, I have no idea.'

'Cottlesham is a small farming village in Norfolk. The nearest town is Swaffham. That's where we go for most of our shopping and where the nearest railway station is. There's a bus that goes from the main road a couple of times a day. You can get to Norwich by bus too, if you want a day out.'

'I'd better get up,' she said. 'I have a feeling today is going to be busy.'

Tommy and Beattie, apparently fully recovered from their journey, had gone out to play when Louise went down for her own breakfast, a huge plateful of fried food which went a long way to making up for the meagre rations of the day before. She had barely finished when Mrs Wayne arrived in a battered Ford and breezed into the kitchen.

'I've come to take you round the village to inspect the children's accommodation,' she said. 'And we'll call in at the schoolhouse to see John Langford. He's the headmaster, you'll need to liaise with him. He lost a leg in the last war but he gets round pretty well on a wooden one.'

Louise realised that not only would she be the children's teacher but responsible for their general welfare as well, especially since she seemed to have lost the rest of her school and the more senior teachers. 'Thank you. I was thinking the same thing.'

'I checked all the accommodation with Mr Helliwell last week,' Edith told her as they set off. 'Some of the villagers were reluctant to take children and found all sorts of excuses not to have them. I didn't feel I ought to insist; it wouldn't be in the children's interests, but most of them were OK about it. Anyway, if we find we have misfits, we can always move them.'

Her cheerful no-nonsense attitude calmed Louise's nerves and she was able to look about her. The village was a typical country village with narrow roads and high hedges. There was a lovely old church and, tucked away up a long drive, Cottlesham Hall, the home, so she was told, of Sir Edward Dryton. Most of the houses were concentrated round the church, the school and a windmill, but further out were farmsteads and smallholdings.

'There's a post office and general store,' Mrs Wayne told her, indicating a shop on the corner. 'There's also a butcher, a baker, a smithy and a cobbler. Mr Chapman comes round once a week with his grocery van, a milkman does his rounds every day with a trailer and a churn on the back of his bicycle, and a baker delivers bread, also on a bicycle, but that's about it, I'm afraid. Not like London, eh?'

'No, but I expect we'll get used to it.'

'You have to go into Swaffham if you need anything the post office hasn't got.'

'I'm told there's a bus . . .'

'Yes, though let me know if you want to go, I might be going myself and can take you.'

'That's kind of you.'

Mrs Wayne pulled up outside the tiny school, beside which was a schoolhouse. 'We'll see Mr Langford first, shall we?'

John Langford was in his fifties and his wooden leg consisted of a peg on which he stumped around quite agilely. 'The kids call me old peg leg,' he told Louise, after they had been introduced. 'Only behind my back, of course.' He had untidy fair hair and a scar on his cheek which disappeared when he smiled.

'How many children do you have?'

22

'Eighty divided into two classes. I take the older ones and Miss Sedgewick the younger ones. Come, I'll show you.' He led the way from the schoolhouse, across a small yard and through a door at the side of the school.

Louise found herself in one large room with a pot-bellied stove in the middle surrounded by a mesh fireguard. There were rows of double desks, two teachers' desks and two blackboards. 'We divide the room with those curtains when we need to teach them separately' he said, pointing.

'It's clear you can't accommodate any more,' Louise said. 'What am I to do? I have twenty-four. Are there any other premises which might be suitable?'

'Can't think of anything offhand. There's the village hall, where you were last night, but that's in use a lot of the time, Women's Institute, Boy Scouts, Girl Guides, parish council meetings, and the doctor comes from Swaffham once a week and uses it as a surgery. I'm afraid we'll have to share.'

'If we are still here,' Louise said. 'I have no idea where the rest of my school ended up.'

'I gather there was a certain amount of confusion,' he said with a laugh. 'But I doubt they'll move everybody round again, it'd be like ring a ring o' roses. Besides, the government has more than enough on its plate dealing with the political situation to worry about where the children are. As long as they have homes and an education, that's all that matters.'

'You are probably right.'

They returned to the schoolhouse. 'Do sit down.' He indicated a horsehair sofa. Louise perched on it next to Mrs Wayne and he took a dining chair. 'Let's thrash this out.'

After some discussion, they decided the village children would use the school from eight-thirty to one, and the evacuees from one-thirty to four one week and then they would reverse it for the following week. 'You will need to find your own books and pencils,' he said. 'Your own LEA should provide those.'

'Of course. I'll write to them.'

'If we find the children's education suffering, we could open the school on Saturday mornings,' he added.

Louise laughed. 'I can just imagine what the children will think of that.'

'Yes, but they will only be in school half the day during the week. Mind you, my lot will have to be given homework to make up for it.'

'And I must do the same.' She paused. 'We are making all these arrangements without having any idea how long it will go on. I thought there might have been a declaration of war before now. Do you think they are still trying to prevent it?'

'Perhaps, but they are wasting their time if you ask me, and in the meantime, Poland suffers, not that the general public feel very strongly about that. Half of them don't know where the place is.'

'Then I think geography will need to be part of the curriculum,' Louise said, then laughed. 'Oh, dear, that sounds pretentious and I didn't mean it to be. I've only been teaching a couple of years and it's a huge responsibility.'

'I'm sure you'll cope, but if you need any help, don't hesitate to ask.'

'And you can call on me for anything to do with the children's welfare,' Mrs Wayne put in. She had been sitting listening to the arrangements without joining in the discussion. 'There isn't much I don't know about the village.'

'Thank you, both of you.' She rose. 'I must go and let the children and their foster parents know about the arrangements.'

He stood up, balancing himself on his peg leg. 'My children

will come to school as usual on Monday morning, so I'll take mornings the first week,' he said. 'Is that agreeable?'

'Yes, perfectly.'

They shook hands and Louise followed Mrs Wayne out to the car.

'He's a good teacher,' Edith said as she put the car into gear and they drove off. 'Strict, but fair, and he doesn't put up with any nonsense. He got four children through the scholarship last term. They'll be going to Hamond's Grammar School in Swaffham next week. Now, I suggest we visit the nearest billets first and then work our way outwards. I live a couple of miles away, so we'll go there last and you can have a cup of coffee while we deal with any problems we've found.'

The children seemed to have recovered from the previous day's events and most had gone off exploring a countryside many had never seen before, so Louise did not see them. Their accommodation varied from the mansion home of Sir Edward Dryton, to substantial farmhouses and two-up two-down cottages with no electricity, mains water or sewerage. Some were a great deal cleaner than others, but unless they were very bad and a danger to the children's health and welfare, their offer of accommodation had been accepted. 'I don't suppose a bit of dust bothers the children as long as they get enough to eat,' Mrs Wayne said as she drove down a narrow winding lane bordered by cow parsley, stinging nettles and blackberry bushes from which most of the fruit had been picked.

'I am grateful for all your work,' Louise said. 'I don't know what I would have done if I'd had to find homes for the children myself.'

'Happy to help.' She braked suddenly to avoid a sheep running in the road. 'How did that get out?' She came to a stop and left the car to catch the animal. Louise followed to help, though dealing with farm animals was outside the scope of her experience and she did no more than watch.

'It's one of Bill Young's,' Edith said when she had her arms round the ewe's neck. 'He's usually careful about shutting gates. Let's get it back where it belongs.' She bundled it through an open gate and shut it firmly, just as a man in his thirties came up the road on a bicycle. 'Your gate was left open, Bill,' she said.

'It's them pesky evacuees,' he said, dismounting. 'I ha' bin behind 'em all morning. Don't know how to go on, they don't.'

'I'm dreadfully sorry,' Louise said. 'They are not used to country ways. I'll make sure it doesn't happen again.'

He turned to look at her, appraising her from head to foot, taking in her tweed skirt, neat blouse and flat-heeled shoes. 'You in charge of 'em?'

'This is Miss Fairhurst, their schoolteacher,' Mrs Wayne told him. 'Miss Fairhurst, Bill Young. He farms at Belmont Farm, just down the road here. He's taken Frederick Jones and Harold Summers.'

Louise shook hands with him. His grip was firm and dry. 'I suppose we've all got a lot to learn,' he said. 'But just you mek sure those childer of yours know how important it is to shut gates.'

'I will.' It seemed the children were all going to be lumped together and called hers. She felt a bit like Mother Hubbard. 'Do you think you could come to the school and talk to them about it?'

'OK. When?'

'The sooner the better. Monday afternoon, if you can manage it.'

'I'll be there at two o'clock.' He went over to the gate to check that all his sheep were safely in the field and the women continued on their way.

'You've made a conquest there,' Edith said. 'He's not usually so tolerant. As for talking to a class full of children, that really is one for the book. I wouldn't mind listening in on that.'

'You can if you like.'

Edith laughed. 'No, I'll leave you to it.' She turned in at a gate and drove up to the door of a substantial farmhouse. 'Here we are.'

The house was large and the kitchen, reflecting its importance, was vast. It had a scrubbed table in its centre which was scattered with papers. 'Sorry about this,' Edith said, gathering them up and dumping them on the pine dresser which occupied almost the whole of one wall. 'WVS business. Do sit down.' She set about making coffee with water from a kettle already on a black range.

With cups of coffee in front of them they talked about the children, the billets they had been given and their individual needs. It was, Louise mused, far beyond the business of teaching for which she had trained. 'Mr and Mrs Young will have their hands full taking in both Freddie and Harry,' she said. 'They are two of the most mischievous in the whole class and egg each other on. Perhaps they should be separated.'

'I'm sure the Youngs are up to it,' Mrs Wayne said. 'Let's leave them for the moment and see how they go on.'

'I wonder what's going to happen,' Louise mused. 'If there's a war we're all going to have to make adjustments.'

'I don't think there's any "if" about it, do you?'

'No, not really.'

She returned to the pub to eat a midday meal with Mr and Mrs Gosport and Tommy and Beattie. Tommy was full of what they had seen in the village and their encounter with two village children. 'I couldn't understand them,' he said. 'I don' think they were talkin' English.'

'Course they were,' Stan said. 'It's just a bit different, that's all. You'll soon get used to it.'

Louise felt a particular responsibility for these two, but Jenny had been designated their foster mother and she was perfectly capable. Louise felt able to spend the afternoon in her room writing letters. There were a great many, one to every child's parents which she piled up with the postcards she had collected on her rounds that morning; and one to the headmaster at Stag Lane. He had elected to stay behind and teach those children who had not been evacuated. And, of course, there was one to her own parents in which she was careful to upgrade the pub into a very nice hotel. By the time she had finished, her fingers ached and she was glad to walk to the post office and explore the village on foot.

Everyone she met gave her a nod and a 'Good day, Miss', which told her the village grapevine had already been to work.

It was not until the children had been put to bed and she sat down to an evening meal in the dining room of the pub that she met the other residents, two young men helping to build an extension to the airfield at nearby Watton. At about thirty-five, Alfred Lynch was the older of the two and was, she learnt, a foreman. He was of stocky build with massive shoulders and a thick neck. Tony Walsh, on the other hand, was only a year or two older than she was, slender but wiry. He had dark hair and amber eyes. He was a quantity surveyor. The two men had been working on airfields for a year, ever since it became obvious that war could not be put off forever and the government had begun a frenzied building programme. They obviously enjoyed each other's company and were full of jokes and laughter. Louise found their good humour refreshing.

'A Hawker biplane tried to land on the airfield this morning,'

Alfred said. 'I think the pilot was lost and didn't know it wasn't operational. Got stuck in the mud. We had a fine old time digging it out. But it was the mud that saved the pilot, I reckon. Gave him a nice soft landing.'

'Was it able to take off again?' Louise asked.

'Yes, after we'd mustered all hands and a tractor with a tow rope and dragged it onto a bit of concrete runway we'd finished.'

'The pilot looked a bit sick,' Tony put in. 'I don't think he'd been flying long.'

'If that's what the RAF is turning out, God help us,' Alfred said. 'We'll be needing good pilots before long.'

'You reckon?' Stan queried.

'No doubt of it. Why d'you think we're building all these airfields?'

'Airfields or no, I've got to open up,' Stan said, getting to his feet. 'If you fancy a drink in the bar later, Miss Fairhurst, just come through.'

'Yes, do come,' Tony said. 'Talking to someone intelligent will be a change from listening to Alfred's nonsense.'

'Talking of nonsense,' Alfred said, grinning. 'Who was it said a couple of Jerry spies had come down by parachute dressed as nuns?'

'I was only repeating something I heard,' Tony said. 'Doesn't mean I believed it. I only said it to illustrate how gullible some people are.'

The men went into the lounge bar and Louise helped Jenny wash up before joining them. It was then she tasted her first glass of beer. She was enjoying the banter, the noise and laughter so much she didn't even notice her glass had been refilled. As she went up to bed that night, she was smiling.

It seemed her head had only just hit the pillow when she was woken by a loud rumbling which turned out to be thunder. She went to the window and drew back the curtains. Outside, lightning lit the sky, followed almost immediately by rolls of thunder. And the rain was lashing down, drenching the garden and the empty car park.

'A fitting end to my first day in the country,' she murmured before going back to bed.

The next morning the rain had gone and the sun was shining. She took Tommy and Beattie to church and it was there that she learnt Mr Chamberlain's efforts to avert war had come to nothing. The Reverend Mr Capstick told his congregation the news after he had finished his sermon. 'It is war,' he said, then offered a prayer for all those involved before giving the final blessing. Afterwards, as he stood in the porch shaking hands with everyone and discussing the situation, Louise introduced herself, knowing her father would expect her to do so. He would be bound to quiz her on what manner of man the incumbent was and his style of delivery. It was very different from her father's, being gentler, more tolerant; there was nothing of the fire and brimstone that characterised her father's sermons. He was younger, of course, not much older than she was, fresh-faced and smiling.

'I am very pleased to meet you, Miss Fairhurst,' he said. 'The village school is a Church of England school and I go there once a week to teach the Gospel to the whole school. I hope your children will join us.'

Louise explained about the arrangements for sharing which meant the London children would not be at the school as the same time as the village children. 'Some of them are Catholic,' she said. 'And I have one or two who are Jews.'

'No matter, my lessons are meant for all. I do not differentiate, but I leave it to you if you feel some should be excused. When you're settled, I'll make arrangements to come to your class separately. That is, if you agree.'

'Yes, of course, always supposing we are not moved again.'

'I do not think that is likely to happen in the near future, do you?'

'No. It is all very worrying. I feel so responsible. I don't want to let the children and the school down. I've only been teaching a year or two and am still groping my way.'

His smile was engaging. 'I am sure you will manage admirably, Miss Fairhurst.'

She hoped and prayed she would. Her life up to then, protected and dominated as she had been, was not the best grounding for the task ahead of her. But she was not the only one to be asked to step outside the comfort of the familiar. Every single person, man, woman or child, young or old, was going to have to adapt if this war was to be won.

Chapter Two

Rulka was filthy and exhausted. The daughter of a doctor and a nurse, she had never considered doing anything else but nursing, but never in her worst nightmare had she envisioned this horror of death and destruction. There had been so many casualties brought to hospital where she worked – torn and broken limbs, appalling burns, smashed faces – it was impossible to keep up with them. She had stayed on duty well over her allotted time but Lech Andersz, the doctor under whom she worked, had seen her exhaustion and sent her home. 'Stay away at least twenty-four hours,' he had said. 'And get some sleep.'

Realising he was right and she could not go on without rest, she left the hospital and picked her way over the rubble, making for the Śląsko-Dąbrowski Bridge over the Vistula and her apartment in Zabowski Street. Warsaw had been known as the Paris of the East, with its wide boulevards, its beautiful parks where people went to enjoy the tranquillity, its shops, ancient churches and magnificent mansions whose window boxes in summer had been vibrant with geraniums. She stopped on the bridge to look back at the city that had been her home all her life. From here she had a good view of the river winding its way northwards and the old town which extended down to the river. By turning a little she could see the Royal Castle, standing proud on its hill despite the bombing.

How much of it would be left by the time the Germans had finished with it? Already half its buildings were in ruins, its parks dug up to make air raid shelters, furniture and even trolley buses were piled up in the streets to make barricades. Every able-bodied person had been called upon to help dig defence ditches on the western outskirts of the city and they had answered the call in their thousands, digging in the mud and diving for cover whenever a German Stuka flew over and dropped its bombs. Many had died there. What good were trenches against bombers? They bombed indiscriminately: churches, schools, hospitals, people in the countryside tending their fields, nothing and no one was safe. And there was little the Polish air force could do about it; their out-of-date aircraft were no match for the German Messerschmitts and Stukas. Jan was flying with the Polish Air Force and she prayed for his safety.

She had met Jan Grabowski in 1938 when he came to the hospital with a broken arm after crash-landing his fighter during a foolhardy manoeuvre. He had been disciplined for it, but as he was one of the famous Kościuszko Squadron's best pilots, he had been let off with a caution. He was so handsome, so full of energy, so courteous and cheerful, she had fallen for him instantly. Theirs had been a whirlwind romance, which was typical of the way Jan went about his life. With the full approval of both sets of parents they had married the year before and made their home in the Praga district on the right bank of the river. They rented a small apartment on the ground floor of a fairly new block which had a comfortable living room, an adequate kitchen, two bedrooms and a bathroom, which she had taken great pride in furnishing and equipping.

But they had had little time to enjoy married life because of the cloud of war which would not go away, in spite of the British prime minister's assurance that he had come to an agreement with Hitler that there would be no more German encroachment of territory. Few in Poland had believed it, but they had believed England and France would instantly come to their aid if they were attacked. The Allies had dithered and then declared war two days after the Germans invaded, but that was all they had done. 'Did they think that simply declaring war would frighten the Nazis into going home?' Jan had said. He had been preparing to leave at the time. Their airfield had been so badly bombed and so many aircraft destroyed on the ground, the remnants had been ordered to scatter to temporary airfields all over Poland. She had not heard from him for some time and was not sure where he was.

German tanks and big guns were coming ever closer to the capital, though according to the news bulletins they listened to every day, a counteroffensive had been launched and was holding them back. But for how long? Already people were fleeing in droves, using whatever transport they could find, cars, vans, handcarts, bicycles and prams, most making for Romania. Some had taken to the river in pleasure boats and were hoping to reach Gdansk and ships to take them to safety. She wanted her parents to go but they had flatly refused and were practically living in the cellar of their home on Jasna Street. She worried about them. Perhaps she ought to stay with them. If the bridges were destroyed, she would have trouble getting to the hospital; it would be better to stay on the same side of the river.

She let herself into the apartment, hurried to have a bath and scramble back into her uniform, donning a clean apron and cap. Then she packed a small bag, tied her cloak about her shoulders and was about to leave when her husband arrived.

'Jan!' She dropped her bag and flung herself into his arms, making him rock back on his heels.

He kissed her hungrily and then held her at arm's length to look at her face. 'You look worn out, sweetheart.'

'Aren't we all? You aren't looking so good yourself. When did you last have a night's sleep?' She had never seen Jan looking so down. His face was pale and his blue eyes had lost their customary sparkle. Even his fair hair looked dull.

'I forget.'

'How long have you got now?'

'Just as long as it takes to say goodbye.'

'Goodbye,' she echoed in dismay. 'Jan, what's happened?'

'We have been ordered to fly to Romania and continue the fight from there.'

'You can't mean you are abandoning Poland?'

'No, of course not, but we can't risk losing the aircraft. The Allies were supposed to send us more, but it was considered too risky to land them on Polish soil and there's been some problem about them landing in Romania. It's probably only a mix-up, but we can't count on them.'

'What you mean is the war is lost.' She was fighting back tears of disappointment and anger: disappointment that no practical help had arrived from Britain and France in spite of their promises, and anger that no one seemed able to do anything against the onslaught. And worst of all, Jan was leaving the country. It wasn't his fault, he had to obey orders, but she railed against those who had issued the orders.

'We have to concede that the battle is lost for the moment,

35

but it is not the end. Poland will fight on.' He spoke with enough fervour to convince her he meant it. 'All the same, I want you to leave, get out while you can.'

'I can't do that, Jan, I'm needed here. There's my work at the hospital. They can't spare me. And Mama and *Tata* refuse to go and I can't leave them.' Unlike Jan who came from Białystok, she was a true Varsovian and no one had given her any orders to leave.

'But I can't bear to think of you here in the middle of all this bombing. And when the *shkopy* come . . .'

'If they come. Perhaps they will be stopped before they get this far.'

'Perhaps,' he said, but he didn't sound very convincing. 'But if they get close, promise me you'll leave. Make for Romania. If you can get to France, so much the better.'

'I'll think about it if I have to. You never know, the situation might improve.'

'If it doesn't?'

'Then I'll leave.'

He pulled her into his arms again. 'I wish I didn't have to go. I should be here, protecting you, not running away . . .'

'You aren't running away, Jan. You'd never run away from anything. I never knew anyone so fearless.'

'You're pretty fearless yourself, my love.'

'I'm doing my job, just as you are doing yours. When do you think we'll be together again?'

'God knows. I'll try and get word to you where I am. Perhaps later you'll be able to join me.'

'Or the war will end and you will come back.'

'Or the war will end and I will come back,' he said.

He stopped only long enough to share a last meal with her and then he hugged and kissed her one last time and was gone. She managed to remain dry-eyed until the door closed on him, then she sank onto a chair at the table, still scattered with the remains of their meal, put her arms on the table and her head on her arms and sobbed her heart out.

But wars were not won with tears. She mopped them up, rinsed her face in cold water and went back to work. Nursing the sick and injured would stop her dwelling on her own misery. There were plenty of people far worse off than she was.

Riding a motorcycle borrowed from a colleague Jan made his way over the bridge and turned south, avoiding the debris of bombed buildings which spilt out onto the streets and the hoses of the men fighting the fires. He hoped and prayed Rulka would see sense and leave. As soon as he arrived in Romania and knew where the squadron was billeted, he would insist she join him. She was a brave one, his wife, and a good nurse too, efficient and compassionate without being sentimental, at least where her patients were concerned. As the woman he loved with his whole heart, she was as loving and passionate as it was possible for any woman to be. He was a lucky devil. If it hadn't been for that foolish episode trying to fly under a bridge and coming to grief, he might never have met her. They came from different worlds.

He was the younger son of wealthy Count Tadeusz Grabowski and his wife Zofia who had an extensive estate near Białystok, in north-east Poland, not far from the Russian border. Intended for the cavalry along with his elder brother, Jozef, he had insisted from his early teens that he wanted to fly. His parents had opposed the idea: his father because the Grabowski men had always gone into the cavalry, his mother because she saw it as foolhardy and dangerous. But he was nothing if not persistent and, after he had finished at the university, they had let him apply for a place at the Polish Air Force Academy at Dęblin, hoping, he thought, though they did not say so, that he would fail in view of the strong competition. But he would not countenance failure. In 1936, he had been one of the ninety young men accepted out of six thousand applicants.

Seventy miles south of Warsaw, the Academy's headquarters was a magnificent eighteenth-century manor house and here he had learnt not only to fly, but to fight. In the classroom they learnt aerodynamics, navigation and maintenance. In practical sessions they learnt to fly several different aircraft, to use the aircraft's guns and to keep their wits and eyes about them at all times. Discipline had been strict but that didn't stop their off-duty escapades and that was how Jan had come to accept the challenge to fly under the bridge, realised too late that it could not be done and crash-landed in a field beside the river. It had been a hard lesson to learn, but learn it he had. On graduation he had, to his great delight, been posted to the Kościuszko Squadron based just outside Warsaw, enabling him to see more of Rulka.

The war had put paid to fun and games. On the first day of September, Hitler had invaded on some trumped-up excuse that Polish troops had raided German territory. Now, so Jan had been told, there were over fifty German divisions on Polish soil, well-equipped with guns and tanks, not to mention hundreds of aircraft waging a war of terror on Polish troops and civilians alike. The fighters of the Polish Air Force were outnumbered and outgunned. Jan, along with his fellow flyers, had adopted a strategy of climbing above the bombers and diving down on them, or if that were not possible, they would fly at them head-on waiting until the last minute before firing their guns and peeling away. It was a question of whose nerve broke first and Jan and his comrades were determined it would not be theirs. They had fought ferociously until, almost out of fuel and spare parts, it became obvious that if they did not withdraw they would lose the little they had left. Hence his unpalatable orders.

He saw a newsboy standing on a corner with a pile of papers, shouting something that sounded like 'Russia'. He stopped and bought a copy, sitting astride his machine to read it. Molotov, the Soviet leader, had made a deal with Hitler and the Red Army had invaded Poland from the east. He thought immediately of his parents. He hoped they would escape and not try to hold onto their lands, though he doubted his autocratic father would give them up without a fight. He stuffed the paper in the front of his jacket and turned the motorcycle round, intending to go back to Rulka and make her come with him. It was probably already too late to do anything to help his parents.

The eerie sound of an air raid siren rose and fell, warning of another raid, making the people on the street scuttle for cover. It didn't occur to him to do the same. He stood astride his machine and watched as the sky became full of Stuka bombers, accompanied by powerful Messerschmitts, the fastest aeroplanes in the world. If only the Polish Air Force had aircraft like those it would be a different story. He saw the bombs falling, heard the explosions, saw the clouds of dust and smoke and then the flames and shook his fist at the sky, a futile gesture if ever there was one. He swore vengeance.

A staff car came speeding along the road and stopped beside him. There was a general in the rear seat. 'Where are you going, Captain?' he asked.

Jan hesitated. Going back to Rulka would be tantamount to desertion; he could not disgrace his name and his squadron by doing that. 'To rejoin my squadron, General, sir.'

'Then don't stand about here. Get going. We can't afford to lose pilots.'

Jan knew that. Air force casualties had been severe but there wasn't a man in the squadron who wasn't prepared to fight and die if necessary. That was where he belonged. He saluted and rode away, turning his back on his beloved wife.

He felt terrible and could hardly see where he was going for the tears that filled his eyes. The road he took was jammed with people and their pathetic bundles fleeing the capital. Where did they expect to find a haven? Would Hungary and Romania take them in? Or were they going east towards the Russians believing they were preferable to the Nazis? And there were columns of troops trying to get through them, marching to defend their homeland and being hindered by this tidal wave. Did the rest of the world know what was happening? Did they care? Poor Poland didn't stand a chance. Between them, Germany and Russia would gobble the country up, as had happened in the past, times without number. Only since 1918, when the Poles had ousted the Russians, had they been an independent republic, their boundaries decided by the Allies at the Treaty of Versailles. It was those boundaries they were set on keeping.

He turned the cycle off the road and bumped off across country, hoping to get ahead of the exodus. The sooner he got to grips with this war, the sooner it would be over and he could go back to Rulka. He had promised her he would.

Romania, fearing for its own safety, reneged on its mutual defence treaty with Poland and declared itself neutral. When the Polish squadrons landed, their aircraft were impounded and the airmen interned, something Jan and his fellow pilots had not foreseen. Jan's spirits, already low at having to leave Rulka, plunged even further when faced with the prospect of spending the rest of the war on the sidelines. But the thought of Rulka facing heaven knew what terrors in Warsaw roused him from his state of apathy. He was determined to escape and fight on, and spent long hours discussing with his comrades how this could be done.

The first they knew that there were forces at work on their behalf was when a Polish go-between slipped Captain Witold Urbanowicz a roll of money and a stack of false identity cards, and told him to distribute them among the men and instruct them to make their way in ones and twos to Bucharest. There the new Polish government-in-exile, headed by General Sikorski, had enlisted the help of the British and French Embassies who were prepared to do all they could to help the Polish flyers escape. 'Guilty consciences, that's what,' Jan murmured when he heard this.

The first of them left that night, their absence covered by the remainder. The next night more went and a few hours later the last of them set off, scattering in the countryside. Some walked, some stole bicycles, others jumped freight trains. Jan and two others hopped on a passenger train just as it was drawing out of the station and hid in the lavatories until they reached their destination. They had been warned that Bucharest was crawling with Gestapo agents on the lookout for Polish military personnel and were told to rid themselves of anything that might label them Polish. They bought themselves civilian suits, but Jan hung on to a snapshot of Rulka and his pilot's wings. 'I might need to prove I can fly,' he told Witold with an attempt at a grin.

They had been told to report to a secret evacuation centre set up in a private apartment, where they were issued with false passports manufactured secretly in the basement of the Polish Embassy. These they used to make their way to the Black Sea and onto ships which would take them to freedom. Freedom yes, but not in Poland, not even in Romania. They were heading for France, away from the people and places they loved. Jan stood at the ship's rail and watched the land disappear and wondered when, if ever, he would see his country and his wife again.

Rulka was burying her parents when a lone Messerschmitt flew over and machine-gunned the cortège. There was nothing and nobody to stop it. The pall-bearers hesitated only a second or two before dropping the coffins and scattering to take shelter among the gravestones as bullets spattered along the cemetery path. Two of them were killed and one injured. The black-clad Rulka, grieving for her parents, went to the latter's help. The living took precedence over the dead. And nowadays there were so many dead.

Her parents, Jozef and Rosa Kilinski, were not alone. They had ventured out between air raids to try and buy provisions. There were so many air raids that the all-clear no sooner sounded on one than the siren went again for the next. Standing in a queue hoping to buy bread, they ignored it and paid for that with their lives.

It was lucky that the family had a plot in the Powązki cemetery, otherwise they could have been buried anywhere. There were so many bodies they were being interred in parks and gardens and even along grass verges, usually by their relatives; there were too many for the city's regular gravediggers. And it wasn't just bombs the people were having to contend with. The Germans were now close enough to train their heavy guns on the city. Walls tumbled, glass was scattered everywhere, fires started and smoke billowed over it all, making the already red-rimmed eyes of those who ventured out of their holes smart and fill with tears. Food was running short and it was a case of risking death or injury in order to find something to eat.

Since Jan had left what had been bad had become infinitely

worse. As far as Rulka was concerned the desecration of her parents' funeral was the last straw. Far from making her cowed, it put steel into her backbone and turned her heart to stone. Not until Hitler and his minions had been defeated and the death of every Polish man, woman and child avenged, would she soften.

She went back to work at the hospital, sleeping on a truckle bed put up in the basement whenever there was a lull in the number of patients needing her, and eating in the hospital canteen. But supplies were dwindling and she didn't like to take food meant for the patients, though most of them were too ill to eat. The defending troops were doing their best, but she knew it could not go on. More than half the city had been destroyed, its houses, shops, cafes, churches and monuments reduced to rubble, many thousands of its citizens killed or injured.

On 27th September, less than a month after the war began, when there was no more food, medicines, water or electricity and the defending troops ran out of ammunition, Warsaw surrendered. The enemy had had to fight hard for their victory, but defeat tasted bitter to those Varsovians who remained and were obliged to watch helplessly as German troops stormed in and took control, shooting anyone who showed the least sign of resisting. And in the east the Soviets, far from coming to the aid of Poland as many believed, were doing the same.

'We are not beaten,' Rulka insisted, when she and Lech were scrubbing up in the theatre for yet another operation; their work did not stop, whoever was in control, though medical supplies were almost impossible to obtain. 'Poland will go on fighting underground and from other countries.'

'Have you heard from Jan?' Lech Andersz was in his thirties, a good, compassionate doctor, but, like Rulka, he had had to harden himself. They worked well as a team and he was as patriotic as she was.

'I had one letter ages ago now, telling me he was on his way to France. He thought I could get away to join him. He can't have realised how impossible that is.' The Germans had taken over the west of the country, including the Danzig Corridor, Poznan, Lodz and Upper Silesia and called it part of the Reich. The Soviets had taken over the east, leaving the middle, including Warsaw, Lublin and Kraków to become the General Government under German control. It was here the population was subjected to particularly harsh treatment.

'So we're stuck here,' he said. 'I've heard there's already the beginnings of an underground army. Shall I find out more about it?'

'Yes. Anything that will help.' The operating theatre was a fairly safe place to talk. Murmuring in undertones, they could have been discussing the operation they were about to perform. There was a German soldier standing guard outside, but he was not allowed in and he did not know if they were working on a Polish citizen or one of his comrades.

'Where are you living?'

'In the basement of my parents' house, it's nearer the hospital than my own apartment.'

'I'm sorry about your parents, Rulka. Doctor Kilinski was a fine doctor. I attended some of his lectures when I was training.'

'Thank you. At least they went together and have been spared this humiliation. It's the only consolation I have.'

'What about your husband's parents? Have you heard from them?'

'No, nothing. They are in the Soviet zone, there's no way to get in touch. I wonder if Jan knows that.'

'I expect he does. If he is in France, then he will know more about the situation than we do. If only the French would do something, invade Germany or something, anything to take the pressure off Poland.'

'I think it's too late for that, don't you?'

'I suppose you are right.'

'Better call in the rest of the team and get on with this op before that fellow outside wonders what we're talking about.'

If Jan thought the squadron would be re-formed when they arrived in France in October, he was disappointed. While the French authorities and the Polish government-in-exile decided how best they could use the Polish airmen, they were confined to primitive barracks with nothing to do but relive the events that had brought them there, to speculate on when they might see some action and wonder what had happened to their loved ones. Jan had heard nothing at all from Rulka. He supposed she was still in Warsaw under the German occupation. He could not be sure she was even alive. The news was as bad as it could be. Warsaw was in ruins and so many people had been killed that they were having to be buried where they died. Worst of all was the report that nine hospitals full of patients had been destroyed with enormous loss of life. It tore his guts and made him even more impatient to get at the *shkopy*.

But the French seemed to be in no hurry to engage the Germans. Life went on as it had before. The shops were still full of goods, the cafés still open and busy. The French air force confined itself to training and flying the occasional reconnaissance sortie. 'They must be blind,' Jan grumbled. 'Hitler won't content himself with half of Poland. And now he has wrapped up his problems in the east, he'll turn west.'

But it seemed he was wrong. The two sides eyed each other over their mutual border and did nothing. The battle-hardened Poles, itching to get at the enemy, became more and more frustrated.

'I've heard the Royal Air Force will welcome Polish pilots,' Witold told him one day just before Christmas. 'I've applied.'

'To go to England?'

'Yes. Do you want to come?

'Anything's better than sitting on our arses here, doing nothing. Yes, put me down.'

As Christmas approached, the children grew more and more excited, speculating on what they would find in their Christmas stockings. Some of them were going home to their mothers for the holiday, but most were going to stay with their foster families in Cottlesham and the adults set about trying to make it as festive as possible. Most of the presents would be second-hand or home-made. There were knitted stuffed toys, model aeroplanes carved from oddments of wood, second-hand dolls with repainted faces and new clothes made from scraps. Adult trousers made shorts for the boys. Jenny pulled out an old jumper, skeined the wool and washed and dried it before rolling it tightly into a ball to take out the wrinkles. Then she knitted it into a pixie hood and mittens for Beattie. Louise wondered whether to give presents to Tommy and Beattie, but knew that they were already branded as teacher's pets and suffered at school because of it. It would be worse if they were to boast they had been given presents by Miss.

Stan spent much of his spare time down in the cellar where they could hear him banging and sawing and whistling to himself. The cellar, containing as it did his beer barrels and bottles of wine and spirits, was forbidden to the children unless there was an air raid and they were supervised, but Tommy was curious to know what he was doing. He took to watching for Stan to leave and would then go and try the door but Stan never forgot to lock it. Jenny caught him once and, laughing, turned him round and gave him a push towards the kitchen.

'Now you know you can't go down there, young man. Away with you.'

'What's Uncle Stan making?'

'Never you mind.'

There was another entrance to the cellar from outside, a trapdoor and a ramp down which the barrels were offloaded from the brewer's dray. The horses were big carthorses but Tommy had overcome his nervousness early on in his stay at the Pheasant and loved to stroke the noses of these gentle giants. He watched for the next delivery and went out as usual with a couple of wrinkled apples for the horses; when the trapdoor was opened, he stepped forward to peer down into the cellar but he could see nothing but beer barrels and racks of bottles. He was getting under the feet of the draymen and they shooed him away. Disappointed he gave up.

In class Louise pointed out to the children that Christmas was as much about giving as receiving and set the girls to work making cross-stitched mats and handkerchiefs, embroidering the corners with initials. The boys made wooden bookends and letter racks under the supervision of Mr Langford. Tommy decided he was going to make a doll's cot for Beattie out of a wooden box, an ambitious project which was only completed after more than one display of temper. Louise helped him by making bedding for it, which did not break her rule of not giving presents to her pupils; after all, the gift was from Tommy to Beattie.

She knew Stan had made a doll's house for Beattie and a sledge for Tommy, but did not stay to see them opening their presents because she felt duty-bound to go home to Edgware, escorting the children who were going home for Christmas. The festival at the vicarage was austere and consisted of going to church three times and having a roast chicken and a small glass of sherry for lunch. They each produced a simple gift for the other two: handkerchiefs, a prayer book, a bookmark or an edifying story with a moral. Louise was pleased to see her mother, but glad to escape her father's constant preaching and return to Cottlesham and a job she loved.

January heralded one of the severest winters the country had had for a long time. Pipes froze, coal and coke ran short and potatoes could not be dug out of the iron-hard ground. Cottlesham was under feet of snow which drifted across the lanes and blocked them. The London children had never seen anything like it – snow to them was slushy pavements, not this powdery white stuff, and they revelled in it. When the new term started they plodded off to school in wellington boots, wrapped in coats, scarves and mittens, often found for them by their foster parents. The fireguard round the pot-bellied stove in the classroom steamed with wet coats, socks and gloves.

Stan dug out some skis and towed Tommy and Beattie to school on the sledge he had made, while Louise battled beside him on an old pair of snowshoes that looked remarkably like tennis rackets. 'I remember going to school on those when I was a nipper,' he told her.

For the most part the villagers had accepted the evacuees and the arrangements for the children's education were working satisfactorily, but everyone was wondering if it had been necessary after all. No bombs had been dropped by either side, except in Poland and, in most people's opinions, that was too far away to worry about.

'I told you there was no need for all that panic,' Louise's father told her one day when she went home for a visit. It was the first weekend of the thaw in March and the difficulties of travel had eased enough for her to go. Apart from the sandbags round the doorways of public buildings, the unused air raid shelters, the anti-aircraft guns in the parks and the blackout, London was as it always had been. Shops, cafes, theatres and cinemas carried on as usual: people still went to football matches, still danced until the early hours – not that Louise knew anything about dancing to the early hours. 'You can come home and go back to Stag Lane. I believe many of the children have already returned.'

She didn't want to do that. For the first time in her life she felt free of oppression, which was strange considering it was wartime. In spite of the identity cards, ration books and the call-up, it didn't feel like war. And living at the Pheasant was fun. In the evenings it was always noisy and full of laughter; there was, so far, nothing to be miserable about. Tony had invited her to go to the pictures in Swaffham with him and, greatly daring, she had said yes. That was another first. The cinema was nearly as bad as a public house for wickedness, as far as her father was concerned, so she hadn't told him. He knew where she was living because, one Saturday shortly after her arrival in Cottlesham, he had come down to inspect the so-called hotel where she was staying. It had not been a happy visit.

He had laid down the law in his quiet, determined way, expecting her meekly to give up and go home, but the presence of Mr and Mrs Gosport – and Tony – gave her the courage to stand up for herself and for the pub. 'There is nothing wrong with staying here,' she told her father. 'It is a decent, law-abiding place and these are decent, law-abiding people. My job is here with the children, especially since the rest of the school has landed up in Yorkshire somewhere and I am the only one here to teach them. If you like, I'll introduce you to Mr Langford, the headmaster of the village school, and the Reverend Capstick. They will vouch for what I say.'

Reluctantly he had agreed to meet the two men. He approved of John Langford, he had been a hero, but the parson was not to his liking at all. 'Too modern, too slack,' was his opinion. 'And to go about in check trousers and a baggy jumper is hardly fitting for a man of the cloth.'

In the end, he had declined Jenny's offer of staying for a meal and had gone home muttering imprecations about Louise coming to a sticky end. But for her mother, she would not have gone home at all, and every time she did she was subjected to the same bullying tactics, and every time she left she felt guilty that she had escaped and her mother had to put up with it all day, every day.

She had another reason for wanting to stay in Norfolk and that was Tony. He seemed to have taken a liking to her and she to him. He had been born and brought up in Essex, the only son of a builder. 'I wanted to do a bit more than just build houses,' he told her. 'So I went to technical college and qualified as a surveyor. That's how I came to be working on the airfields.'

'What will you do when the airfield is finished?' They were strolling back to the pub from the bus stop on the main road after a visit to the cinema. He had hold of her hand. She thought that was greatly daring, but did not take her hand away.

'I've done it already. I decided not to wait for call-up. I've enlisted in the air force.'

'Oh, Tony, you didn't say.'

'I'm saying now. I've always wanted to fly ever since I was a boy. There was a chap with a Tiger Moth came to an airfield near us when I was about fifteen. He was giving people half-hour trips and Dad paid for me to go up. I loved it. The ground was all spread out below me like a map: roads, rivers, buildings. I was so excited I forgot to be afraid.'

'A bit different from flying in wartime, though, isn't it?'

'Yes, but if I'm going to do my bit, then that's the way I want to do it. It's better than going into the army or the navy, poor devils.' The navy was the only service that had been in serious combat and had suffered significant losses. Nothing much was happening on land.

'Then you'll be leaving Cottlesham soon?'

'That was always on the cards. But we'll keep in touch, won't we?'

'Yes, if you want to.'

'Of course I want to. I've grown very fond of you. In fact . . .' He hesitated then rushed on. 'I was thinking of asking you to marry me.'

'Marry you?'

'Yes. Oh, I know it's a bit sudden and you might want some time to think about it, but I had to tell you what's on my mind. It's been on my mind since Christmas.' He chuckled suddenly. 'When we kissed under the mistletoe in the bar parlour, you remember . . .'

'I remember.' How could she forget? There had been a crowd in the pub and they had all laughed and clapped and made her blush to the roots of her hair.

'That's when I knew I'd fallen for you, hook, line and sinker and nothing would please me more than if you felt the same way.'

'You've bowled me over.'

He laughed. 'That was the general idea.'

'Oh, Tony, I don't know what to say.'

'You could say yes.'

She stopped to turn and face him. 'It's a big step and I don't know what my parents will say.'

'I'm not asking to marry your parents, just you, my darling.'

She put a hand up to touch his face. He grabbed it and kissed the palm. The feel of his lips on the inside of her wrist sent shivers down her spine. 'Well?' he queried. 'How long do you need to make up your mind?'

She laughed. 'Will ten seconds do?'

Solemnly he counted to ten and ended. 'So what is it to be?'

'Yes,' she said. 'Yes, Tony, I will marry you.'

He picked her up from the ground and swung her round and round until they were both giddy. 'I promise you will never regret it,' he said, setting her on her feet, then kissing her as she had never been kissed before. 'We are going to be so, so happy.'

With their arms round each other, they continued on their way. 'I'll have to tell my parents,' she said.

'And I'll have to tell mine.'

'What do you think they'll say?'

'Mine will be happy for me. We'll go down at the weekend and tell them, shall we? We could call in on your mum and dad afterwards. And I'll buy you a ring, make it official.'

'Hang on, you're going a bit fast for me.'

'Oh, do you want to wait?'

He sounded so disappointed, she laughed. 'No, no, let's get it over with – telling my parents, I mean.'

Mr and Mrs Walsh lived in a substantial four-bedroomed house next to the builder's yard just outside Witham. Philip Walsh had built it to his own design and Peggy had added touches of her own in the decor and furnishings; it was not only a beautiful house, it was a home full of love. They welcomed Louise with hugs and kisses, inspected her small diamond engagement ring and said how happy they were that Tony had found himself a nice girl, and Tony had grinned, half in pleasure, half in embarrassment and said he knew how lucky he was.

'Are you going to stay the night?' Peggy Walsh asked. 'I can soon make up a couple of beds.'

Tony looked at Louise. 'We planned to go on to Edgware and tell Louise's parents our news.'

'You can do that tomorrow. You've got the whole weekend, haven't you? I see so little of you and I want to get to know Louise.'

Louise knew it was cowardly but she seized the opportunity to delay what she knew would be a confrontation, and they stayed until Sunday morning, leaving after breakfast.

Her parents had just come back from church when they arrived at the vicarage. 'You could have made the effort to get here in time to attend morning service,' her father said.

'I'm sorry, Reverend,' Tony put in before Louise could speak. She was hugging her mother. 'We would have been but the train was late getting into London.'

Henry looked at Tony. 'Who are you?'

'I'm Tony Walsh, a friend of your daughter. We met when you came to Cottlesham, you remember.'

'So we did.'

'He is more than a friend, Father,' Louise said, holding out her left hand to display her ring. 'We are engaged to be married.'

'Engaged? Since when?'

'Since last week when Tony asked me and I said yes.'

'Without consulting your parents, what is the world coming to?'

'I do not need to consult you, Father. I am of age.'

'Years don't necessarily make you wise. I should like to know a little bit more about this young man.'

'Of course,' Tony said, squeezing Louise's hand to reassure her that he had the situation under control. 'I'll be pleased to answer all your questions.'

'I must go and see about lunch,' Faith said and disappeared into the kitchen, followed by Louise.

'You are happy for me, Mum, aren't you?' Louise asked as her mother set about preparing vegetables. There was already a small joint of beef in the oven.

'Of course I am, darling. He seems a nice boy.'

Louise picked up a knife and stood at the kitchen table to shred a cabbage which she had brought with her along with other produce Jenny had given her. Vegetables were much easier to obtain in the country than the town. 'Oh, he is. He's kind and considerate and we agree about almost everything. And I love him dearly.'

'I'm glad for you, but I wish you had said you were coming. I used up nearly all my meat coupons to buy a joint, your father does like his Sunday roast, but it's so tiny, I'm afraid it won't stretch to four.'

'Never mind, Mum, I'm sure we'll manage. You don't need to give me any meat, just the gravy and Yorkshire pud. You always make such lovely puddings and gravy.' She paused. 'I wonder what they're talking about.'

'No doubt your father is grilling the young man about his prospects. I do hope he doesn't mind.'

'No, I warned him it might happen and he said that was as it should be.'

'Have you decided on the wedding? I expect your father will want to officiate.'

'We aren't getting married for the moment. There's the war, and Tony has joined the air force. He'll be called up any day now, so we'll wait a bit. It will give us a chance to save up.'

Louise went back into the sitting room to find her father in what was, for him, a genial mood, opening a bottle of sherry to celebrate. She breathed a sigh of relief. How Tony had done it she did not know, but it made her realise just what a treasure she had in him. He would always be a bulwark against her father's tyranny and she loved him all the more for it.

'I was afraid there'd be a row,' she said when they were in the train on the way back to Cottlesham. 'How did you manage to win Father over?'

'By keeping my temper and being as cool as he was. I'm not sure he is convinced I am good enough for his daughter, but at least he accepted the inevitable.' He laughed. 'I had to assure him I was a churchgoing Christian.'

'Tony, that's a whisker.'

'No, it isn't. I go to church at Easter and Christmas and for weddings and funerals.'

'That wouldn't count. You didn't tell him that, did you?'

'No, of course not. Look, sweetheart, I don't think this phoney war will last, something is bound to happen before long and then everyone's lives will change. I don't think we need to worry too much about your father's stuffiness.'

'Oh, Tony, I'm so glad I've got you.'

'And I you.'

Tony's prediction proved only too true. The following month Hitler, whose occupation of Poland was complete, invaded Norway and then Denmark, ostensibly to protect the neutrality of those countries against a French and British invasion. The Allies did go to the aid of Norway but had to withdraw in the face of more compelling problems in the rest of Europe. Hitler ignored the neutrality of Belgium and Holland and sent his tanks and guns across both countries and into France. At the end of May, the British Expeditionary Force, which had been in France all through what had come to be called 'The Phoney War', was driven back to

Dunkirk. Three hundred and thirty-eight thousand troops were evacuated, thanks to the little pleasure craft which went with the naval ships to bring them off the beaches. But they had to leave all their guns, ammunition and equipment behind.

There was no doubt that it was a military disaster but the rescue was claimed as a miracle. Winston Churchill, now prime minister, while warning that 'wars are not won by evacuation', was at his most defiant and promised that the country would defend itself at whatever cost and would never surrender. France signed an armistice with Germany on the 22nd June, and everyone knew the British Isles was next on Hitler's agenda and prepared for invasion. In Churchill's words, the Battle of Britain was about to begin.

Chapter Three

Louise bade a tearful farewell to Tony whose call-up papers had come through, and settled down to teach those London children who were still in Cottlesham, including Tommy and Beattie. Their mother came to visit them occasionally, but not as often as she would have liked. She was now working in a munitions factory and, having no one to look after Beattie while she worked, was glad to leave her with Jenny. The two women got on well, mainly because Jenny, though she had come to love the children dearly, never tried to usurp the place of their real mother.

Some of the other children were not so lucky and Louise and Edith had had to soothe ruffled feathers on more than one occasion. Freddie Jones and Harry Summers had set up a gang of Londoners dedicated to fighting the village children and the battles were fierce and unmitigating and the two boys had to be separated at school, but it was impossible to keep an eye on them out of school hours. The situation was eased when Harry's mother decided to fetch him home.

Tony was training somewhere in the north of England. He

wrote loving letters to Louise as often as he could and she replied, telling him about the happenings in the village and the school, trying to amuse him and not be too gloomy. 'Several of the young village men have gone into the army, even though farming is a reserved occupation,' she reported. 'The farmers have taken on land girls in their place, and Stan has joined the Home Guard. They are digging trenches all over the place and learning to shoot with their new rifles and to throw hand grenades, so you can be sure we will be well defended.

'Half the cellar at the Pheasant has been made into an air raid shelter with a few chairs and a cupboard full of emergency rations. There's a primus stove down there and a kettle and teapot, so if we have to go down there, we won't starve. All we've got to do is remember to take some milk down when we go. So far we haven't had to use it. The council came and built a brick shelter in the school playground and the children have been practising marching out to it in an orderly fashion and donning their gas masks. They don't seem a bit frightened and think it is great fun and a good excuse to miss lessons. That may change if we get a real raid close by.

'Beattie is way ahead for her age, which comes from going to school early, I suppose. And the rest of the children are doing well. I'm going to coach the brightest of them for the scholarship next year. That is, if we are still here, which I assume we will be. Are you going to have a passing out parade when your training is done? I suppose then you will become operational. I am dreading that, but you must know that wherever you are or whatever you are doing I shall be with you in spirit always. Your very loving Louise.'

The reason Louise was dreading Tony becoming operational was that the Battle of Britain was being fought in the air and every day they would learn from the Home Service bulletins how many aircraft had been lost, and aircraft meant airmen too, though some were able to bail out. The Luftwaffe started by attacking British ships in the Channel and bombing Channel ports and airfields around London. It was happening mostly in the south but with so many airfields in East Anglia the people there were far from immune. Cambridge and Norwich and some of the Norfolk airfields were bombed. When the first bombs were dropped on London, Louise went home to try and persuade her parents to move to the country.

The train as far as Ely had spare seats but after Ely, where she changed to a London-bound train, it was a different story and she resigned herself to standing all the way to Liverpool Street. A young airman with a Poland flash on his shoulder stood up and bowed to her. 'Please, take my seat.'

She thanked him and sat down. He went to stand in the corridor but when another passenger left the train at Cambridge, he returned to sit beside her. He took a cigarette packet from his pocket and offered her one.

'No thank you, I don't smoke.'

'Do you mind if I do?'

'Not at all.'

He lit up, blowing the smoke towards the open window.

'How long have you been in England?' she asked.

'I arrived just before Christmas.'

'It's a pity you didn't go straight back again,' another passenger put in. She was a middle-aged woman, wearing a light linen coat and a felt hat with a sweeping red feather. Her lips, drawn into a thin line of disapproval, were scarlet. 'We don't want you here.'

'How can you say that?' Louise demanded. 'The Poles are our allies, our only allies at this moment.'

'It's their fault, this war,' the woman went on, to a murmur of agreement from the fat man sitting beside her. 'They brought it on themselves, sending troops into Germany – asking for it, that was. And then they expect us to dig them out of it.'

'I think you have been badly misinformed,' Louise said, furious with her. Whether the other occupants of the carriage agreed or disagreed, she did not know; they remained silent. 'Poland was overrun by the Germans, just as the rest of Europe was. You should blame Hitler for this war, no one else.'

'What do you know about it?' the fat man demanded. 'A mere slip of a thing not long out of the schoolroom, I shouldn't wonder.'

'I know better than to believe German propaganda. Anyone with half an eye can see that Hitler has been planning this all along.'

'Please,' the Polish airman said, laying a hand on Louise's arm. 'Do not argue with them.'

'Aren't you going to stick up for yourself?'

He smiled. 'It would make no difference. They believe what they want to believe. I have heard it all before.'

'I'm very sorry. I am sure not everyone agrees with them.'

'You are very kind.'

'Kind be blowed! I hate injustice.' She opened a packet of tomato sandwiches Jenny had made up for her and offered him one.

'I cannot take food meant for you,' he said.

'Goodness, I'm not starving. There's more here than I need. Do have one.'

He thanked her and took one and the women in the feathered hat snorted. 'Jezebel,' she said.

Louise took a deep breath. The woman was not worth fighting. She smiled. 'Takes one to know one.'

A laugh from a soldier sitting in the corner defused the situation and the rest of the journey was completed in silence.

When they all gathered up their belongings and left the train at Liverpool Street, the Polish airman, his kitbag slung over his shoulder, walked alongside Louise towards the barrier. 'Are you in a hurry, Miss?' he asked. 'I would like to buy you a cup of coffee. To say thank you, you understand.'

She turned to look at him. He was tall and good-looking and his blue eyes appealed. 'You do not have to thank me, but yes, I'd love to have a cup of coffee.'

They went to the station canteen. 'I am Jan Grabowski,' he told her, when he came back to the table after queuing for two cups of coffee. Neither had wanted anything to eat. 'In my own country I am a captain, here I am just a flying officer.'

She was aware that he was trying to make a joke of what must have seemed a humiliation, and smiled. 'I am pleased to meet you *Captain* Grabowski. My name is Louise Fairhurst.' She held out her right hand but instead of shaking it, he took it in his and kissed the back of it.

'I am very pleased to meet you, Miss Fairhurst.'

She suppressed the impulse to giggle at this extravagance of chivalry and sipped her drink. It was hot but didn't taste a bit like coffee.

'Do you live in London?' he asked, sitting down opposite her.

'No, my parents do. I lived with them until war broke out and then I took my class of children to Norfolk to be safe.'

'You are a teacher?'

'Yes.'

'Then that is why you keep yourself better informed than some of your compatriots.'

His English, she noted, although heavily accented, was very good. 'I don't think of myself as well informed, but I do read the newspapers. We all know what Poland had to go through, or we ought to. It must have been terrible. Were you in the Polish Air Force at the time?'

'Yes. And you are right, it was terrible. We were heavily outnumbered and our aircraft were no match for the Messerschmitt. The worst was when we realised we could not win and that to have any chance of continuing the fight we had to leave the country. When I came away Warsaw was in ruins but still fighting, still hoping the Allies would come. The people believed the promise made to them by your Mr Chamberlain, but it was not to be.'

'I am sorry,' she said softly. 'I don't think people should make promises they can't keep, but perhaps he didn't know he wouldn't be able to honour it.'

'Perhaps.' It was said with a resigned sigh. 'We had to leave our loved ones behind to live under the German occupation.'

'You are married?'

'Yes, we had been married a year. Rulka is a nurse. She could not leave with me. I have written to her many, many times, but I have heard nothing from her.'

It was evident he wanted to talk to someone and she was prepared to listen. 'I imagine it must be almost impossible to get news in or out.'

'Yes, that's what I tell myself all the time. I say, "Jan Grabowski, be sensible. The Germans are beasts, but not even they would harm doctors and nurses needed to tend the wounded."'

'There you are, then. You must not give up hope.'

'No, it is hope that keeps me going, that keeps all my countrymen going. In spite of everything . . .'

'Everything?' She sensed there was more to come.

'The loss of our country. That comes hard and is bad enough, but unlike France we did not ask for an armistice. Poland will never surrender.'

'That's what Churchill said about this country; we will never surrender.'

'Yes, I like his spirit. He welcomed us, not like that woman on the train and the air marshals who think we Poles cannot be trusted in one of their precious aeroplanes without an Englishman to hold our hands. We have been in combat, we know what it's like, the British pilots are – how do you say it? – still wet behind the ears.'

Said in his strange accent, the phrase sounded excruciatingly funny, and she laughed. 'Your English is very good. Where did you learn it?'

'I was fortunate that my father was able to send me to a good school where English was on the curriculum and I read English at the university in Warsaw. Since I have been in England I have been employed teaching my compatriots the language and learning more myself. The Air Ministry will not let us fly in fighter squadrons until we have all learnt it. We have been put in the Volunteer Reserve of the Royal Air Force and are subject to King's regulations. They wanted us to swear allegiance to the King but we refused. I have nothing against your king, you understand, but we are Poles, our allegiance is to Poland. It has made some of my countrymen very frustrated and angry. They cannot fight the Germans so they quarrel with each other.' He sighed. 'It is not good.'

'No, but understandable. Is that all you have been doing, teaching English?'

'No, I have been learning to fly in a Blenheim bomber with a British crew. Bombers are necessary but that is not the flying I know. I am a fighter pilot and my aim is to shoot down as many

German aircraft as I can. Then when there are no more, then I can go back to Poland and Rulka.'

'Rulka is a pretty name. Is she pretty?'

'She is beautiful. Here, I will show you.' He felt in his breast pocket and produced a snapshot. 'It is the only thing I brought out of Poland, except my wings.'

Louise studied the image. Rulka, standing beside Jan, was petite; the top of her head hardly came up to his shoulder. It was a black and white photograph but she could see that the girl's hair was dark and she was indeed pretty. 'She looks very young.'

'She is small. I call her my *myszka*.'

'What does that mean?'

'Mouse. She is my little mouse, but she has the heart of a lion. She will be twenty-four next week and I cannot even wish her a happy birthday.'

'I am sure she knows you would if you could. Have you any other relatives in Poland?'

'My parents live in Białystok – that's occupied by the Soviets now. I have no idea what has happened to them. And I have an older brother, Jozef. He is in the cavalry and I haven't heard from him since the war started. He might be dead. They all might be dead.' His voice caught as he said this and she was afraid he was going to cry, but he pulled himself together suddenly. 'What about you? Are you married?'

'No, but I am engaged. Tony is in the air force, like you. He is doing his flying training.' Afraid that he was going to ask where Tony was, and remembering all the posters that told everyone careless talk costs lives, she added, 'He gets moved around a lot. I don't always know where he is, but at least he's in the same country as me and we can write to each other.'

'Do you like writing letters?'

'Yes, I suppose so. I haven't really thought about it. It's just something I do.'

'Would you write to me? Just now and again, just so I have . . .' He paused, searching for a word. 'An anchor.'

She felt truly sorry for him; he was in a strange country, not always welcome, his wife was thousands of miles away under Nazi tyranny, how could she refuse him? 'Yes, if you like.'

He beamed with pleasure, tore the corner off a discarded newspaper, wrote his address on it and handed it to her. 'Now, you give me yours. If I am moved, I shall write and tell you.'

She complied and they left the canteen together and made for the Underground, where they parted, she to go to Edgware, he to cross London and take another train to Tangmere.

Louise sat in the crowded underground train, musing on the encounter. There were people all over Europe suffering a great deal more than those in Britain. She could not imagine what it would be like to be occupied by a foreign army, nor the emotional upheaval of being parted from loved ones as Jan Grabowski had been from his Rulka. Not to know if she was alive or dead must be a terrible thing to live with. She hoped he would hear from her soon and in the meantime she would write to him, try to cheer him up, let him know he was not forgotten.

Leaving the Underground and walking to the vicarage, she braced herself for her encounter with her father. It was always like that; it tied her insides up in knots. Once back in the vicarage she became a little girl again, subject to his punishment for her wickedness. The beatings had stopped when she went to college but she was still more than half afraid of him. He sapped her self-confidence until it was easier to agree with him than to fight, which was how her mother coped. But deep inside her was an ember of rebellion she hardly knew she had. It had showed itself

65

when she had insisted on accompanying her class to Norfolk and again when she had become engaged to Tony. Dear Tony. He gave her strength, encouraged her to stick up for herself. 'Do it quietly,' he had said. 'Just be firm. He can't hurt you.' But even Tony did not know the whole truth.

She found her mother lying on the sofa, with a cold compress on her forehead. She scrambled to sit up when she saw Louise. 'Darling, how lovely to see you. Why didn't you let us know you were coming?'

Louise hugged her. 'I wasn't sure I could get away. What's the matter, aren't you well?'

'Just a headache, that's all. I'll be fine now you're here.'

'Where's Father?'

'Visiting his parishioners. I didn't feel up to going with him.'

Louise knew what it was like accompanying her father on his rounds. He had little sympathy for some of his flock, calling them idle and feckless and preaching hell and damnation when what they really needed was a little understanding and a helping hand. Others were sycophants and reminded her of the false humility of Uriah Heap. Going with her father had always embarrassed her and she knew her mother felt the same. Headaches, genuine enough, were her excuse not to go.

'Shall I make us a cup of tea?'

'Yes, please, then you can tell me all your news.'

It was lovely to have a couple of hours alone with her mother and she was soon recounting the doings at Cottlesham. She told her about the battle between the rival gangs which had culminated in bruises and bloody noses on the both sides. 'John Langford called all the children, his and mine, into the classroom and gave them a long lecture about how wars start with little quarrels and they ought to learn tolerance and cooperation and helping each other,' she said. 'I think it worked. Anyway Harry Summers, who was the ringleader of the Edgware lot, went home and that eased the situation somewhat.'

'A lot of them came home, didn't they?'

'Some did, but that was before the war got going. I'm wondering if their parents made the right decision, after all.' She paused. 'Mum, I worry about you, what with the bombing and everything. Couldn't you and Father move somewhere safer?'

'He would never leave his parish, Louise, you should know that.'

'Then you leave. Come to Cottlesham and stay with me.'

'Without him? Oh, no, child, I could never leave him.'

Louise knew it was useless to argue, though she did mention what was in her mind when her father came home at lunchtime. He reacted predictably. Duty came before his own comfort and he would continue to do his duty and it went without saying that his wife would support him in that. The Lord would take care of them and keep them safe.

After they had had their meal, Louise and her mother did the washing-up while her father went to his study to compose the next day's sermon. Louise had a feeling it would be centred on duty.

'How is Tony?' Faith asked.

'He was well last time I heard from him. Sent you his regards.'

'What's he doing?' She put a washed plate on the drainer. Louise picked it up to dry it.

'Training to be a pilot.'

'Do you worry about him?'

'Of course, all the time, but I don't let him know that. He's hoping to get some leave when he finishes his training. Then he'll be posted.'

'Do you know where?'

'No idea.'

'I hope it's not to one of those airfields being bombed.'

'So do I, but I don't expect he'll be given a choice.'

'How long can you stay?'

'Just tonight, Mum. I'll have to go back tomorrow afternoon.'

'But it's the school holidays.'

'I know, but that doesn't alter the fact that I am responsible for the children, even in the holidays. And I have to prepare for next term and liaise with Mr Langford over the arrangements.'

'Of course, I understand. You'll come to Communion in the morning?'

'Yes, I'll leave after lunch.'

Her father was so engrossed in preparing his sermon that he hardly noticed Louise was there. Perhaps he was softening towards her or perhaps he had given her up as a lost cause. Whichever it was, she was careful to say nothing that might cause dissension. She certainly said nothing of her meeting with Jan Grabowski. That would have been asking for a lecture on the perils of picking up strange men in railway carriages. But she had not forgotten him or her promise to write to him.

After persistent lobbying and in the face of a great shortage of pilots, Jan had been transferred from Blackpool, where they had been training, to an English fighter squadron in Tangmere, and though it wasn't exactly what he had hoped for, it was a step in the right direction. He would teach those stiff-necked Britishers how to fly.

He arrived to find Witold already there, ensconced in the officers' mess, a favourite of the WAAF waitresses who served him. It hadn't taken his friend long to convince the RAF he could fly as well as any of them, and the next day Jan did the same. He found himself in combat for the first time with those he had called 'wet behind the ears' and discovered they had plenty of courage, if little experience. But they learnt quickly, at least those who survived did. The casualty rate was horrifying. Jan's first 'kill', a Messerschmitt 109 shot down into the Channel, brought great rejoicing. At last he was having a crack at the enemy and his first taste of revenge.

A week later Witold came to him with momentous news. Short of hearing from Rulka, it was the best news in the world. 'They're giving us our own squadrons,' Witold told him gleefully. 'The Polish Air Force flies again. Get your things together, we're off to join them.'

It wasn't quite what they expected, they discovered when they arrived at Northolt and joined their compatriots, many of whom they had not seen since leaving Poland. According to the agreement thrashed out between the Air Ministry and the Polish government in exile, every senior Polish Officer would have an equivalent British one and they would still be under British command. Officially designated 303 Squadron, it did not take the Polish flyers long to rename it the Kościuszko Squadron and to paint the squadron's emblem on the Hurricanes they were to fly.

But they were still not operational. The station commander was adamant they had to learn English and understand what was meant by angels and bandits, scramble and tally-ho and how to count at least to twelve because the clock face was used to convey bearings. And they needed to measure their speed in miles not kilometres, and fuel in gallons not litres. Every day they went to classes while every day the Luftwaffe came and bombed airfields, coastal towns, shipping and important installations. It frustrated Jan and his companions until they were ready to explode. What they wanted was to get at the enemy, to defeat him and get their country back so they could go home.

While they were learning English and going on training flights, the Luftwaffe continued trying to bring the country to its knees and losses were frightening. Aircraft were coming off the production lines in vast quantities but there weren't enough trained pilots to fly them. When one of Jan's compatriots broke formation during training to chase after and bring down a Dornier bomber, the Air Ministry at last agreed the Polish flyers were ready for action. On the last day of August, the eve of the first anniversary of the invasion of Poland, 303 was made operational. It was the day on which the German High Command decided to send everything it had to finish the job they had started and sent wave after wave of bombers, escorted by fighters, to put an end to the stubborn resistance of the Royal Air Force. In that it failed. But only just. It was the most momentous time of Jan's life.

It was one of excitement and danger, of jubilation mixed with sadness when friends were lost. There were times he was so overcome with exhaustion, he fell asleep as soon as climbed out of the cockpit and found a convenient armchair. At other times when given a few hours' respite he and some of his fellow pilots would go to The Orchard in nearby Ruislip, where they were always made welcome and where they whiled away the time in false jollity. In between there were times of intense melancholy, when Jan thought about Rulka and their parting in the ruins of Warsaw. Was that the last time they would be together? Ever? Was she alive? How was she coping? And his parents, what had happened to them?

The tales coming out of Poland of imprisonment and executions and hardship were horrific. If his countrymen and women were not being ill-treated by the Germans, they were being rounded up by the Soviets as 'enemies of the people' and sent to Siberia in cattle trucks to work as slave labour. Among them were the elite of Polish society: army officers, professors, lawyers, doctors, anyone who might be a threat to the indoctrination of the people into the Soviet way of life, and that would certainly include aristocrats, his parents among them. He tried telling himself that no one really knew the truth and it was probably nothing but exaggerated gossip. He wrote to Rulka, telling her what he was doing, reminding her of the good times they had had and how he was looking forward to being with her again and how happy they would be when the war was won and they could live again in a free Poland. He couldn't send the letter – he did not know how to – and simply folded it and put it away in a drawer with his clothes.

He wrote to Louise too. She had kept her promise to write to him and she seemed his only contact with the outside world, a world that was not one of scrambling into kit, of flying with nerve ends tingling, of falling asleep and getting drunk. She represented tranquillity in a world gone mad. She had indeed become his anchor.

'You don't mind me writing to Flight Lieutenant Grabowski, do you?' Louise asked Tony. Having finished his training, he had forty-eight hours' leave before being posted to a squadron and his first port of call had been the Pheasant at Cottlesham. There was little privacy in the pub and they had decided to go for a walk. She was holding his arm in both hands and her head rested on his shoulder. The day was unusually warm for the time of year and she was wearing a cotton print dress with a nipped-in waist and puffed sleeves. He had taken off his jacket and was carrying it over his other shoulder. A camera hung from a strap about his neck.

'No, of course not,' he said. 'I feel sorry for the blighters being so far from home and loved ones. But don't you go falling for him.'

'As if I would! Don't you know how much I love you?'

'So you say,' he teased. 'But I've heard tales of their exploits with the ladies. Since they turned out to be such heroes, there's no holding them back.'

The Polish flyers had distinguished themselves in the Battle of Britain, bringing down more enemy aircraft than any other squadron with fewer casualties, although those were far from light. Not until Churchill told the nation 'Never in the field of human conflict has so much been owed by so many to so few' did the people of Britain realise what a narrow squeak it had been and the extent of the contribution of the Polish airmen. They were feted everywhere and invited into people's homes. In the public houses they hardly ever paid for their own drinks and the clippies refused to take their fares on the buses and received kisses for a thank you. Articles appeared about them in newspapers and magazines, all of which they lapped up. London society hostesses held lavish parties in their honour, where there seemed to be no shortage of food and drink. Girls almost threw themselves at them to the chagrin of the British airmen. In the air, fighting for their lives, they concentrated on what they were doing, but on the ground they had an endless capacity for enjoyment and causing mayhem.

Louise, who had come to know Jan from his letters, understood what lay beneath the surface. 'I don't think Jan is like that,' she said. 'He is pining for his wife. All I'm doing is trying to cheer him up.'

'Then you do that, sweetheart. How could I begrudge the man a letter or two when I have so much more?'

'I knew you'd say that. Where are you going to be stationed?'

'Coltishall, 2-4-2 Squadron. It's commanded by Squadron Leader Douglas Bader. He lost both legs in a flying accident nine years ago. I've been told he doesn't let that hamper him and he's still flying. The good thing is that the station is near enough to take advantage of a twenty-four-hour pass when I get one.'

'It's near enough for me to come over and see you for a weekend too.'

'That's an idea, though I don't know how long I'll be there. I might not come up to scratch.'

'What makes you say that?'

'Oh, I don't know. I'm nervous, I suppose, going on ops for the first time. Will I have the guts to do it?'

'You'll be all right, more than all right, I should say.'

'How do you know that?'

'Because I do.'

They wandered down a grassy path just wide enough for a horse and cart or a very small car if you didn't worry about its springs on the rutted surface. On either side were meadows dotted with bright yellow buttercups where cattle grazed. Tony took several pictures of Louise, positioning her with a wild rose hedge as a background.

'I want one or two of you,' she said. 'Show me how to work the camera. It looks complicated. I've only ever had a Brownie Box.'

'That was my first one, I had it for my tenth birthday and that started me off. It won't help me much in the building trade, but I find the subject fascinating. When I go to the pictures I find myself thinking of camera angles and different shots, when I should be concentrating on the story.'

'Would you like to do that sort of thing after the war, be a film cameraman, I mean?' Louise asked

'No, I don't think so, taking pictures is only a hobby. Look, all you've got to do is look through the viewfinder and when it looks OK, press this knob.'

She did that, though she doubted her hand was steady enough, and then he set the camera up to take them both together and by then he had used up all the film. 'They will be something to look at during the long, boring days and nights,' he said.

'You expect to be bored?'

'I don't know, but you can't be on the go the whole time, can you? Not even the air force would expect that. Then I will sit and look at my snaps and think of you.'

'And I of you.'

They found a quiet spot and sat down on Tony's jacket. She opened her bag and took out a packet of tomato sandwiches and a bottle of lemonade made with crystals. Real lemons were a thing of the past.

'It's so peaceful here,' she said, offering him a sandwich. 'You would never believe there was a war on, that people are being killed and injured every day. And for what? One man's thirst for power.'

'Let's not talk about it. Let's talk about what we'll do after the war.'

'What do you want to do?'

'I expect I'll join Dad in the family business. I've no doubt there will be plenty of work for us to do. And I'll build us a house.'

'Like your father's?'

'Something like that. It will have all the latest mod cons and be big enough for a family.'

'A family?'

'Yes. Don't you want a family?'

'Of course I do.'

'How many?'

She laughed. 'How many do you want?'

'Four would be nice, two boys and two girls. But it's up to you, of course.'

'It's up to both of us, surely?' She giggled. 'I can't do it on my own.'

He laughed and grabbed her shoulders pulling her down beside him to kiss her. When his hand strayed along her leg and up her thigh under her skirt, she knocked it away. 'No, Tony.'

'Sorry.' He looked aggrieved. 'I wasn't . . . I mean . . .'

'I know, but we mustn't get carried away.'

'Why not? We are engaged, after all, and who knows what the future holds.'

'I don't want to get pregnant. Not before . . .'

'You won't, I promise.'

'All the same, I'd rather wait.'

'If you say so.' He sat up and opened the bottle of lemonade to take a swig.

'Now you are angry with me.'

'No, of course not, just disappointed that you don't trust me.'

'I do, oh Tony, I do, but I'm nervous. And that's something that should only happen on your wedding night, isn't it?'

'Oh, my poor innocent.' He was smiling now; the little spat was over. 'Kiss me again. I'll be good, I promise.'

She kissed him. 'I do love you, Tony, really I do, and sometimes I wonder what it will be like to, you know, be married and all that, but . . .'

'But you aren't ready to experiment.'

'I suppose that's it. It feels wrong.'

'Point taken. Now, let's go back. Jenny told me she is making us a special tea, seeing as we didn't have an engagement party.'

They walked back to the village and were met on the way by Tommy and Beattie. Unlike Tommy, who sometimes longed for his Edgware home, the little girl was content in Cottlesham, spoilt by all the grown-ups around her. 'Auntie Jenny sent us to find you,' she said, taking Louise's hand. 'Tea is nearly ready and she has made a special cake. Is it your birthday?'

'No, but it's in honour of Uncle Tony. He is a qualified pilot now.'

'You mean he's going to shoot down Germans?' Tommy said, holding out his arms in imitation of an aeroplane, running in circles and making a noise like a gun firing.

'I don't know about that, you bloodthirsty little monster,' Tony said.

Later that evening, they were listening to the news on the wireless in the bar parlour of the pub when they heard about the air raid on London that afternoon. Hundreds of German Heinkel, Dornier and Junkers bombers escorted by double the number of Messerschmitts had come out of a cloudless blue sky and subjected the capital to an all-out assault. The previous raids on places like Croydon, Wimbledon and Enfield became insignificant in comparison. The bombers concentrated on the docks and the Woolwich arsenal and oil storage tanks, causing huge fires that could be seen for miles. And close by the docks were the overcrowded homes of the poor, where the damage and loss of life were worst. But the bombing was not so accurate that the rest of London did not suffer. Other places were an inferno too.

The BBC newsreaders had a dry way of delivering the news that somehow seemed to diminish the horror of it, but not even the most determined ostrich could be blind to the terror of what had happened. Louise's first thought was for her parents. She tried ringing them but the telephones were out of action. She spent a sleepless night worrying about them. And the next morning the news was even worse. The afternoon raid had been followed almost immediately by an even greater one in the evening, the bombers guided to their target by the fires.

'I'll have to go and see they are all right,' she said, after again trying and failing to reach her parents by telephone.

'I'll come with you,' Tony said. 'Then I must go and see my folks.'

London was recovering from the most terrifying night most of its inhabitants had ever experienced. The fires in the east could easily be seen from the west. Even in streets where the buildings still stood, there were heaps of broken glass and everything was covered in grey dust. Louise found her mother stoically trying to clean the house. Her face was chalk white and her eyes red-rimmed. Strangely she was not so much afraid as angry.

'Louise! Where have you sprung from? And Tony too. How nice to see you.'

'And you,' he said.

'I couldn't get you on the phone, so we came to see how you are,' Louise explained.

'The lines are out of action, but we're all right, not like some poor souls, but if I could get hold of that Herr Hitler, I'd personally wring his neck.'

This was so unlike her normally timid mother, Louise laughed. 'That's the spirit.'

Faith put down her dustpan and brush. 'I'll make some tea.' She took three cups from hooks on the dresser. 'I'll have to wash these before we can drink from them. There was a bomb dropped in the next street and it set everything shaking and wobbling and some of the ceiling came down and covered everything in dust.' She filled the kettle as she spoke. 'We're lucky we've still got gas.

So many have lost everything. According to your father it won't be the last of it and there'll be more to come.'

'I'm afraid he is right,' Tony said. 'Have you thought any more about evacuating?'

'Henry won't do that.'

'Where is he?' Louise asked, washing up cups and saucers.

'Gone to see what he can do to help. He was out in the thick of it last night, came home for his breakfast and went out again.'

'He left you alone all night?'

'I went into the church. There were lots of others there.' She smiled suddenly. 'We had sing-songs, and not always hymns, either. I didn't tell your father that, though.'

They all laughed. Louise was amazed at the resilience of her mother. It was as if the raids had imbued her with a stoical courage she had never shown before. They sat drinking tea, making use of a tin of evaporated milk because the milkman hadn't turned up, and discussing the raids, the casualties and the damage, and then moved on to talk about what was happening in Cottlesham and Tony's posting to an operational squadron.

'Do you think you'll be flying against that lot?' Faith nodded her head skywards. 'The RAF boys did their best to knock them out of the sky, but there didn't seem to be enough of them.'

'Well, there aren't, are there?' he said. 'They've taken a pasting themselves.'

'I shall pray for you,' Faith said. 'Not that I don't pray for everyone in danger in this war, but you shall be mentioned especially.'

'Thank you,' he said.

Henry returned just as they were leaving to catch their trains. His black frock was thick with dust; there was even a layer of it in the brim of his hat. He had a scratch on his face and looked exhausted. 'How are you, Father?' she asked.

'I am, as ever, in good heart myself, but I despair of the world.' He took off his hat and punched it to knock off the dust. 'Such wickedness and corruption, such godlessness, is it any wonder we have to be punished, the good along with the evil?'

Louise opened her mouth to comment, but changed her mind when she saw Tony shaking his head at her. 'We have to leave to catch trains,' she said instead. 'Tony is going to see his parents and I am going back to Cottlesham. The new term starts tomorrow.'

'Yes, go before they come back, for assuredly they will.' He had evidently abandoned his crusade to persuade her to come home.

'I wish you and Mum would leave London for somewhere safer.'

'Our duty lies here, Louise. I told you that before. Now go, both of you, before it's too late.'

Chapter Four

Tony saw Louise safely onto her train and watched as it drew out of the station before going to find one to Witham. The siren wailed as he waited for it and everyone scuttled into the Underground to take shelter. It was the early hours before he left London and by that time there were more fires, more damage, more loss of life. Soon he would be part of the fight, and though he hated the idea of deliberately killing another human being, he could not honestly say he was a pacifist. If he found himself face to face with an enemy who was attacking those he loved, he would not hesitate to hit back and kill and so he would do his bit to shorten the war in whatever role he was given. The sooner it was over, the better. He wanted to show Louise what a loving relationship really meant.

She was such a compassionate soul, worrying about that stiff-necked father of hers, caring for her class of children and befriending strange men in railway carriages. Ought he to have tried to squash that? She was so naive, the man might easily take advantage of her. He smiled suddenly. If she could say no to him, whom she loved – and he did not doubt that – she would be impervious to anyone else. And if he were the one to have to leave a wife behind in an occupied country, he might be glad of a pretty girl to cheer him up. There could be no love without trust.

His parents were well and unharmed and made a great fuss of him before he left them the next day for Coltishall, just a few miles north-east of Norwich. The base had been built early in 1939 as a bomber station but switched to fighters in 1940 because the many bomber stations in the region were being targeted by the Luftwaffe and fighters were needed to protect them. The station seemed to be a transient base for several squadrons on the move from one place to another: there were Canadians and South Africans as well as 242 and a squadron from Yorkshire. There was a rumour going round that 242 was going to be moved to Duxford in Cambridgeshire, and Tony supposed he would be going with them.

He was lounging in a comfortable chair in the mess two evenings later, looking through his prints of Louise, when he felt a shadow over him. He looked up to see Wing Commander Blatchford and sprang to his feet, scattering the pictures.

'Like taking photographs, do you?' Blatchford queried, bending down to help pick them up and return them.

'Yes, sir. I'd rather shoot pictures than shoot guns.'

The Wingco smiled. 'At ease, Flying Officer. Shall we sit down?' He took the next chair and Tony returned to his seat, wondering what was coming next – a dressing down for some misdemeanour, he supposed, though he had only been on the base two days, not really long enough to get into trouble, but that last landing had been a bit bumpy, he had to admit.

'Tell me about yourself,' Blatchford went on. 'What's your background? Professional photographer, are you?'

'No, sir, an enthusiastic amateur. I am a surveyor in civilian life.'

'May I see?' Tony handed over the handful of small prints,

which the other man spread out on the table, shifting Tony's glass of beer to do so. 'Your girlfriend?'

'My fiancée. Louise.' He pointed to another. 'That's Cottlesham village taken from the church spire. I believe it's one of the tallest spires in Norfolk. There's an amazing amount of detail considering how far up I was.' He pointed to another. 'That's an inscription on an old gravestone in the churchyard. It's a funny thing, but when I first looked at it the words were indecipherable, worn away by the years, and I couldn't read any of it, but suddenly the sun came out and slanted across it and every word was clearly visible. I took the picture and then the sun went behind a cloud and I couldn't read it any more. It was completely blank again.'

'Interesting,' the Wingco murmured, examining the images carefully. He put them down and looked across at Tony. 'Have you seen any action yet, Flying Officer?'

'I was in the air yesterday and saw a couple of ME 109s in the distance, but they were chased away before I got near enough to join in.'

'But you would rather use a camera than a gun, isn't that what you said?'

'Yes, but—'

'Never mind trying to explain.' He laughed. 'Would you like a job where your only weapon is a camera?'

'What sort of job, sir?'

'I've been asked to recruit suitable men to take pictures on reconnaissance flights. Are you interested?'

'Yes, sir.'

'Come and see me tomorrow morning, eight o'clock.' He stood up and strode away, leaving Tony wondering why he had been singled out. It surely wasn't the pictures of Louise. He picked up the photographs and studied one of a smiling Louise. Behind her, pale dog roses bloomed in the hedge, throwing a dappled shade over her dress but leaving her smiling face in full sunshine. He tucked it with the others into his breast pocket.

It was purely coincidence that the wing commander had seen Tony studying his handiwork on the same day as he had been asked if any of his command were handy with a camera. His comment about preferring cameras to guns clinched it, the Wingco told Tony the next morning. 'It isn't an easy option.' he explained. 'So I want you to think about it carefully. You will be flying a specially adapted Spitfire. Because speed and distance are paramount, it will have no guns, only extra fuel tanks and the latest camera technology. You will be flying over enemy territory completely unarmed and alone. Your only defence if you are spotted will be your speed and manoeuvrability. How's your navigation?'

'Not bad, sir.'

'Want to give it a try?'

'Yes, sir.'

'Right. I'll get in touch with the Photographic Reconnaissance Unit and if they want you, they'll send for you.'

'Thank you, sir.'

'The work is highly classified, so no talking about it, understand?'

'Yes, sir.'

Three days later he was on his way to Heston, just west of London. Before the war, the airfield had been a private one used by civilian flyers, but had been taken over by the Photographic Reconnaissance Unit. It was commanded by Wing Commander Geoffrey Tuttle to whom Tony reported.

'Glad to have you,' the Wingco said, after the formalities of introduction were over and they were both seated. 'The Luftwaffe seem to know what we're doing here and we've taken a battering in the last few weeks, but, we've been given some extra aircraft and need pilots to fly them. I see you have only just completed your pilot training.' He turned over the page of a document as he spoke. 'Came out top of your class for almost everything.'

Tony smiled. 'Not so good at take-off and landing, sir.'

'No, but that will come with practice and it's not so important for the work we do here. The be-all and end-all of the PRU is to take good pictures and get them back to the Photographic Interpretation Unit for analysis. That's housed at Wembley.' He smiled suddenly. 'All three services seem to think they have first call on our time and it's my task to prioritise. You may be taking pictures of shipping one day for the navy, aircraft on the ground for the air force the next, troop deployment for the army the next, factories or the damage our bombs have caused for Bomber Command, and it all needs precision. Pictures that can't be interpreted are a waste of fuel, time and often lives. You understand?'

'Perfectly, sir.'

'Your kite will not be armed. The guns and armour plating have been taken out to lighten the aircraft and give it some extra speed. You are not in the air to fight and must avoid it at all costs. The cameras and their film must not fall into enemy hands, not to mention aircraft and pilots.'

'I understand, sir.'

'Do you want to change your mind?'

'No, sir.'

'Good. I'll take you out to have a look at the aircraft. If you want to take one up and get the feel of it, then do so. Then have the rest of the day to settle in and explore. Tomorrow, you will be assigned your task.' He stood up and Tony stood too. 'Go and get into flying kit. I'll meet you by the hangar in half an hour.'

Tony followed him out and a sergeant conducted him to his quarters where he unpacked and changed, then hurried out to the hangar, where a Spitfire was taxied out onto the runway for his benefit. It looked a little different from an ordinary Spitfire; there was a new bulge under each wing. The port one contained extra fuel tanks and the starboard one three large cameras, which took the same view at different angles. The whole aircraft had been polished to a mirror finish to get an extra knot or two of speed out of it. After a few instructions from Sergeant Drayton, who was in charge of the ground crew, he adjusted his oxygen mask and took to the air.

He was not sure how he felt. There was elation, apprehension and quivering nerves, especially as the Wingco watched him take off, but once in the air, he felt the power of the aeroplane. He took it up to twenty-five thousand feet and nearly four hundred miles an hour. It was a clear day and below him the airfield was spread out like a map. Although he should have been able to see London, it was invisible beneath a pall of smoke. Beneath that, the citizens were trying to get on with their lives, going to work, eating, sleeping when they could.

He operated the cameras from a box in front of him where the gunsight would have been, had he had guns. Turning to return to base he noticed a formation of bombers and fighters below him and realised they were enemy aircraft. His heart started to pound and his gut seized up. Could they see him? What should he do?

The Wingco's words echoed in his brain: *You are not in the air to fight and must avoid it at all costs.* He did not have important film on board, but he did have a valuable aircraft. He climbed even higher and circled, waiting. In spite of his extra clothes and warm flying gear he was frozen with cold and could hardly feel his fingers and toes. He saw some Hurricanes on the tail of the enemy aircraft and three of the enemy fighters went down in flames. The bombers droned on. Once again alone in the sky, Tony brought the Spitfire down and taxied to a stop.

'How was it, sir?' Sergeant Drayton asked as he climbed out of the cockpit.

'Bloody cold, but the aeroplane is out of this world. It flies like a bird. I couldn't believe the speed of it.'

'The boffins are making it faster all the time. I should go and get warm, sir. We'll take over here.'

Tony took his advice. He had a hot bath and went to the mess for dinner and afterwards he wrote to Louise. She would be disappointed that he was no longer at Coltishall and the weekend they had planned would have to be postponed. He couldn't tell her in a letter what he was doing, but hinted that it was something different and very much to his liking because he would not be killing anyone. She might assume from that he was working with the ground crew or in an office. Well, that didn't matter. The bulk of the letter was a reiteration of his continuing love for her and he found himself carried away by that. 'I will love you to the end of time and beyond,' he wrote. 'I can't wait to hold you in my arms again and kiss you until you cry for mercy.'

'Soppy,' he told himself as he read it through, but it was how he felt and it was the sort of thing he wanted to hear from her. The censors might have a good laugh at his expense, but what the hell! He folded it into an envelope and propped it beside the framed photo of Louise on his bedside cabinet ready to take to the post. He was fast asleep when his roommate came in and tumbled into bed.

The next day he was flying over the Channel ports, where the Germans had been assembling a fleet of barges, presumably in preparation for an invasion. Only by taking photographs on a regular basis could it be seen how the number had grown all the time the Battle of Britain was being waged in the skies, but the pictures he had taken on the last few days had shown the number shrinking. Today there were hardly any. Had Hitler given up his idea of invasion and sent the barges back where they came from? He turned for home.

As soon as he landed, the ground crew removed the film from the cameras and took them to the processing unit on the base for a preliminary examination before sending them to the Photographic Interpretation Unit at Wembley where there was technical equipment for more detailed analysis. Tony, anxious to see if what he had surmised was borne out by the pictures, went over and watched them being developed.

'Thank God, it looks as though they've gone,' he was told. 'I'll get these over to PIU. Good work, Flying Officer Walsh. Better get some rest.'

Tony went to his room to strip off his flying gear and stretch out on his bed. It had been nerve-racking, wondering if he might come up against enemy aircraft or be caught by the anti-aircraft guns protecting the ports, but the speed and height of the Spitfire made him feel comparatively safe, even when he had dived low to make sure he was over the target. It gave him a feeling of euphoria, of being invincible. He picked up Louise's photo from his bedside locker. It was that image that had started it all off. 'I'm back safe and sound,' he murmured. 'I'll write to you after I've had some shut-eye. I love you.' He kissed it and put it back on his locker and in no time at all was fast asleep.

Jan, high in the sky above London, looked down and felt a great lurching in his stomach that had nothing to do with the eggs and bacon he had consumed a couple of hours earlier. It was because the burning city reminded him of Warsaw and Rulka and their parting. It was something he relived in his mind over and over again, everything they had said, every touch, every poignant look, every tear bravely withheld. Could he have done more, said more, reassured her more, left her with more optimism? Should he have disobeyed his orders and stayed with her? Was she alive even?

The stories reaching the Polish fighters from goodness knows what sources were so horrendous he was almost inclined to hope she was dead and not having to suffer. Any show of resistance was being put down with mass public shootings. 'Rulka, my love,' he murmured to himself. 'Don't do anything rash. Stay safe.'

He saw a lone Messerschmitt below him to his starboard and banked away to go after it. The pilot didn't see him until he had fired his cannon and then it was too late; the *shkopy* was spiralling downwards in flames. 'That one is for Rulka,' he said, looking about him for more. His blood was up and he was in a white-hot fury. But the sky was empty and he turned back to the airfield. Tomorrow would be another day and he did not doubt the bombers would come again just as they had to Warsaw. The only difference was that Hitler had to cross the English Channel to invade the British Isles and while there was an air force he would not risk it.

When he first came to England he had doubted the people's will to resist. He had wondered if they might, like the French, seek an armistice, but he soon realised they were every bit as determined as his own countrymen to win. Led by Winston Churchill, who had replaced Chamberlain as prime minister, they were stoically fighting on. The 'wet behind the ears' British pilots had turned out not to be so wet; they were as gallant a crew as you could meet anywhere. He was proud to call them comrades.

As soon as he landed he went to debriefing and claimed his 'kill', then to his quarters and flung himself on his bed and slept. Waking three hours later he realised he was still in his flying kit. He stripped off, had a bath and went to the mess for dinner. With luck he might be able to eat his meal in peace, but that hadn't happened for days. The only thing that would stop the bombers coming over was bad weather, and there hadn't been any of that. After the terrible winter, the summer had been glorious.

So much for the stories that England was a country of rain and yet more rain, and if it wasn't raining the fog was so dense you couldn't see a hand in front of your face. It was a beautiful country, just as the girls were beautiful, not the ugly freaks they had been told to expect. Louise was lovely, not only to look at, but in her temperament. They had been writing to each other for weeks now and with every letter, he learnt a little more about her, about her life at Cottlesham and the children she taught. She made it all seem so pleasant, a million miles away from the death and destruction he witnessed every day. And she understood about his frustration and misery over leaving Rulka and always made him feel better about it. Next time he had a few days' leave, he'd write and ask if he could visit her.

There were always airmen from Watton enjoying what free time they had in the bar of the Pheasant and Jan was made welcome and was soon exchanging hair-raising stories with them and making jokes. His English was very good, but sometimes he did not see the point of the humour and had to have it explained to him, which caused more hilarity. Louise, glad to see him so relaxed and enjoying himself, sat quietly in a corner and listened.

'Where did you find him?' Jenny asked, pausing from collecting glasses to sit down beside her. 'He's dishy. He clicked his heels and kissed my hand when he arrived. And he was loaded with flowers. I'm not sure if they were meant for me or you, but I put them in water.'

Louise had guessed where the flowers came from, a glorious bouquet in a range of vibrant colours. 'I think all the Poles do that. It's the custom with them.'

'Where did you meet him?'

'On a train. The other people in the carriage were being nasty to him and I stuck up for him.'

'Does Tony know about him?'

'Of course. I don't have secrets from Tony. Besides, he's married.'

'That doesn't mean anything these days.'

'It does to me and it does to him. He adores his wife but he had to leave her behind in Poland and he doesn't know what's happened to her. I've been trying to cheer him up.'

'Very successfully, it seems,' Jenny said, as a gale of laughter came from the other side of the room.

Jan was laughing but Louise detected the underlying strain he was under. There were dark rings round his eyes and the blue eyes themselves were bleak. This was a man almost at the end of his tether.

'Where's Tony now?'

'Near London somewhere.'

'Not the best place to be right now.'

The first raid of the Blitz had been bad enough but that had only been the beginning; the constant bombing night after night was exhausting the population and the night before had been the worst yet. According to Jan, a pall of acrid smoke hung over the city, bits of blackened paper and charred rags drifted about on the breeze and there was broken glass, brick and cement dust everywhere, even some distance from the destruction. The government had admitted in news bulletins that thousands of people had been made homeless and thousands more were without water, gas or electricity. The House of Commons had been reduced to rubble and many other famous landmarks damaged. And it wasn't only Londoners who suffered; other big cities had been subjected to their share. It was a bad time everywhere. Greece had fallen, Germany had invaded Crete, there was fierce fighting in North Africa where the Germans had gone to the aid of the Italians, and Malta was being bombed out of existence. Everyone was feeling and looking drab. What was needed was some good news to cheer everyone up.

'I know,' Louise said. 'But he tells me he isn't in active combat. I think he's got a desk job.'

'That's a waste of a good pilot, don't you think?'

'Perhaps, but I'm not complaining. Jan has been getting more and more exhausted and I don't want that for Tony.'

'When will you see him again? Tony, I mean.'

'He's due some leave, but hasn't been able to get away. Soon, I hope.'

'Time, gentlemen please,' Stan called from behind the bar.

The RAF men drained their glasses and left to pile into the Humber car that had brought them from the airfield and were soon gone. Jan came and sat down beside Louise. 'I like your friends,' he said, watching Stan slide the bolts in place on the door. Jenny was hanging tea towels over the pumps on the bar.

'And I'm sure they like you.'

'They fly Blenheims. That's what I was doing when I first came to England.'

'Yes, and I recall you didn't think much to it.'

He laughed. 'We have to do the job given to us, don't we?'

'Yes,' she agreed.

'I am glad I met you. I think I was going a little bit mad before, becoming reckless, and that is not good.'

'Glad to help. Have you heard any news of your wife?'

'No, none. The people at home have ways of communicating with the Polish government in London and sometimes we hear things, but not often and then we don't know how reliable it is, or how old. I think it is perhaps dangerous for the people at home to send messages and the London government-in-exile cannot waste time trying to find out about individuals. It is not easy, so many have died . . .' His voice faded.

She put a hand over his. 'Don't despair, Jan. The war will end one day.'

'That was almost the last thing I said to Rulka, "The war will end and I will come back . . ."'

'Hang on to that thought.'

'I am trying. Have you heard from your Tony?'

'Yes. He writes that he is busy, though what he's busy doing, I have no idea.'

'But he is in England?'

'Yes.'

'And he doesn't mind that you write to me and let me come and stay with you?'

'You are not exactly staying with me, are you? We are both staying at the Pheasant which is a respectable public house. Yes, he knows. He said if he was in your shoes he would be glad to have someone to cheer him up.'

'You do cheer me up. You make my stay in England not so bad. If I did not have Rulka and you did not have Tony . . .'

'Yes, I know.' She stood up, unwilling to continue that topic. 'It's time I went to bed.'

He followed her from the room and up the stairs. On the landing, she stopped outside her door. 'Goodnight, Jan.'

'Goodnight, Louise.' He took her hand and put it to his lips in his usual fashion, then grabbed both her shoulders and pulled her forward to kiss her cheeks, first one, then the other. 'That is the kiss of a true friend and I am your friend, should you ever need one.'

'I know,' she whispered and fled into her room, closing the door and leaning back against it. Was Jan getting a little too amorous? How could she tell? She had so little experience of the ways of men, particularly of men living with danger every day of their lives. Did it change their character, make them more impulsive, less likely to consider the consequences of what they did? Did they care more, or less?

She crossed the room and stood looking out of the window at the night sky. It was a clear night, the half-moon was bright; the bombers would be back and Jan's colleagues would be up there, fending them off. But not Jan, not tonight. He was probably already asleep in the next room, dreaming of his Rulka. Poor man, he had so wanted a friend and it had only been a friendly peck on the cheek to say thank you. She pulled the blackout curtains shut and switched on the light so that she could see to undress. Tomorrow, after church, she would take him round the village and introduce him to a few people, so that he could make more friends.

Jan returned to Northolt at the end of his leave more relaxed than he had been since leaving Poland. The nightly terror visited on London hardly touched the people in the rural communities and, unless they had friends or relatives in areas being bombed, they had no real idea of what it was like to crouch in shelters night after night and listen to their houses crumpling and burning. The Cottlesham people were aware of aeroplanes droning overhead, heard about the raids on the daily BBC bulletins and read about them in the newspapers, but that was second-hand and not real. Jan would not have dreamt of trying to explain it to them, instead he had enjoyed talk of farming and country lore, watched Cottlesham men playing cricket and laughed when Louise tried to explain the game to him. 'There are eleven men in each team,' she said. 'The idea is for the team that's in to get as many runs as possible before getting out. When they are all out, they come in and the other team goes out.'

'I see, it is a game of in and out,' he said laughing. 'Which is the team that's in?'

'Cottlesham. Bill Young and Graham Wayne are batting. Swaffham are fielding.'

'But there are only two Cottlesham men out there. Where are the rest?'

'Waiting to go in to bat when the other two are out. Watch and learn.'

He was no nearer an understanding at the end of the game than he had been at the beginning, but it had been enjoyable just sitting in a deckchair next to Louise, doing nothing but tease each other.

He liked England; it was so green, with its narrow lanes and hedges, it's gently rolling hills, its bustling towns and picturesque villages, its farms and grand houses. It wasn't Poland, of course, but it would be a good country to settle in if he could not go back home. Whatever put that idea into his head? Of course he would go home. Rulka was there. He had to keep telling himself that because she was becoming more and more distant as if she were floating out of his reach, up among the stars, further away each day, and it was difficult to see her face when he shut his eyes. All he had was that well-thumbed snapshot to remind him what she looked like and he consulted it constantly. If he didn't see her soon, touch her, talk to her, his love for her would become a thing of dreams, ephemeral, not real. And dreams fade . . .

He pulled himself together as the train drew into Liverpool Street station and came to a stop. He picked up his haversack and left the train. The reality was that he had a job to do, a war to win, and he had better concentrate on that. Rulka would wait for him.

Chapter Five

With the threat of invasion over, Tony and his colleagues were kept busy monitoring the German navy. It was vital to keep the Atlantic sea lanes open so that supplies could get through. In spite of everyone's best efforts too much shipping was being sunk, by surface craft and submarines. Two German battle cruisers, the *Scharnhorst* and the *Gneisenau* had left the docks at Kiel and were creating havoc with shipping, but could not be found and engaged. Then regular reconnaissance pictures being taken of Brest harbour showed them in dock being refitted. Tony had braved frightening anti-aircraft fire to bring back his pictures but he had come back with only a few holes in his fuselage and was jubilant when he heard the *Gneisenau* had been so badly damaged by torpedo bombers it would be out of commission for months. The job he was doing was definitely worthwhile.

But the prize was the *Bismarck*, Germany's newest, biggest and fastest battleship, but so far it had stayed in its moorings in the Baltic, out of range of reconnaissance aircraft. But that was to change. The British naval attaché in Stockholm alerted the

Admiralty in May 1941 that the ship had been spotted crossing the Baltic, presumably on its way to the Atlantic. Two pilots in the reconnaissance team stationed in Wick in Scotland were sent out to investigate. What the cameras on Pilot Officer Suckling's aircraft had recorded was confirmed as soon as he landed and the film was processed and sent down to RAF Medmenham where the interpretation unit had relocated after the Wembley station had been bombed. There was no doubt he had filmed the *Bismarck*.

The find caused great excitement and all the resources of the PRU were used to keep track of her while the navy assembled an armada to sink her. Tony was sent to Scotland to reinforce the small team there, and was soon flying over the Norwegian fjords. He was not as familiar with this coastline with its jagged cliffs and tiny offshore islands as he had been of the coast of France and the Low Countries; it took all his navigational skills to identify where he was. Finding his way back to Wick after taking his pictures was even more nerve-racking. Below him was three hundred miles of cold, grey ocean. Even a tiny error in navigation could result in him missing the Shetland Islands where he could pinpoint his position and turn south. Miss those and he would find himself heading out into the north Atlantic and running out of fuel.

He was keyed up to fever pitch as he peered out of the cockpit, looking for the tiny islands. He dropped down low to check on something he had caught sight of below him. It was not an island but a ship, a very large ship, and it had spotted him. The big guns opened up. He had no defence. He was hit but still hoped to climb out of trouble, but the aircraft refused to respond. And then the cockpit exploded in a ball of fire. He didn't feel a thing as the Spitfire spiralled out of control and hit the sea like a fiery comet . . .

The sinking of the *Bismarck* was the good news everyone had been praying for. The great ship had been tracked going all round the north of Iceland and then turning south into the mid Atlantic. On the way it had sunk the *Hood*, the navy's biggest battle cruiser which went down in four minutes with only three survivors out of a crew of nearly one and a half thousand. Bent on revenge, the ships of the navy went after the *Bismarck*, and though they lost her for a time, reconnaissance found her again, apparently making for Brest. The armada subjected her to a series of torpedo attacks, one of which damaged her steering gear so badly she lost control and could only drift round and round in circles. *HMS Rodney* and *George V* went in for the kill. Hundreds of shells set the great ship on fire. It finally went down two hours later. The newspapers made a great story of it and the country rejoiced.

Louise had agreed that it was good news, but other matters, closer to home, had claimed her attention. It had been a trying day at school. Tommy had had a fierce fight with Freddie Jones which had resulted in bloodied noses on both sides. Neither would say what they had been fighting about. Louise was well aware that some of the children called Tommy 'teacher's pet', an epithet he hated and one which made him react ferociously; it might have been that. She had given them both a dressing-down and sent them to John Langford, the ultimate punishment as far as the children were concerned. John didn't like using the cane, but sometimes he felt it was necessary, and on this occasion the boys had stinging hands to add to their bloody noses. Tommy felt he had been victimised and looked to her for comfort, but of course she could not give it; if anything she had to be extra strict with him or he would suffer more. She resolved to have a serious talk with him after tea and find out what was really going on.

'There was a phone call for you this afternoon,' Jenny said as soon as she arrived home that sunny afternoon.

Louise brightened. 'Tony?'

'No, his father. He said to ring him back. I left the number on the pad.'

Louise went out into the hall where there was a pay phone and asked the operator for the Witham number. It was picked up as soon as it rang. 'It's Louise, Mr Walsh.'

'My dear, I'm afraid I have some bad news.'

She listened to what he said, but couldn't take it in. 'What on earth was he doing in the North Atlantic?' she queried. 'He's stationed at Heston, not Scotland, and he wasn't flying at all. It can't be true.'

'Seems he was moved to Wick two days ago and he *was* flying, Louise, he had been all along.' The voice at the other end of the line was quiet but his words were clear enough.

'Are you sure there hasn't been some dreadful mistake?'

'No, Louise, no mistake. His squadron leader has been to see us. He told us Tony disappeared on a mission.'

'Disappeared doesn't mean dead.' She was fighting growing panic by questioning everything. Her hands were shaking so much she could hardly hold the receiver.

'In this case, I am afraid it does.'

'I don't believe it.'

'We didn't want to believe it either but we had to face the truth, just as you have to. Peggy is devastated. I must ring off to look after her. Come over if you want to talk.'

Of course she wanted to talk! She replaced the receiver and wandered into the kitchen, too numb to think straight. Jenny stopped what she was doing to go to her. 'Louise, what's happened? You look white as a sheet. Is it Tony?'

She nodded and then the dam burst behind her eyes and she fell against her friend sobbing.

Jenny put her arms round her and said nothing. When the

tears had subsided a little, she led her to the sitting room and sat down beside her on the sofa. 'Tell me what happened,' she said.

'He was on a reconnaissance mission tracking the *Bismarck* and he didn't come back,' she managed to say between sobs. 'I didn't know he was flying. He told me he wouldn't be asked to kill anyone and he was pleased about that. He lied, Jenny, he lied to me.'

'Perhaps he didn't want to worry you. In any case, do the reconnaissance people fight? Aren't they just supposed to take pictures?'

'I don't know. Oh, Jenny, what am I going to do without him? I loved him so and we had such plans . . .' Stricken, she twisted her engagement ring round and round until it dropped off in her lap. Appalled, she grabbed it and put it back on her finger and started to cry again. Jenny took her in her arms and rocked her like a baby. Stan came in, took one look at them and silently disappeared again.

At last Louise stopped crying, mopped her eyes with her already sodden handkerchief and said, 'I must go to his parents. We have to talk.'

'Of course. First thing in the morning. I'll tell Mr Langford, he'll look after your class. Stan will take you to the station in the pony and trap.'

It didn't seem real and yet she knew it was and cried all night until exhaustion overtook her just before dawn and she managed an hour or two's sleep. She rose next morning and looked in the mirror at red swollen eyes and blotched cheeks. There was nothing she could do about them. And it didn't matter anyway. When she arrived in Witham, she saw that Peggy's face was just as bad. They clung to each other and wept, before either of them said a word.

'Tell me what happened,' Louise said, when they recovered enough to talk and Philip had made them tea.

'Squadron Leader Tuttle came and broke the news to us,' he said. 'Tony went out to track the *Bismarck* and he didn't come back.'

'Could he have landed somewhere?'

'That's what I asked,' Peggy said. 'But the Squadron Leader said there was nowhere for him to land, it's just miles and miles of sea, but they had checked everywhere within his range in case he had got lost and put down, but there was no sign of him. And then another aircraft reported seeing a fighter being attacked by a ship and going down into the sea. He wasn't able to identify it, but it was exactly where Tony would have been on his way back to base. And all other missing aircraft had been accounted for.'

'He was a first-class navigator, he wouldn't have got lost,' Philip put in. 'The Squadron Leader was sure of that.'

'So he's really gone?' Louise felt numb. The tears had dried up and she had no more to shed. 'What are we going to do?'

'What can we do, but carry on?' Philip said. 'Other people are suffering just as we are suffering. We are not alone.'

'That doesn't help,' Peggy retorted sharply.

'I know, my love, I know. Shall I make us some lunch?'

'I can't eat anything.'

'Neither can I,' Louise added.

He made more tea and they sat drinking it and talking about Tony. Philip and Peggy recalled incidents in his life, some of them amusing enough to raise a wan smile, and Louise listened and tried not to think about the plans they had made which would never come to fruition. Tony, her love, was gone. She would never see him again.

She left them in the middle of the afternoon and went home

to Edgware to tell her parents the sad news. Her mother was sympathetic but her father was non-committal. The fact that Louise was desperately unhappy seemed to pass over his head. 'It's happened to a lot of people in this war,' he said. 'You'll get over it.' Which was not something she was ready to hear.

'Don't you care?'

He shrugged. 'It is God's will. Whether I care or not is irrelevant.'

She gave up, hugged her mother and said, 'I must get back to Cottlesham.'

She had intended to stay the night but in the face of her father's indifference could not bear to spend a moment longer with him. At Cottlesham she would learn to pick up the pieces of her life among friends and do the job she was paid to do.

'If the siren goes, mind you take shelter,' her mother called after her as she walked down the garden path.

Jan read Louise's letter for a second time and his heart went out to her. She was trying to be brave and practical but it was obvious it was a struggle. He knew how that felt. She had befriended him and cheered him up when he needed it and he had said he was her friend. Saying it was one thing, now it was time to prove it. He applied for a long-overdue pass and went down to Cottlesham.

'She is at school,' Jenny told him when he arrived. 'Her lot are on mornings this week, so she'll finish at half past twelve. She'll be pleased to see you. Poor thing, it's been hard for her, but she's coping.'

He went to meet her, standing outside the school gate as the London children tumbled out and ran off for an afternoon of freedom, and the village children filled the playground in their place. Tommy, with Beattie tagging along, spotted him. 'Uncle

Jan,' he called. 'Are you going to walk home with us?'

'Not today, Tommy. I'll wait for Miss Fairhurst. You go along. We will follow.'

The road emptied, the evacuees had gone, the village children had disappeared inside the building. He began to wonder if he had missed her. And then she was crossing the playground towards him. Her head was down and she did not immediately see him standing beside the gate and he was able to watch her. She was thinner and paler than he remembered and she walked without the usual spring in her step. 'Louise,' he said softly.

Startled she looked up to see him standing there, holding out his arms to her. She ran into them. 'Jan! Oh, Jan, I hoped you would come.'

'And I have come. My friend needs me, so here I am.'

He took her by the hand and led her away from the school. 'Do you want to go home or shall we go for a walk?'

'Let's walk.'

They turned onto the common. It was rough ground, dotted with blackberry brambles, elderberry bushes and crab apple trees, which provided the villagers with fruit in due season. It was also used as rough pasture; there were a couple of tethered cows grazing its lush grass and a rabbit scuttled away as they approached. At that time of day there was no one about but the animals.

He put the hand he held to his lips. 'Tell me,' he said softly.

'He was on reconnaissance and was shot down. He didn't even have a gun on his aeroplane. I didn't know he was flying, he told me he wouldn't have to kill anyone. I didn't realise he meant he was unarmed.'

'It might not have made any difference.'

'Perhaps not. I'll never know, will I?'

'He died doing what he wanted to do, to be of use and yet not kill. Take comfort from that.'

'I do try.'

'You are very brave.'

'Me? No, I am not brave. I am hurt and angry and miserable.'

'Oh, my dear one, I feel for you. If I could take away that hurt and anger and help you to smile again, I would. Tell me how.'

'I don't know how. Just be you.'

He stopped to fold her in his arms, holding her tight against him. 'I am as lost and uncertain as you are,' he murmured. 'But for what it's worth, I'm here for you.'

'Thank you.' She lifted her head to kiss his cheek. 'I needed someone to give me a cuddle.'

'Cuddle, what is that? I have not heard that word.'

She sometimes forgot that his English vocabulary had gaps. 'Holding someone to comfort them.'

He pulled her down beside him on the grass in the shade of an elder tree. 'Then I will cuddle you.' He held her against him and brushed her hair with his lips. 'Sometimes, I too, need a cuddle.'

They clung to each other while a blackbird chirruped in the branches above their heads. Neither spoke. After a while he stirred and kissed her lips. 'You are not alone,' he said.

'But Jan . . .'

'Hush, sweetheart. Now is not the time for doubts.' He opened her blouse as he spoke, each movement slow and careful, oh, so careful. And he did care. He cupped one exposed breast in his hand and lowered his head to kiss the nipple. She shivered but did not stop him as he pulled her blouse off her shoulders and his hands roamed further over her body. And then from simply being passive, she clung to him all the more fiercely and welcomed him inside her. It was not an act of lust, it was an act of healing.

'I've never done that before,' she murmured some time later as they sat side by side, properly dressed again. He was smoking a cigarette. 'I wouldn't let Tony and ever since . . .' She stumbled, then went on, 'Ever since, I've regretted it. He went to his death thinking I didn't love him enough.'

'I am sure he did not think that at all.'

'I didn't want to lose you the same way, sort of unfulfilled.'

'I understand.'

'I've been unfaithful to Tony, haven't I?'

'No, you haven't. Tony is – forgive me, sweetheart – dead and you are alive. You are young . . .'

'. . . and I'll get over it, that's what my father said.'

He was shocked by the insensitivity of the man, but did not comment. 'No, I didn't mean that, but you have a life to live and life without love is only half a life. It is not good.'

'You too?'

'Me too.'

'But you don't know, not for sure, do you?'

'No, not for sure.' He stubbed out his cigarette. 'Are you ready to face the world again?'

'Yes, I think so.'

He stood up and held out his hand to haul her up.

Together they walked back to the village side by side, but a little apart. He understood she could not be seen holding hands with another man so soon and, besides, she had to maintain her role as the prim and proper schoolteacher.

He returned to duty next day, leaving a different Louise behind, one that walked with her head up and had a spring in her step again. His own emotions were in turmoil. He had not gone to Cottlesham with the intention of making love to her, but it had seemed the natural thing to do. Unlike his compatriots who took full advantage of the young ladies who adored them, he had always held back. He told himself he was a married man and faithful to Rulka, but that wasn't the whole of it. Louise had always been in the background, growing in importance to him. He prided himself on being a man of honour; he would never have made love to her if Tony had not died or if she had resisted. Had Rulka died too? Some of his compatriots had heard positive news of their loved ones through messages being sent, along with intelligence, to the Polish government in London and it had been passed on. Some were dead, some sent to prison, some getting by as best they could in occupied Poland. When this happened he asked about Rulka but the answer was always the same: 'No information. Sorry.' Not knowing was the worst of it.

The German invasion of Russia towards the end of June seemed to sound the death knell of his hopes. The British government conveniently forgot the non-aggression pact Stalin had made with Germany before they both invaded Poland and embraced the USSR as an ally, an ally who would be given all the help it needed to resist the invader. Jan viewed this new development with misgiving. It was true it would divert Hitler's attention from the west, but it made a battleground of Poland all over again.

The nightly terror over London and the other big cities came to a halt and the people gave a huge sigh of relief. It wasn't the end of the war – far from that, because there was fighting in North Africa and the Mediterranean, and ships were still being lost at sea – but it gave the people of Britain, and that included the Polish airmen, a much needed breather. From defending the skies over Britain, Jan's role changed and he found himself flying the new Spitfire and escorting bombers on their way to bomb Germany and important targets in occupied Europe, tempting German fighters out to do battle. At other times, after crossing the Channel, he would fly low, almost at treetop height, and strafe airfields, railway stations, freight trains and troops on the move with his cannon. They were taking the fight to the enemy at last.

'You're pregnant, aren't you?' Jenny was standing in the doorway of the bathroom, having heard Louise throwing up her breakfast.

Louise, who had been kneeling on the floor with her head over the lavatory pan, looked up. 'I think so.'

'Only think so?'

'Well, yes, I am.'

Jenny ran some water onto a flannel and mopped Louise's face with it. 'It's not Tony's is it?'

'No.'

'You're an idiot, do you know that?'

'Yes.'

'What are you going to do about it?'

'Nothing I can do.'

'Does Jan know?'

'Not yet . . .'

'Don't you think you should tell him?'

'I will. I'll have to tell my parents too and I'm dreading that.' She stood up and tottered back to her room, followed by Jenny. 'I must get ready for school.'

'You're not fit for school.'

'Yes I am. I'm over it now. And I've got to keep going as long as I can.'

She knew as soon as her condition became known she would lose her job and if she did not have a job how could she go on living at the Pheasant? Something had to be done but she was too emotionally confused to think clearly.

'Too right, you do.'

'You're not very sympathetic.'

'What good's sympathy now?'

Louise managed a wan smile. Jenny's abrupt manner hid a soft heart. 'None at all.'

'Take the day off and go and see your mother. A girl needs her mother at a time like this.'

'I'll go on Saturday.'

If she hoped to catch her mother alone, her hopes were dashed. She arrived just as both parents were sitting down to lunch. Her mother jumped up to hug her. 'How lovely to see you, dear.'

'You'd better sit down,' her father said, indicating an empty chair at the table. 'We can probably stretch this Woolton pie to three.'

'I'm not hungry.' She was so keyed up with nerves that even the contemplation of food was liable to make her sick again.

'Why not?' her mother asked. 'Aren't you well? You don't look very well. The country air is supposed to put roses in your cheeks not make you look pale. You've got dark rings under your eyes too.'

'I'm all right. I've got something important to tell you.'

'We're listening,' her father said, ladling pie onto his plate.

'I'm pregnant.'

Henry's eyes nearly popped out of his head as he stopped what he was doing to stare at her and Faith caught her breath in a little whimper of concern.

'Are we to assume you are not married and this is the product of the devil?' he said coldly.

'The devil has nothing to do with it,' Louise said. She was calm now and would not allow him to browbeat her. 'It is the product of love.'

'Love, bah!'

'You and Tony were simply carried away,' her mother put in, trying to defuse the situation. 'No doubt if you stay down in Cottlesham no one here will know about it and you can have it adopted.'

'It will not be adopted. And Tony and I were never carried away. The baby is not his.'

'What?' Henry sprang to his feet, knocking over his chair. 'I have begotten a whore.' He pulled her from her chair and forced her to her knees. 'Pray for forgiveness. Go on, pray.'

His bony-fingered grip on her shoulder was hurting her, but she ignored it. Any sign of pain would make him worse, she knew that from experience. 'Father, if I need forgiveness, I shall ask it privately of God, not you.'

He turned and grabbed a thin stick that was always kept leaning against the wall in the alcove by the fire and brought it down with all his strength on her shoulders. 'I'll beat the evil out of you. You have always been a thorn in my side with your wilful ways. Now we are all to be punished. God knows what I have done to deserve such a daughter.'

'Henry, stop! Please stop!' Faith cried, trying to grab his arm as he continued the thrashing. He knocked her away. She fell into a chair.

Louise, angry as much on her mother's behalf as her own, turned suddenly, grabbed the stick and hauled herself to her feet, making him almost lose his balance. Then she took the implement of her torture and broke it across her knee. 'You will never beat me with that again, Father.'

'I am no longer your father!' He was panting from his exertion and red in the face. 'I renounce you. Get out of my sight. I never want to see you again.'

'But Henry—' Faith began.

'And you will not see her again either. She is lost to us. We never had a daughter.'

Louise looked at her weeping mother, but dare not go to her. She pulled the remnant of her blouse about her stinging shoulders, found her jacket and slipped it on. Then she left the house without looking back.

She found a public call box and asked for the number Jan had given her. She had to wait while someone went to fetch him, then he was at the other end of the line. 'Jan, I'm in London. Can you get away? I must see you.'

He didn't ask what was wrong, he simply said, 'I'll be with you in an hour, less if I can borrow a car. Where are you?'

'I'm in Edgware but I'll come into town to meet you.'

'Go to the station hotel at Liverpool Street. I'll meet you in the lounge.'

Jan knew Witold had a little sports car and dashed off to find him. 'Matter of life and death,' he said, when Witold wanted to know what he wanted it for.

His friend smiled. 'A lady in distress?'

'Yes. It's urgent, She would not have called me if it wasn't.'

'You are on standby, aren't you?'

'Yes, but you can square it with Squadron Leader Krasnodebski, can't you? Stefan will stand in for me. Tell him I'll do two of his duties to make up for it.'

Witold grinned and tossed him the keys 'Mind you bring it back in one piece.'

Jan thanked him and was gone.

The car was a speedy little roadster and he was soon approaching the suburbs where he had to slow down. Even so, he made the journey in record time. He had no idea what Louise wanted him for, but he had known by the sound of her voice that it was important. He left the doorman to park the car and rushed into the lounge. She was sitting hunched in a corner, her whole body screwed up as if in pain. As soon as she saw him, she jumped to her feet. 'Oh, Jan.'

He went to embrace her and felt her flinch at his touch. She had never done that before and it puzzled him. 'Louise, what is wrong? Not the right time for a cuddle?'

'Yes, it is, but . . .' She gave a sharp little cry as he put a hand on her shoulder.

'Are you hurt?' He took his hand away and noticed a dark-red stain on her jacket. 'You have been hurt.' He slipped the jacket off her shoulder and saw the shredded blouse. 'Wait here.' He dashed off and spoke to the receptionist, then he came back with a room key and took her hand. 'Come with me.'

'Now,' he said, when they were sitting side by side on the bed. 'Let me look.'

'It's nothing,' she said, as he carefully took off her jacket.

Her blouse was sticking to her raw flesh. He knew the marks of a beating when he saw them. He went into the bathroom and soaked his handkerchief, then went back to tenderly dabbing the wounds to remove the blouse. 'Who did this to you?'

'My father.'

'Your father! My God, what father would do such a thing to his own child?'

She winced as he touched her but managed a crooked smile. 'He was trying to beat the wickedness out of me.'

'Wickedness! The man is mad.'

'Not mad, angry. I let him down, shamed him . . .'

'How?'

'I went with you.'

'Oh.' He paused. 'Did you have to tell him?'

'Yes, I did.' She paused. 'You see, I am going to have a baby. *We* are going to have a baby.'

He stared at her, then his face broke into a grin. 'Is that bad?'

'From my father's point of view, it is. He has thrown me out, said he never wants to see me again.'

'I see. Were you afraid I would say the same?'

'No, Jan, I know you better than that.'

The last of the torn blouse came away. 'You need some ointment on that. I'll go and buy some and come back. Then we will decide what to do. I'll buy a blouse too.'

'You will need some clothing coupons.' Painfully she reached for her handbag and handed him a sheet of coupons. Clothes had only recently been rationed and she had not used any of them yet.

He left her to find a chemist and a shop selling blouses. He needed to come to terms with what she had told him. How did he feel? Sorry? Ashamed? Elated at the thought of being a father? Fatherhood was something he had talked to Rulka about, but somehow her work, the war and their enforced separation had put paid to their plans. He told himself he still loved Rulka, but with Louise's news, she had slipped even further from him. And he loved Louise too.

He hurried back to her. She was lying face down on the bed with her arms at her sides. He sat down beside her and applied the ointment with gentle fingers. 'I ought to fetch a doctor,' he said.

'No, he'll only ask questions and I don't want anyone to know.'

'It's not the first time he's beaten you, is it? There are old scars here.'

'I was a wicked and wilful child.'

He bent and kissed the nape of her neck. 'You don't believe that, do you?'

'I tried not to be bad, but the harder I tried, the more I displeased him.'

'What about your mother?'

'She is afraid of him and believes very strongly in her vows to honour and obey. Sometimes she would try and stick up for me, but it didn't do any good. If anything it made him worse. It's a terrible thing to say, but the war helped me. I got away.' She scrambled into a sitting position and turned to face him. 'Now I have to manage as best I can.'

'I cannot marry you, you know that, don't you?'

'Yes, I know.'

'But that does not mean you have to manage alone. I will look after you.'

'Oh, Jan.' The tears she had not shed when she was being beaten, rolled down her cheeks.

'Cuddle?' he queried with a lopsided grin.

'Yes please.'

Tenderly he took her in his arms and they lay down together. She turned on her side to face him. 'Jan,' she said tentatively. 'Will you mind being a father?'

'Mind, my sweet? I shall love it, as I love you.'

'Do you? Really? But what about your wife? What about Rulka?'

'Rulka was my first love. I thought she would be the only one, until I met you. Now she has drifted away into the clouds where I cannot reach her. Just as your Tony has.'

'You think she is dead?'

'I don't know. Perhaps.' He paused, dwelling on that thought for a moment, then set it aside. 'We must decide what we are to do.'

'I shall keep my job as long as I can, but as soon as I begin to show, I'll have to leave.'

'Will you stay in Cottlesham?'

'I'd like to. It depends on whether Jenny will have me and if I can afford to.'

'Money is not a problem. I will make you a regular allowance, and if anything happens to me, I will make sure you and our child are provided for.'

'You don't want me to have it adopted?'

'Certainly not! You do not want it either, do you?'

'No, but some people might think I should.'

'Then they have no heart.' He paused. 'Shall we stay here tonight? Tomorrow you will be better able to face your friends in Cottlesham.'

'I haven't got a toothbrush.'

He produced two from his pocket. 'I bought them in the chemist when I bought the ointment.'

She laughed. 'Oh, Jan, I do love you.'

Chapter Six

February 1942

'I think it's time you disappeared,' Lech murmured. It was not a good idea to speak too loudly, even in the hospital. 'The Gestapo are getting too close for comfort.'

'I'm not leaving. I'm needed here and I've nowhere to go in any case.' Rulka, never very robust, was thin as a rake, but her small frame concealed a courage and determination which would not have shamed a gladiator.

'You could go to the grave,' Lech said, looking down at the body of the girl who had just died in spite of their efforts to save her. 'She's about your size. I'll sign the death certificate in your name. Then you can disappear.'

'You are not serious, are you?'

'Yes, I am. The Germans have rounded up hundreds of innocent people since that ammunition train was sabotaged two days ago. Is it any wonder one of them told all she knew and the name Rulka Grabowska was mentioned? Simply trying to lie low will not be enough. The only way they'll give up looking for you is if you are officially dead.'

The Germans had instituted what they called 'collective responsibility', which meant the whole community was punished for the deeds of the few and any acts of sabotage brought on merciless reprisals which they hoped would deter the resistance. Rulka found it heartbreaking, but if they stopped their work, it meant that the occupiers had won and that could not be allowed to happen. 'How do you know all this?'

'I know someone on the inside. I won't tell you his name . . .'

'No, don't.' She knew Lech was allowed into the Pawiak prison to treat the prisoners, not that there was much he could do for them, but no doubt his information had come from someone there.

'You haven't any family to mourn you, have you?'

Rulka looked down at the girl in the hospital bed. She was no more than skin and bone. Brought into the hospital with pneumonia, her emaciated body had had no resistance and she had soon succumbed. 'No,' she said. 'Except Jan. When he comes back, it is to Warsaw he will come. I must be here so that he can find me.'

'Do you even know if he is alive?'

'No, I don't. How could I? But until I am certain he will never come back, I will continue to wait for him.' She had not heard from Jan since that brief letter sent from Romania told her he was going to France. Whether he arrived there, she did not know or whether, having arrived, he had been rounded up by the Germans when France fell or managed to escape, she had no idea. She liked to picture him, free and happy, flying aeroplanes, and like her, doing his bit to win the war so they could be reunited. It was that hope and her gritty determination not to admit defeat that kept her going.

Lech sighed. 'You have to face facts, Rulka, and the facts are that life will never be the same as it was before the war, even if the Allies win, which is looking more and more unlikely. Save your own skin, no one else will.'

'My skin is not important, the fight for freedom is.'

'You cannot fight for freedom or be reunited with your husband if you are dead, can you? If and when the war ends and you are still alive, then is the time to worry about the name you use.'

It was not as if changing identities was something unheard of. She knew it happened frequently. Taking the identity of a dead person had its risks because of the chance that relatives or people who had known them would turn up, but it was a risk the underground deemed worth taking in certain circumstances. A safer method was to use birth certificates of dead babies from twenty-odd years before. Priests in sympathy with the underground, and that was most of them, would find suitable ones in their registers and pass them on and with these a new identity was forged, work permits and ration cards obtained. Some underground workers had two or three of these, providing them with extra rations and different addresses, to which they could move in the event of searches.

'What is her name?' she asked.

'Krystyna Nowak.'

'What about her family?'

'All dead. She was brought in by the janitor of the building where she lived. Her mother and sisters died in a bombing raid at the beginning of the war and her father was shot in a round of reprisals last year, so the man told me. She was living alone in the cellar which is all that's left of the building.'

Rulka knew what that was like. Ever since she had buried her parents, she had lived in the bombed-out cellar of their home. There was no gas or electricity but thankfully the chimney still stood above the ruins of the building and she could light a fire in the grate, burning furniture and odd pieces of wood, not only what had been in the house but what could be dragged from elsewhere. Keeping warm was a major concern as well as keeping fed. The hospital, though damaged, still functioned and she availed herself of the opportunity to have a bath in the nurses' quarters while she was there. Sometimes she was given food, sometimes she queued for hours for half a loaf of black bread.

'What about the underground? You are not suggesting I should stop that work, are you?'

The Polish underground was the most organised of any of the occupied countries. It was a state on its own, answerable to the government-in-exile in London. It had a political wing, an army with a proper military hierarchy, medical staff, schools and university. Afraid of an educated population who could challenge them intellectually, the Germans had shut the schools, retaining only those producing skilled manual workers who could be useful to the Reich as labour. The Ministry of Education building in Szucha Street had been turned into the Gestapo headquarters. Nevertheless, the young people of Poland were being educated, usually by teachers and lecturers who had been turned out of their jobs. But the most important function of the underground army was sabotage, propaganda and the collection of intelligence to pass on to the Polish government in London. Communication between Warsaw and London was difficult, though not impossible, and agents, money and supplies had been parachuted in, but not nearly enough. Lech and Rulka had been involved from the start.

'No, but how many of them know your real name anyway?'

'I am not sure that any do. They know me as Myszka.' Everyone used a code name without a surname for security's sake and she had chosen Jan's pet name for her: Mouse. Apart from one's immediate superior there was no upward contact. No one at the lower level knew who was really running things. 'How did my real name come to be mentioned?'

'I don't know. You have lived in Warsaw all your life, so perhaps someone recognised you on that last operation, an infiltrator or someone terrified out of their lives.'

'Do you know who?'

'No, but if it was an infiltrator, he or she will be rooted out and dealt with.'

She shuddered, knowing what that meant. 'What about my job here? We're short-staffed as it is.'

'You can be replaced. Your life is more important.'

'Very well.' She sighed. 'Rulka Grabowska dies and Krystyna Nowak lives – for the moment.'

He signalled to someone waiting outside the room to come in and take the body away and quickly filled in the death certificate. 'Pneumonia', he wrote as the cause of death, refraining from adding 'starvation'. The little cortège had no sooner disappeared along the corridor than a new patient was wheeled in.

Why Rulka went to the mortuary when she went off duty she did not know; sympathy, she supposed, because there was no one else to mourn the girl and she was taking something precious from her. She found old Father Karlowicz kneeling beside Krystyna's body, praying. Rulka dropped to her knees beside him, as he intoned a prayer for the dead.

'Amen,' he said, when he finished and crossed himself, but he did not immediately stand up. 'Someone came to my church for confession this morning,' he went on in the same sing-song murmur he had used to pray. 'He needs help.'

'Who is he?'

'A British prisoner of war. He ran off from a stalag work party. He has been hiding in the forest.'

'Are you sure he is genuine?'

'I think so. Can you help him?'

'What makes you think I can do anything?'

'I don't, but I hoped you could, or would know someone who can.'

'Where is he?'

'I've hidden him in the crypt.'

'I will come this evening after I have taken advice about what to do with him. Seven o'clock.'

'Come to the confessional. I will be waiting.' The confessional box was the safest place to talk; so far the Germans had respected it.

'Father, I am not ready to confess my sins, though they are many. At a time like this it seems an irrelevance.'

He sighed. 'More relevant than ever, I think, but never mind, we will forgo it for the sake of helping the young man.' He crossed himself again, rose and blessed her, then left.

Rulka followed a minute or two later and set off through slushy streets heaped with the rubble of half-demolished buildings. It was strange, but the starkness of the ruined cityscape, with its covering of snow, was almost beautiful. Mounds of snow-covered earth and little wooden crosses dotted along the verges marked burials and on a corner near the station the paving stones had been torn up to make a mass grave for the soldiers who had died defending the city. In summer it had been covered with flowers and visited daily by people who knelt to pray. It had infuriated Ludwig Fischer, the German governor, who ordered the bodies to be dug up and buried in the cemetery, but that had not deterred the people who still came to the spot to pray. Rulka paused to cross herself, then turned up a side street where Stanisław Roman, her immediate superior in the underground movement, lived.

He was in his thirties, a thickset man going prematurely bald but with a large drooping moustache. He was, according to his papers, an undertaker, someone so necessary to the functioning of the city he was usually left unmolested to get on with his work. It was he who hid guns and ammunition in his coffins, whose men dug graves all over the city that contained more than just bodies, who decided on who was going to sabotage what. He was fanatical, uncompromising and courageous. But he was also very careful and a stickler for security. Rulka was one of the few people who knew what he did and she worked for him as assiduously as she did for Lech at the hospital, but even so, she was reluctant to disturb him at an unscheduled time.

He answered the door himself. 'Did anyone follow you?'

'No. I came by a circuitous route.' It was something they were all trained to do and he did not really need to ask her.

'Come in.' He opened the door wider and led her into a comfortable sitting room. There was a crumpled newspaper, a glass and a bottle of vodka on a small table beside an armchair. 'Sit down.' He motioned her to take another chair and fetched another glass from a cupboard to pour her a measure of the spirit. 'What brings you here?'

'A young girl died in the hospital today with no one to arrange her funeral and I thought I would do it for her and thought of you.'

He knew perfectly well she would not do such a thing; unclaimed bodies were disposed of with little ceremony but, though she knew his wife had been killed in the bombardment in the early days of the war, she was unsure if he were alone in the apartment. Until that had been established she could not speak openly.

'Very well,' he said, returning to his seat. 'Now tell me the true reason. You have intelligence?'

'No. There is an escaped prisoner of war hiding in the crypt of the Church of the Holy Cross. He is asking for help.'

'Is he Polish?'

'No, according to Father Karlowicz, he is British. He ran away from a stalag work party and has been hiding in the forest.'

'Why did he come into the city? The forest is by far safer.'

'I don't know. Looking for help to go back to England, I assume.'

'What do you expect me to do?'

'You know how other escaped prisoners have been helped.'

He was thoughtful for a moment. 'He'll have to be thoroughly checked. There have been Nazi infiltrators. And I do not want him here. Take him home with you. Does he speak Polish?'

'I do not know, but I speak a little English. Jan taught me.'

'I will send Boris Martel to you at ten o'clock. Don't open the door to anyone else. I assume you are still living in Jasna Street?'

'Yes, but my official residence is still Zabowski Street. I go there now and again to make sure everything is as it should be.'

'Don't go there anymore. It is the first place they will look for you.'

'Oh, you know—'

'That there is a search on for you, yes. I told Dr Andersz to warn you.'

'He did. He suggested I should change names with a dead patient.'

'What was her name? What do you know of her?'

Rulka told him what she knew which was little enough. 'I have no idea of her background at all,' she said. 'Dr Andersz knows where she was living but as far as he could tell she had no surviving family.'

'How many of your neighbours know who you really are?'

'None that I know of. The original tenants of neighbouring

houses, who might have known my parents, were all killed in the bombs that destroyed the street.'

'Good. Leave it with me.'

He saw her to the door and looked up and down the street carefully before letting her out. On the way to her cellar home, she queued up for bread, a single skinny sausage and beetroot with which she could make *ćwikła*. It was little enough to feed her, let alone a hungry escaped prisoner, but it was all she could find. Since Germany had invaded Russia, the food situation had become worse; the Reich needed all the supplies they could get to feed their hungry army battling the Russian winter as well as the stubborn Russians, and if it meant starving the Poles, so be it, they were only *Untermenschen*, after all.

Before the war, Jasna Street had been the home of exclusive shops and expensive apartments. Now it was a heap of broken stone, splintered wood and shattered furniture. She clambered over the rubble to what appeared to be a broken door, but which was the entrance to a staircase. She felt her way down, then stopped at the bottom to light an oil lamp. It lit a room furnished with a table, a cupboard, a couple of upright chairs and a sofa salvaged from the wreckage of the house above her. In a bowl on a small table in an alcove were the plate and cup left from her breakfast. She washed them up, using water from a standpipe, which Lech had set up for her when she first moved in. It was connected to the boiler in the next room which was fed from the mains, although the boiler didn't work anymore. Then she tidied the room and prepared a camp bed in the boiler room, fetched an old overcoat of Jan's from the room where she slept, and set off for the church.

Father Karlowicz found her sitting in one of the pews in quiet contemplation. She turned when she heard the rustle of his skirt. 'Come,' he said.

She followed him through a side door, down some steps and into the crypt. On the far side was an altar covered with a cloth. He walked over to it and rapped on the top. 'Come out.' A man scrambled out from beneath it. He was young, about her own age, tall and dressed in the remnants of a British soldier's uniform. His face was grey with fatigue, his cheeks hollow from lack of food.

'Hallo,' Rulka said in English.

'Thank the Lord,' he said, giving her a brilliant smile which lit his blue eyes. It reminded her of Jan; he, too, had a smile that could light up a room. 'Someone who speaks English.'

'I only have a little. What is your name?'

'Colin Crawshaw. Sergeant, Royal Engineers.'

She handed him Jan's coat. 'Put that on, please, and come with me.' To the priest, she said, 'Thank you, Father. You may forget he was ever here now.'

'Where are we going?' the soldier asked as she led the way through the streets.

'Do not ask questions,' she murmured. It was gone curfew and only those with passes could venture out. Rulka had one because her work at the hospital meant she worked odd hours, but Nurse Grabowska was supposed to be dead, so it was better to avoid being asked for it. 'The *shkopy* are everywhere and they have their spies. Please do not speak again until we are inside.'

He fell silent. Once in the cellar of her home, she set about lighting a fire in the open grate and boiling a kettle on a primus stove.

He was shivering with cold and reluctant to remove the coat. 'You live here?' he asked, looking about him.

'Yes.'

'It is very spartan.'

'Spartan? What is that?'

123

'Bare. Uncomfortable.'

'It is better than some. I am warm and dry and I can cook what little food there is.'

'Do you live here alone?'

'Yes, but I am expecting someone later this evening. He might help you. Tell me about yourself.' When he hesitated, she added, 'You may trust me.'

He shrugged. 'I suppose I have to trust someone. Besides, there's nothing much to tell. I was taken prisoner in France, left behind at Dunkirk, and shipped from prison to prison until I ended up in Poland. The Poles are our allies, so I told myself that if I could escape I had as good a chance as any of getting back home. I managed to slip away from a working party.'

Rulka had to interrupt this frequently to ask him to explain and speak more slowly. He knew a few simple Polish words and a little German, but when she discovered he could speak reasonable French and it was a language she had learnt at school, they communicated in a mixture of all three which, together with a lot of expressive hand actions, caused a great deal of hilarity. She had not laughed so much for months.

'Poland is a very long way from England, Sergeant, and the ports are in German hands.'

'Yes, but maybe I could get to the Russian lines. Aren't they supposed to be our allies now? Would they help?'

She gave a bitter laugh. 'I doubt it. They would probably send you to Siberia. That would be much worse than a German prisoner of war camp, believe me.' Rulka, like many Poles, trusted Stalin no more than she trusted Hitler.

'Then what do you suggest? I won't give myself up.'

'Let us wait and see what my friend says, shall we? In the meantime, eat.' She put a plate of food on the table in front of him.

'What about you? Where is yours?'

'I have my food at my place of work.' This wasn't strictly true but he looked as though he needed a meal more than she did.

He tucked in and by the time he had finished eating, Boris had arrived.

Rulka had met Boris once or twice before and had no hesitation in letting him in. Dressed in an ill-fitting overcoat and worn-down shoes, he was tall and slim but his slimness hid a wiry strength. Born in Poland in 1918, his parents had fled with him to England during the war with Russia in 1920 and had become British citizens. He had been brought up in England, but his parents never forgot their roots and always spoke Polish at home, with the result he was completely bilingual. How he had arrived in Poland, or even if Boris Martel was his real name, she had no idea and knew better than to ask.

He had brought a half-bottle of vodka with him which he poured into three glasses, then took his to the settee where he sprawled with his long legs out in front of him. He appeared completely relaxed, but appearances were deceptive, as Rulka knew. 'Tell me about yourself,' he instructed Colin, who had stayed at the table, while Rulka busied herself clearing away the plates and washing them up. Colin repeated what he had told Rulka. At the end of it, Boris questioned him closely. He wanted to know where he had lived in England, where he had gone to school, what work he did in civilian life, when and where he joined the army, his regiment and his company within it, how he had been captured and what other camps he had been sent to. He asked him which football team he supported at home and the names of the players. He even asked him what picture had been on at the local cinema the last time he had been in England, all of which Colin patiently answered. Then he asked him his mother's maiden name and where and when he had been born and whether he was married or had a girlfriend.

'I am unmarried and unattached,' he said, growing impatient with the cross-examination. 'My mother was Ethel Rutherford. I was born on the last day of October 1917 in Royston. That's a small town in Hertfordshire, in case you didn't know.'

'I do know,' Boris said quietly. 'We have to make these checks, you know.'

'And am I entitled to make checks myself? Are you going to tell me who you are?'

'No.'

'Is that it, then?'

'For now.'

'Are you going to help me?'

'Perhaps,' Boris said, watching the other man carefully, as he had been doing all through the interview, which had been conducted in English. He turned to Rulka and spoke in Polish. 'Can you keep him here while I make enquiries?'

'I suppose I can, but I'll need a ration card for him and some money . . .'

'I'll see about it. Now I must go.' He stood up and withdrew a sheaf of papers from his pocket which he handed to her. 'Arkady sent these. He said to meet him at the cafe at nine tomorrow morning for further instructions.'

Arkady was the code name for Stanisław Roman. She glanced down at them. They were identity papers for Krystyna Nowak. She thanked him and he left.

'What did he say?' Colin asked her. 'Did he say he would help me?'

'He said you are to stay here while he makes the arrangements.'

'He would not tell me his name. Are you going to tell me yours?'

'It is Krystyna,' she said. 'I have made a bed up for you in the next room. I suggest you go there. I have left some clothes and some toilet things on the bed.'

'Are you in the habit of entertaining men?' he asked, smiling.

It was a moment before she understood him. 'No. They are my husband's.' She had brought most of Jan's civilian clothes to the cellar, mainly to keep them from being looted from the empty apartment and also because they helped to keep her warm.

'Where is he? He isn't going to come home and beat me up, is he?'

She gave a wry smile. 'No, he is dead.' It was easier to say that than explain the truth.

'Oh, I am sorry. Clumsy of me. Please forgive me.'

'Come with me.' She led him to the boiler room, showed him where the lavatory was and left him.

Back in the living room, she sat down in front of the fire to study the papers Stanisław had sent. According to her new *Kennkarte*, she was now Krystyna Nowak, a qualified nurse, born in Lwów on 15th March 1917. Her father was Ludwik Nowak and her mother was Rosa, maiden name Lipska. There was also a certificate of ethnic origin, a ration card and a work permit supposedly issued by the German *Arbeitsamt* for her to work at the Hospital of the St Elizabeth Nuns, both stamped with apparently authentic German stamps. Another sheet of paper contained a potted history of her life, her school, where she qualified, where she had been up to this point. It was a private clinic in Krynica, a spa town on the River San, in Russian-occupied Poland. She had smuggled herself to Warsaw, preferring the Germans to the Russians. Rulka had no idea how much of the history was true, nor did she know where they had obtained the rather fuzzy picture of her on the official documents. But the forgers had done a good job.

It was hours later before she felt confident enough to put the life story on the fire and go to bed. 'I am Krystyna Nowak,' she told herself, over and over again as she lay sleepless. 'And tomorrow, I begin a new life.' She realised suddenly that she had told Colin she was a widow. That was a slip and she must guard against slips like that in the future. It felt bad, not only taking the identity of another person, but denying the existence of Jan. It was for Jan she fought, for Poland and everything about it she held dear. She went to sleep thinking of their last meeting and his assertion: *I will come back*.

She woke late and wandered into the living room in her dressing gown to find Colin raking out the fire, ready to re-lay it. Her heart missed a beat when she saw him dressed in Jan's clothes. He was so like Jan it was uncanny, but it made her warm towards him and she hoped the checks Boris was making would clear him.

'Good morning, Krystyna,' he said cheerfully.

'Good morning,' she responded. 'I hope you were not going to light the fire.'

'Why not?'

'I can't keep a fire going all day, there isn't enough fuel. I only light it when I come home from work.'

'It's freezing in here.'

'I know. You'll get used to it.'

'I was looking at that boiler. If I had a few tools I might be able to get it going again.'

'Could you?' The thought of a little heat and hot water seemed like heaven. 'It used to run on gas, but the pipe was sealed off when the house was bombed. I have no idea if there's any gas there.'

'Get me some tools and I will soon tell you.'

He poured the boiling water on the ersatz coffee, a concoction of ground acorns, while she fetched out half a loaf of bread and a tiny scrape of margarine. 'It's all I have until I get a ration card for you,' she said.

'Ration card? How will you do that?'

'There are ways. It is important you do not ask questions. What you do not know cannot hurt you. I have to go out, but I want your word you will not venture outside and if anyone should come you will not answer the door. Lock yourself in the boiler room . . .'

'I understand. But don't forget the tools, a set of spanners particularly.'

'I'll see what I can find. If you want to help, you can chop up that cupboard in the boiler room.' She had dragged it home over the snow from two streets away.

He stood up, came to attention and saluted in an exaggerated manner that made her laugh. She put on her coat, scarf and gloves and left him. A weak sun was glistening on the half-melted snow, but a bitter wind cancelled out any warmth that might have brought.

The cafe was on Ujazdowskie Boulevard, once a thriving street, but now as dilapidated as the rest of Warsaw. Painted on some of its ruined buildings in an act of defiance were the words: *Polska walczy* – Poland fights. The cafe owner only managed to keep going by serving the German troops who came in for coffee and snacks and because of that he was allowed extra rations. He was vilified as a collaborator, but he was a good Varsovian and often passed on titbits of information he had overheard to Arkady. Rulka had met the undertaker there by appointment on several occasions. Today she felt a shiver of trepidation as if her new identity were written all over her as a lie.

As soon as she arrived, she was shown upstairs to a private room where he was already waiting for her. 'The sergeant passed all the tests,' he told her. 'You may assume he is who he says he is.'

'I'm glad. I like him. What can you do to help him?'

'Nothing at the moment. We'll try and get him to Gdansk, but the guides and safe houses will have to be alerted and then only when we hear of a neutral ship arriving in the harbour. We can't have him wandering about on the loose. Does he speak any Polish at all?'

'A few odd words he learnt in the camp and he knows a bit of German, not enough to be useful, but his French is quite good.'

'Can you keep him?'

'Yes, if I'm given a ration card for him and a little money.'

'You shall have it just as soon as we have established a life story for him, probably as a French worker. In the meantime, teach him a little more Polish. We won't be able to say he's Polish, but it might help him to understand what's going on around him. Don't, whatever you do, let him out alone.'

'No, I have emphasised that.'

'According to the information I have been given he is an engineer and explosives man. We could use him. Do you think he would agree?'

'He might, but I think not if it delayed his return to England.'

'Promise him it won't, but tell him we cannot arrange to send him on for some time.'

'Very well. He said if he had some tools he might be able to mend my boiler. It would be a real help to have that working again.'

'I'll see what I can do.'

'There's my new identity . . .'

'Is there a problem with it?'

'No, I do not think so, but the work permit is for St Elizabeth Hospital. Are they expecting me?'

'You start on Monday. Do not go anywhere near your old

hospital and do not, whatever you do, be tempted to attend Rulka Grabowska's funeral. You were a popular nurse and good friend to many, so there will be a congregation, headed by Dr Andersz.'

She did not need to be told and was miffed that he felt the need to remind her. 'I know better than to go anywhere near it.'

'Stay indoors until next Monday. From then on you are Krystyna Nowak.'

'I understand.'

She left him and wandered about a few streets to put any followers off her trail, and returned to the cellar soon after midday. She and Colin had barely finished their cabbage soup and an apple they shared which had cost her several hundred *zloty*, when a man arrived with a bag of plumber's tools. He handed them to her without speaking, turned and left.

Colin soon had them out, told her he would have to turn off the water to her tap while he worked and disappeared into the boiler room. He worked all afternoon and then she heard a pulsating rumble and rushed in to see him standing admiring his handiwork. Already the room was a little warmer. 'I have turned off all gas connections to the upper part of the house,' he said. 'If I had a bit of piping I might be able to rig up a hot-water tap.'

'Finding that won't be easy and if I could, it would cost too much. You have no idea how prices have shot up.'

He pointed upwards. 'You had a kitchen and bathroom up there, didn't you?'

'Yes, more than one. It was once a well-appointed house, it even had central heating in the downstairs rooms.'

'Let me out. I'll see what I can salvage. I'll take care not to be seen.'

She hesitated. Her orders were clear not to let him out, but if he dressed in an old overcoat with a scarf tied over his head and anyone saw him clambering over the rubble, they would assume he was a looter. Looting might be frowned upon by the occupiers, but to the Varsovians it was a legitimate way of surviving. 'Very well,' she said.

Taking a few spanners, he disappeared. He was gone a long time and she was on tenterhooks, listening for the sound of jackboots. When he did come back he was covered in cement dust and his hands were grazed, but he was loaded with mangled lengths of piping and a couple of taps. He dumped them in the boiler room and disappeared again, returning a few minutes later with a bathroom basin. A third trip produced a small radiator.

'You've got a whole plumber's shop there,' she said.

'I don't know how much I can use, but I'll see what I can do.'

She became his plumber's mate for the next three days, at the end of which, connected by a maze of joined pipes, she had a basin and hot water and the living room was cosily warm from the radiator. The first time she turned on the hot tap, she threw up her hands in delight. 'Colin, you are a magician.'

'My pleasure,' he said. 'Mind you, I don't know how efficient it will be. If the gas pressure drops or is cut off, we'll be back to square one.'

'Square one?' she queried.

He laughed. 'Back to where we were.'

'Well, I am going to take advantage of it, while I can. Go into the boiler room and stay there, while I strip off and wash. You can take your turn later.'

They were both feeling more civilised when Boris arrived. He commented on the warmth of the room immediately.

'Colin mended the boiler and now we have hot water and heating.'

'Sergeant Crawshaw seems to be a good innovator,' he said,

taking off his coat and revealing a crumpled brown suit.

This was translated for Colin's benefit and the rest of the conversation between the two men was conducted in English.

'Your story checks out,' Basil said.

'I did not doubt it would. So, are you going to help me?'

'As soon as we can, we hope to get you to Gdansk, that's Danzig to you, but there are complicated arrangements to be made first and it may take some time. In the meantime, you stay here.'

Colin grinned at Rulka. 'That's no hardship for me, but I do not want to put Krystyna at risk.'

'The risk will be minimal if you do exactly as you are told. There are a lot of French workers in Warsaw due to the collaboration of the French Vichy with the Germans. They are mainly technicians and engineers. You will become one of those. Krystyna tells me your French is reasonable.'

'Nothing like good enough to pass as a Frenchman among Frenchmen.'

'No, but you will avoid your so-called countrymen. It will explain your accent if you are questioned by the *shkopy*, that's the Polish equivalent of Jerry, by the way.'

'I do know that word,' Colin said, laughing. 'Krystyna uses it all the time. She has been trying to teach me Polish, but with little success. It's a diabolical language.'

Boris smiled. 'A few words would help.' He paused. 'I have been instructed to make you a proposition. You may refuse, but I hope you will not.'

'Go on.'

'While you are a guest of the Polish people, we can use you.' He spoke warily, waiting for a reaction, and when none came, went on, 'You are, according to the information we have, an explosives man; a skill that could be very useful.'

'You mean to the underground?'

'Yes. Since the beginning of this month it has been called the *Armia Krajowa* or AK, the Home Army.'

'And Krystyna is part of it?'

'Do not ask.'

'Very well, I will not ask. All I can say is that it was a fortunate day for me when the good father brought her to me. I would die rather than expose her to risk.'

Rulka looked sharply at him but did not comment.

'Is that a yes?' Boris asked him.

'Yes.'

'Then you will be given your new identity, a work permit and a ration card, together with a potted biography which you will memorise until it becomes second nature. When we are satisfied, you will be assigned your task.'

He shrugged himself back into his coat and took his leave, leaving Rulka and Colin facing each other. They stood in silence for several moments. There had, they both realised, been a subtle change in their relationship. It was no longer simply a business one, but had become personal. They were comrades together in the universal fight and though Boris had not said so, they knew that whatever role they played in the future, it would be together.

Chapter Seven

May 1942

It was Saturday and Louise was pegging washing on the line in the garden at the back of the Pheasant. It was closed off from the public area of the pub by a six-foot wall and was a sun trap where she would sit, reading or knitting. Today there was a stiff breeze; the cot sheets, nappies and tiny nightdresses would be dry in no time. Not far away, three-month-old Angela slept in her pram. She slept peacefully, unaware of the turmoil of the world about her. She knew nothing of the fall of Singapore, when thousands of British soldiers had been taken prisoner, many from Norfolk and Cambridgeshire, two from Cottlesham. She didn't know that British shipping was still being lost at an alarming rate, that Tommy was old enough to worry about his father on board a merchant navy ship carrying vital supplies, that Rommel had the upper hand in North Africa and poor old Malta was still taking a pounding. She was innocent of the suffering of the defenders of Stalingrad or the plight of the Polish people.

Louise was determined to protect her from all harm. She knew when the war ended Jan would return to his wife and she would be left to bring up Angela alone, but she tried not to think of that. While she had him, she would cherish him, just as she cherished his daughter. He had supported her all through her pregnancy, not only with money and extravagant presents for the baby but, more importantly, by coming to see her as often as he could, helping her to hold her head up in the village, where she felt everyone's eyes were on her. She would have moved away but Jenny had been adamant she would not allow it. 'You're staying right here, where I can look after you,' she had said. 'You'll need your friends when the time comes. And just because one or two round here look sideways at you, doesn't mean everyone is like that. Most are right behind you. They like you and they like Jan.'

Jenny's friendship meant a great deal to her, especially as she had no contact with her parents at all, in spite of writing regularly to her mother. 'I thought she might have found some way of getting in touch, if only to let me know she was OK and thinking of me,' she had said to Jenny. 'I would be notified if anything dreadful happened to her, wouldn't I?'

Jenny, who had found the Reverend Fairhurst rude and overbearing, had seen the marks on Louise's back when she returned from that fateful visit and knew how matters stood. 'Yes, of course. Perhaps when the baby is born, she will come to see you.'

'Perhaps,' she had agreed, but she didn't hold out much hope.

She had given up her job as soon as her condition became obvious and a new teacher had been appointed. Fresh out of teacher training college, she was unsure of herself and too diffident to manage ten-year-old scamps like Freddie Jones and Tommy Carter. As far as Louise was concerned the evacuees were still her children and she kept a motherly eye on them. They, in turn, often came to her with their troubles, either a grievance against another child or a sense of injustice over a punishment, or they would have bad news from home and needed a shoulder to cry on. Her shoulder and lap were always there, even when her lap disappeared beneath her bump.

By Christmas, she had felt huge and ungainly, but the pub had been warm and cheerful and, in spite of rationing, Jenny had somehow managed to provide plenty to eat and drink. Jan had managed a forty-eight-hour pass and was able to join in the festivities, bringing with him a silver brooch for Louise in the shape of the squadron's emblem, besides small presents for everyone else: perfume for Jenny, tobacco for Stan, a model of a Spitfire on a stand for Tommy and a doll with a china face for Beattie. Louise had knitted him an air force-blue scarf which he said was just what he needed to keep him warm in the air. Some of the time he was boisterous and laughing and then suddenly he would become sober and thoughtful and Louise knew he was thinking of home. When he was like that she didn't try to jolly him out of it and he soon recovered. And then he was his usual loving self. As far as Jenny was concerned, they were a married couple and she was not going to spoil things for them by insisting on separate rooms.

The baby girl had been born on 22nd February in Louise's bedroom in the Pheasant with Jenny to hold her hand and the local midwife to deliver the baby. The arrival had been a cause for great rejoicing in the bar that evening, where many a toast was raised to her and her child and to Jan, who was looked upon as something of a hero. He had come down the following weekend, loaded with flowers and a big teddy bear, which he told her was to be called Cuddles.

He had found Louise sitting in a chair by the window of her room, nursing the baby and looking out at the leafless trees in the lane, the tops of which were bowing in a strong breeze. She turned when she heard him come into the room. 'Jan! You came.'

'Of course I came.' He strode over to kneel at her side and gaze at his little daughter with eyes full of tears, which he brushed impatiently away. 'She is perfect,' he murmured. 'A little cherub, an angel.'

'She is like you.'

He looked from the baby to Louise and grinned sheepishly. 'Do you think so?'

'Definitely. Everyone says so. Especially her eyes. She has a way of looking at me so knowingly, which reminds me of you.'

'Knowingly?' he queried.

'As if she knows what I'm thinking, how I'm feeling.'

'Do I do that?'

'Yes, you do.'

'That's because I love you.'

'Oh, Jan!' She had been feeling emotional herself and the least thing seemed to set her off

'Hey, it's not something to cry about,' he said, leaning over to kiss her. 'What are you going to call her?'

The tears turned to a watery smile. 'You said she was an angel, so what about Angela?'

'Angela,' he repeated. 'Yes, I like that, but can we have a Polish name too?'

'Of course. What would you like?' She hoped he wasn't going to suggest Rulka.

'My mother's name was Zofia. It's spelt with a Z, by the way.'

'Then Angela Zofia she shall be. We'll have the christening here in the village church the next time you have leave.' She paused. 'You don't object to that, do you?'

'No. You must do what you think best.'

It was, she knew, a reference to the fact that he would not always be with her and Angela would be brought up in England.

Insisting on his daughter being christened in the Catholic faith would not help to bring about a reconciliation with her parents. 'Thank you, Jan.'

'Don't thank me. I have to thank you. It is thinking of you and this little one that keeps me going.'

'You are looking very tired. Can't you get a spot of longer leave?'

'When my turn comes.' It was said flatly and she wondered if he was talking about leave at all.

'There's something wrong.'

'No, nothing. How could there be?'

'Come on, out with it.'

'My friend, Miroslav Feric died two days ago. His Spitfire broke up in the air and crashed into the runway. We stood on the ground and watched it happen. The aircraft buried its nose in the concrete. Mika was half hanging out of the cockpit as if he had been trying to bail out. He didn't even die in combat. It might be easier to bear if he had. He was one of the best. I had known him for years and I can't believe he's gone.' He paused, gulping back tears, but when she did not speak and simply put her hand over his, he went on. 'I've lost many friends in this war, but no one like him. He was always so optimistic. He kept a journal and everyone was expected to contribute. As soon as we came off an op, there he was with his book and a pen. We teased him unmercifully about it. Now the book is all that's left of him.'

'Perhaps you should keep it up in his memory.'

'We have already decided that. It is a chronicle of all the squadron has been through. One day, when Poland is free again, it may be important.'

Christenings had a low priority when it came to the conduct of the war and Angela's had to be postponed twice because Jan's leave was cancelled, but eventually it had taken place on Easter Sunday with Jenny and Edith as godmothers and Stan as godfather. Louise looked for her mother in vain. Jenny had somehow managed a christening tea and a little cake which she said she had made with carrots. Louise would not have believed it if she had not seen the cake in the making. It tasted exceptionally good. Jan had gone back next day and she had not seen him since but letters went back and forth regularly.

The new teacher at the school had enrolled in the ATS, where she would probably be more at ease and a replacement was hard to find. John asked Louise to step in and fill the breech and when Jenny offered to look after Angela while she was at work, she jumped at the chance to be useful again. Gradually she was losing all her evacuee children, either to grammar school, and that included Tommy Carter, or because they had gone home. Now employed by the Norfolk education authority, her pupils were a mix of Londoners and natives of Cottlesham. Her life was full to overflowing and, but for the estrangement with her mother, she was content.

She had just finished pegging the washing out and was picking up the empty clothes basket, when she became aware of an aeroplane flying very low, almost at rooftop height. Thinking it was a stricken bomber coming in to land at Watton, she glanced up and found herself looking at a huge black cross, painted on the wings of a German Messerschmitt. It was so low she could clearly see the pilot. She grabbed Angela from her pram and dashed for the back door. 'It's a Jerry,' she shouted, and flung herself into the Morrison shelter, followed by Jenny. Outside they could hear the spat-spat of machine gun fire as the pilot raked the village. 'The cheeky devil,' Jenny said lightly to cover her terror.

After a while there was silence and they crawled out from the shelter and went outside. One of the cot sheets was in shreds and Angela's pram had a hole clean through it. Louise stood clutching

Angela to her bosom, and stared at it in disbelief. 'He was low enough to see exactly what he was doing,' she said furiously. 'How could anyone who calls himself a human being do anything so callous? I hope he gets shot down and dies a horrible death.' Until that moment she had not known what it was to hate. Now it consumed her.

Stan, returning from an errand to the post office, came running up the road towards them. 'Are you all right?'

'We're fine,' Jenny said because Louise was still looking at the pram, still shaking at the thought of what might have happened. 'Is anyone hurt?'

'Only a cow belonging to Bill Young. Everyone else dived for cover. Pauline Johns fell over trying to hide in a ditch and it looks like she's broken her wrist. Edith is taking her to the hospital in Swaffham. It's a good thing the children weren't in school. The bullets ripped into the playground.' He stopped when he saw the pram. 'God! What happened there?'

Louise found her voice to tell him. He swore softly. 'No one's safe in this war, not even babies. I'd kill the fellow with my bare hands if he came anywhere near me. Let's get indoors and make a cup of tea. A bit of the strong stuff in it wouldn't go amiss by the look of you. You're shaking.'

'I am shaking with fury,' she said. 'You can't even put babies out in prams now.' She had been in the habit of putting Angela in the garden in her pram for some fresh air while she helped with the housework, assuming she was safe there. She would be brought in if the air raid siren went, which it did sometimes because they were so near the airfield. This time there had been no warning. 'If I hadn't been outside myself . . .' Now the danger was over, she was crying softly. 'Oh, it doesn't bear thinking about. I'll never be able to put her out again, not while this war lasts.'

Angela herself was unperturbed and continued to thrive. By the beginning of the autumn term she was crawling and investigating everything about her with wide blue eyes and inquisitive fingers. Tommy and Beattie hauled her about like a living doll, treatment she bore with good humour. Louise's letters to Jan were full of his daughter's progress. Occasionally he came to see for himself. His daughter fascinated him. He would help to look after her and croon a lullaby in Polish when she was put to bed, and when she slept he would sit watching her. He knew about the German fighter machine-gunning the village and it had affected him deeply. 'It is for her and all children I fight,' he murmured on one occasion. 'They must live in a world at peace, a very different world from the evil we see around us now.'

If he came in the middle of the week, Louise, being at school, wasn't able to have much time with him, but he would spend the day helping out at the pub and wheeling Angela out in her new pram, much to the amusement of the men of the village: such domesticity was not manly in their eyes. He didn't seem to mind their ribaldry. If he managed a weekend, he would ask Jenny to look after Angela so that he could take Louise to the cinema in Swaffham or for a day's outing in Norwich, though that had been badly damaged in air raids earlier in the year. He always appeared cheerful, but Louise was not deceived.

The strain he had been under was showing, though he still smiled and joked. She knew he had been escorting bombers raiding German targets and worried about him being shot down. She loved him unreservedly and knew she would do so for the rest of her life, but she also knew that she was destined to lose him. She would rather it was to his wife than to enemy action.

Privacy was hard to come by in the Pheasant, especially in the evenings when the bar was crowded, so on one visit towards the end of July, she suggested going for a walk after Angela had been put to bed. Leaving Jenny in charge of her they strolled, hand in hand, through the village to their favourite place on the common. It was a warm evening and would be light until late. The grass on the common was turning brown, the blackberry bushes were laden with green fruit and elderflowers spread their heady scent. It was a peaceful summer evening in rural England, but the peace was illusory.

'How long have you got?' she asked. It was the first question anyone asked when loved ones came home on leave. It was as well to know when the next parting would be and cram everything into a few hours.

'I must go back tomorrow.'

She looked at his face. He looked thin and gaunt and there were dark pads of fatigue below his eyes. Was it his work, the daily brush with death that caused it? After all, the Polish airmen had been enduring it longer than most. Or was it worry about what was happening in Poland? 'Any news from home?' she asked.

'Of Rulka? No, none. We know the Polish people are resisting and we hear of dreadful atrocities, but neither your government nor ours seem able to do anything about it. I don't think they believe it.'

She put a hand on his arm. 'I'm sorry, Jan. I do understand.'

He took her hand and put it to his lips. 'I know you do. You are still my anchor. When I am here I can relax. Let's not talk about it anymore.'

'Are you still on escort duty?'

'Some of the time, but just lately we have been training American flyers in aerial combat.' He paused to smile at her. 'They are even more wet behind the ears than the Britishers were, but they are learning.' He did not add that they had also been escorting American bombers in daylight raids over Germany. They called it 'precision bombing' and maintained that going in daylight gave them a better chance of finding their target. Jan didn't think they were any more accurate with their bombing than the RAF who went at night and their chances of being shot down were a great deal higher. The Spitfires of the Polish squadrons did not have enough fuel to take them all the way to distant targets and back, but even so, escorting the slower bombers as far as they could, they were vulnerable and their losses were high. The heroics of the Battle of Britain were behind them and the fickle public forgot them to embrace the new arrivals.

'There are some stationed near here,' Louise said. 'They seem so well fed and even the privates dress like officers. And they are generous with their presents of chocolate and nylons, is it any wonder they are popular with the girls, if not the men?'

He laughed. 'They have quite put our noses out of joint.'

The way he had picked up colloquial English amused Louise and his accent had improved considerably. She sometimes forgot he wasn't British, then something he said or did would remind her of his roots and she found herself dwelling on her situation. It was not unique; there were other women who had children by Poles and some had been lucky enough to marry them. At times like that she would wonder if the fact that Jan had no news of his wife meant she was no longer alive. She told herself sternly that it was unchristian to wish anyone dead but, like Jan, she wished she knew for sure.

Occasionally, when something triggered off a memory, she thought of Tony. Their love for each other had been genuine, she did not question it, but he seemed to belong to a different world, and though he had died in action, it was a kind of peaceful, pre-war world which would never come again. This was borne out every day when the BBC, to which everyone listened for reliable information, spoke of losses and bereavement. But then it came closer to home. Agnes Carter arrived one Sunday morning to break the news to her son and daughter that their father had been lost on an Arctic convoy taking supplies to Russia. The news of the loss of two-thirds of the convoy and thousands of lives had not been kept from the public and there were many who questioned whether the supplies were worth the loss of men and ships. Seeing the white-faced Mrs Carter, twisting the handle of her handbag while she waited for Jenny to fetch Tommy and Beattie, Louise wondered it too. 'They don't stand a chance once they're in the water,' Agnes said. 'It's the cold you see . . .'

Beattie had never seen much of her father even before the war. He was a shadowy figure her mother and brother talked about and she received the news with a kind of indifference which upset her mother. Tommy, on the other hand, had idolised his father. When he was at home between voyages, they had gone to football matches together, fishing and camping. It was for his father he worked hard at school, to make him proud. He had stared at his mother for fully a minute, then rushed out of the house. He was gone for hours.

'If he's not back by teatime, we'll go looking for him,' Louise said. 'He won't have gone far. It's just his way of coping.'

'I've got to get back tonight,' Agnes said. 'I'm on early shift tomorrow.'

'Can't you ask for some time off?'

'What would I do with it if I had it? I'd only mope about the house. It's better to keep busy. I've got mates at work. We keep each other going.'

'Yes, of course.'

Tommy came back at four o'clock, dawdling up the lane, kicking viciously at stones as if everyone of them was a Jerry. Ignoring those who had been watching his progress, he went straight up to his room. His mother followed him. There was silence for a few minutes and then they heard the unmistakeable sound of sobbing. 'He'll be all right now he's got it out of his system,' Jenny said.

Louise knew it would not be as easy as that and she might very well be called upon to try and soften his anger in the days and nights to come. She went to telephone Bill Young to ask him if he would run Mrs Carter to Swaffham station in his car. Being a farmer, he had a petrol allowance. Mrs Carter was coming down the stairs as she rang off. 'I've arranged a lift for you to the station,' she said.

'Thank you.'

'Try not to worry. I'll keep an eye on the children for you.'

'I should think you have enough to worry about without concerning yourself with my children,' she said, looking down at Angela who had crawled after her mother and was trying to hug her leg.

Whether it was a reference to her single state, Louise neither knew nor cared. She picked Angela up and opened the door just as Bill's car drew up. Beattie ran out to kiss her mother goodbye, but Tommy stayed in his room. He came down the following morning, dry-eyed but subdued. Breakfast over, he took Beattie by the hand and set off for school. Louise saw to Angela's breakfast, kissed her goodbye and followed. Like everyone else she was feeling the weight of her responsibilities.

It was obvious the men of 303 Squadron, especially those who had been with it since the beginning, could not go on much longer without casualties escalating, not only through enemy action but as a result of accidents through fatigue. They were taken off operations for rest and recuperation. Jan's leave coincided with the school's summer holiday, so he took his little family on holiday to the Lake District, hiring a small cottage tucked away on the slopes above Lake Windermere.

It was a wonderful two weeks, the longest they had ever spent together. Jan put Angela in a sling on his back and they walked all over the hills, taking picnics, even swimming in the cold water of the lake, returning to the cottage to eat and go to bed to make love and go to sleep in each other's arms. They didn't talk about the war or the future, what might have been or what might yet be. The present was all that mattered and they made the most of it. They returned to Cottlesham, refreshed and ready to carry on with the work they had to do. Jan went back to Northolt and Louise set about preparing her lessons for the new term.

The first person Jan saw when he arrived back was Witold coming out of the mess.

'I'm being posted,' he said after they had greeted each other.

'When? Where?' Jan knew that Witold had asked to be assigned to a special RAF squadron that had begun smuggling supplies and men into occupied Europe, Poland included. 'Special operations?'

'No, more's the pity. I'm going to America.' It was said bitterly. Witold had been in at the start and worked his way up from pilot to command the first Polish fighter wing and the posting was not to his liking.

'America? Why there?'

'I am being attached to the Polish Embassy in Washington and I'm supposed to go round drumming up support for the war. Apart from the ones who have come over here, the Yanks have little idea what it's all about.'

'I'll miss you.'

One by one Jan's old comrades were disappearing, either killed, injured or moved on. A few new flyers had arrived in Scotland, freed from Soviet camps, and Witold and Jan had had the job of training them in RAF ways, just as they themselves had been trained, but the old comradeship was slowly being eroded.

'When do you go?'

'Tomorrow. Jan Zumbach is taking over from me.'

'So soon? We'd better have a celebration tonight, then.'

'It's all arranged at the Orchard. Oh, and I nearly forgot, there's a letter for you. I put it on your locker.'

Jan was puzzled. He had just left Louise, so it couldn't be from her. He hurried to his room. There on his locker was an envelope with several official-looking stamps; letters like that usually meant news from home, smuggled out by agents to the government-in-exile. He snatched it up and ripped it open. Inside was another envelope which had been opened and resealed. He recognised the handwriting of his brother. Jozef was alive! He sat down heavily on his bed to read it.

'I do not know if you will ever get this,' Jozef had written. 'For all I know you never left Poland. You might have died there. You might have died anywhere, but I live in hope that you have survived. When I heard that the Kościuszko Squadron had distinguished itself in the Battle of Britain and that Witold Urbanowicz and Mika Feric were still with it, I thought maybe you were with them and if not they might know what happened to you.

'I was taken prisoner by the Russians in 1939 and sent to Kolyma. It is the most desolate and coldest spot on earth. I cannot begin to describe the conditions there, for civilians as well as soldiers. Hard labour, starvation rations and a cold that freezes your blood. Many, many succumbed. How their families will ever find out what happened to them, I do not know. How I survived, I have no idea – stubbornness, I suppose, but survive I did and then we were suddenly set free, if you can call it freedom. We had been on the march for weeks and many died on the way, before we learnt the reason for it. The Germans had turned on the Soviet Union and the Soviets needed more manpower to defend themselves. Manpower! We were living skeletons.

'Some of us went into a Polish army in Russia, but others, me included, became part of General Anders' army and spent last winter in a tented camp and more people died. When we had gained enough strength we were marched to Tashkent. We spent eight months there and then began another trek, this time to Iran and then Palestine. And here I am, back in the fight. There were very few officers among us; they were separated from the troops when we were captured. Heaven knows what their fate was, but it means I have been promoted to major.

'Father and Mother died during the early fighting. I heard that the day before I was taken prisoner, but perhaps you know that already. In a way I am glad because they would never have survived Siberia. Is Rulka with you? I would like to think she is. Write to me.'

Jan lost no time in doing just that, and took it to the post before leaving the camp for the Orchard, where they had a noisy and drunken carouse to say goodbye to Witold.

By the end of that autumn term, Angela was able to pull herself to her feet, hanging onto whatever came handy: a chair, a table leg, the seat of the sofa and Tommy's hands. He was very good with her and she adored him. It was Angela, with her sunny nature, who had eventually pulled him out of his gloom. She was trying to talk too, though whatever it was she was chatting about was unintelligible to the adults. Sometimes Beattie would report what she said, whether accurately or not no one knew.

By this time, too, the Battle of El Alamein had been won, Malta had been relieved and the Russians were fighting back outside Stalingrad. The Allies had landed in force in North Africa, determined to flush the enemy out of that continent, which frightened the Germans into thinking an invasion of southern France might be on the cards and they swiftly occupied the whole of France. At home the population struggled with shortages and air raids – nothing like as bad as they had been during the Blitz, but frequent enough to cause deaths, injury and hardship. The fourth Christmas of the war was at hand and everyone hoped it would be the last. Already there was talk of a second front. Louise wanted the war to end as much as anyone but she knew it would mean parting from Jan. He would, she knew, not abandon his wife if he thought she was alive. And that was, so she told herself sternly, as it should be.

Jan had hoped to go down to Cottlesham for Angela's first birthday, but it was not to be, and he spent her birthday in the air, sticking close to an American bomber on its way to Dusseldorf.

The tide of war was beginning to turn in the Allies' favour. The Germans had given up their attempt to take Stalingrad, nine hundred miles inside Russia, when an apparently defensive action turned into a full-scale counter offensive. The German commander Marshal Paulus, his chief of staff and fifteen generals, surrendered. Hitler, like Napoleon, had been defeated by stubborn resistance and the Russian winter and now those troops who had not surrendered were retreating westwards. Jan rejoiced at the ignominy of the German army, but he wondered what would happen if and when the Russian army pursued them all the way back to Poland. He feared for Poland and he feared for Rulka – if she were still alive. Louise had told him that the English had a saying, no news is good news, and he hoped it was true. But at the end of the war, if he survived, he was going to have to make a choice.

In the air, droning on at the speed of the Liberator he was escorting, his mind had time to wander. He could think while he searched the sky for enemy aircraft but his thinking led him to no conclusion. He had loved Rulka from the first moment he set eyes on her. She shared his pride in his nationality, spoke the same language, liked the same food, enjoyed the culture of Warsaw, just as he did. But how much of the nationality, the language and the culture would survive the war? If Rulka were alive, had she changed? Had he? Would she even recognise the prematurely ageing man who had promised her he would be back? If conditions in Warsaw were as bad as they had been led to believe and she had lived with it for years, how would that affect her attitude towards him who had escaped from it?

And then there was Louise. His love for her had not been a sudden revelation, it had grown slowly and inexorably as a result of a mutual need, but it was no less real for that. She was a steadying influence, a calm presence; she understood his changeable moods and soothed him, so that he was able to return to the fray with renewed vigour. He had called her his anchor and she remained his anchor through thick and thin. It was because of him she had become estranged from her parents. He despised her self-righteous father, but Louise loved her mother and he felt guilty about that. And there was Angela. He adored his daughter and the thought that he would not see her grow into womanhood wrenched his heart in two whenever he thought about it. How could he leave them?

Louise did not recognise the voice at the other end of the telephone, but she knew from the accent it was Polish. 'Miss Fairhurst, I believe you knew Flight Lieutenant Grabowski?'

'Knew?' She immediately picked up on the past tense. 'What's happened? Where is he?'

'I am afraid he is missing. He did not come back from the last sortie. According to the others the outward trip was uneventful, it must have happened on the return. They realised he was not with them as they crossed the Dutch coast. There was heavy flak. They think he might have been brought down . . .'

'He's not dead, then?'

'We do not know. If he survived and was taken prisoner we shall soon hear. He might have been picked up by the Dutch people and is being sheltered by them. News of that might take longer to reach us.' He paused, but when she did not answer, added, 'Are you still there?'

'Yes.'

'Jan gave me your phone number some time ago and said if anything happened to be sure and let you know.'

'Thank you.'

'If there's anything we can do for you?'

'Let me know if you hear anything.'

'Yes, I will.'

She put the phone back on its cradle and wandered into the kitchen in a kind of stupor.

'What's up?' Jenny asked. 'You look as if you've seen a ghost.'

'Jan's missing.' Her voice was flat. 'They think he was shot down.'

'Oh, my dear girl.' Jenny came to her at once and put an arm round her to draw her to the settee. 'I don't know what to say.'

'It's not fair!' Louise burst out. 'Twice! Why should I lose them both, when others get off scot-free?'

'I don't know, Louise. But they said "missing", didn't they? When Tony was lost, they were quite sure, right from the first.'

'Yes, I know. They said Jan might be a prisoner or he might have been picked up by the Dutch people.'

'Then you mustn't give up hope.'

'Oh, Jenny, I am so tired of this damned war. Will it never end?'

'One day it will and we must soldier on until it does.'

Angela, who had been playing with Cuddles under the kitchen table, a favourite spot of hers, toddled across the room on unsteady legs and tried to scramble onto Louise's lap. Louise picked her up and hugged her, kissing the soft curls on the top of her head. She did not cry. What she was feeling was too deep for tears.

Jenny made tea and persuaded her to drink. 'Is tea your cure for everything?' Louise asked with a wan smile.

'It helps.'

'I suppose so. I'm so glad I've got you, you and Stan. Without you, I'd be lost.'

'Yes, well, you are part of the family now.' She paused to sit down beside her friend. 'You mustn't let this defeat you, Lou. Think of Angela. One day, she is going to grow up into a lovely young woman in a world at peace. Think of that.'

Louise looked at her daughter, sitting on her lap. She seemed to sense there was something wrong with her mother. She pulled at the ears of the teddy bear. 'Cuddles,' she said, endeavouring to give the toy to her mother. Louise kissed her soft cheek, set her on her feet and she toddled off. 'Your daddy didn't see your first steps,' she murmured as she watched her. 'He didn't hear your first word.' It would have made him laugh, because it was not 'Mummy' or 'Daddy', but 'Cuddles'. It was then she cried.

Chapter Eight

Faith looked down at the man who lay unconscious in the hospital bed and wondered why she had ever been afraid of him. He was only flesh and blood, after all, just like any other man. He didn't see himself like that. In his eyes he had been put on earth to eradicate sin wherever he found it. The trouble was he saw it everywhere except in his own soul. He was a man so driven he could see no good in anyone. Thirty years they had been married. Thirty years she had endured, even allowing herself to be cut off from the daughter she loved at a time when she was most needed. But Louise could be stubborn too. She had not answered any of the letters she had written to her in secret and given to the daily help, Mrs Phillips, to post.

'He's had a stroke,' the doctor told her. 'He must have hit his head on something when he fell which caused the head injury. But we've got to work on him, so I think he has a good chance of recovering.'

He wasn't dead, wasn't even dying. She was thankful for that or she would have been an accessory to manslaughter, if not murder.

Henry had been out all day visiting his parishioners and had come home in a filthy temper, complaining that they were a godless lot. 'Mrs Green is obviously pregnant and her husband is a prisoner of war,' he told her. 'I spoke sharply to her about her wickedness and told her to get on her knees, but she laughed. She laughed at me, Faith. Laughed.'

'Oh, dear.'

'And Felicity Barlow is going about dressed like a tart. She *is* a tart. I saw her in the high street, standing on the corner with her skirt up to her backside, talking to an American serviceman. When I intervened, the man told me to get lost and pushed me over. Me, a man of the cloth. It was humiliating.'

'Are you hurt?'

'Of course I'm hurt. What do you expect? Everyone was laughing.' He had been very red in the face and pacing up and down the study in his agitation.

'Calm down, Henry.'

The doorbell rang and she had gone to answer it to find Felicity Barlow's father on the step. He had stormed past her into the study without speaking and slammed the door shut leaving her on the other side of it. She heard him ranting at Henry about his abuse of his daughter. 'You've no right to speak to her like that. In front of a crowd of people, too. Who are you to judge? My Felicity is a good girl. I want a public apology.' She heard Henry's equally angry answer as she made her way down the hall to the kitchen. He had really overstepped the mark, this time. The sound of a crash had sent her rushing back.

Mr Barlow was standing over an unconscious Henry and blood was pouring from Henry's head. 'I only gave him a little push,' he had said. 'He just fell and hit his head. Honest to God, I didn't mean to harm him.'

Believing he had caused the injury, she had bundled him out of the back door with instructions to go home and then called an ambulance. She told the ambulance men and the doctor that she had been in the kitchen when she heard a crash and had run back to find him on the floor. She said nothing of Mr Barlow; she didn't want to have to explain what he was doing there and why the men were quarrelling. It would have resulted in an investigation which would have made public the sort of man Henry was and the kind of life she led with him. She could not bear it. Being told it had been a stroke didn't change anything.

'Will you be all right?' the nurse at the bedside asked as the bell went for the end of visiting time and she stood up to leave. 'Is there anyone who could come and stay with you? A relative perhaps?'

'No, there's no one. I'll be fine.'

She went back to the vicarage and tried to clear up the mess in the study. She righted the desk lamp, picked up papers that were strewn about, set an overturned chair back on its legs and tried to scrub the blood off the carpet. The stain defeated her, so she abandoned it and went into the kitchen to make herself a meal which she could not eat. She scraped it into the bin and set about washing up. Her mind was whirring like an overworked fan; what had she not done that she should have? What had she answered to all the questions put to her? Had she contradicted herself? She could not remember.

Hearing the front doorbell, she dried her hands and went to answer it to find an agitated Mrs Barlow on the step. 'What happened?' the woman demanded.

'What do you mean?'

'My Wally stormed out of the house saying he was going to kill the Reverend. He was angry enough to do it too. Then my neighbour said the Reverend had been taken off in an ambulance and now Wally's disappeared. He didn't come home.'

'My husband is not dead, Mrs Barlow. He's had a stroke.'

'It wasn't anything to do with Wally, then?'

'No.'

'Oh, thank the Lord for that. I'm sorry to have troubled you.'

Faith watched her hurry down the drive, then went back into the study and used Henry's keys to open his desk and took out his diary. She would have to cancel his appointments and the confirmation class he took every week. She had not realised before how many young girls he was giving instruction to and the book was full of instances of the wickedness of his parishioners and the need to chastise them. They revealed a man not quite right in the head. Would he need that again? She made a note of the appointments, then tried the next drawer. It was then she found Louise's letters, a whole pile of them flung unopened, together with those she had written herself. How had Henry come to possess those? She had begged and begged him to let her write to their daughter but he had been adamant and must have guessed she would try and do it in secret and browbeaten Mrs Phillips to hand them over.

She sat down heavily on the high-backed chair Henry used at his desk and began reading. She had kept her self-control all through the day's ordeal, answering the doctor in monosyllables, careful not to give anything away of the turbulent emotions that seethed below the surface. But that facade cracked as she read, and tears streamed down her face. 'Louise, oh my dear child,' she sobbed. 'It's too late, all too late.'

Jenny had talked it over with Stan and they had decided that Louise would have to know sooner or later. 'Better do it this evening, after the children have gone to bed and I'm in the bar,' he had said.

So here she was pretending to read the newspaper, while Louise marked school exercise books.

'Lou, I think you ought to see this,' Jenny said, tapping the newspaper.

'Why, what's in it?'

'See for yourself.'

Louise took the paper and scanned the headlines. 'The tide of war is turning in the Allies favour' was one. 'The enemy faces defeat in Tunisia' was another. Others were about the air campaign against European targets and one, more disturbing, reported that the Germans had unearthed thousands of bodies in Katyn Forest in western Russia, more than four thousand of them, nearly all Polish army officers. They had their hands tied behind their backs and each had been shot in the back of the neck and tumbled into a mass grave with their identification still on them. 'The Germans are accusing the Russians,' it said. 'They have asked an independent medical team to investigate it. The Russians are blaming the Germans. They say it is a ploy on the part of the Nazis and Polish government in London to undermine the Soviet Union. The Polish government is asking for a Red Cross enquiry.'

'This is dreadful,' she said. 'Jan said something about officers disappearing when he heard from his brother . . .'

'I didn't mean that,' Jenny said, pointing at an article headed: Crime soars in the capital. 'I meant this.'

Louise dutifully read it. Besides a flourishing black market, looting and robbery were escalating, it said. It went on to give examples, some of them violent in nature, and ended: 'No one is immune. The Reverend Mr Henry Fairhurst was attacked on the street in Edgware yesterday. It is a sorry state of affairs when a man of the cloth, a highly respected churchman, going about his business of preaching the gospel and succouring the needy, should be attacked in this way. He is in hospital. His wife is at his bedside. The police are looking for the culprit and ask anyone who has information about this or any other crime, to contact them immediately.'

Louise let the paper drop in her lap. 'I'll have to go to her.'

'Of course. I'll see John and tell him what's happened. I'm sure he'll stand in for you.'

Louise was unsure of her welcome but as soon as her mother opened the door, she knew it would be all right. They hugged each other and then Faith made some Camp coffee and they sat on the sofa in the drawing room to drink it and talk. 'And this is Angela,' Faith said, drawing the child onto her lap, but she wriggled so much Faith let her go and she climbed onto Louise's lap, sucking her thumb.

'How do you know her name?' Louise asked. 'Did you get my letters after all? Why didn't you write?'

'I did, lots of times. I found the letters two days ago when I was going through your father's desk, every single one of them, and all yours to me.'

'He kept them from you?'

'Yes.'

'Why?'

'You know your father, Louise, better than most.'

'Yes. So tell me about this attack. I read about it in the paper.'

'As usual the paper got it wrong. He did have an altercation in the street and was pushed over, but he wasn't hurt. I don't know how the paper got hold of it, but there were a lot of people about at the time so I suppose it's not surprising. The truth is he had a stroke after he got home and hit his head on the corner of his desk when he fell. It cut his head open.'

'How is he?'

'He's alive, though it is too early to say whether he will recover fully.'

'I'm sorry, Mum. Is there anything I can do? Should I go and see him?'

'No, I shouldn't. He looks dreadful and he won't know you. Let's have some scrambled egg. I've got some dried egg and some bread I can toast. You can tell me all about Angela while I get it ready.' It was obvious that her mother did not want to talk about what had happened. 'She is like you, don't you think?'

'She's more like Jan. Her hair is fair like his.'

'Is that her father?'

'Yes.'

'It's a funny name.'

'It's Polish.'

'Polish! Oh, Louise, how could you?'

'He is the most wonderful man you could ever wish to meet,' Louise said. 'He is kind, considerate and generous and he adores his daughter.'

'But you have not married him?'

'No, he has a wife in Poland.'

'Oh.' She paused to absorb this. 'But he will divorce her and marry you?'

'He can't. For one thing he is Catholic and for another he loves his wife.'

'I don't think I want to meet this Jan, if that's the way he goes on.'

'You couldn't anyway. He's been posted missing.'

Faith stopped buttering toast to look at her daughter who met her gaze unflinchingly. 'Judge not lest you be judged,' she said.

Louise managed a laugh. 'Whatever do you mean by that?'

'It was something I thought of when I read your letters. I was not there to help and guide you when you needed me. I am to blame that you went off the rails and I am truly sorry for that.'

'Mum, I make my own decisions. You don't have to blame yourself. I know how it was with Father but I hoped you would defy him and come and see us.'

'I dare not, Louise. I was brought up to believe in the sanctity of marriage and the marriage vows I made: love, honour and obey. The love and honour were eroded years ago but I could not break myself of the habit of obeying.'

'And when Father recovers and comes home, will you still obey him?'

'No. I am stronger now.' She put scrambled eggs and toast on two plates and put them on the kitchen table. 'Come on, let's eat this while it's hot.'

Louise stayed two days and during the whole time she felt that there was something her mother was not telling her, but however much she hinted she learned no more. She needed to get back to school; John couldn't stand in for her indefinitely.

'I'll come again soon,' she said as she hugged her mother goodbye.

Faith stood at the garden gate and watched until Louise had turned the corner, then she went back inside. There was joy in her heart. Henry's stroke had had one happy result.

It was a lovely day, the sun was shining and, though it was still cold, people were out on the streets, going about their business, visiting the parks with their children and trying to pretend all was right with the world. Everything was far from all right. Looking out of his attic window, Jan could see the grey of German uniforms and the black muzzles of rifles interspersed with the civilian suits and colourful frocks of the inhabitants and it was the presence of those uniforms that kept him incarcerated in the attic.

He was lucky to be alive and he knew it. If half his tail fin had been shot off after crossing the coast, he would have had to come down in the sea and that would almost certainly have been the end of him. He had watched the other aircraft disappear out of sight, knowing the Spitfire was going to crash. But there were houses below him, a church and a busy market square. If he bailed out, the aeroplane would dive into the town, causing untold damage and loss of life and he couldn't let that happen. He had deliberately turned away from it, not easy with only half a tail, looking for a way to bring his Spitfire down without it costing anyone's life, his own included, if he could manage it.

He had been losing height rapidly and by the time he had left the town behind he was too low to bail out safely. He just missed the top of some trees and then there was a strip of farmland in front of him. It rushed up to meet him. The Spitfire buried its nose in the ground and juddered to a stop. He was thrown violently forward over the control panel and hit his head on the Perspex of the canopy.

He had regained consciousness to find himself in a bed with his leg encased in plaster and a nurse bending over him. 'Where am I?'

'In hospital,' she answered in English. She was a pretty girl, very young with soft grey-green eyes that reminded him of Louise.

'A prisoner of war?'

'No.' She laughed. 'The Germans don't know you are here. This room is right up under the rafters. They don't search up here.'

'How did I get here?'

'A farmer saw the plane come down and dragged you out. He carried you to his barn and sent word to us. We fetched you in an ambulance.'

'The Germans must be looking for me.'

'Perhaps, perhaps not. The farmer who found you set fire to the aeroplane. He said it burnt fiercely and the petrol tanks blew up and scattered debris everywhere. With luck it will be assumed the pilot died inside it. Let us hope they don't examine it too closely.'

'You speak English very well.'

'Most Dutch children learn English at school, or they did before the occupation.'

'What's your name?'

'You may call me Yaan. Where are you from?'

'Poland, but I have been in England since 1940. Can you help me get back there?'

'When the doctor says you are fit to move we will start you on your way. You have a broken leg and the plaster will need to stay on at least six weeks . . .'

'Six weeks!' He struggled to sit up but fell back again.

She smiled. 'Apart from the broken leg and many bruises, you have suffered serious concussion which will make you dizzy if you try to get up. You are lucky you were not killed. You are safe here, as long as you do not walk about or make a noise.'

He smiled. 'I will be good.'

She left him to lie there and think. He castigated himself for not seeing that Messerschmitt until it was too late and now he was paying the penalty for his inattention. He would be reported missing, they might even assume he was dead, especially if the Dutch had a way of communicating news to London of downed aircraft that had apparently exploded on impact. Tad would tell Louise as he had asked him to because she would not have been informed officially. He could imagine what that would do to her. And there was his beautiful little daughter. Somehow he was going to have to get back to them.

Three months on and he was still in the same place. His wounds had healed, the muscles in the mended leg had been built up by exercise, so that it was once again the same size as the other one, and his brain seemed to have recovered from its jolting without permanent damage; it was not Dr Van Stoek or Yaan who held up his move, but the Dutch underground. Gerard, whose surname he was not to know, was a bicycle salesman by day and a saboteur by night. He was a thickset middle-aged man with a decided limp from polio as a child, which was the reason he had not been conscripted to work in Germany like so many others.

'These things take time to arrange,' he had said when he had first come to interrogate Jan, something Jan had expected and even welcomed. Once the Dutch underground were satisfied he was who he said he was, they might be more forthcoming about helping him on his way. 'It is like a chain: we need each link firmly in place or the chain gets broken. And broken chains are not safe.'

And so he endured his cramped conditions where the roof was so low he could not stand upright, and tried to stretch his legs without making a noise. The hospital was in the centre of the town and by standing on a chair he could see out of the skylight to the street below him. He became familiar with its pattern of movement: the time when the workers entered and left the nearby factory; the time when the shops opened; the time the Germans patrolled the street opposite the hospital; the time on Sundays when the townsfolk went to church. What he could not see, however much he craned his neck, was the entrance to the hospital immediately below him.

At last, towards the end of June, plans were afoot to take him to a safe house outside the town, which would be the start of his long journey to freedom. Civilian clothes, identity card and travel documents had been assembled and he had begun to learn his cover story. His nerves were keyed up for the journey, which he knew would be perilous, but his hopes were dashed when Gerard came to him with the news that the Germans had captured one of their number and would almost certainly try to make him talk. 'Everyone is lying low until we are sure it is safe to resume operations,' he told Jan. 'The great fear is that one of our number is an enemy agent. Until we are sure, no one moves.'

'I could try going on my own.'

'No. It's too risky. If the Boche have been told we have an evader in hiding and they know the name we have given you, they will be looking for you. The documents we have given you must be destroyed and new ones prepared when it is safe.' He held out his hand. 'I'll take them now, if you please.'

Jan handed them over reluctantly. 'Will they also know where this evader is hiding?'

Gerard gave him a crooked smile. 'There are only three people who know exactly where you are, that is Dr Van Stoek, Yaan and me. We intend to keep it that way. I will send you some more books to help you while away the time.'

He left and Jan flung himself on the bed and swore.

Several days passed and Gerard did not return and Dr Van Stoek and Yaan were even more careful than usual. Consumed by frustration, Jan would lie on his bed, staring at the roof timbers and recite poetry to himself and when that palled his thoughts would go to Rulka and his home in Warsaw, then to Louise and his little daughter. She would be walking by now, perhaps saying her first words. It was then he pummelled his pillow and muffled his groans of anger in it. Was anyone doing anything to get him out of here?

He was woken a few nights later by a hand on his shoulder. Still half asleep, he sprang up, ready to fight or run. 'It's me,' the doctor whispered. 'Get dressed quickly and follow me.' He put a bundle of clothes on the bed as he spoke.

He had a torch in his hand and by its light Jan scrambled into the garments: a flannelette shirt, a well-worn suit and down-at heel shoes. 'Who am I supposed to be?' he asked.

'Nobody. There's no time. Follow me and don't speak.'

He led the way out of the tiny room. In front of them the roof space stretched the whole length of the building. Unless someone compared the external measurements with the internal, no one would know about the hidden room. The wooden partition did not appear to have a door. Anyone venturing up there to search would have seen nothing but an empty space.

Jan was led down three sets of stairs until they arrived on the ground floor. Because it was the middle of the night, the lighting was minimal. He was hustled into a small office where a man in a white coat waited with a stretcher. He was asked to lie on it and was covered with a blanket. 'You are extremely ill with smallpox,' Doctor Van Stoek murmured. 'We are taking you to a fever hospital for quarantine. If we are stopped, it should be enough to prevent anyone coming too close.'

They carried him out to a waiting ambulance; Doctor Van Stoek took a seat beside Jan's stretcher and the white-coated attendant climbed into the driver's seat, and they set off at speed through the deserted streets. Jan, taken aback by the pace of what had happened, was silent for some time, but he wanted his curiosity satisfied. 'Where are you taking me?'

'To a safe house just outside Brussels. They will take charge of you and send you on.'

'What happened to Gerard?'

'He has been arrested.'

'Oh, I'm very sorry to hear that. Will he talk?'

'Not he. Unfortunately there was a traitor in our midst and he has been busy telling the Boche all about us. The whole network has been blown. You are the last one we will be able to help until a new circuit has been built up.'

'You are all very brave people and I am grateful for the care and help I have received, but I hope my presence has not made matters worse for you.'

The doctor smiled. 'It is our way of continuing the struggle. We do not submit to tyranny.'

'Do they know in London what's happened?'

'We don't know. The wireless operator was the first to be arrested. They tortured him and shot him. If they got his call sign out of him they might be using it. When you get back to Britain, we want you to tell them that. Tell them the Dutch circuit is not safe. They will know what to do.'

'I will. Is there anything else I can do?'

'Just get safely back.'

Jan knew there was a long and dangerous journey ahead of him before that happened, but at least he was on his way.

It was dawn when they pulled up in a farmyard on the outskirts of Brussels. Their arrival set up a frenzied barking. Jan waited with some trepidation while the doctor went to the door to make sure it was safe for him to leave the ambulance. The barking stopped and two minutes later he came back. 'All is well. Come with me.'

Jan scrambled off the stretcher and followed the doctor into the house, where he was met by a man with an untidy ginger beard and watery green eyes. 'I am Philippe,' he said, as they shook hands.

'I'll leave you now,' Dr Van Stoek said, holding out his hand. 'Good luck.'

Jan shook the hand vigorously. 'Thank you for everything,' he said. 'I will not forget you. Perhaps after the war we may meet again, who knows.'

'Who knows,' the doctor repeated, then turned on his heel and left.

'Come,' Philippe said, beckoning Jan to follow. The big mongrel padded after them.

They went through the hall to a kitchen where a woman was stirring something on the stove. 'This is my wife, Hortense,' Philippe said. 'Sit down and eat. You are safe here. The dog will warn us if anyone comes and we will have time to hide you. In a few days, my son, André, will take you to France.'

It was a week before André arrived. Thin as a rake and businesslike, he had little to say except to give Jan his instructions and his identity card and travel documents, which was apparently why he had had to wait so long. It took time to produce the forged paperwork to fit individual circumstances. There were a great many foreign workers in France, from many occupied countries, and Jan's papers stated he was one of those. They would not appear to be travelling together, but Jan was to take his cue from his guide and follow at a safe distance.

Philippe took them to the railway station in a farm cart where they boarded a train for Paris. The first time a German guard came along demanding to see their papers, Jan's heart was in his mouth, but they passed muster and he breathed again. They changed trains in Paris and once again his documents passed scrutiny. His next stop was Toulouse, once in the so-called free zone but now under German occupation like the rest of France. Here, they left the train and took a bus to a small village. His guide took him to a cafe, where the owner provided them with ersatz coffee and a lump of bread and cheese. After that was consumed André left to return home, leaving Jan sitting on his own, wondering what would happen next. He watched the customers coming and going, ready to bolt if necessary. No one paid him any attention. When at last the cafe was closed for the night, its owner beckoned Jan to follow him. 'Do not follow too closely,' he said. 'But do not lose me. I shall not look back.'

They left the village behind and began climbing a steep hill at the top of which was a picture book chateau. It was his next stopping point. His hostess was a *comtesse*, though he was never given her name. She was in her forties, he guessed, very elegant and self-assured. She provided him with the best meal he had eaten since leaving England, and a sumptuous bedroom which had its own bathroom. 'Please use the bathroom,' she told him. 'There is plenty of hot water. And then go to bed, I am sure you are tired after your journey. If you should hear noises downstairs, do not be alarmed. My unwelcome guests will not come up here. They think I am a collaborator and do not search my house.'

On the way back from the bathroom, feeling civilised once more, he heard the sound of laughter and music and crept onto the landing to listen. The voices were German. So that was what she meant. He went back into his room but took the precaution of locking his door and sleeping on the bed fully clothed. He need not have worried. The *comtesse* knocked on his door next morning. 'It is quite safe for you to come downstairs,' she called.

He opened the door and she laughed at the sight of him. 'Oh, dear, you did not go to bed. I told you there was no need to worry. Have a shave and come down.'

A little later, having shaved and brushed his suit, he joined her at the breakfast table. 'I have sent for Marius who will take you as far as the border,' she told him while he made inroads into a couple of fried eggs. 'Other people will take over from there. But beware, Spain guards its neutrality and not all Spaniards are sympathetic towards escapees and you could easily be interned for the duration. Stick with your guide but if you do become separated, make for a British consul.'

Marius duly arrived, a thin man in peasant clothing, who was taciturn to the point of speaking in monosyllables. Jan followed him to a local railway station where they took a train to Tarascon close to the Spanish border. He was installed in a house on the outskirts where his host spoke a dialect Jan could not understand, but he was eventually made to understand he was to wait. What he was waiting for, Jan had no idea. He was so near to freedom, and yet so far, this final delay was galling, but he knew he could not find his way over the mountains without a guide.

During the next few days, five more escapees arrived one at a time: two English airmen, a Frenchman determined to join De Gaulle's army in North Africa and two Polish prisoners of war. Jan did not know them, but he was soon in animated conversation with them. They had been prisoners since 1940 and knew very little more about what was happening in Poland than he did; what they did tell him was hearsay, gleaned from other prisoners, but it was enough to make his blood curdle. Warsaw was in ruins, the people half starved and frequently arrested and tortured on the least excuse, or no excuse at all. Executions were commonplace, and as for the Jewish population, they had been rounded up and forced into a walled ghetto, where living conditions were even worse. How true all this was, Jan did not know, but it made him fear for Rulka.

The next morning, all six set out to cross the Pyrenees on foot behind their guide. It was a steep climb and the going was rough with stones and boulders. And at that altitude it was very cold. A biting wind tore through their inadequate clothing. They were glad to spend the night in a rough mountain hut, but even then they dared not light a fire for fear of the smoke being seen by German patrols. The food they had brought with them was soon eaten and they were faced with more climbing the next day.

There was a major scare when they almost ran into a German patrol and had to scatter into the forest. It took some time to round them up again when the danger was passed and it was then too late to go on. They returned to the hut, and rose, cold and damp, next morning ready to try again. There was more climbing and then a descent. If they thought this meant they were nearly at their journey's end, they were soon disillusioned. There was still another mountain to cross. On they trudged, so cold they could not feel their fingers and toes and as they went higher they encountered snow, which made it even more difficult. Some of the party were not as fit as Jan, particularly one of the Poles who had suffered badly at the hands of the Germans. Jan, whose own leg was beginning to ache, put his arm round him and helped him along.

In the late afternoon of the next day, their guide held up a hand to stop them. They froze, thinking it might be another patrol, but all he said, with a huge grin on his face, was '*Espagne*'.

He left them there and they made their way down to a village. They were not the first escapees to arrive there and they were taken in by the local schoolmaster who gave them food and a bed for the night. Unsure from the villagers' demeanour whether they were friend or foe, Jan hardly dare close his eyes. Early next morning they were roused and directed to the next village where they were told they could take a bus to Barcelona. They had no Spanish money and only Jan had papers and these were of no use since they said he was a Polish worker in France. He felt it would be folly to attempt it, but the two Poles, who were so exhausted they could walk no further, and the Frenchman, decided to risk the bus. Jan and the British airmen, being healthier and stronger elected to keep walking.

At the end of that day, when they had managed forty kilometres in searing heat, Jan began to wonder if they had made the right decision. Hungry and thirsty they went to the church in a small Catalonian town and threw themselves on the mercy of the priest. He fed them and let them sleep in the church and the next morning gave them money to take a train to Barcelona. The consul there sent them on their way to the embassy in Madrid and from there, after a good meal and a night in a real bed, they took a train to Gibraltar. The frontier there was well guarded because the British authorities were on the lookout for German agents and everyone's papers were scrutinised. They had no papers but they did have letters from the consul and that ensured they were allowed through. They were once again on British territory and in the hands of the British authorities.

Louise was reading Angela a bedtime story, but the child fell asleep long before it was finished. She shut the book gently and sat looking down at her sleeping daughter, her heart swelling with love for the little scrap. She was Jan's gift to her. She heard the telephone and wondered if it was her mother.

Faith had been rehoused by the Middlesex County Council in a ground-floor flat where she was looking after Henry with the aid of a nurse who came in daily. He had regained consciousness but was unable to leave his bed and could only speak in angry grunts; no one had any idea what, if anything, he remembered. Louise had suggested her mother ought to put him in a nursing home and then come to live with her in Cottlesham, but she had refused. 'I couldn't,' she said. 'I must look after your father, it is my duty, and in any case I would never fit in with your friends. Their lifestyle

and yours now is so very different from what I have been used to.'
All of which sounded like an excuse to Louise.

She had begun to wonder if she ought to change her job and move away herself to make a new start in a different area, just the three of them. But she hesitated to take the first step. She and Angela were content where they were, she loved her job and the children she taught, and there was always the hope that Jan was alive and would come back – at least in the beginning, but even that was starting to fade. It was August and the school had broken up for the summer holidays. Soon the war would have been raging for four years and still there was no sign of it ending, no news of Jan either. His Polish friend had promised to tell her if he heard anything, but he hadn't contacted her again and she had begun to think Jan must be dead. But still she clung to a stubborn hope, as if refusing to admit he had gone from her life would bring him back.

'It's for you, Louise.' Jenny's voice drifted up to her. She put the book down on the bedside table and went to answer it.

'Louise, it's me.'

'Jan!' she screamed, and then more moderately, 'Oh, Jan! Thank God, oh, thank God. Where are you?'

'In London.'

'Oh, Jan.' She couldn't stem the tears that ran down her face. 'Are you all right?'

'I'm fine. How are you? And Angela?'

'We're both fine.'

He was in a public call box and the pips were going. 'Damn,' he said. 'I've no more pennies. I'll be back with you tomorrow. See you then.' She heard the telephone click as he replaced the receiver. Her legs suddenly gave way and she sat down heavily on the nearest chair. Jan was alive. Jan was safe. She had got him back.

He arrived the following morning, a gaunt, hollow-cheeked man with a slight limp, but the blue eyes still danced and his smile was just as captivating. Louise threw herself into his arms and cried.

'I thought I'd lost you,' she said, after he had mopped up her tears.

'I am not so easy to lose, my love.'

'You look dreadful.'

'Thanks for that,' he said, grinning. 'I'm a lot better than I was.'

'Sit down and tell me what happened.'

'After I have seen my daughter. Where is she?'

'In the kitchen. Jenny wanted to give us a few moments on our own.'

Followed by Louise, he dashed off to the kitchen and scooped Angela up from the floor where she was playing. She was not sure she liked that and squirmed to be put down again. 'She's forgotten me,' he said flatly, letting her go.

The child toddled away. Her little legs were quite sturdy now and she was into everything. Ornaments and medicines had to be put out of her reach, but she was learning the meaning of 'No'.

'It has been a long time, Jan,' Louise said. 'She'll get used to you again, give her time. How much time do you have, by the way?'

'Two weeks, a whole fortnight. Shall we have another little holiday?'

'Lovely. If it can be arranged before the autumn term starts.'

They managed to rent the little cottage they had taken before and travelled up to Windermere two days later. Little by little, Louise learnt what had happened to Jan. He was a little quieter than he had been before and often seemed lost in contemplation and she wondered how bad it had really been. 'Do you want to talk about it?' she asked on the evening they arrived. They had eaten a light meal and put Angela to bed, clutching Cuddles, and were sitting together on the settee. His arm was about her and her head rested on his shoulder.

'Not much to tell,' he said. 'The Dutch people were marvellous, particularly the doctor and nurse who looked after me. Even when the Germans infiltrated their underground network, they still managed to get me out. I learnt later they had all been arrested and shot.'

'That's dreadful.'

'It happens all the time. I get so angry.'

'Doesn't help though, does it?' she said.

'No. Their wireless operator was the first to be arrested so they lost their contact with London. I couldn't let anyone know I was OK.'

'But you were wounded.'

'I broke my leg when I crash-landed. It mended. The trouble was I couldn't move until the plaster came off. You have no idea how frustrating that was.'

She smiled. 'Knowing you, I can imagine. So how did you escape in the end?'

'I was passed from hand to hand, from Holland to France to Spain. It was an interesting experience, travelling through occupied territory.'

'Interesting!' She laughed. 'I'm sure it was more than that.'

'I can't tell you any more. I've been warned . . .'

'"Careless talk costs lives", eh?' she said quoting the posters that were everywhere.

'Something like that. They spent a week debriefing me and until that was done I couldn't return to my unit or contact you.'

'I understand. And when you got to Spain?'

'Oh, that was interesting too. We still had to be careful . . .'

'We?'

'There were six of us in the end. We walked a lot, took trains and buses, rode in taxis, walked, and eventually arrived in Gibraltar, a week after General Sikorski was killed taking off from there.'

She knew General Sikorski, the prime minister of the Polish government in England and C-in-C of their armed forces, had died in an air crash after visiting Polish troops in the Middle East. His dual role had been shared; the new C-in-C was General Sosnkowski, while Stanisław Mikołajczyk became premier. 'I read about that.'

'There was a lot of talk about it being sabotage,' he said. 'I can't see it myself, but it did make us nervous. I was glad when we were safely airborne and even more glad when we touched down in England.'

'All's well that ends well.'

'But it's not the end, is it?' he said. 'There is a long way to go yet.'

'You think so? We're winning, aren't we? After all, we've invaded Italy and the Russians are chasing the Germans back where they came from.'

'And they'll overrun Poland if no one stops them. I fear for my country, Louise. I don't think people in the West understand.'

She lifted her head to look into his face. She had never seen him so down and knew he was thinking of Rulka as well. 'Try me.'

'It's complicated, but I'll put it in a nutshell. Poland originated in the valley of the Vistula and spread eastwards while the Russian state began around the Volga and spread westwards. The territory in between has always been a bone of contention; the boundary has gone back and forth according to who was in the ascendancy. It was not until 1920, after Poland won the war with the newly emerged state of Soviet Russia, that the internationally recognised boundaries were established, but even those have been disputed. When Hitler and Stalin decided to carve Poland up in 1939, the area the Soviets took they consider theirs. I doubt they will concede anything less, and, if we are not strong, they will take the whole of Poland.'

'You don't think they will be allowed to get away with it?'

'I don't know – I wish I did. I feel so cut off from it all, when I wish I should be doing something.'

'You are doing something. You are helping to win the war, aren't you? Nothing can be done until that happens.'

'Yes, you are right.' He smiled suddenly. 'Let's not be miserable. Let's plan what we'll do tomorrow. A long walk perhaps, a picnic and a lazy afternoon?'

'Sounds heavenly. But what about your leg?'

'Oh, that's fine. It won't stop me doing what I want to do and right now I want to make love to you. Let's go to bed.'

Not wanting to spoil an idyllic holiday, she did not tell him about her father's stroke until they were packing to leave. 'Mum is in a poky little council flat, looking after my father and refusing to put him into a nursing home,' she said, folding Angela's little garments into her case. 'She said something about retribution, but whose I am not sure.'

'I am sorry, Louise, but perhaps it was your father's retribution she was talking about. I know he is your father, but I cannot find it in my heart to pity him, not after what he did. He could have killed you and our unborn child.'

'I know. But at least Mum and I are talking again. She came to Cottlesham once and stayed a couple of days, but she was uncomfortable, I could see that. Being an unmarried mother is a terrible sin in her eyes, and she couldn't understand how I could still be friends with everyone, nor why the rector hadn't publicly condemned me, which is what my father would have done to any of his flock who transgressed. I go and see her occasionally. Usually we meet in a hotel. I rarely go to the flat.'

'Poor you.'

'I told her all about you, how much I love you, what a good father you are and she seems to have accepted that.'

'Does she know about Rulka?'

'Yes, I told her. It only made my sin more terrible. She loves Angela, though.'

'That is something.'

She fastened the suitcase. 'There, that's that done. Do you want me to help you with yours?'

'No, I've done it.'

She turned to face him. 'What happens now, Jan?'

'We go back to the real world, me to my flying and you to your teaching, living life as best we can until this terrible war is over.' He took her in his arms and pulled her close to him. 'It will be time enough to worry about the future then, but whatever happens, you must always remember I love you.'

'And I love you too,' she said, fighting back tears. Every parting seemed like a last goodbye and every reunion to be treasured in case there would never be another. She didn't suppose she was the only one to think like that. It was happening to thousands, millions, of couples all over the world. Knowing that didn't make it any easier.

Jan returned to duty, as undecided about the future as he had been on the day he had been shot down, more so, since he had spent two weeks with Louise and Angela and even saying goodbye to them for a short time was hard. How much harder if it had to be forever? He had been debriefed at the Baker Street headquarters of the Special Operations Executive, the people who had most to do with underground movements in occupied countries, and their questions had been searching. He had felt sometimes as if he were a criminal being investigated, but in the politest way. If anyone knew what was going on in Poland, they would. They would not divulge secrets but he had asked them, as a favour, to see if they could find out what had happened to Rulka. They had said they would see what they could do, but made no promises. It was all he could hope for.

Chapter Nine

July 1944

The story had gone round Warsaw like wildfire the month before. It had been whispered in the bread queues, muttered on the trams, passed from one to the next as they knelt in church in prayer, discussed among the members of the Home Army. 'The Allies have landed in France. It can't be long now.'

Everyone in Warsaw who had a secret wireless listened to the BBC and passed on what they heard. London news differed greatly from what the German broadcasts were saying, but there was no doubt the fight in Western Europe was slower than had been expected. The greatest seaborne invasion in the history of the world was being met with stiff resistance. It had taken over a month for the Allies to capture Caen which had been one of the first day's objectives and Paris had still not been liberated by July. By that time the Russians were within twelve miles of Warsaw. Artillery fire could clearly be heard all over city.

Rulka and Colin had been summoned to a meeting of their section of the Home Army to discuss the implications. Colin had turned down the offer of an escort to Gdansk in favour of staying with the Polish underground and they were happy to have him. He was undoubtedly an asset and had been given the code name *Buldog*, though his *Kennkarte* named him as Pierre Saint-Jules. He could defuse a bomb as easily as he could make one and he was ingenious in using the most unlikely components, most of them brazenly stolen from the Germans themselves. And he could be ruthless. The gentle domesticated man he was when in Rulka's cellar could turn himself into an assassin when the need arose.

It was a fine July evening and the ruins still reflected the heat of the day. Rulka was wearing a blue dirndl skirt and white cotton blouse, shabby but clean. Her dark hair, once so lustrous but now lank, was tied back in a ponytail with a bit of blue ribbon. The neat clothes did not disguise the fact that she was painfully thin. Food was becoming harder and harder to find. Without Colin's ability to scrounge and steal from the Germans – usually blank ration cards – she did not think she would have survived.

They were accepted in their company as a team, the Bulldog and the Mouse, and were often given the most risky and dangerous jobs to do. Nothing was too difficult for them and they found themselves blowing up railway lines and freight trains, gunning down Nazis as they rounded people up for deportation, breaking AK leaders out of Pawiak prison, and generally making a nuisance of themselves. They were both on the Nazis' most wanted list, but as their real identities were known only to a few, they had managed to evade capture. How long it could last they did not know and would not think about.

It was inevitable that they would become close, working together and living together as they did, and it had become more than just the closeness of friends and colleagues on the day they blew up a packed German troop train on its way to the Russian front. It had been a particularly risky operation but they had both said they could do it. The idea was to lay charges at intervals along the track, to cause the maximum disruption. Colin and Rulka were sent to a section of line that went through the forest and over a bridge where, if they were on time, two trains were expected to cross going in opposite directions.

They left the city environs by night, evading the German guards, and made their way on foot to the bridge, arriving just before dawn. It was still dark but they dare not use torches because Germans patrolled the bridge. Colin set the charges while Rulka kept watch armed with a Bren gun. It had seemed hours to Rulka, but could only have been thirty minutes, before he came back to her, carrying the detonator and paying out the fuse. 'All done. Now we wait.'

The first train had been bang on time, its engine followed by several carriages and then some freight trucks. It rattled onto the bridge. Colin watched and waited, his hand on the plunger. 'Where's the other one?' she whispered.

'Don't know.' He daren't wait any longer. The explosions, from end to end of the bridge and some along the line each side, coincided with the arrival of the second train. The result had been spectacular. Engine, wagons, carriages flew everywhere. Rulka turned to Colin, eyes alight, and flung her arms round him. 'We did it, *Buldog*, we did it!'

'Yes, let's get out of here.'

He took her hand and they ran as fast as they could deeper into the forest, leaving behind a burning train, buckled railway lines and dead enemy soldiers. When they could no longer see it or feel its heat, Rulka stopped to bend over and catch her breath. 'Give me a minute,' she said.

He sat down with his back to the trunk of an oak tree and pulled her down beside him. 'We are safe here for the moment.'

The forest had been eerily silent: no voices, no birdsong; no gunfire, no explosions. 'It's as though we are the only two people left in the world,' she said.

He put his arm about here and drew her head onto his shoulder. 'Let's pretend we are. Let's pretend there are no yesterdays, no tomorrows, just today.'

It was impossible to be a hardened warrior every minute of the day and Colin represented the warmth of another human being in a city where humanity seemed to have died along with so many of its inhabitants. And so they had become lovers, though they never spoke of love; that was an irrelevance, but they had the next best thing: trust.

It was obvious to everyone that the Germans were staring defeat in the face and those occupying Warsaw were twitchy and liable to shoot without provocation. The rumour was that Hitler had refused to allow them to withdraw.

'What do you think will happen?' she asked him as they walked to the meeting place in the crypt of the Church of the Holy Cross that July afternoon.

'No idea,' he said. In the two years he had been with Rulka he had learnt enough Polish to get by but his accent often had Rulka in fits of laughter. Laughter helped them to endure the terrible conditions under which they lived. 'I suppose it depends on how much the Home Army trusts Stalin.'

'As far as they can throw him,' she said. 'Arkady told me that when the Red Army have encountered units of the AK, they have disarmed and arrested them. That's not the action of an ally.'

'No, it's not.'

The crypt was already crowded when they arrived, with about fifty people of both sexes; among them were several Boy Scouts, called the Grey Ranks, who acted as runners and distributors of

183

secret underground publications. Arkady and Boris Martel were standing on the altar under which Father Karlowicz had hidden Colin. Boris was their intelligence officer and though Rulka could not be sure of it, she thought he was in direct communication with the government in London. He also seemed to have access to a certain amount of German intelligence. If not, he was singularly successful in gauging what they would do next. She suspected it was he who had told General Bór-Komorowski, the C-in-C of the Home Army, about the AK units being arrested by the Russians. It did not bode well for the future.

Arkady lost no time in outlining the situation. 'The Soviets are sweeping all before them and will soon be on our doorstep,' he said. 'We have been instructed by our government in London to cooperate with them, but that comes with the proviso that diplomatic relations broken off after the Katyn affair are resumed between the Polish government and the Soviet Union, so we are once again allies.'

This pronouncement was received by some with groans and ironic laughter, and by others with cheers. 'The Soviets have already set up a Polish government of Communists and traitors,' someone called out from the middle of the crowd. 'So who do we obey? The one that arrives first?'

Independent of the Western Allies, the Soviets had been preparing for the future of Poland and had formed what it called the Polish Committee of National Liberation to take over the administration of the country as soon as the Germans had been ousted. According to the Soviet Foreign Office, their objective was to help the Polish people to become once again an independent democratic state. They had, so they said, no wish to acquire any part of Polish territory.

'London,' Arkady answered. 'That is the government we have

obeyed since 1939 and we shall go on doing so.'

'It is thousands of kilometres away,' someone else said. 'Do they know what is happening here in Poland?'

'Yes, they do,' Boris told them. 'We are in constant communication with them. And the Western Allies have promised their support.'

'The kind of support we had in '39, I suppose.' The speaker spoke bitterly.

'It is different now. Britain is no longer on the defensive and the Americans are with us,' Arkady went on. 'But there is one thing we must do and that is free Warsaw before the Soviets arrive. Our flag must be flying everywhere. We have to welcome them as allies and not occupiers.'

'You know what happened to the Jews,' another reminded him.

When, in April the previous year, the skeletal inhabitants of the Ghetto had tried to rise up with stolen rifles, home-made bombs, sticks and stones they had been crushed mercilessly with tanks and flame-throwers. If they were not burnt in their cellars and tenements, they had been shot as they tried to escape and their bodies piled in the streets and burnt on massive funeral pyres. Those that managed to survive were herded into cattle wagons to die in the camps. Rulka and Colin had saved as many as they could, hiding them and feeding them and sometimes supplying them with false papers to hide their ethnicity. The Ghetto, the largest in Poland, was no more. It had been completely destroyed.

'We are better prepared than they were,' Arkady told them. 'Britain will drop supplies and Polish paratroopers to help us fight and they will bomb all the airfields in the vicinity so the *shkopy* cannot use them. General Bór has also asked for the transfer of Polish bomber and fighter squadrons to Poland.'

'Jan,' Rulka murmured to herself. Was he with them? Did

it mean they might soon be reunited? Her heart missed a beat. Could it happen? But she still had no idea if he were alive, so what was the point of getting excited about something that might never be? It was more important to set aside personal feelings until the war was won.

'What did you say?' Colin whispered as everyone began discussing possibilities.

'Nothing, just praying it's true.' Close as they were, he did not know about Jan, nor her real name. And she knew no more about him than he had revealed when he first arrived.

'The Home Army is to be recognised by the Allies as a legitimate combatant,' Arkady went on. 'We will no longer be an underground army, we will be out in the open.'

'When?' someone shouted.

'When everything is in place and the time is right. In the meantime we stockpile weapons and ammunition, carry on with sabotage operations, and gather as much information about enemy troop movements as we can. If you have hidden weapons or know anyone who has them, make sure they are made serviceable and available.' Then he brought the meeting to a close. One by one, they drifted away, mingling with the populace taking the early evening air. They knew that similar meetings were going on all over the city.

Colin took Rulka's hand as they pretended to be a courting couple out for a stroll, but they were wary and their glances darted left and right and occasionally he stopped to turn and kiss her, while at the same time looking back to see if they were being followed. They reached the cellar in Jasna Street without incident. In winter the cellar had been icy cold but in the warm days of July it was like an oven. With no windows, all they could do to let in a breath of air was to prop the door open at the top of the stairs. It was risky, so they only left it open while Rulka was cooking.

'I wonder what the Nazis will do,' she said, setting about making dumplings stuffed with a couple of boiled potatoes and some mushrooms Colin had gathered in the Kampinos forest just to the north of Warsaw. He often went there to confer with partisans who lived there in hiding and visit the elderly couple who had befriended him when he first escaped. It was because they were so poor and had little enough for themselves he had left them to come to Warsaw. 'Perhaps they will withdraw and let us take our city back unmolested.'

'You don't really believe that, do you?'

'No, just wishful thinking. I think we are in for a battle.'

'Not only here,' he said. 'In France, Holland and Belgium. It is a long way from Normandy to Berlin.'

'Surely Hitler will give in before that happens, then we won't need to welcome the Soviets.'

'I doubt it,' he said.

'But the end can't be far off.'

He came and stood beside her as she dropped the dumplings into a pan of boiling water. 'Then what will you do? In the end, I mean.'

She turned to face him. 'I don't know. We can't make long-term plans, can we?'

'No,' Then he lapsed into English. 'Let's eat, drink and be merry for tomorrow we die.'

'Is that an English saying?'

'Yes, though I don't know who said it first.'

'Let's eat anyway,' she said, dishing the dumplings onto two plates while he climbed the stairs to shut and bolt the door.

'Colin,' she said, as they were eating. 'Is there anyone in England who should be told if anything happens to you?'

'My parents. Boris knows how to contact them. What about you?'

'No one. All dead.' It sometimes helped to say it aloud in order to make herself believe it. It was better that way.

'I'm sorry.'

'Don't be. Not your fault.'

'Hey, I thought we were going to be merry,' he said, fetching half a bottle of vodka and two mugs from a cupboard. 'Let's drink to . . .' He looked up from pouring the drink. 'What shall we drink to?'

'To us,' she said.

'You mean you and me?'

'Yes, why not?'

'To us,' they said together, clinking the mugs against each other, and drank.

'Confusion to our enemies,' he added and refilled the mugs.

'And peace. And freedom,' she said. 'It will happen, won't it? In the end, I mean.'

'Yes, my love, it will happen.'

She was startled. He had never called her love before. 'Colin, I—' She stopped, undecided what to say.

'Don't worry, sweetheart,' he said. 'I'm not going to make fulsome protestations of undying love, but here and now it's what I feel, and here and now is all we have.'

She rescued her hand and picked up the plates to wash them up, turning away from him. Over the years since she had said goodbye to Jan and buried her parents, she had not allowed herself to cry, but now tears were streaming down her face and she could not stop them. He came to stand beside her and took her shoulders to turn her towards him. 'I didn't mean to make you cry, sweetheart.' He put his forefinger under her chin and tipped her face up to his.

She looked into his face, thin as hers was, grey with fatigue too, but there was concern in his blue eyes. 'Give me a smile.'

She sniffed and managed a watery smile. 'I don't deserve you.'

'Nonsense. You are the deserving one. For a little'un you pack quite a punch.'

'I don't understand that.'

He laughed suddenly. 'Never mind. It's time for bed.'

To the dismay of the Varsovians, the German troops prepared to stand and fight. German civilians and wounded soldiers were evacuated and they mingled with hundreds of refugees, blocking the roads to the west. In the city the Nazi administration set about making bonfires of their files. Governor Fischer decreed that all able-bodied Varsovians were to assemble in the main squares to help build defences, with the threat that if they disobeyed they would be punished. They were offered extra rations as an inducement.

'If we go, it will leave us without men to fight,' Arkady said at a second meeting in the crypt. 'But if we don't, there will be the usual bloodthirsty reprisals.'

'On the other hand,' Colin said, 'the foolish man is inviting us to congregate, something he has never allowed before. He must be desperate.'

'And desperate men are dangerous men,' Rulka added. 'When do we rise?'

'When we hear from London that help is on its way. Colonel Monter is to be in command of the rising and he has called a state of alert.' Arkady went on to outline everyone's role, which unit was to take which objective and who was to supply support services such as radio communications, medical aid and food. Already communication rooms, kitchens, first-aid centres and workshops had been established in the city's warren of cellars. The Grey Ranks would hold themselves in readiness to convey the order to assemble. With that he called the meeting to a close. One by one they dispersed, careful to avoid German patrols.

The next day, which was a fine, sunny Saturday, Colin and Rulka watched in silence, along with hundreds of others, as reinforcements arrived for the beleaguered Germans in the form of a Panzer division which marched through the streets and crossed the river with their tanks, making for the front line. 'He's not going to give in, is he?' Rulka murmured, referring to Hitler.

'No, but then he thinks he's indestructible.' An attempt on the Führer's life by his own officers, had recently failed and the plotters were being hunted and executed.

They turned to go back to their cellar. On the way, Colin ripped a poster from a lamp post which was leaning at a crazy forty-five degrees. 'What's that all about?' he asked, handing it to Rulka. Unlike German proclamations, it was not in German and did not have the German Eagle at the top of it. It was in Polish and headed with a red star. 'The Polish government in London has been disbanded,' she translated. 'The Union of Polish Patriots is assuming command of the underground. All patriotic Poles are expected to join them in cleansing the city of its Fascist invaders.'

'For patriots, read Communists,' he said.

'Yes.' The Union of Polish Patriots had replaced the pre-war Polish Communist party which had been dissolved when, according to both the Nazis and the Soviets, Poland had ceased to exist. Now it had become politically expedient for Moscow to admit it did exist after all. 'It's worrying.'

'Let's tear them down.'

They began systematically going from street to street, pulling down the posters but they wondered if the damage had already been done. There were a great many people on the streets, enjoying the sunshine, trying to pretend all was well; the sound of guns was not yet near enough to drive them into shelters. They could not fail to see the posters.

Colin and Rulka had just turned into Jasna Street when they heard the sound of aircraft coming from the east. They ducked into the remains of a building already destroyed by German bombs and waited with their heads down, expecting Russian bombs. But it was not bombs the aircraft dropped but leaflets, repeating what had been said on the poster and calling the people to arms.

'If we don't move now, we never will,' Colin said. 'Let's go and find Arkady.'

They found him at his apartment listening to a broadcast on behalf of the Polish Committee of National Liberation, now based in Lublin. 'Soviet forces are advancing on Praga. They are coming to bring you freedom. People of the capital to arms! Strike at the Germans. Blow up their public buildings. Assist the Red Army in crossing the Vistula . . .'

He turned it off when they arrived. 'London cannot help,' he told them flatly.

'Why not?' Colin demanded.

'They say that even if they had sufficient aircraft with a long enough range to transport troops, there is nowhere they can safely land them, or drop parachutists. To attempt it would be suicidal.'

'What about fighters?' Rulka asked, thinking of Jan.

'Same thing. Can't get here, can't land. Nowhere for them to be kept and maintained. And they have to fly from Italy over German occupied territory. Previous flights have proved unacceptably costly.'

'Oh,' she said. There would be no reunion with her husband, not yet. 'We are alone, then?'

'No. As the British government pointed out to our people, there is the Red Army, which is in a better position to render aid. We have to work with the Soviets whether we like it or not. General Mikołajczyk has been flown to Moscow for talks with Stalin . . .'

'Fat lot of good that will do,' Colin said in English.

Arkady asked Rulka to translate, which she did. 'I am inclined to agree with you, my friend,' he told Colin. 'But it means there's no one in London to say yes or no. General Bór will have to make the decision himself and he is inclined to seize the moment. If the Soviets cross the river before we have secured the city, the battle will be between them and the retreating German army and our moment will be gone. We have to take the city and hold it before the Russians come . . .'

'Don't you think we can?'

'Of course we can,' he snapped. 'The Soviets will be here in two or three days at the most. I just wish we had more weapons, that's all. I spent all morning digging up graves and retrieving the guns I buried. There was a nosy SS sergeant who came and wanted to know what I was doing. I told him we had run out of suitable burial plots and I was having to put one body in on top of another.' He chuckled. 'It is as well he did not look into the coffin I had beside the grave. I had to pretend it was a body and bury it again. I'll go back after dark and retrieve it.' He paused. 'Are you ready, Bulldog?'

'Yes.' Colin was to take part in the assault on one of the German army stores. 'I have rifles, ammunition and hand grenades, enough to arm each man in my unit to start with. After that we will take them from the Germans we kill.'

'What about me?' Rulka asked.

'You will stay out of it,' Colin said.

'I will not! Haven't I been with you all along? Haven't I done everything you asked of me and more besides? I won't be left out.'

'You are not going to be left out, Myszka,' Arkady said patiently. 'Your skills as a nurse will undoubtedly be needed. Your orders are to report to the church of St Stanislaus Kostka. It is to serve as a hospital for our casualties. Dr Andersz will join you there.'

Colin and Rulka went back to the cellar, more than usually subdued. The streets had somehow emptied. The population, who had been trying to make the best of the sunshine, had gone to wherever they called home: an undamaged apartment, a cellar, the basement of a church, an empty shop or office. There was an eerie calm. Even the boom of heavy artillery to the east had fallen silent.

Rulka was keyed up to fever pitch and these last few hours were going to take a toll on nerves already frayed. She clung to Colin's hand until they regained the cellar, where she made a meal of sorts but neither had much appetite. Colin went into the boiler room, now no longer his bedroom, and set about cleaning his rifle and laying out his ammunition. Unable to settle, she went and watched him. He looked up and smiled. 'Feeling fidgety?'

'Yes.'

He left what he was doing and came over to take her in his arms. 'We can't do anything but wait, sweetheart, but I can think of something to pass the time.' He paused to lean back and look into her face. 'That's if you want to.'

'Yes. I want to feel your arms about me, your body next to mine, to pretend the world is at peace, to feel human for a change. To feel safe.'

'Your wish is my command,' he said, leading her into the bedroom. He was a tender and patient lover and, for a little while, they were able to forget what was happening elsewhere. Afterwards they lay with bodies entwined, waiting for dawn.

But nothing happened the next day or the day after that and

they were beginning to wonder if anything was going to happen at all, when, on Tuesday morning the first day of August, a runner in the person of a Boy Scout came to tell them Liberation Hour would be at five o'clock. Everyone was to be in position by then. Rulka donned her uniform, clung to Colin for a moment, then left for the church.

In a light drizzle, welcome after a hot dry spell, Varsovians from all over the city, men and women as well as children, were emerging in small groups. The adults were carrying pistols and ammunition disguised as briefcases and shopping bags, while the children shouldered rucksacks of food and medical supplies. Rulka gave no sign that she had seen them, as she hurried to her own station. She knew, before the day was out, she was going to be busy.

A few minutes after Rulka had left, Colin set out to join his unit in the grounds of a school next to the stores. He was under no illusions about the difficulty of the task ahead of them. Because he wasn't a native Varsovian or even a Pole, he could be more objective than people like Arkady and Krystyna who were passionate about their city and Polish independence. He would probably have been the same if the Germans had occupied London. That they had not was, so he had learnt while a prisoner of war, due to the Royal Air Force and that included Polish airmen. He felt disappointed, angry and embarrassed that no one from the country of his birth would help the Poles now.

He could have taken the help that was offered and left Warsaw two years before, but there was no guarantee he would have reached England safely, so he had stayed. To begin with he had stayed because he admired the courage of the Poles and hated the Germans and it had seemed like an adventure. The adventure had turned into a nightmare, but by then he had fallen head over heels in love with Krystyna and hoped one day to wear her down into admitting she loved him too. He didn't blame her for holding back when life itself was so uncertain, but please God, they would survive the next few days and then he would really tell his mouse what was in his bulldog's heart.

They called her Myszka because she was so small and swift and could squeeze through holes and apertures that a larger person could not. But she was no mouse when it came to courage; she had more than her share of that and he had often had to hold her back from doing something foolish. It was he who had suggested to Arkady that she should be ordered to the church. He wanted her to be safe where he could find her when it was all over.

He found the rest of the platoon at the appointed place. He was wearing his old army uniform which was far too big for him now, and the others were dressed in a motley range of uniforms, many of them stolen from the Germans. Others had donned old uniforms, some their own, some belonging to their fathers from the Great War. A Scout handed them all the red and white armbands to denote they were part of the Home Army. The Germans must have guessed there was something afoot but they didn't know where or when the strike would be. By three o'clock, Colin and his men occupied the school without opposition. At precisely five o'clock, they climbed over the back fence of the school and raced across to the stores, guns blazing.

At the same time, doors and windows all over the city were flung open and any Germans in the streets were subject to a hail of small arms fire. Home-made grenades, called *filipinki*, and Molotov cocktails were hurled at German strong points. Those not involved in the fighting – housewives, teachers, children – dragged furniture, carts and paving stones into the streets to build barricades, and many of them were shot while doing so.

There were casualties on both sides, but Colin survived unscathed, as they overcame German resistance and took control of the stores which were immediately raided for uniforms, boots, helmets and camouflage jackets. They could hear fighting going on all over the old city, but had no idea of the outcome. By evening a Polish flag was flying from the top of the Prudential Building, the tallest structure in Warsaw. They saw it when they moved out to their second objective, leaving the populace to loot the stores of flour, sugar, cereals and anything else they could carry.

That evening Colin met Arkady in the Kammler furniture factory which had become command headquarters, and his feeling of euphoria at a job well done evaporated when Arkady told him they had failed to take several important objectives. In spite of valiant efforts and heavy losses, Castle Square, the Police District, the airport and the State telephone building were still in enemy hands and they had not managed to seize control of the bridges. What was even more worrying, the Germans were bringing in reinforcements and the Soviet advance had been halted.

'It's early days yet,' Colin said.

'Yes. No one said it would be easy.'

'Have you seen Mouse?'

'No.'

Colin could not leave to see if she was all right, he could only hope that in the hospital she would be safe.

The casualties had been coming in all day and Rulka had not had a moment to spare, but it was obvious from the tales filtering through to her the fighting was bitter and unrelenting. She worried about her friends, especially the women who were fighting alongside the men, and Colin, of course. He was her rock, the one person she could turn to when she had doubts or felt low. You couldn't live with someone for two years as she had been doing without having feelings for him, but was it more than that? It was certainly enough for her to rush to look at every new patient who came in and breathe her relief when it turned out not to be Colin.

She slept in a makeshift rest room that night, while others took over her duty, but the next morning it all began again. The enemy was not going to give in and responded with savagery. Not only were Home Army personnel killed and injured but the civilian population as well: men, women, children and babies, it was all one to the Nazis. And fire was their principal weapon. They used tanks and flame-throwers to telling effect.

Day after day, night after night, was the same and by the end of the week everyone was exhausted. The Home Army was still in control of the old town, the city centre and some of the southern suburbs and they had become masters at surviving bombardments and retaking positions they had lost the day before, but they hadn't been able to drive the Germans out. It was stalemate.

'We've been on to London again,' Colin told Rulka on the sixth day. He had been to visit another small outpost on behalf of Arkady which took him past the church and he had taken the opportunity to find her. They had gone out to the forecourt to share a cigarette. 'If they don't do something, General Bór doesn't know how much longer we can hold out.'

'Is it as bad as that? I saw the RAF bombers fly over yesterday and drop supplies into Krasinski Square. Everyone waved and cheered. How they got through the guns, I'll never know.'

'Yes, brave men those pilots, coming in over the rooftops to make sure they dropped accurately, but according to Boris, who seems to know these things, there won't be any more.'

'Why not?'

He smiled ruefully. 'They were Polish pilots who had been

ordered to drop the supplies into AK rural areas outside Warsaw. They disobeyed orders not to fly over the city and one of them was shot down. The mission as a whole took heavy casualties and so future sorties have been cancelled.'

'I can't believe that.'

'True, though.'

'What are the Russians doing?'

'Nothing.'

'We can't surrender.'

'No, that's not an option.' He paused. 'I suppose it's no good telling you to try and get out of Warsaw.'

'No good at all,' she assured him.

'Then take care of yourself.'

'And you.'

He kissed her and was gone. Rulka tucked a tendril of escaping hair into her cap and went back into the hospital. Beds were being emptied as people recovered or died, but they were quickly filled again as more casualties were brought in.

The fight went on and the longer it went on, the greater the atrocities. From wanting to retake control of the city, the German occupiers and their reinforcements seemed bent on destroying it and every living being in it. Rulka, trying to cope with burns, gunshot wounds, people crushed by falling buildings or flattened under tanks, worked like an automaton; her senses reeled and then became numb. She could only pray, 'Please God, let it end soon.'

But that plea was not to be granted immediately. As the days and then weeks went by, the Home Army turned from attack to defence in an effort to hold the ground they had. They had lost the element of surprise and with nothing but small arms and a few captured tanks, they had no hope of dealing a knockout blow. General Bór sent out urgent messages to AK units outside Warsaw to come to their aid, but they couldn't get through the cordon the Germans had put round the city. The German artillery, bombers and tanks gradually reduced the ground held by the insurgents and by the end of the month, even though the RAF had relented and dropped more supplies, and American Flying Fortresses had also dropped supplies on their way to Russia, more than half of which landed among the Germans, it was all too little and too late. Food and fresh water were running out; people were eating horses and pigeons and taking water from the river which was at a low ebb due to lack of rain, a dangerous undertaking since they risked cholera as well as being seen and shot. Soon Rulka was treating the sick as well as wounded. General Bór ordered a withdrawal of all outlying posts from the Old Town into the city centre, through the sewers. They all knew the end could not be far off.

'Will you give me permission to go and fetch Mouse?' Colin asked Colonel Mentor. They had climbed a ruined stairwell and were looking from a blackened window embrasure at a city that was a mass of rubble – whole streets had disappeared.

The colonel, exhausted and worried as he was, smiled. 'She means a great deal to you, doesn't she, Sergeant?'

'Yes, sir.'

'Then go with my blessing. You know where to take her?'

'Yes, sir.' He raced down the stairwell to the street and set off for the hospital, stumbling in his effort to run. Several times he had to duck when enemy artillery shelled the area. Some of the way he was able to run underground where the people had hacked holes in the walls leading from one basement to the next. Hopping over the people who were sheltering there, he emerged at the end of the terrace to find German tanks in the street using flame-throwers. He ran back and shouted to the occupants of the cellars. 'Get out! Get out that way!' Picking up two small children, he led the way, ushering them all out to safety, as, one by one, the basements behind him went up in flames. The heat, as the buildings caught fire, was intense; even the tarmac of the road was hot. He would not be able to return that way.

Rulka stayed at her post, doing what she could for the dead and dying, but in the end Lech had told her to go out for a breath of fresh air. The rumble of tanks told her the Germans were moving in. She ducked into the doorway as they came round the corner and saw a group of teenage members of the Grey Ranks dart out from surrounding buildings and hurl petrol bombs at the tanks. The boys were met by murderous fire. She rushed out to try and help one who had been wounded and was kneeling beside him when a dozen German troopers appeared from behind the tanks and ran into the hospital, firing indiscriminately. One of them came over to Rulka and ordered her back into the hospital. She ignored him. He kicked her over and put the muzzle of his rifle into her side. 'Get up!' he shouted.

She struggled to her feet, though standing upright hurt her ribs, and made her way back into the hospital. The Germans ordered everyone, staff and patients alike, into the crypt and were kicking the heads of the patients lying on the ground and shooting others when they were slow to obey. Rulka protested over and over again, only to be knocked down and kicked. Too winded to move, she watched in horror as the troopers flung petrol-soaked straw into the basement and set light to it.

Colin heard the shrieks long before he reached the scene. The church was an inferno, but the attackers had moved on. Desperate to find Krystyna, he dashed into the burning building, but was driven back by the fire. Again he tried and again was beaten back, choking on the thick smoke. 'Krystyna!' he yelled above the roar of the flames. 'Myszka! Where are you?' By now the shrieking had stopped and there was nothing to be heard but the crackling of the fire, nothing to be seen through thick black smoke.

Choking and consumed with fury and misery, he turned to go and nearly fell over a bundle of clothes by the door, but then he noticed it move and bent down to look more closely. It was Mouse, battered and bruised but alive. 'Thank God!' he said, lifting her up. She weighed very little. 'Let's have you out of here.'

That was easier said than done. He was now behind what could be called enemy lines, though lines was a misnomer. Urban warfare was nothing like fighting in the countryside. It was done house by house, street by street, and each side held pockets or small enclaves. He had to find his way back without accidentally finding himself on the wrong side of a barricade. It was bad enough scrambling over ruins when he had his hands free, but with the burden of Rulka in his arms he often stumbled and had to stop frequently to rest and get his bearings. And several times they were held up by gunfire too close for comfort.

She stirred. 'Colin, put me down, I can walk.'

'Are you sure?' She was bruised and in shock but he knew he could not carry her much further.

'Yes.'

He set her on her feet and they set off again. There was fighting all around them as the insurgents launched diversionary counter attacks to cover the withdrawal of the main forces. They did not speak, there was no time for that, they had to concentrate on finding their way through unrecognisable streets to the corner of Dluga Street, where members of the Grey Ranks were to conduct people through the sewers. Darkness fell, but the fires lit up the ruins in a smoky glow. Colin feared they would be too late and everyone, including the boys, would be gone.

They were within fifty yards of the manhole and could see the head of a boy sticking out of it, looking about him to see if there were any more wanting to leave. Colin shouted at him to wait. He heard them, but he also heard the whoosh of a German rocket. His head disappeared and the manhole cover clattered back into place. Colin and Rulka, hiding behind what had once been a barricade, felt the force of the explosion, as more stones, bricks and cement dust flew into the air. Colin flung himself over Rulka.

'We've got to make it to the sewer before the next one,' he said when the dust settled. 'Are you ready?'

As he spoke the manhole cover rose again and the boy's head reappeared. 'Run!' he yelled.

Rulka went first and, gagging on the stench, was helped down onto the rungs of a slippery ladder by the boy. Colin was following when he was caught by the next rocket. His body was flung into the air and came down on the road with a sickening thud. 'Colin!' Rulka screamed and tried to scramble back to him, but was held back by the boy. 'I must go to him.' She squirmed from his grasp and scrambled back onto the road.

She had seen enough dead and dying to know that there was nothing she could do to help him. She crouched over him, tears streaming down her face.

He gave her a crooked smile. 'I love you, Mouse,' he murmured. 'Live. Live for my sake and for all the people of Poland. Go on. Leave me.'

'I can't.'

'Yes you can. Don't keep the boy waiting.'

The boy was shouting to her to come back, that he could not stay there much longer.

She looked down at the man who had given his life for her and kissed him for the last time. He died with a smile on his lips. She closed his eyes, muttered a prayer and left him.

The journey through the sewers was worse than any nightmare as the boy, with a torch, led her through thick noxious sludge, sometimes ankle deep, sometimes as deep as her chest. She knew if she fell she would not be able to get up again and she had to concentrate on each tiny step. They passed underneath German-held positions; she could hear the rumble of tanks which reverberated along the slimy tunnel. If the boy spoke to her, she did not hear him, all she could hear were Colin's last words which went round and round in her head. 'I love you. Live for my sake and for all the people of Poland.' She had lived through so much misery already, she would live through this, she had to.

Three hours later, they climbed out of the sewer onto the street, the last to do so, and were greeted by cheers. Those fighting the rearguard would fight on while their ammunition lasted, then they would be taken prisoner or meet their end as Colin had done. Rulka found the cheers wholly inappropriate and angrily burst into tears.

Chapter Ten

October 1944

Jan had always loved going to Cottlesham and thought of it as his second home, a place to relax away from the stress of combat and enjoy some time with Louise and his little daughter. Angela, trotting about on her sturdy little legs and chatting away ten to the dozen to people she knew, always ran to him to be hoisted on his shoulder. But the news of the uprising in Warsaw had sent his thoughts careering back to Rulka and he had not been to Cottlesham for over six weeks – the whole time the Rising was in progress – for fear of upsetting Louise, who had an uncanny knack of reading his mind.

The latest public announcement from the Polish government that the insurgents had been forced to surrender only served to deepen his gloom. 'The cessation of military operations took place after all supplies had been exhausted,' it said. 'The garrison and the people were completely starved. Fighting ceased after vain attempts to fight their way out . . . and finally after all hopes of relief from outside had vanished.' It was small consolation that the Germans, recognising their courage, had agreed to treat the Home Army as prisoners of war and not rebels and that included the valiant General Bór. Nothing at all was said about the Russian part in the affair, or rather lack of it. According to information circulating among the exiled Poles, Stalin encouraged them to take up arms and then sat on the other side of the river and refused to help, publicly condemning the 'adventure' as foolhardy. Honest reliable information was hard to find and Jan had no way of gauging the truth of that, but the reported casualties had been horrendous. Was Rulka in the thick of it? Had she survived? Had she even lived beyond 1939?

His repeated requests to the Polish government in London had finally produced a kind of answer. 'No one by the name of Rulka Grabowska has been found in Warsaw,' he had been told. 'She may have perished or been taken prisoner or she may have escaped to the countryside. The situation in Warsaw is confused to say the least and it is difficult to trace people. Perhaps after the war . . .' *After the war.* It seemed to be the answer to every query nowadays. Would it also show him the way to go?

He missed Louise and his daughter more than he thought possible and keeping away from them was not helping as he had thought it might. He had a forty-eight-hour pass due to him and telephoned to say he was on his way.

Louise realised as soon as he arrived that he was not his usual self and not even Angela could coax him out of his brown study. She had recently been given a room of her own and a proper bed of which she was very proud and nothing would do but he must go with her to admire it as soon as he came through the door. Having done so, he sat on it with the child on his knee, absent-mindedly nuzzling her soft curls with his chin.

'What's wrong, Jan?' Louise asked. She had been folding

Angela's newly laundered clothes and putting them away in a chest of drawers, but left the task to come and sit beside him. 'Are you thinking about what's happened in Warsaw?'

'Yes, not that there is anything I can do about it. When we first heard about the Rising and were told everything was going according to plan, we had a party to celebrate. But we were premature. As soon as the true state of affairs filtered out from our government, the whole squadron wanted to do something to help. Jan Zumbach lobbied for us to be allowed to go to Warsaw but he was turned down. There were logistical problems, he was told, and in any case we were needed to combat the flying bombs.' The latest menace to hit London and the south-east arrived without warning and caused untold damage and loss of life. People were calling it a second Blitz.

It was so unlike Jan to be miserable, but when he was down, he was really down and Louise guessed he was thinking of his wife. She felt selfish that she had him and Rulka did not, but there was nothing she could do but sympathise. 'I'm sorry, Jan,' she said. 'But do you think your going would have made any difference?'

'Why didn't the Allies do something to help?' he went on without answering her question. 'We Poles fought alongside the Allies from the very first. We were there at the Battle of Britain, North Africa, Italy and Monte Cassino, D-Day and Arnhem. We had all the difficult jobs and we did them and never counted the cost. And for what? To be deserted in our hour of need . . .'

'I'm sure there must be more to it than that.'

'Of course there is. Churchill and Roosevelt are afraid of upsetting the Russians. Roosevelt has no idea what it is like in Europe and is more concerned about the presidential elections. Churchill is an old man and can't stand up to him or to Stalin. Now Stalin can walk into Warsaw whenever he likes and take over with his puppet government. They can't or won't do anything to stop him.'

'The Russians are our allies.'

'Only because it suits Stalin to say so. He has no love for Poland, never has had.'

'I'm sorry, Jan,' she said, putting her hand on his arm. 'I wish there was something I could do to cheer you up.'

'Just be you,' he said, turning to kiss her. 'My anchor.'

'You can rely on that,' she said. 'Always.'

And then his mood suddenly lightened and he grabbed her and rolled her over onto her back and began tickling her until she cried for mercy. Angela climbed over both of them, wanting to be a part of whatever game they were playing. Jan turned and took his daughter into his arms. 'Give *Tata* a cuddle,' he said.

She was used to him now. He was the man who came with presents and flowers, who made Mummy laugh. She put her little arms about his neck and hugged him tight. Louise, watching them, felt her heart would burst, especially when she saw how affected he was. His blue eyes were bright with unshed tears. She did not doubt his love for his daughter, nor for that matter, his love for her, but it was a love she had to share. Was it too much to hope that he would choose to remain in England when it was all over? Had she any right to ask it of him? He had never said what he would do, it was something they did not discuss, nor had he spoken of Rulka by name by the time he left to go back on duty. She was left wondering . . .

The end of the war was not as near as they had hoped. The Germans were fighting every inch of the way and the Normandy invasion, begun so optimistically, had turned into a long grind of hard-won objectives. An Allied scheme to shorten the war by dropping parachutists, including Poles, far behind enemy lines at Arnhem, had been a dreadful failure. It looked very much as if they were in for a sixth Christmas of war. Everyone was feeling tired and drab and longed for peace.

The flying bombs, which everyone called doodlebugs or buzz bombs, were driving the evacuees out to the safety of the countryside again and Louise found her class swollen by a new intake. Some of them, like Harold Summers who had been in her infant class in 1939, had moved up to secondary level, but unless they passed the scholarship to Swaffham Grammar School, they would remain at Cottlesham, taught by John until the war ended and they went home for good.

As usual the children were looking forward to Christmas. Not for them to worry how the grown-ups had managed to hoard enough ingredients to make Christmas dinner and tea special. Nor were they concerned with what was happening in Europe and the Far East where the Japanese were no more inclined to give up than Hitler. They had spent most of their formative years in a world at war. They didn't know what it was like to be at peace, not to have air raids or rationing, to eat oranges and bananas, to wear new clothes, not hand-me-downs or make-do-and-mend, not to suffer the news that fathers had been killed, as Tommy and Beattie had done. But there were already some changes: the blackout had been partially lifted and was now called the dim-out. Even given the menace of flying bombs and the latest V2 rockets, the adults could look forward to Christmas in the confident expectation that this really would be the last one of the war.

The children had been rehearsing carols and a nativity play, something they did every year. This year Beattie had been chosen by Mr Langford to play the Virgin Mary and wrote a letter to her mother, begging her to come and see her in the play. 'Please,

please, Mummy, please come,' she wrote. 'I want you to see the blue dress Miss is making for me. And the halo. It is made of silver paper wrapped round wire.' Louise, who had vetted it for spelling mistakes, could not break the children's habit of calling her Miss without a name attached.

Agnes arrived the afternoon before the big day to Beattie's intense delight. 'You're going to stay for Christmas, aren't you?' she begged her.

'If Aunty Jenny can find a room for me.'

'I think we can manage that,' Jenny said. 'We'll be pleased to have you. We're going to have a party in the pub on Boxing Day. Everyone's welcome. The boys from the RAF base will be coming, English and American. It should be fun.'

'Thank you. I should be thinking of having the children home but what with the buzz bombs and all, and me still working in the factory, I don't think it would be a good idea. Can you keep them a little longer?'

'Of course. They are no trouble.'

Louise, engrossed in making the nativity play a success, had little time to speculate on when Tommy and Beattie might leave. Harold Summers, one of the wise men, forgot his lines and kicked Freddie Jones when he said them for him, resulting in retaliation, which was stopped by a withering look from the headmaster. And Beattie, so proud of her part, sat regally upright, beaming at everyone, quite unable to utter a word of the lines she had so carefully rehearsed. The audience were not inclined to be critical and the end was received with warm applause. This was followed by carol singing and then a tea party, with sandwiches, cake and lemonade provided by the mothers and foster mothers. All in all, a successful and happy end of term.

'I must go and see my mother,' Louise said to Jenny on

Christmas Eve. Stan was in the cellar, checking his stocks and hoping there would be enough to last the holiday, and Jenny was plucking a turkey that had been on order from a local farmer since the autumn.

'Oh, Lou, you don't mean to desert us?'

'I ought to. Mum will be alone with my father but, to be honest, I can't face it. My father's idea of Christmas is to attend church three times, listen to his extra long sermons and have a glass of sherry with our dinner, but only if we have been good. Not that he can attend church now, but I bet my mother will. I'll go on Boxing Day.'

'You'll miss the party.'

'I know, I'm sorry about that but it can't be helped.'

'Do you want to leave Angela with us?'

Louise did not usually take Angela to Edgware for fear of enflaming her father. 'Thanks, but I'll take her with me. Mother has been complaining that she never sees her. I've arranged to stay at a hotel. Jan is hoping to get some time off to be with us. He won't go anywhere near the flat.'

'Has he met your parents?'

'No.'

It was not only the war and what Jan would do when it ended, that worried her, it was the situation at home. Her mother waited on her father hand and foot and never grumbled. It was as if she was trying to atone for some guilt on her part. But what guilt? Louise could only guess.

Faith took the pillow from behind Henry's head and stood looking down at him with it in her hands. It would be relatively easy to put it over his face and hold it there until his breathing stopped. Then she would be free of this terrible burden. But would she? Would she ever be free of guilt? Walter Barlow had returned to his wife, relieved when he discovered his victim could neither walk nor talk and no one was looking for him. He did not appear to be bowed down by his guilt. Hers was, of course, the wish that Henry had died and that was a wicked sin.

Between the nurse's visits, she had to wash and shave him, give him a bedpan, feed him, and answer the imperative knocking on the wall with his stick, which he preferred to ringing the brass bell he had been provided with. He had bought a new stick the day after Louise destroyed the old one and had somehow managed to persuade Nurse Thomson to give it to him. The nurse knew nothing of the story behind the attack on him and she was all sympathy, doing her best to make him comfortable and placate him when he raged. 'It's frustration,' she told Faith. 'You would be frustrated and angry if you were in his shoes.'

Even knowing she could step out of range, Faith was still afraid of that stick. When he required personal attention she took it from him and put it out of his reach until she had finished what she was doing for him. If she forgot to give it back, she could hear his bellows of rage in the kitchen. But bellowing and grunting were all he could do. He could not speak, except with his dark eyes, which followed her as she moved about the room. One day she might give herself the pleasure of telling him that she had found Louise's letters and was in touch with their daughter again in defiance of his wishes.

She loved her daughter and little granddaughter but it was not enough to overcome her repugnance at what Louise had done. As for that Polish airman, she had made up her mind not to like him, even though she had not met him. It would have been much better if he had died when his plane crashed and not come back to continue the sin. Louise made no secret of the fact that they had been on holiday together, which made her as guilty as he was. But everyone said the Poles could be charming and left a trail of broken hearts and illegitimate children behind them and Louise had obviously been taken in by him.

The trouble, as far as Faith was concerned, was that her sin was just as great, and she had no right to condemn anyone, not Louise, not the Polish airman whom she refused to think of by his name, not Walter Barlow. Instead she blamed the war and Hitler. It was easier that way, though if she were honest with herself Hitler had nothing to do with Henry's cruelty. That had begun years before, when Louise had been a small, mischievous child. Her efforts to try and protect her daughter had led to Henry turning on her and to her eternal shame she had more often than not let him get away with it. That Louise had grown up as well balanced as she had was a miracle. At least she had been before she met the Pole.

She sighed, pulled Henry up to put the pillow behind his back, then sat down on the side of the bed and started to spoon-feed him with his Christmas dinner.

Louise arrived just before noon the next day, entering by the back door. She kissed her mother and then stood back to look at her. Faith was wearing an old tweed skirt and a beige-coloured twinset. Her hair had escaped from the pins that were supposed to hold it in a bun and wisps of it hung untidily round her face. Her eyes were dull and her skin sallow. 'How are you, Mum?' she asked, concerned to see how she had let herself go.

'Plodding on as usual,' Faith said with an attempt at cheerfulness. 'You are looking well.'

'It's the country air and good living,' Louise said. 'Why don't you try it?'

'You know why. Don't let's go into all that again.'

She bent down to Angela who was looking up at her as she would a stranger, and one she wasn't at all sure of. 'How's my little Angela? Are you going to give your grandmother a kiss?'

Angela's answer was to hide behind her mother's skirts. Louise turned and lifted her up. 'Come on, sweetheart, give Granny a cuddle.'

Angela cuddled her mother, she cuddled Auntie Jenny and she cuddled her *Tata*, but she'd be blowed if she'd cuddle this woman who smelt funny. She dug her face into Louise's shoulder and refused to budge.

'It's because she doesn't see you very often,' Louise explained. 'She's not old enough to remember you from one visit to the next.'

'And who's fault is that?'

'Mine, I suppose, but you know, Mum, I do have to work, and you could just as easily come to see me. Nurse Thomson would stay with Father for a day or two. I'm sure it would do you good to get away for a bit.'

'I'm not coming to Cottlesham to stay in a pub, Louise. It would be different if you were married and had a home of your own. Can't you find a nice young man to take you on?'

'I've got a nice young man, Mum.'

'I meant one that isn't married to someone else.'

'Yes, well, that can't be helped. Let's not quarrel over it.'

'You know how I feel about it so I won't say any more. Besides, what's done is done and can't be undone. Would you like a cup of coffee? It's only Camp, I'm afraid.'

'Camp is fine, Mum.'

Faith busied herself boiling the kettle and fetching out cups and saucers. 'Would Angela like a glass of milk? I got an extra half pint from the milkman today. People round here are so helpful. They know how it is with your father and they often say how they admire me for looking after him so well. Mind you, the nurse is a great help.'

'How is Father?'

'Just the same, neither better nor worse.' She put a small glass of milk and a cup of coffee on the kitchen table in front of where Louise was sitting with Angela on her lap. 'He manages to make his wishes known, though. He points and grunts. Nurse Thomson seems to understand some of what he is trying to say.'

'Did he know I was coming?'

'I told him when I gave him his lunch. He had it early so I could have more time with you.'

'I'd better go and see him after I've drunk this.'

'Leave it until after you've had something to eat. I've got the remains of yesterday's roast chicken and I can easily do some more vegetables.'

Louise was thankful to concede this and helped her mother to prepare the meal. By the time they had finished eating it, Angela had lost some of her shyness and slipped from the table to explore the flat. Louise, helping her mother wash up, did not at first miss her, but then a bellow from the bedroom sent her scurrying to find her.

The child was standing just inside the door looking at Henry who had picked up his stick and was waving it at her while he tried to speak. Louise grabbed Angela up. 'It's all right, sweetheart,' she said. 'The man won't hurt you.' Then to the man in the bed, who appeared to be in a purple rage, 'How are you, Father?'

His answer was unintelligible, but she could guess the gist of it. 'I'm sorry you cannot even be civil to a small child who has done you no harm,' she said. 'We are leaving now. I won't trouble you again.' She turned to come face to face with her mother who was looking terrified. 'Is he often like that?'

'All the time.'

Louise carried Angela back to the kitchen followed by Faith. 'You can't go on like this, Mum. I had no idea. Look, won't you think again about putting him in a nursing home? We'll manage the cost somehow.'

'No. It's a cross I have to bear.'

'That's nonsense. What are you afraid of? He can't hurt you now. He's helpless.'

'God isn't. God sees all. He knows what's in our hearts.'

'Anyone would think your heart was black as sin.'

Faith promptly burst into tears. Louise shut the kitchen door and put Angela down so that she could go to her mother. 'Don't cry, Mum, please. It just goes to show you can't cope any longer. You're worn out. I'm going to talk to the nurse, see what she thinks.'

'She thinks he's a saint.'

'Well, we know differently, don't we? Sit down. I'll make a cup of tea and we'll talk about it sensibly.' She picked up the kettle, filled it from the tap and put it on the gas stove.

'I don't want to talk about it. I'm all right, really I am. It's this dratted war, it's been going on too long.'

'You are changing the subject.'

'No, I'm not. What will you do when it ends?'

'I don't know. It all depends. If Jan goes back to Poland . . .'

'You aren't planning to go with him, are you?'

'No, Mum, I'm not. I suppose I'll go on teaching. I'll need to if I'm to keep myself and Angela.' It was the first time she had said that aloud and it brought home to her just how difficult it was going to be.

'Are you hoping he won't go?'

'Yes. I suppose, if I'm truthful, I'd say I want him to stay.'

'Will you ask him to?'

'No, Mum, I won't ask him.'

'Will you come back to Stag Lane School?'

'No, I don't think so. I really don't know. Let's wait and see shall we?'

Jan was still a little preoccupied when she met him later that day and she supposed the nearer they came to the end of the war, the more he thought of home. He had told her in one of his letters that the civilian population of Warsaw had all been evacuated and dispersed into camps, and then the Germans had systematically destroyed the city; there was nothing left but empty ruins. The Russians would walk into it almost without opposition. Determined not to let him dwell on it, she chatted about her Christmas and how Angela loved the doll he had sent her. 'I don't think she has replaced Cuddles in her affection, even though he is looking a little bedraggled.' she told him. They had put Angela to bed and arranged for one of the hotel staff to listen for her while they went to have a meal in the dining room. There was cold turkey on the menu.

'I'll buy her a new one.'

'I shouldn't. It wouldn't be her beloved Cuddles.'

'Beloved Cuddles,' he murmured. 'Do you remember . . .'

'Of course. How could I forget?'

'I didn't do you any favours, did I?'

'Jan, what are you talking about?'

'I mean having Angela. It can't be easy for you, bringing her up and going to work.'

'My love for her and for you makes it easy. I wouldn't change either of you for the world.'

'You love me?'

'Oh, Jan, you know I do. I always will.'

'Even if I behave like – what is the word in English? A cad, yes, even if I behave like a cad?'

'But you don't. Whatever gave you that idea?'

'I cannot marry you.'

'I know that. I knew it from the first; you never made a secret of it. Why all this sudden soul-searching, Jan?'

'I am thinking of what will happen when the war ends.'

'What will happen?'

He sighed. 'I don't know, I really don't know.'

And for the second time that day, she said, 'Then let's wait and see, shall we?'

The Russians entered the snowbound ruins of Warsaw on the 17th January with little opposition. They overran the rest of Poland, the Baltic states, Romania, Hungary, Czechoslovakia and Austria and crossed the frontier into Germany the same month. If there had ever been any idea on the part of the Allies to race for Berlin, they did not pursue it, although they crossed the Rhine and some Americans made contact with Russian forces on the Elbe towards the end of April.

The advance of the Allies also revealed the horrors of the concentration and extermination camps in Germany and Poland, which people in Britain would never have believed but for the newsreel pictures. Jan and Louise had gone to the cinema in Swaffham to see Laurence Olivier in *Henry V*, which had received mixed reviews from the critics but was hailed by the populace who enjoyed the colour, the pageantry and the patriotism which fitted in with their mood. But the news that followed it had the audience gasping and hurrying out of the cinema. 'I can't watch this,' Louise said, letting her seat up with a clatter. 'I'll be sick.'

'It is true, isn't it?' she queried when they were outside in the fresh air. 'They couldn't have made it up.'

'It's true,' he said. The images of ragged, starving people and piles of naked corpses had sent his thoughts winging back to home and Rulka. Had she had to endure anything like that? Was she among those wretches? Had she been killed? It made him boil with frustrated rage. Here he was, well clothed, well fed, happy with the job he was doing, while all the time others, including his wife if she were alive, had had to endure this horrendous suffering. 'I just hope that those who allowed it to happen get their just deserts. I'd willingly tie the rope round their evil necks myself.'

'I'm sorry, Jan,' she said, laying a hand on his arm. 'I can guess what you must be thinking, but please, don't be bitter.'

He pulled himself together. 'I wouldn't have brought you if I'd known they were going to show it.'

'But I think people ought to know, don't you?'

'Yes, I do,' he said quietly.

Stalin's troops took nine days to win the battle for Berlin, a city in ruins whose people were as tired of war as everyone else and whose Führer committed suicide rather than face retribution. Admiral Dönitz was named his successor and it was he who made the decision to surrender. The war in Europe was over. May 8th was Victory in Europe Day and a public holiday.

There were wild celebrations all over the free world, particularly in London. Crowds thronged into the Mall and congregated round Buckingham Palace where the King and Queen and the two princesses appeared on the balcony with Winston Churchill and everyone sang 'Land of Hope and Glory' and 'There'll Always be an England'. Total strangers hugged and kissed each other and the pubs ran out of beer. When darkness fell London blazed with light. Buckingham Palace, the Houses of Parliament, St Paul's Cathedral and Big Ben were all floodlit. In towns and cities and small hamlets all over the British Isles, the people celebrated. Cottlesham was not to be outdone.

All day children and adults had been dragging wood and anything combustible onto the village green to make a huge bonfire. Some of them made an effigy of Hitler, draped in the blackout curtains from the Pheasant, and set it on top. The butcher donated a whole pig which had been roasting on a spit for hours. Bill Young provided a sackful of potatoes for cooking in the embers. Edith Wayne had discovered a box of bunting in the attic of the village hall and this had been supplemented with more made by the village ladies from odd scraps of colourful material, and strung between poles. The bunting was not the only thing to come from the village hall; the men hauled the piano onto Bill Young's farm trailer and took it to the green. Stan brought a table and stacked it with beer and spirits. The WVS had a portable kitchen acquired at the beginning of the war in case they had to feed the homeless but which had never been put to use, except in training. It was fetched out and the ladies were soon boiling kettles, making tea and heating soup.

Louise and Angela, Jenny, Tommy and Beattie, joined the whole village to celebrate, but more than a few tears were shed for those, like Tony, Mr Carter, Honor Barker's son, Daniel, and Mrs Johns' WAAF daughter, Doreen, who would never come home. The war against Japan had yet to be won and many men from Norfolk were still in captivity in the Far East, Greta Sadler's twin sons with them. More than a few had died out there on the other side of the world. Before the festivities began, the rector presided over a moment of quiet reflection, thankfulness and prayer.

But nothing could quell the need to rejoice. The bonfire was lit, the beer barrel tapped and Edith Wayne sat at the piano and played all the old favourites: 'Roll Out the Barrel', 'It's a Long Way to Tipperary', 'When the Lights Go On Again All Over the World', Don't Sit Under the Apple Tree With Anyone Else But Me', and 'There'll Be Bluebirds Over the White Cliffs of Dover'. They sang and danced and burnt their tongues on baked potatoes. A group of American airmen from the nearby base arrived in a jeep to join in the fun.

Louise smiled as Angela ran to her with an orange one of the Americans had given her. She didn't quite know what to do with it. Louise squatted down and peeled it for her and broke it into quarters. 'It's for eating,' she said, popping a piece into her own mouth. 'It's lovely and juicy.'

The child wandered off again eating the orange. The juice dribbled all down her clean frock.

Tomorrow would be time enough to think about the future, a future, so they had been told, where everyone had work, everyone had somewhere decent to live, where no one was poor or hungry, where the people would be looked after from the cradle to the grave, and all children would enjoy a good education, regardless of their parents' ability to pay. It would be a very different and more prosperous world than the one they had left behind. At the time they believed it, because they wanted to believe it and only the most sobersides asked how it was all to be paid for. The country was almost bankrupt.

It was the middle of the school summer holiday when the Japanese surrendered, after the dropping of two atomic bombs which had devastated two of their cities, killing thousands. The celebrations for what was called VJ Day were more muted than those earlier in the year. Peace had not brought prosperity; rationing and shortages were as bad as ever. There was a new

Labour government, headed by Clement Attlee, who had made all sorts of promises about public ownership, social reform and the rapid demobilisation of the forces, but that was all going to take time and in the meantime people were being urged to tighten their belts, as if they hadn't been doing just that for the last six years.

One by one, the men came back from wherever they had been serving and tried settling back into civilian life. For some it was easy, for others, almost impossible. One of Greta Sadler's sons returned from Japanese captivity towards the end of the year, but he didn't know what had happened to his brother. Three months later she learnt that he, too, was on his way home. Both young men were painfully thin and their stomachs could not take the good food Greta dished up for them. Peace was going to take some adjustment on everyone's part.

Nearly all the London children had left Cottlesham, although Tommy and Beattie remained. Agnes had not been to see them for a couple of months and Louise wondered why. It wasn't that she wanted to see the children go, she had become very fond of them, but surely they should be back with their mother by now?

She learnt the reason for this when Agnes Carter arrived one evening towards the end of August, accompanied by an American sergeant, a bomber pilot in the United States Army Air Force, whose name was Russ Forrester. He was tall, dark and smart in his uniform and he smiled a lot, mostly at Agnes. She was looking exceptionally smart herself in a new fur coat and green felt hat with a matching feather. She wore sheer nylon stockings and high-heeled shoes and rather more make-up than when she had come visiting before. There were some people who were not looking drab.

'Russ is my fiancé,' she said as she introduced him to Louise, Jenny and Stan. 'I've brought him to meet the children. We are going to take them away for a few days for a little holiday so they can get to know each other.'

'We'll take off tomorrow morning,' Russ said. 'And bring them back next Saturday, if that's OK with you.'

'Of course,' Jenny said, giving Louise a meaningful look. 'I am sure they will enjoy it.'

'Where are they?' Agnes asked.

'They've gone to bed, but I doubt they're asleep. They will have heard you arrive.'

'Let's go up to them,' Agnes said, and led Russ from the room.

'Well, that's a turn up for the books,' Jenny said when they were out of earshot. 'What do you think the children will make of it?'

'No idea, but they are used to Americans, aren't they? There's enough of them round here.'

'Yes, but not ones who want to marry their mother.'

'I suppose something like it had to happen,' Louise said. 'Agnes is only in her late thirties and she's not a bad-looking woman, especially when she's dressed to the nines. I wonder where she got that fur coat.'

'I expect he bought it for her. You can get anything if you've the money to pay for it.'

They learned at breakfast next day that Agnes was planning a wedding later in the year and would take her children to make their home in America. 'Russ has to have written permission from his commanding officer to marry,' Agnes told them, smiling at Russ who was devouring eggs and bacon, oblivious to the fact that it was a whole week's ration for two people. 'Until that's signed we can't arrange the wedding. I was wondering . . .' She paused and turned to Jenny. 'Do you think you can keep the children until then?'

'Of course.'

Bill Young took Agnes, Russ and the children to the station in his taxi. Tommy was a little subdued. Louise realised he was torn between wanting his mother to himself and the excitement of going on holiday to a real hotel. Beattie was happy to go along with whatever was suggested, especially as the American had brought her a new doll, dressed far more grandly than she was, in lace and frills. Tommy had been given a baseball bat with the promise that Russ would teach him the game. Angela was left without her playmates but it meant she would have her mother to herself.

Their departure left Louise feeling flat. She was glad to see the end of the conflict, the end of death and destruction but she had no illusions about the difficulties they would be facing. So much was bound to change, though it was slower coming than some people liked. The troops would come home eventually, though there was a strict order in the way they would be demobbed; guns, aeroplanes and ships no longer needed to fight would be laid up. The Americans, like Russ, would go home. And that inevitably led to thoughts of Jan. Would he leave her? Would she be able to keep her job? Where would she live? The London children, who had not yet left, would go home and Jenny would almost certainly want her bedrooms back. She had been talking for some time of making the Pheasant into a proper country hotel. And what was she to do about her mother? All these questions had to be faced, but the overriding one was what Jan would do.

The euphoria of the celebrations for the end of the war had passed Jan by. London, Paris, Rome, Amsterdam, Oslo, Copenhagen and Moscow might celebrate, with singing and dancing in floodlit streets, but in Warsaw, empty, defeated, ruined Warsaw, there was nothing but darkness and bitterness and rows and rows of wooden crosses.

Like his fellow Poles Jan felt out on a limb. Roosevelt, Churchill and Stalin had met at the Tsar's old palace in Yalta the previous February and decided the fate of Europe between them. Germany was divided into four zones of occupation under the British, American, French and Russians. Berlin was similarly split. And, as he had predicted, Stalin had got his way over the boundary with eastern Poland. The land he had annexed when he invaded in 1939 was now designated Western Belorussia and Western Ukraine, part of the Soviet Union. Poland had been compensated for the loss of nearly half its eastern territory with a chunk of Germany in the west, which meant whole populations were on the move westwards. The Polish administration in London was no longer recognised as the government of Poland and the Soviet puppet government had been formally accepted by the Western Allies as the interim government until elections could be held, which Stalin had promised would be 'free and unfettered' and held a month after the end of the war. Few of Jan's comrades believed that.

All over Europe there were thousands of people in the wrong place, wandering about like lost souls with nowhere to go. Camps had been set up for them until they could be helped to go back to where they belonged, or to find new homes elsewhere. They were called displaced persons, which exactly described how Jan felt.

Chapter Eleven

January 1946

Agnes had decided to be married in Cottlesham. 'I prefer the Reverend Capstick to your father's replacement,' she had told Louise on a previous visit. 'Besides, people I used to call my friends frown on me for marrying a Yank.'

'Why?'

'I dunno. Perhaps they think I should wear black for the rest of my life. They don't like to see me enjoying myself.'

'Perhaps they're just jealous.'

'Maybe. Anyway, I've asked the rector if he'll marry us and he said yes, so that's what we're going to do. Stan said he'd give me away. Will you be a maid of honour?'

'I'd love to.'

'Beattie will be a bridesmaid. Will you let Angela be another one?'

'She's very small, not yet four.'

'I know, but she's so pretty and I don't want her to feel left out. And you'll be there to look after her.' She laughed suddenly. 'This wedding is going to be different from my first. I was three months gone with Tommy and we had to get married. It was done in a registry office with only a couple of Dan's friends for witnesses. My parents had washed their hands of me.'

Louise knew what that felt like. 'I'm sorry.'

'Water under the bridge now. They both got killed in the Blitz. There's only me and the kids left. This is like a first wedding for me, so I want it to be special.'

'Then we'll do our best to make it special, Agnes.'

'You and Jenny are better friends to me than all my neighbours in Edgware. You understand, don't you, about wanting to make a fresh start?'

'Yes, of course.' Louise said, wishing she could do the same.

Jan didn't talk about it. It was almost as if he were afraid to bring the problem out into the open. The longer he was silent, the more she thought he was intent on going back to Poland. Would he stay if she asked it of him? Had she any right to do so? He was a Catholic and Catholics did not divorce. If he stayed she would still be an unmarried mother and would remain so until the end of her days. Unless his wife were dead. That was not beyond the bounds of possibility, but he would have to be sure.

In the meantime, she had to support Agnes and help to make sure the wedding went off without a hitch. Besides a crowd of Russ's friends, Jan and half the village had been invited and Jenny had been kept busy organising the catering, not made any easier because everything was still rationed and, for the first time ever, bread was rationed. Queues and shortages were as bad as ever. They were lucky Russ was able to buy almost anything from the PX stores and he brought cheese, ham, tinned fruit, as well as dried fruit and icing sugar, so that Jenny was able to make a real wedding cake.

The wedding dress was made from parachute silk which Russ had also provided. Parachutes had to be flawless, he told them, and this one had been rejected. White, they decided, would not be appropriate, so Jenny dyed a swathe of it powder blue. Something borrowed would be a rather flamboyant hat with a wide brim and a big artificial rose on the front which had belonged to Jenny's mother. 'I don't know why I kept it,' she said. 'Except that it seemed such a shame to throw it away. It was part of Mum's outfit for my wedding.'

Beattie and Angela would be in pink dresses, also of dyed parachute silk, with tiny silk rosebuds in a coronet, made up by Louise, and they would carry more in little baskets. Being January, they might be cold in thin frocks so she and Jenny had knitted white ponchos for them. Louise went off to Norwich and spent a whole Saturday searching for something for herself and came back with a dove-grey silk dress and matching jacket that cost her five guineas as well as fifteen clothing coupons.

Everyone was up early on the day of the wedding, all getting in each other's way. Beattie was sick with excitement and came down to breakfast looking like a ghost. 'You can't go to church looking like that,' Agnes said. 'Perhaps a little rouge . . .'

'A spot of fresh air should do the trick,' Jenny said. 'Stan's taking the pony and trap into Swaffham to pick up the flowers. She can go with him. It will keep her occupied until it's time to get her dressed.'

And so Beattie went to Swaffham and Tommy, bored with it all, went for a walk. It was frosty, the cobwebs hanging from dead stalk to dead stalk glittered like jewels. So far there had only been a light dusting of snow, nothing like the first winter he was here when Stan had pulled them to school on a sledge. It seemed an age ago, a whole lifetime. Now everything was up in the air.

He had left his mum having her hair done and Miss fluttering round her and Aunt Jenny sorting out the food. Getting all worked up over it, they were. As for the navy pinstriped suit they had bought for him, he hated it. Why couldn't he go to church in his school blazer and flannels? It wasn't as if he had a major role to play. All he was required to do was show people to their seats.

He wasn't at all sure about this wedding idea. The last time he had seen his father, he had said, 'You're the man of the house while I'm away, son, so you look after your mum and sister until I come back.' How was he to know he would never come back or that they'd be evacuated? He had tried to look after Beattie, but he'd failed when it came to his mother. He thought she had gone off her head a bit. It was Russ this and Russ that, the whole time; she had no time for anyone else. So instead of going home to Edgware, they were going to be shipped off to America.

He wondered what that would be like. All he knew of America was what Russ had told him about his home in Illinois and the cowboys and Indians he saw at the pictures in Swaffham on a Saturday morning, both of which he was sensible enough to take with a pinch of salt. And what about school? He was due to take his school certificate in June and had been hoping for a scholarship so that he could go into the sixth form and then to college. Miss had been helping him to swot for it.

He would miss her when they left. She was all right, was Miss Fairhurst, and he liked Jan, though he couldn't say his name properly let alone spell it. Would Miss marry him and go to Poland? Jan had showed him where it was on the map and told him a little about it. Warsaw seemed a bit like London, what with the bombing and all, but German troops had never come to London. Now they never would. The war was over.

It was difficult to remember what it was like before it began. They hadn't been starving or dressed in rags, but he didn't think they had had much in the way of possessions. Being in Cottlesham had shown him a different life and he liked it. Would he like America? Russ didn't seem short of money and he always came loaded with presents and today he would marry his mum and he had been told he should call him 'Dad'. He'd told them right out, he couldn't do that, Russ wasn't his dad. His dad was at the bottom of the Atlantic. Mum had been angry but he had stuck to his guns and, to give Russ his due, he had agreed that calling him 'Uncle' would do.

They were going on honeymoon after the wedding. Tommy wasn't sure where but he and Beattie would stop with Aunt Jenny until they came back and arrangements were made to go to America. A lot of GIs had married over here and the American government was going to lay on special transport for all the brides and their children to go to America. They would be going on the *Queen Mary*. Dad had taken him on board one of his ships once, when he was little, but it had been on the quayside; he hadn't actually been to sea. Half of him was looking forward to it, the other half was apprehensive about the future. Supposing it didn't work out? Supposing he couldn't go to college? He had set his heart on being an aeronautical engineer.

He looked up from kicking a stone to see Jan coming towards him. 'There you are, old chap,' he greeted him. 'Your mother is worried about you. It's time you got ready.'

'I was just coming.'

They turned to walk side by side, off the common and along familiar lanes bordered by leafless hedges where here and there a few red berries hung for the birds, to the pub which had been his home for the last six years. He would miss it when they left, miss the people too.

'Do you think it will be all right?' Tommy asked Jan. 'Going to America, I mean.'

'Are you worried about it?'

'How do I know Mum will be happy? It's a long way to go if she doesn't like it.'

'I'm sure she has thought of all that and decided that's what she wants. She seems very happy about it, so don't spoil it by being gloomy, eh?'

'OK. Are you going to marry Miss Fairhurst?'

'That's a very personal question, young man.'

Tommy sighed. 'I just wondered. Will you go back to Poland?'

'I don't know. I might.'

'You wouldn't go and leave Miss and Angela behind, would you?'

'She might not wish to come.'

'Then you had better stay here, don't you think?'

Jan did not answer that. The boy was old for his fifteen years. He had grown up in wartime and learnt to shoulder responsibility at an early age. Now he was worrying about the future, as they all were. And he had put his finger on the core of Jan's unease. There were, according to estimates, some sixty thousand Poles in Britain and nearly twice that number in Allied camps overseas, many of whom, like him, had been fighting alongside Britain since 1940, and they were becoming an embarrassment to the British government. Most of them were reluctant to return to a Poland under Russian domination, certainly not before the 'free and unfettered' elections promised by Stalin had been held and there was a democratically elected government. It hadn't happened yet and only the most naive believed that it ever would. But the pull of home was strong and some had decided to return.

Those left behind were being transferred from the Royal Air Force and the Polish armed forces into a Polish Resettlement Corps, whose aim was to help find employment for those who were staying. They would be on a two-year contract on full pay while they decided what they were going to do. After that the Corps would be disbanded. Jan could foresee trouble finding jobs. There was the language barrier for a start and the lack of qualifications except fighting, and already some Poles had been turned away on the grounds that jobs were for British men being demobbed. People's memories were short and the old antagonism was beginning to surface again. He had seen a large poster fixed to the wire surrounding the holding camp where he was quartered which proclaimed: 'England for the English'. If he decided to stay, what could he do? He knew nothing but how to fly. Many of his comrades were talking about going to the United States, Canada or South Africa, rather than return home. It was to South Africa Jozef was heading.

His brother had written to him from Italy where he had survived the slaughter of the Battle for Monte Cassino and was with the Polish 2nd Army stationed in Rimini, an army that was mostly made up of men who had been taken prisoner when the Soviet Union invaded Poland in 1939 and were only released when Hitler invaded Russia. 'Having been on the receiving end of Soviet hospitality myself,' he had written, 'I could have told anyone who asked what would happen. Everywhere they go, they intend to be masters and Poland is no exception. It is naive of anyone to expect them to grant democratic freedom to Poland when they do not even allow it for their own people. I shall not return. Mother and Father are dead, there is no longer an estate for me to inherit and I might as well make a new life for myself. I fought alongside the South Africans here in Italy and many of them are my friends. I think South Africa will do me very well. What are you going to do? Any news of Rulka?'

It was easy for Jozef, Jan decided; he had no wife to worry about, nor a loving girlfriend and a precious little daughter. He had been avoiding discussing it with Louise, but before long it would have to be faced.

*   *   *

The Pheasant was in an uproar, but in the middle of it Agnes was serene. She appeared to have no doubts about what she was doing. 'I'm going to have a wonderful life with Russ,' she told Louise. 'His family have a huge farm with thousands of cattle.' She giggled suddenly. 'I shall be a farmer's wife.'

Louise laughed. 'You're terrified of cows. I remember when you first came here, you met a herd in the lane being driven home for milking and you ran for your life.'

'I'll just have to get used to them, shan't I?' She surveyed herself in the mirror of the dressing table. 'Do I look all right?'

'Lovely.'

'You look smashing. What about Beattie and Angela?'

'They are both ready. Beattie is fine now and reading Angela a story to keep her out of mischief.' The sound of someone running upstairs came to them. Louise went to the door. 'It's Jan and Tommy.'

'Tommy!' shouted his mother. 'Where have you been?'

The boy appeared in the doorway. 'Out for a walk.'

'Well, go and get changed. You should be on your way to the church by now. Mr Young will be here to take the bridesmaids any time now.' Agnes was going to church in Stan's pony and trap suitably decorated with garlands and ribbons.

Tommy disappeared and Louise noticed Jan behind him. 'Will you make sure he gets to church on time?'

'Yes, of course. You are looking exceptionally lovely, sweetheart.'

'Well, it will be your turn next,' Agnes called from behind Louise.

Neither commented. Jan dashed off to make sure Tommy looked his best and they both took up their usher's duties, leaving Louise feeling a little down. She pulled herself together and accompanied Agnes down to the sitting room until it was time to leave for the church. Today was Agnes's day and she would not spoil it by being sad.

The wedding was a triumph. The church was full and the villagers and Russ's American colleagues mingled happily together. The bride was radiant, the bridegroom was looking pleased with himself, the bridesmaids and the best man remembered what they were supposed to do and the Reverend Capstick delivered a homily which was neither too short nor too long. Afterwards they all crammed into the Pheasant for the reception. Not until the newly-weds had left for their honeymoon and everyone else had gone home and the children were in bed, could Jan and Louise have any time to themselves. They went up to the room they shared.

Louise, worn out with the excitement of the day and her own brimming emotions, kicked off her shoes and sat on the bed with her hands idle in her lap. Jan went to the window and stood looking out on the garden, although there was nothing to see except a light on the corner of the building that illuminated the car park. The garden, bleak at that time of year, was in darkness. There was a constraint between them that had never been there before.

'I'm whacked,' Louise said, breaking a long silence. 'But it was a good day, wasn't it?'

'Yes.' He turned towards her. 'Tommy was a little apprehensive when I talked to him. He was unsure about America and whether his mother would be happy in a foreign country.'

'I think if you love someone, then you adapt, don't you?'

'Yes.'

He came and sat beside her and took her hand. 'I love you, sweetheart. You are precious to me and so is Angela, more precious than you'll ever know.'

'I love you too, I always will. But I also understand about Rulka.'

'I know you do and I love you all the more for it.'

'It's been a long time,' she murmured. 'Anything could have happened.'

'I know. Nothing can ever be the same as it was before the war. Poland has been swallowed up by the Red menace. I don't want to live in a place like that. On the other hand . . .' He stopped, his anguish visible on his face. 'I don't know what to do, really I don't. I'm being pulled apart.'

'Can't you find out what has happened to Rulka before you make the journey? After all, if she – forgive me, Jan, for being blunt – if she is dead, it would change everything, wouldn't it?'

'Yes, but is she? When the Germans were in Poland, I couldn't find out anything about her, and since the Russians took over it's worse. There's been a complete blackout on communication and no one can tell me anything. Supposing she is alive, supposing she is waiting for me to come back?'

If he was being pulled apart, then so was she, but it was up to her to be strong, for everyone's sake. 'In that case you must go to her.'

He looked surprised. 'I didn't expect you to say that. I thought you would beg me to stay.'

'For what, Jan? You cannot marry me. Are we to live in sin while you mope about wondering if you have done the right thing? That is not a recipe for happiness.'

'But I want to be with you.'

'You are with me now.' She paused. 'Let's not be miserable, let's make the most of our time together. You never know what's round the corner.'

Their lovemaking that night had an extra dimension. The emotion they both felt was heightened to such a pitch, they were carried away to somewhere not of this earth. It left them drained. They slept, tangled in each other's arms.

They woke next morning to reality with Angela scrambling over them to snuggle down between them. Jan put his arms about her while tears rained down his face. She put her finger up to touch his cheek. '*Tata* sad.'

'No, sweetheart, *Tata* is not sad. He is happy he's got you, his little Angel.' He put her from him and gave her to Louise, then made a dash for the bathroom, where he locked himself in and gave way to the despair he felt. How could he leave them?

Louise did not see him again until breakfast time. He had dressed and gone out, she had no idea where. She was as emotional as he was and finding it difficult not to burst into tears herself. She had been right to tell him to go home, but it had taken every ounce of her strength. Would he go? How long before he left?

He came back as she was sitting down to breakfast with Angela and Jenny. Stan was in the cellar, taking stock. The wedding had almost drained the pub dry.

'Enjoy your walk?' Jenny asked as he sat down and helped himself to coffee.

'Yes. I think I had rather too much to drink last night, I was decidedly hungover.' He did not need to ask for translations of English sayings now and used them readily, rarely in the wrong context.

'I doubt you'll get much tonight, we're almost out of beer.'

'I must get back to Framlingham.'

'Must you?'

'Can't overstay my leave. We haven't been demobbed yet.'

'When is that likely to be?' Louise spoke for the first time.

'I don't know. I suppose people will start to leave when they

235

have places and jobs to go to. The trouble is that I don't know about anything except flying. Some of the chaps are learning to be publicans, waiters, car mechanics or gardeners. I know one who has set up a scrap metal business, there's plenty of that around, and another has rented a smallholding and is rearing chickens and pigs.' All this, Louise guessed, was simply to make conversation; she did not think he was seriously considering any of it.

'Being a publican is not a bad life,' Jenny said, going to the oven to fetch the rasher of bacon and scrambled dried egg she had been keeping hot for him. 'If you don't mind the hours.'

'It's a thought,' he said. 'We will have to wait and see what turns up.'

'I'll give you a good reference. You've helped in the bar many a time when we've been busy.'

'Thank you. I enjoyed it.'

He and Louise went to church, came back for lunch and then spent the afternoon wandering about the village with Angela in her pushchair, well wrapped up against the cold. They didn't talk much, neither could think of anything to add to what had already been said. Everyone they met greeted them and said what a grand wedding it had been, and looked knowingly from Louise to Jan. If this embarrassed him, he did not show it. At teatime they returned to the Pheasant, and after picking at a meal neither had an appetite for, they put Angela to bed and Jan told her a story which had to include Cuddles. She was fast asleep with the teddy bear in her arms when they crept from the room.

He left in Bill Young's taxi soon afterwards. Louise clung to him as they said goodbye. 'Hey,' he said, using his forefinger to tip her chin up. 'Cheer up. It might never happen.' Then he kissed her, settled his cap on his head and picked up his holdall. One more swift kiss and he was gone.

236

Louise watched the taxi out of sight and went back indoors. Goodbyes in wartime were taken on the chin as a necessary evil, but just lately they had become harder and harder to bear.

A week later Russ and Agnes came back from their honeymoon and took Tommy and Beattie away. Russ was going back to his camp to wait his turn to be sent home, but Agnes and the children were going to a camp at Tidworth in Hampshire. This was a holding camp for GI brides and their families where all the paperwork and checks would be made before they embarked on the *Queen Mary* for New York. Russ hoped to be back himself by then and would meet them there.

'We'll come back one day and visit,' Agnes told Louise and Jenny. 'And you must come and visit us. Isn't that right, Russ?'

'Sure,' he said. 'Anytime.'

'I'm grateful to you for looking after my children so well,' Agnes went on. As a parting present she gave Jenny and Louise a large dish each, painted with a picture of the King and Queen and inscribed 'VE Day May 8th 1945.'

'Can we go to the station in the pony and trap?' Beattie asked.

'Course you can,' Stan said. 'But I don't know about all that luggage. Poor Beauty won't be able to manage it and four passengers as well.' There was a mountain of it, though Russ had said there was no need to take so much; they could buy what they needed when they found a home of their own. In the meantime they would be living with his parents. Louise wondered how that would work out but kept her thoughts to herself.

'Tell you what,' Russ said. 'You children go in the trap and your mum and I will follow in Mr Young's taxi with the luggage. How's that?'

This suited everyone and Stan went out to hitch up the pony.

The pub seemed empty after they had gone. For over six years it had echoed to the sound of children running up and down, shouting to each other, laughing, crying, making their presence felt, and now there was only Angela. Louise felt the time was fast approaching when she must do something about finding somewhere of her own. She had been putting it off, hoping that the situation with Jan might resolve itself, but she was slowly coming to the conclusion it wasn't going to happen.

One by one Jan's comrades were disappearing, finding jobs, going on training courses, taking the risk to go back to Poland or, like Jozef, emigrating to the Commonwealth or America where there was already a sizeable Polish population. It was about time he did something himself and he enrolled on a bricklaying and stone masonry course. Bombed houses needed rebuilding and new houses built, in Britain as well as Poland. This meant he was away from his base Monday to Friday but his weekends were often spent in Cottlesham.

On 22nd February, which was a Friday, he dashed straight from his training course to Cottlesham to be there for Angela's fourth birthday, taking a small wooden rocking horse, which he had bought from another Polish airman who was learning to make toys. It was white with brown spots and had a mane of grey hair.

She had been allowed to wait up for him and ran to be hugged. 'I'm four,' she told him solemnly.

'I know. And young ladies of four need a horse to ride, don't you think?' He undid the bulky package he had brought and stood the horse on the living room floor. He picked her up and sat her astride it.

'You spoil her,' Louise said, smiling at the child's round-eyed delight, as he showed her how to make it rock.

'She is worth spoiling, and so are you.' He kissed her

hungrily. 'What do you want to do this weekend?'

'You could help me look for a house to rent.'

'Why? You don't have to leave here, do you? Jenny isn't throwing you out?'

'No, of course not. But the time has come to move on. Stan and Jenny have plans of their own.'

'Where do you want to go? Back to London?'

'No. John Langford is retiring at the end of the summer term and I've been offered the headship. Angela can start school then, so it fits in very nicely.'

'You've got it all worked out, then?'

'Sort of. I will be able to move into the schoolhouse when John leaves. He is going to live with his sister in Dereham, but until then I need a home of my own.'

'Where do I fit in?'

'Wherever you want to fit in, Jan. It's up to you.'

She was throwing the ball back into his court. It made him feel uncomfortable, as if he were surplus to requirements. And yet he knew it was his own fault. 'OK,' he said. 'I get the picture.'

She laughed. 'You use more slang than an Englishman.'

'I'm not though, am I? I'm a Pole.'

'I know. I wouldn't have you any other way except for one thing and that is something we cannot help. Let's not talk about it.'

The next day they left Angela with Jenny and went to Swaffham to call on an estate agent there. They might have saved themselves the bus fare. There was a housing shortage everywhere, even in places that had not suffered the Blitz, and they found nothing suitable. Either it was too big, too small, too derelict or too far from Cottlesham. They returned to the Pheasant with nothing accomplished.

'I could have told you that,' Jenny said. 'You had better stay here.'

'But I can't get into the schoolhouse until August.'

'So what? We are in no hurry to make the alterations. We can't get the labour and materials to do them anyway. And the place is like a morgue without the children. If you and Angela go it will be worse. And you do help with the housework and in the bar. I can't think why you took it into your head we wanted you to go.'

So she decided, unless something turned up that was ideal, she would stay where she was. The Pheasant had seen her happy, had seen her sad, had witnessed her growing love for Jan and the birth of her daughter, had been her liberation as a woman. She had so much to be thankful for.

'Jan, there's someone to see you,' Tadek Sawicz, the Camp Administration Officer, said, catching Jan crossing the grass towards the Nissen hut he shared with several others. 'He's in my office.'

'Who is he?'

'He says his name is Boris Martel.'

'Never heard of him.'

'Nevertheless he must have heard of you.'

He made his way to the office and found a man he had never seen before sitting in a chair by the window. He was thin as a rake, his complexion pasty and his civilian clothes all seemed too big for him. He rose when Jan entered. 'Flight Lieutenant Grabowski?' he queried, holding out his hand. His fingers were long and bony, Jan noticed, as he nodded and they shook hands. 'My name is Boris Martel.'

'What can I do for you, Mr Martel?'

'I have come from Warsaw.'

'Warsaw?' Jan sat down hurriedly on another chair. 'You have news of my wife?'

'Yes.' He returned to his seat. 'She asked me to try and find you.'

'She is alive?'

'She was when I left her, six months ago.'

'Thank God. Tell me what happened? We get so little reliable information here. How is she? Is she well? How has she managed?'

'Hold on!' Boris smiled. 'I can understand your anxiety, but let me tell it in my own time.'

'I'm sorry.' He fumbled in his pocket for cigarettes and lighter and offered one to Boris.

'No, thank you. I have a chest complaint and cigarettes make me cough. But don't mind me, go ahead.'

Jan lit his cigarette and inhaled deeply. 'Go on, please.'

'Your wife, Flight Lieutenant, was one of the heroines of the resistance. She was brave, selfless and resourceful. She deserves a medal, but she won't get one, there is no one to give it to her.'

'You were there?'

'Yes.'

'But you are English.'

'I was born in Poland, but my parents brought me to England when I was three years old. I have dual nationality. It was why I volunteered to be dropped into Poland to help the Home Army. I was one of the *cichociemni*, "the dark and silent" ones.'

'Is that where you met Rulka?'

'Yes'

'Tell me what it was like.'

'With the Germans in control you could not call your life your own. There were so many rules and regulations, you could not avoid breaking them at some time – and then, woe betide you.

Executions were commonplace.' While Jan smoked his cigarette, Boris went on to describe in graphic detail what it had been like: the resistance in the early days, the reprisals, the Ghetto where thousands of Jews were crowded into one small area of the city and its complete destruction after their ill-fated uprising, and the Home Army Battle for Warsaw a year later in which he and Rulka had been involved. 'There were shells and mortars landing everywhere,' he said, 'and tanks rumbling about shooting anything that moved and they didn't stop if someone got in their way. They detonated mines and set fire to buildings, even churches. The church where Rulka was working with the wounded was torched with the patients inside. Rulka was lucky to escape. There were dead bodies all over the place. Without the help we had been promised, we were lost. Casualties were in their thousands and those of us that were left, ran out of ammunition and starved. In the end, there wasn't a horse, a dog, a cat or a pigeon alive in our sector of the city centre. We had to surrender. When I left in October, they were still finding bodies in the rubble.'

'And Rulka?'

'We didn't use real names. She went by the name of Krystyna Nowak, code name Myszka.'

'Mouse,' Jan murmured. 'That was my name for her.'

'Yes. When she knew I was coming back to Britain, she asked me to try and find out what had happened to you. She had no idea whether you were alive or dead and could give me no address, but knowing the name of your squadron in Poland led me to you.'

'Why did she change her name?'

'She was wanted by the Nazis for sabotage and the gunning down of a senior German officer who was known for his brutality.'

'She is a nurse, dedicated to saving life, what was she doing getting involved with assassination and sabotage?'

'She managed to fulfil both roles, and very efficiently too.'

'And now? Where is she living? I understood Warsaw has been destroyed.'

'So it has, but there are still a few hardy souls living in the ruins.'

'Why didn't she try and get out? I heard the civil population had been evacuated.'

'Yes, the old, the sick and the dying, as well as the healthy, were marched twelve miles to German transit camps which were later "liberated" by the Russians. Most of them were arrested by the Reds on the grounds they were collaborators and sent to the gulags.'

'Rulka too?'

'No, she was a member of the Home Army, not a civilian. She marched out to captivity with the army, but she managed to get away from the German guards taking the women to a prisoner of war camp and made her way back to Warsaw. I had been arrested by the Soviets and taken to jail in Moscow, but I kept insisting I was British and the British government knew where I was. I don't know if they checked on that, but they must have decided it would be expedient to let me go. I went back to Warsaw which was when I met Rulka again and she talked about you. I'm sorry it's taken me so long to get here. It was not easy to get out. I offered to bring her out with me, but she said Warsaw was her home and having fought so hard for Poland's freedom, she would not abandon it now. I could not persuade her.

'I left her in the ruins of Warsaw and made my way to Odessa, which meant going on foot or hitching lifts, earning my bread and butter on the way and dodging Russians and Ukrainians, but I've had plenty of practice at that, and I managed to board a Greek ship going to Athens. There I was taken on board a British destroyer which took me to Gibraltar, from where I was eventually flown home. Once here I had to be debriefed and that also took time, but I came as soon as I could.' He paused. 'Your wife, Flight Lieutenant, is waiting for you.'

'Oh.' His own words came back to him: *I will come back.* It crossed his mind to try and fetch her to Britain, but he knew that was a foolish idea. How could he live with her here, knowing Louise and Angela were not far away? And in any case, would Rulka come? She had already refused Boris Martel's offer. 'Can you get a message to her?'

'Possibly. I can't guarantee it. It's harder now than when the Germans were in control.'

'Tell her I will join her as soon as I'm discharged.'

'I'll see what I can do.'

Boris stood up to leave. 'Glad to bring you good news, Flight Lieutenant. Now I have a less pleasant task. I have to visit Mr and Mrs Crawshaw. Their son, Colin, escaped from a German prisoner of war camp in '42 and spent the rest of his time fighting in our sector of the Home Army. I have to tell them he was killed in the Rising. He died saving Rulka's life.'

'Then I owe him a deep debt of gratitude.'

'I will tell them that. It might be of some comfort.'

They shook hands and Boris left. Jan sat down again and put his head in his hands. It seemed Fate had made up his mind for him. But, oh, how was he going to steel himself to say goodbye to Louise and Angela?

Chapter Twelve

1946-47

Ever since Jan had been told his wife was alive, Louise had known there was no alternative; he had to fulfil a promise he had made over seven years before. He was too honourable to do anything else. But she also knew he was going back into danger. The Soviet Union had installed puppet governments in the whole of Eastern Europe and made a kind of fortress of it. Churchill in a speech in America had said, 'From Stettin on the Baltic to Trieste on the Adriatic, an iron curtain has descended across the Continent.' Jan was voluntarily going behind that iron curtain to an uncertain future, so he must love his Rulka very much. It was all very well to be practical and try to do what was right, but it was hard to subdue the feeling of jealousy that it roused in her.

'If I can, I'll let you know I've arrived safely,' he said on his last visit to the Pheasant. 'I'll write to you too, just to keep in touch.'

'No, Jan, don't do that. You have to make a life with your wife, you can't hang on to the life you had here with me.' He could not have known the effort it took to say that when all she wanted was to keep him with her. A clean break was the only way she was going to be able to cope. 'Try to forget me.'

'Louise, how can you say that? How can I forget? You and Angela mean the world to me . . .'

At any other time his words would have pleased her, but now it only made matters worse. 'Jan, you cannot live in both worlds, you must know that. Please don't make it harder than it is already.'

They clung to each other, sitting on the bed in their room at the Pheasant, both of them weeping. Only when there were no more tears to shed and they felt stronger, did they go downstairs so that he could say goodbye to Angela, who didn't understand what all the fuss was about. He found a pair of scissors and took a snippet of the child's fine blonde hair, wrapped it in his handkerchief and put it in his top pocket. Then he took his leave of Stan and Jenny, who shook his hand and wished him good luck. When Bill Young arrived with his taxi to take him to Swaffham station, Louise went out to see him off. One last embrace and he was gone.

She turned to go back indoors, fighting back tears. She was not only weepy, she was angry. Why did it have to be like this? Why? Why? Love was not always easy or joyful; it could tear you apart. Angela ran towards her and was lifted up and hugged so tightly she cried to be put down.

Louise let her go and went into the kitchen, where Jenny was preparing vegetables for lunch. Silently, she gave Louise a knife and a cabbage. They worked side by side in silence for some time, until Louise, with a monumental effort, pulled herself together. 'It's just me and Angela now and I've got to get on with it.'

'No, you're wrong. You have us and your work and friends all round you. You are not alone.'

'I know. I appreciate that, I really do.'

'He needn't have gone.'

'He had to. His wife takes precedence over a wartime love affair.'

'Is that what you call it?' Jenny said indignantly. 'I thought it was a lot more than that.'

'Let's not talk about it.'

'OK. Fine by me. Are you going up to London for the Victory Parade?'

'I don't know. I don't feel much like celebrating.'

'No, there doesn't seem to be much good news, does there? But things can only get better. And we did win the war, after all.'

'Jan said we won it, but the Poles lost it.'

'Yes, I can understand he would be bitter. But that's no reason for us to be miserable. Stan and I are going up on the train. Come with us. It will take you out of yourself.'

So she went and stood in the crowd, lifting Angela so that she could see the long columns march past. Every service was represented, people from every remote corner of the British Empire, every ally except Poland, the oldest ally of all. The interim Polish government, behind its iron curtain, declined to attend and efforts to get those who had served with the British forces to take part were met with refusal. The Poles remained proud and stubborn to the last. After it was over, Louise took the opportunity while she was in London to visit her mother.

Faith had been listening to the commentary on the wireless in Henry's room, but switched it off when her daughter arrived and they went into the kitchen to drink tea and talk. 'Well, it's all over now,' Faith said. 'The Victory Parade put the finishing touch to it. Now we can get on with our lives in peace.' She made it sound simple. 'Are you coming back to Edgware?'

'No, Mum. I've taken on the headship of Cottlesham School, starting in September. It means I'll be able to live in the schoolhouse.'

'I'm very proud of you for that, Louise, but what about that Polish airman? Do you still see him?'

'He's going back to Poland, back to his wife.'

'Oh. I could have told you that would happen. Wives always win in those situations.'

'It is only right and so I told him. Now I must live the life I've been given. I shall enjoy my new job and I'll have Angela . . .'

Faith looked at the child, who was sitting at the table eating a biscuit, taking tiny little bites all round it, making it last. 'Growing up with the stigma of illegitimacy,' she said flatly.

'I'll make sure she never suffers because of it. It's one reason why I want to stay in Cottlesham. I have good friends there and Angela is accepted for what she is, a lovely little girl.' Tired of explaining herself, Louise changed tack. 'How is Father? Is he any better?'

'Slightly, I think. He seems a little more mobile. Nurse Thomson is talking of getting him on his feet again. She thinks the doctor and hospital gave up too soon and she's looking for a specialist physiotherapist.'

'Oh.' Louise was not sure that would be a good thing. While he was helpless her mother could walk away from him when he became angry. If he could get out of bed and move around, there was no telling what he might do. 'Do you think it will work?'

Faith shrugged. 'We shall have to wait and see.'

There was no more to be said on the subject. Faith's prickly defensiveness and her own only half-concealed misery which her mother could not share seemed to be keeping them apart. The loving mother of her childhood had disappeared. Louise supposed it was her own fault; she had fallen far short of being the perfect daughter. What hurt her most was that her mother did not even try to understand about Jan.

In spite of telling him not to write to her, she had hoped, deep down, that he would let her know if he had arrived and found his wife, but there was nothing. It was unsettling. Did it mean he had never arrived back in Poland? Had he found his wife or hadn't he? He had been worried about being arrested, but she found it hard to believe that would really happen. She ought to stop worrying about him and concentrate on her move into the schoolhouse and her new job.

She moved in during the second week of August. It was a substantial Victorian building meant to accommodate the schoolmaster's family. It had a kitchen, living room and dining room downstairs and three bedrooms upstairs. John had had a bathroom extension put on the back of the kitchen. He had taken some of his furniture with him but Louise had bought the rest from him and added a few pieces of her own. Good furniture was very hard to come by; people who had been bombed out and newly-weds had precedence for what there was, and most of it was utility. She managed to find a second-hand dining room suite and a couple of beds which would do until she could replace them. She and Jenny had been busy making curtains and acquiring linen. Everyone in the village had been kind and generous, giving her bits and pieces, but at last she had a home of her own, even if there was no husband to share it.

The challenge of a new job fulfilled her to a certain extent and stopped her dwelling on what might have happened to Jan. The Education Act passed in 1944 had to be implemented and that meant that now the school only catered for five-to-eleven-year-olds. The eleven plus had replaced the old scholarship and after that the children went on to grammar school or secondary modern, according to their capabilities. There was talk of doing away with grammar schools altogether, but she couldn't see that happening, and going to Hamond's Grammar in Swaffham was still the goal of the majority of her pupils and she was determined to do her best for them.

They were a happy household of two, supported as ever by Stan and Jenny, who would always look after Angela if she had to go to a meeting or visit her mother. The term rolled by and she found herself preparing for Christmas again, which meant a carol service, a nativity play and a school party, catered for by the parents. Christmas Day was spent at the Pheasant and Boxing Day visiting her mother.

The physiotherapist Nurse Thomson had found to help her father was confident he could improve the patient's mobility, given time, Faith told Louise. 'He massages and exercises his legs twice a week. He lifts him into a wheelchair to do arm exercises and other movements to strengthen his core muscles. In the days he doesn't come, Nurse Thomson does it.'

'And is it working?'

'I think so. I'll be glad when they start this National Health Service and we don't have to pay for it any more.'

'Are you finding it difficult to make ends meet? If, so I'll try and help.'

'I can manage. After all, I've got nothing else to spend our money on. I don't go anywhere, except to the Townswomen's Guild and the church. As long as I've got enough to pay the rent, keep us warm and fed, I must give thanks. There are plenty of people worse off than me.'

Louise went to speak to him and take him the book she had bought him for Christmas because he still liked to read, and then set off home.

January brought arctic conditions with snowdrifts fourteen feet deep; there were icebergs reported off the Norfolk coast and in some places the sea froze. Children floundered on their way to school and it was a problem for Louise to keep the stove going in the classroom. 'Bring a change of shoes and socks,' she told them. 'And wear your warmest clothes.' She kept a supply of garments begged from the WVS for those who forgot or who were too poor to have many changes of clothes. Some, who came from outlying farms, stayed away altogether.

There was unrest in the newly nationalised coal and power industries: the railways, only barely maintained during the war years, could not deliver stocks of coal quickly enough and power stations started to run out. The housewives in the village resorted to the old custom of digging peat from the common to stoke their fires and the old oil lamps and candles were brought back into use, but even the oil and candles had to be queued for. Some of the outlying village homes still did not have electricity, and though it had been promised, it had yet to materialise. Everyone was grumbling. 'I don't know what we won the war for' was a common complaint. The brave new world was as much a dream as ever.

Louise's life was full to the brim, trying to teach her pupils and overcome the difficulties they all faced with as much cheerfulness as she could muster. It didn't stop her following the news and picking up on what was happening in Poland. There had been elections there. Stanisław Mikołajczyk, the only one of the old government to return to Poland and serve in the new one as head of the Polish Peasant Party, protested that the elections had neither been fair nor unfettered, the ballot had not been secret, there had been intimidation and arrests and he was going to demand that they be declared null and void. Slandered as a foreign spy, he had fled back to London. The West might protest and condemn, but it did not bode well for an independent Poland. Sometimes she imagined Jan coming back to her, saying his return to Poland had been a mistake, but she knew she ought not to allow herself such fancies and did her best to banish them. And when Angela sometimes asked her where her *tata* was, she fobbed her off with half-truths until the child stopped asking. Jan was as lost to her as Tony had been, but, oh, how she missed him. She missed his broad grin, his teasing voice, his laughter; his arms about her, his kisses and murmured endearments. Sometimes she lay in her lonely bed, aching for him. And then the tears would flow afresh.

Unlike buildings on the other side of the river, the house in Zabowski Street was still standing, although there were a few slates off the roof and some of its windows had been blown out. Jan did not need to use a key, the door had been forced at some time and stood drunkenly on one hinge. He stepped into the vestibule and knocked on the door of the apartment he had shared with Rulka. It was opened by a stranger who stared at him in hostility. 'What do you want?' He was middle-aged, dressed in a shabby pre-war suit that hung on him loosely.

'I'm looking for someone who used to live here before the war. Her name is . . .' He stopped. According to Boris, Rulka Grabowska was dead. 'Krystyna Nowak.'

'There must be hundreds of women by that name, it's common enough, but I never met any of them.' He peered at Jan suspiciously. 'Where have you come from? Police, are you?'

'No, I'm from Lublin. I'm sorry to have troubled you.'

'If she should come,' the man called after him as he turned away, 'who shall I say was looking for her?'

'Doesn't matter,' Jan told him. 'She wouldn't remember me anyway.'

He hurried out into the street, glad of his thick air force overcoat, for the January cold was penetrating. Snow lay where it had fallen, made filthy by the passing of feet and vehicles. It clothed the ruins in a white blanket, but did nothing to disguise the devastation. He stood looking about him. Now where?

It had taken him months to return to Warsaw, even after his demob came through, long enough to make him wonder exactly what he was coming back to and whether he might be on a wild goose chase. He had crossed the Channel into France and then taken trains and buses and begged lifts all the way to the Italian border, stopping at cheap hotels and *estaminets*. France, he had noted, was slowly coming to life again, but travelling was chaotic, not made any easier by heavy snow. It was December by the time he crossed into Italy at Modane. No one questioned him or asked him who he was or where he was going. From Modane he had taken a train to Milan, where he had an emotional reunion with Jozef, who had postponed his move to South Africa to meet him.

His brother was battle-scarred and seemed to have aged prematurely, but he was robust and cheerful. 'You are a fool to go back,' he had told him as they sat in the hotel room Jan had taken in the suburbs. They had exhausted the tales they had to tell of their exploits during the war. Jozef told Jan about fighting in the desert, where the heat was almost unbearable and sandstorms blew grit into their food and into every crevice of clothing and body. He spoke of Italy and the hell that was the Battle for Monte Cassino, which had been taken by the Poles after several failed attempts by the British and Americans. Jan had told him about the Battle of Britain and escorting bombers to Germany and what had happened to some of his comrades in the squadron whom Jozef had known. He said nothing of Louise and Angela. It didn't seem relevant when he was on his way to be reunited with his wife. Both had agreed they had been lucky to come out of it in one piece. But Jozef was gloomy about Jan's decision to return to Poland. 'You won't last five minutes.'

'I promised Rulka I would go back. According to what I have been told, she survived and is waiting for me.'

'How can you be sure of that? She is dreaming and so are you. Poland does not exist as we knew it. Those so-called free elections were a sham. The new government is under the thumb of the Soviets and as far as they are concerned anyone who fought with Britain is a fascist and therefore an enemy. Instead of being reunited with your wife, you will find yourself in Siberia, or at the very least, a Polish prison. You know that, don't you?'

'I have to try. I'll invent a new identity and enter the country incognito. I've been given the name of a contact in Budapest who used to arrange for undercover agents to travel back and forth during the war. He is apparently still doing it.'

'Who gave you his name?'

'Boris Martel, the man who told me about Rulka being alive and working in the resistance.'

'Can you trust him?'

'Yes, I'm sure I can. He was a Polish-born English agent who worked with Rulka. He said she had been rounded up as a prisoner of war after the Rising, but escaped and returned to Warsaw. He saw her there, a year ago, alive and well.'

'How are you going to get to Budapest?'

'By train. I won't be in any danger before I cross into Poland, will I?'

'If you have made up your mind, then I won't try and change it, but don't say I didn't warn you.'

'I won't.'

They had stayed in Milan that night and spent the next day sightseeing and visiting the cathedral, and the subject was not returned to until they were standing together at the railway station, about to part. 'Good luck,' Jozef said as they embraced.

'Let me know how you get on. And if you can't find Rulka or it doesn't work out, get yourself out and join me. I'm not at all sure I shouldn't try and persuade you to come with me now.'

'You would not succeed.'

'Then goodbye, brother. Maybe one day we'll meet again.'

A last hug and Jan had boarded his train, leaving Jozef to find his way back to his regiment and from there to embark for Cape Town.

From Budapest Jan made his way northwards to a village on the Hungarian side of the Tatra mountains. The area was well known for its skiing. He hired skis and pretended to be enjoying a Christmas vacation while he tried to find a guide to take him over the mountains into Poland. He knew it would be hazardous, not only because of the depth of snow, but because the border was patrolled and anyone caught trying to cross was liable to be imprisoned and interrogated. The Communist rulers were paranoid about spies and he wasn't sure whom to trust. He had eventually found an exiled Pole who was making a living as a ski instructor, who agreed to take him across. It had taken several days of floundering in blizzard conditions and he had begun to wonder if his guide really knew where he was going, but apparently he did because he suddenly announced, 'We are in Poland. I will leave you here.' And with that he had shaken Jan's hand and turned back the way he had come.

Jan had found his own way to Zakopane, a ski resort he had often visited in his youth, and from there boarded a train for Warsaw. His papers had been examined but no comment had been made as they were returned to him.

Looking about him now at the devastation that had been Warsaw, he was beginning to realise his brother had probably been right. The population of the once beautiful city was sadly depleted but even so, searching for someone among the thin, pinched people whose main occupation seemed to be finding enough to eat, was like looking for a needle in a haystack. He smiled wryly to himself; his use of English idiom had not left him, though England was now only a pleasant memory, and Louise and Angela a happy dream from which he had awakened to this awful reality.

He crossed the pontoon over the river which had been hastily erected after the Germans blew up the bridges. A way had been cleared for traffic through the rubble of Karowa Street, but scattered bricks, blocks of stone and broken glass were still piled either side and the smell of death still hung in the atmosphere in spite of the cold. He almost lost his way as he negotiated more rubble-strewn streets looking for the hospital where Rulka had worked. She might have taken up her old job again or, if not, there might be someone who could tell him what had happened to her.

The hospital had been badly shelled but seemed to have escaped the ministrations of the German fire squads with their flame-throwers, and parts of it had been repaired in order to make it operational. Jan went in to be assailed by the smell of putrid flesh, urine and carbolic. Nurses and doctors and bewildered patients, some missing limbs, came and went along the corridors and ignored him.

He approached a nurse. 'Excuse me, I'm looking for Rulka Grabowska. She was a nurse here before the war . . .'

'I don't know anyone of that name, but I've only been here a year myself. Ask the director.'

'Where can I find him?'

She pointed. 'His office is down that corridor on the right.'

He thanked her and went off in the direction she had indicated, knowing she was watching him. He felt as though the word 'illegal' was emblazoned on his back. He was glad when he turned the corner and found himself facing a door with the label 'Director' on it. He knocked and was answered by a low voice saying, 'Enter.'

Opening the door, he found himself face to face with Lech Andersz, who was seated at a desk, a pile of documents in front of him. It was a gaunt and white-haired Lech, but still recognisable.

'Good God! Jan Grabowski,' he said, getting up to offer his hand. 'What are you doing here?'

'Looking for Rulka.'

'Rulka died in '42.'

'I know, but I believe she was reborn as Krystyna Nowak.'

'Who told you that?' He motioned Jan to a chair and returned to his own seat.

'A gentleman by the name of Boris Martel.'

'Where did you meet him?'

'In England last year.'

'I see. What else did he tell you?'

'As much as he felt he could. I have no doubt there was a lot he didn't say, but he told me Rulka had escaped from POW detention and returned to Warsaw and was waiting for me. I've been to our old apartment. There's someone else living there now.'

'I do not doubt it. People squat wherever a building is halfway habitable.'

'Do you know where I can find her?'

Lech turned to look out of the window at a lifeless poplar tree, its whitened trunk stark against the pale blue of a wintry sky. He seemed to be hesitating. 'The last time I heard anything of Krystyna Nowak,' he said carefully, 'she was in prison.'

'Prison? Which prison?'

'I hope, my dear fellow, you are not planning to try and have her released. I fear it would have no consequence except to deprive you of your own freedom.'

'I can't just leave her there.'

The doctor laughed. 'She was left over seven years ago and managed to survive.' It sounded like an accusation.

'I could not help that.'

'I am aware of that. She never held it against you and she would not now, if you were to go back where you came from.'

'I can't do that. What is she being accused of?'

'Being a member of the Home Army.'

'But that's not a crime.'

'It is now.' He paused, evidently uncomfortable. 'If you want to know more, I suggest you speak to Father Karlowicz at the Church of the Holy Cross. You'll find him busy about the rebuilding of the church. It may look to you as if nothing is being done, but the church is being given precedence when it comes to restoration. The rest of the city has to make do with ugly concrete blocks for new buildings, as you must have noticed.'

Jan, aware of Lech's caginess, did not press him further, but thanked him and left.

The church, opposite Warsaw University in the city centre, had been in the thick of the war right from the start. It had been seriously damaged in 1939 when its crypt had been used as a hospital and the German police had plundered it of its treasures during the occupation. It had been under constant attack during the Rising and, towards the end, when the Germans had reoccupied the area, they had detonated two Goliath remote-controlled mines inside it which destroyed much of the interior and brought down the facade.

As Jan approached it, he noticed people going through the rubble picking up pieces of stone and statuary and fragments of coloured glass from the broken windows and carefully placing them in separate heaps. He asked one of them where he could find

Father Karlowicz and was directed to a grimy figure bending over a broken statue.

'Have you come to help?' he asked Jan. 'We need to salvage as much building material as we can to guide us in reconstructing the church. It has to be restored as good as it was.'

'Perhaps I will later.' He paused, wondering how to begin. 'Father, will you hear my confession? Doctor Lech Andersz sent me.'

'Come,' the priest said, and led the way into a corner of the building still standing where a hasty confessional had been erected. 'Sit,' he said, indicating a bench.

When they were seated side by side, Jan went through the ritual and received his penance, but it was not so much absolution he wanted as information. 'Dr Andersz said you might be able to help me trace someone. Rulka Grabowska.'

'Rulka Grabowska died. I conducted her funeral service myself.'

'I'm sorry, I meant Krystyna Nowak.'

'Aah.' The word was drawn out. 'Who are you?'

'Jan Grabowski, Rulka's husband. I have not seen her since 1939.'

The priest looked Jan up and down. 'Where have you been?'

'In England with the Royal Air Force.'

'I guessed as much. There is too much meat on you to have been in Poland. No doubt you will learn to starve like the rest of us.'

'Perhaps I will, but what about Rulka?'

'Rulka is dead and Krystyna Nowak is in Pawiak prison.'

'So I have been told. Has she been tried and sentenced?'

'Not yet. The new Polish justice works very slowly, when it works at all.'

'Can she be defended?'

'A defence lawyer will be allocated.'

'Will I be allowed to see her?'

'On what grounds? Officially Krystyna Nowak is a single woman and has no near kin.'

'Are you allowed to see her?'

'Yes. I visit the prison, as does Dr Andersz.'

'Then you can tell her I am here in Warsaw and will do my utmost to have her released. Tell her not to give up hope.'

The old man laughed. 'She has had seven years of fighting and not giving up hope. I do not think she will start now.'

'Yes, that was silly of me. But tell her I am here, will you?'

'Very well, on my next visit. In the meantime, what are you going to do?'

'I must find work and a place to live. In England I took a short course in stone masonry and bricklaying.'

'Then we can use you. Warsaw has to be rebuilt. Do you have identity and ration cards?'

'Yes, but they are probably forged. I obtained them in Budapest.'

'Then no doubt they are,' the priest told him. 'Go and see Stanisław Roman, the undertaker. He was allowed to live because there was no one more needed and he has connections everywhere. But take my advice. Whatever thoughts you have about the Soviet Union or the Rising, keep them to yourself.'

Jan knelt to be blessed and then left to go in search of the undertaker. The joyful reunion with Rulka he had dreamt of was not to be. But he was here now and he had to make the best of it.

Rulka counted each step she took round the courtyard of the prison. Counting and reciting poetry kept her sane, considering the prisoners were forbidden to speak when on this daily fifteen-minute exercise. She was weak from hunger and the steps she took were small shuffles. It was ironic to think that she had escaped the German POW camp and made her way back to Warsaw, only to be caught because of the young Boy Scout who had guided her through the sewers when the Rising collapsed. She didn't blame him; he had no doubt been threatened, perhaps tortured, to get the information out of him. She hoped that by giving it, he had saved his life and that of his family.

It was over a year since she had asked Boris to find Jan. Whether he had she did not know, perhaps never would. Rumour had reached her that Polish pilots returning from Britain were immediately arrested as fascists. Perhaps that had happened to Jan and she began to wish she had not told Boris to find him and tell him she was waiting for him. Jan could do nothing for her. Her future would be decided by a judge in a mockery of a trial and she did not hold out much hope that she would be released.

When the war ended, Polish prisoners of war in Germany were released to find their own way home or become displaced persons, but those 'liberated' by the Russians had no such luck. As far as the NKVD, the Russian Secret Service, was concerned anyone who had been in German hands had been contaminated and was a collaborator. The same was said of the members of the Home Army. They had obeyed the orders of the government in London and were therefore fascists and capitalists, enemies of Communism. They were accused of using the Home Army as a cover for clandestine activities against the Soviet Union, and in partnership with the German Reich, which was laughable considering the Rising had been all about driving the *shkopy* out of Warsaw. It did not stop many of those still at liberty from forming a new resistance movement, the Freedom and Independence Organisation, dedicated to preserving democracy and restoring Poland's independence; as far as they were concerned, the war was far from over. Rulka, once back in Warsaw, lost no time in joining it.

The new Communist government of Poland had formed an internal security corps, the KBW, an equivalent of the Soviet NKVD. It was mobile and heavily armed and a law unto itself. It was this body that had arrested Rulka and thrown her into Pawiak prison. She had been here six months, enduring daily brutal interrogation aimed at forcing a confession out of her, until she had begun to wonder how she was going to hold out. Her cell was a cold stone room with a straw palliasse to sleep on and food that was just enough to keep her alive, no more. Her clothes were in rags and certainly inadequate in winter and what sleep she managed was frequently interrupted by being hauled out for more interrogation from which she returned battered and bruised.

But the years of privation in occupied Warsaw and her years with the resistance had made her tough. There was no room in her life for sentimentality, for mercy, for weakness of any kind. She had learnt to kill without compunction when the necessity arose. It was almost as if she were devoid of feeling. And yet she could still remember what her life had been like before the war, when she had been happy making a home with her husband. She had loved him and looked to him for protection. Her faith had been misplaced because he had left her. The Home Army had become her family, people like Lech, Arkady, Boris and Colin, the Bulldog, who had died saving her. Jan had become a distant memory, part of another world, that could never come again. She had been foolish to hold onto it and even more foolish to want or expect him to come back.

'Inside!' the guard shouted and the line of women dutifully turned and made their way back to their cells to be locked in again. Rulka supposed they were all awaiting trial as she was but as she had had no contact with them, she had no idea what they were being accused of. The list of crimes against the state was endless.

She had hardly sat down on the end of the bench that served as a bed, when the door was unlocked again and she was ordered out. Without a word she rose and followed the guard to the office of the prison governor for more interrogation. She knew the drill. She would be kept standing and a strong light shone into her face. There would be a guard on either side of her armed with truncheons and pistols, while her interrogator would either be sitting at a desk on the other side of the light or pacing back and forth, throwing out questions, always the same questions. When had she joined the Home Army? Which unit had she served in? Who had been her commanding officer? When had the unit been in contact with the German forces? How had they communicated with London? Who had been her co-conspirators plotting against the Soviet Union? Why did she not answer their questions and save everyone a lot of trouble? If she confessed, she would be dealt with leniently.

She was perfectly aware that they already knew the answers and all they were after was confirmation and a confession. Confessions saved them the trouble and expense of a proper trial. But she would not give them the satisfaction. The result was always a beating with the truncheons until she lost consciousness and was dragged back to her cell to await the next time.

But today was a little different. For a start, the two guards were not standing quite so close to her and her interrogator was smiling. 'I have good news for you, Krystyna Nowak,' he said. 'Your trial has been fixed for tomorrow.'

If he had hoped for a reaction from her, he was disappointed, her expression remained wooden.

'Are you going to confess, throw yourself on the mercy of the court and save us all a lot of time and trouble?'

'I am not interested in saving time and trouble. I want a proper trial.'

'Then you shall have one. You will be assigned a defence lawyer.' He turned to the guards. 'Take her back and make sure she is prettied up, get her a better dress and some decent shoes and stockings. And have her hair washed. We can't have the press thinking we do not treat our prisoners well.' He waved a hand to dismiss them and she was wheeled about to return to her cell. From this she deduced she was going to be the subject of a show trial meant to tell the world that there was justice to be had in the new Poland.

A nurse arrived the next day and treated her sores, sponged her bruises and set about ridding her of the vermin who had made their home in every crevice of her emaciated body. Later she was taken for a shower. It was only lukewarm but it left her feeling a little more alive. After she had dried herself she was handed a pile of clothes. They were far from the latest fashion and second-hand but much better than the rags she had discarded. There was underwear, a cotton dress, a knitted cardigan and shoes and socks; stockings were impossible to come by. The next arrival was a hairdresser who trimmed her hair and combed out the lice.

'It won't make a jot of difference,' she said, looking at the rough blanket and the straw mattress on the bench. 'They'll be back tomorrow.'

'Won't matter, will it?' the woman said. She was a huge Polish woman. Rulka could not be sure where her sympathies lay and did not risk trying to find out. 'It will all be over by then.'

When the hairdresser had left, Rulka sat on, waiting. Her head was full of what might be about to happen and the answers she might give to the questions asked of her. Her reverie was interrupted by the arrival of her defence lawyer, a small wiry man with dark hair and a pale face, who introduced himself as Tomasz Gorski. It soon became evident he was one of the establishment and as far as she could see there was little to distinguish him from the prosecution, except for telling her to plead guilty and beg for mercy. She'd be damned if she would do that. She hadn't fought for all those years to buckle under now.

He sighed at her intransigence, as if her refusal had personally hurt his feelings. Calling to the guards who stood outside the door, he gathered up the papers he had spread over the bed and which he said contained damning evidence against her. 'Then let us go and get this over with,' he said.

She followed him from the cell to a waiting room, where she was told to sit, while he paced the floor. Five minutes later, Father Karlowicz arrived. He had evidently come in great haste because his frock was dust-laden and his shoes scuffed.

The lawyer looked at him with contempt. 'You will not be needed until after the verdict,' he said.

'On the contrary,' the priest answered calmly. '*Pani* Nowak needs the support of the church for the ordeal ahead of her. I come to offer that support.'

'Oh, very well, you may have a few words with her, but make haste, the van will be here soon to convey her to the court.'

Rulka was puzzled, but decided to go along with this little charade; there must be a reason for it. She stepped forward and knelt before the priest. He laid a hand upon her head and murmured a prayer and then took her hand to help her up. She felt something being pressed into her palm and closed her fingers over it. Father Karlowicz turned to the lawyer. 'I shall see you in court, my friend, for there are others who need me.' And with that he took his leave, just as the prison van came to convey her to the courtroom.

Not until she was sitting in the waiting room and the lawyer had gone off to speak to colleagues, dare she look at the piece of paper in her hand. It was only a scrap and the handwriting was tiny, but its message was clear. 'Your husband is in Warsaw and working towards your release.' Could it be true? Was Jan really here? Her state of lethargy, the feeling that nothing mattered any more, was suddenly transformed into hope. She put the paper into her mouth and swallowed it and then resettled her expression into one of lethargy and hopelessness. But inside she was seething. It made her change her mind about her intransigence.

'I want you to plead mitigating circumstances,' she told Gorski when he came back. 'I was, and am, a nurse, committed to saving lives, no matter who they are. I was coerced into helping during the Rising, but only as a nurse. It was made very plain to me what would happen if I refused. I was never a fighter. I have nothing against the present regime. All I want is get on with the job I am trained to do. Nurses are needed.' The last statement was true, even if the previous ones were not. The hospitals were working flat out in appalling conditions. She knew typhoid, tuberculosis and rheumatoid arthritis were rife.

'You have left it late to say this,' he said.

'I'm saying it now.'

'Have you any witnesses to attest that you were forced to help?'

'Most of them are dead.'

'What about Father Karlowicz?'

'Ask him. He said he would be in court.'

He went off again and she sat there for several minutes, which seemed like an eternity. Would the good Father swallow his scruples to help her? There was no necessity to swear on the bible, so he might. Perhaps she ought to have suggested Lech. He was a doctor and had either not been suspected or had used the same argument as she had to keep his freedom. But was it fair to draw attention to him?

She watched other people come and go, some stoical, some in tears, a very few jubilant. Her turn came and she was conducted into the courtroom. It was an austere room and there were few people there. The general public were not admitted, but she noticed several members of the press, invited no doubt to witness her humiliation and report on the wonderful justice of the new Polish government. Father Karlowicz was there and so was Dr Andersz.

Her crimes were read out to her. She was accused of being a member of the *Armia Krajowa* who allegedly used it as a front to prepare terrorist activities and espionage against the Soviet Union. The organisation had cooperated with the Germans and given them supplies that had been dropped by the British and Americans. It was so palpably false it was almost laughable. But Rulka did not laugh.

Her cross-examination went on and on, the same questions she had been asked in her interrogation, the same answers, except that she now admitted to being coerced into the Home Army. At the end of it, Tomasz Gorski was allowed to speak on her behalf. He repeated what she had told him in the waiting room and then called Father Karlowicz, who attested to her good character and her skill as a nurse. He was followed by Lech Andersz, who said much the same thing. 'I have known Krystyna Nowak since 1942 when she came to Warsaw to nurse,' he said. 'She has always been conscientious and honest. She nursed wounded Russian soldiers with the same devotion to duty as she did her Polish brethren. There are many who owe their life to her skill.'

The outcome was a mild sentence of six months which she had already served and a fine of a thousand zloty. It was better than she had hoped. She thanked the judge and was taken back to prison. Until her fine was paid, there she would remain. She had no money, so who would pay it for her? Jan?

Jan had joined the people clearing rubble from the church, separating what could be used again from mere hard core. It was hot, back-breaking work and at the end of each day, his face, nose and mouth were caked in grey dust. He was glad to get back to the cellar of Jasna Street and clean himself up and make himself something to eat. Stanisław Roman had provided him with identity papers in his own name, but there was a fictitious reason for his eight-year absence. It was borrowed from his brother, so that if enquiries were made they could at least find a Grabowski in their records. 'You were taken prisoner by the Russians early on in the war and sent to a gulag,' Roman had said. 'You were released during the general amnesty when the Soviets became an ally of Britain and America, and joined General Anders' army. On release you came back to your homeland. You have recently come to Warsaw to help with the rebuilding. Have you got that?'

'Yes. Am I Jan or Jozef?'

'It doesn't matter, they both have the same initial letter, easily confused. But make sure you do not fall foul of the authorities.'

He was back in his home city, under his own name, but it was not the homecoming he had dreamt of. The wife he had come back to find was in prison. His home had been requisitioned, there were still bodies being unearthed as the rubble was cleared, and unexploded bombs and shells were still killing people. Sappers were still going from house to house, district to district, clearing them, after which they posted a notice: 'Checked, no mines.'

He straightened his aching back as the undertaker's hearse drew up alongside him and a gaunt figure, in a dress too big for her, emerged from it. He stood and stared. 'Rulka?' he queried.

'Jan.' She smiled, revealing a broken tooth. 'Don't you know me? Have I changed that much?'

'Myszka. Oh, Myszka.' He held out his arms and she went into them. She seemed tinier than he remembered and the feel of her in his arms was nothing but skin and bone. She was laughing as the tears rained down her face. She brushed them impatiently away. 'I haven't cried in years.'

'They said you were in prison.'

'So I was, but they let me go with a fine. Good nurses are hard to find.'

'Who paid the fine?'

'The organisation.'

'What organisation?'

'Never mind. Can you leave? Where are you living?'

'In the Jasna Street cellar.'

'How did you find out about that?'

'Stanisław Roman suggested it. It was filthy, blackened by fire, but I cleaned it up.'

She turned back to the undertaker who had remained sitting in the driving seat. 'Thank you, Stan,' she said. 'Thank you for everything.'

'My privilege,' he said. 'You two must have a lot to talk about, so I'll leave you. Good luck.'

Hand in hand, they found Father Karlowicz, who congratulated Rulka on her release, and sent them both home with his blessing. 'Be good to each other,' he said. 'The missing years will be hard to fill. You are neither of you the same people you were when you parted, so be tolerant of each other.'

Jasna Street had been cleared of most of the rubble and a start made on rebuilding, but there was a chronic shortage of labour and building materials and progress was slow. What new buildings were being constructed were concrete blocks of tiny flats with shared kitchens and bathrooms and there was a long waiting list for one of those. The cellar it would have to be. It reminded Rulka of her years with the Home Army and Colin and their life together. She found it difficult to relax and respond to Jan's lovemaking, even though he was gentle and tender. She was only too aware of her emaciated body, which he must surely find repulsive. It was not only her body, but the broken tooth which had happened during one of the interrogations in the prison, and the hollowness of her cheeks. In the end, he gave up. 'There's plenty of time,' he said. 'The rest of our lives.'

'I'm sorry.'

'Don't be. I should be the one who's sorry. Shall we talk instead?'

'Yes, tell me what your war was like.'

And so he talked about England and flying and being shot down and escaping, of meeting Jozef, and finding his way over the mountains and back to her. He did not mention Louise or Angela; they were locked away in his heart and in his memory, where they would have to stay. 'Now tell me about what you were up to,' he said. 'Boris Martel told me you were a heroine.'

'He found you, then?'

'Yes. I had no way of knowing what had happened to you, but when he told me you were alive, I had to come back.'

'Did you know what you might be coming back to?'

'I had a rough idea. What about you? It must have been grim.'

'It was. I don't want to talk about it.' She couldn't put into words what it had been like, the danger and the exhilaration, the slaughter and the suffering, the comradeship and the determination not to be subdued. But it had been in vain. They had lost and yet the will to resist was still there, still strong. It was why she had joined the Freedom and Independence Organisation to continue the fight, this time directed against the Soviets. Lucky for her, her accusers did not know that and her 'crime' had been that she belonged to the Home Army. How could she explain all that to Jan, a Jan who had never known real hunger and repression. His body was pink, well-nourished, muscular. He had all his teeth and his hair was as thick as ever. He had known comrades die, she did not doubt that, but he had never had to see women deliberately run over by tanks, never had to eat cats and dogs, or walk through sewerage up to his armpits.

'It doesn't matter,' he said, breaking into a long silence. 'Tell me when you're ready.'

She rose from the bed and went to gather up her clothes. 'Is there anything to eat?'

'Some sausage and a cabbage, a little beetroot too.'

She finished dressing. 'I'll make *barszcz* and *bigos*, then. Can you get the fire going?'

He dressed and went off in search of firewood. Life would get better, he had to believe it. One day they would learn to live like human beings again. They would have a proper home and enough work to keep them out of penury and then, maybe, Poland would be free and independent again.

Chapter Thirteen

Early summer 1960

Jenny stared at the tall young man in casual slacks and a donkey jacket who stood on the back doorstep of the Pheasant. His smile was mischievous and vaguely familiar. 'It isn't . . . It can't be . . . Not Tommy Carter.'

'The very same,' he said, laughing.

She grabbed his arm and pulled him over the threshold. 'Come on in.' Then, 'Stan! Stan! Look who's turned up like a bad penny.'

Stan appeared from the cellar where he had been tapping a new barrel. 'Well, I'll be damned. Where have you sprung from?'

'I'm back.'

'So I see. Are your mother and Beattie with you?'

'No, I left them in the States. Beattie got married last year. He's a car salesman. Mum and Russ divorced. It didn't work out. She's got a new fellow now. I didn't fancy playing gooseberry, so I decided to come home.'

'Home? You still call this home?'

'Definitely, have done ever since the war drove us out of London.'

'Sit down. We were just about to have lunch. We have to wait until the bar closes, so it's always the middle of the afternoon by the time we have it. My goodness, there's so much catching up to do. I don't know where to start. Where are you staying? How long are you here for?'

'I'm here for good, I think. I didn't take to life in the States and I was homesick, but I stuck it out until Beattie married and Ma took up with Randy; it was then I began to think of coming back.'

'You'll find a lot has changed.'

'So I noticed. There are houses all over Mr Sadler's meadow and there's a bypass. I wasn't sure I was in the right place when I got off the bus. And the Pheasant has changed, hasn't it? It's twice as big as it was.'

'We've expanded into providing restaurant meals. And we've got more bedrooms. It was the only way to survive; the old idea of the village pub only serving alcohol wouldn't provide a living nowadays, in spite of Macmillan telling us we never had it so good.'

'What happened to everyone else, Miss Fairhurst and Angela?'

'They live in the schoolhouse. Louise is headmistress. The school has been expanded too, though children are only there until they are eleven now. Then they go on to secondary school or Swaffham Grammar. Angela goes there. You must go and see them.'

'I will. Do you think you can put me up for a bit, just until I find a job and somewhere to live?'

Stan laughed. 'Oh, I think we can manage that.'

Jenny had been laying the table and dishing up while they talked. 'Come to the table,' she said. 'You can tell us all about what you've been up to while we eat.'

* * *

'Are you coming to the dance on Saturday?' Rosemary Richards asked Angela, as they sat side by side on the bus on their way home from school. 'Toby's taking me.'

'I dunno. I've got no one to go with since I ditched that creep, Nigel Barker.'

'Why did you ditch him?'

'He was spreading tales about me.'

'What tales?'

'Doesn't matter. I told him if he repeated them again, I'd have the law on him.'

'Good for you. I could ask Toby to get one of his mates to partner you, if you like.'

'No thanks, I don't fancy blind dates. Anyway, Mum likes to approve of my boyfriends, and as for Granny.' She laughed suddenly. 'She's oh, so Victorian. She doesn't think you should have boyfriends before you're at least twenty and then only chaperoned.'

'Did your mother approve of Nigel?'

'She didn't exactly disapprove. After all, she's known Nigel's mother for years and years . . .'

'Did you tell her what Nigel said?'

'No, course not.'

'Why not?'

'Because it's all lies and it would hurt her.'

The bus drew up at the end of the road leading to the village and Angela left it to walk home. 'Ring me if you change your mind,' Rosemary called after her.

It was only half a mile to the schoolhouse, a walk Angela had made every day of every school term since she passed her eleven-plus and gone to the grammar school. She could have done it in her sleep. At the end of this term when all her exams were finished, she would go out into a wider world. Living in a village was so restricting, nothing ever happened. Everyone knew everyone else's business – or thought they did. And if they didn't know it, they made it up. Nigel Barker had been all over her trying to get her to have sex with him, just because he had taken her out once or twice and she had allowed him to kiss her. 'What are you holding back for?' he had demanded. 'It's what you want, isn't it?'

'No, it is not.'

'Don't believe you. Girls always say no to start with when they really mean yes.'

'Not me.'

'Can't see why you're so particular,' he had grumbled. 'Your mother never was.'

She couldn't help herself; she had to ask. 'What's my mother got to do with it?'

'You know.'

'No, I do not.'

'Well, I'm not going to be the one to tell you.'

She had been furious and when he tried to kiss her, had thumped him over the head with the tennis racket she was carrying. He had winced and put his hand to his head, so it must have hurt. Serve him right. But things like that were difficult to forget and his words festered. She might have confided in her mother, but when it came to it, she couldn't, didn't know how to begin.

She didn't remember her father. According to Granny, he had been killed in the war, though that didn't account for the fact that her surname was Fairhurst, the same as Granny's. She had come to the inevitable conclusion her mother had never married. It didn't bother her. Mum was still Mum, whom she loved. She was not only Mum, but her best friend. She would not allow anyone to say a word against her, especially creeps like Nigel Barker.

She went in at the back door of the schoolhouse to the kitchen where her grandmother was preparing their evening meal. Granny had come to live with them when Grandfather had died of a stroke. He had been an invalid; she had never known him when he was fit and healthy, but even bedridden he had frightened her on the few occasions she had seen him. Granny sometimes smiled, but she never laughed. And she was so strait-laced she found fault all the time. Her arrival in the household had not made for harmony, but Mum had told her to be tolerant, that her grandmother had had a hard life and needed understanding. It was difficult when Granny criticised her clothes, her love of rock and roll and dancing and nagged her to do more about the house. If there had been a man in the home, it might have been different.

Mr Young had been trying to court Mum for years, ever since his wife had died of cancer, but Mum would have none of it. 'I've got enough to keep me busy without having to look after a husband,' she had said, laughing.

'Where's Mum?' she asked her grandmother.

'In the front room marking books.'

Angela put her head round the door of the sitting room. 'I'm home, Mum. Just going up to change.'

Louise looked up from the exercise book she was marking and smiled at her daughter. At eighteen she was growing into a lovely young woman. With her blonde hair and blue eyes and determined chin, she was the image of Jan. Every day she noticed it more and more, a constant reminder of the man she had loved and lost. He had taken her at her word and never tried to communicate with her, but she wondered if he ever thought of her and his daughter. Perhaps he had other children, half-brothers and -sisters to Angela, but they would never know.

The years had passed incredibly swiftly. The horrible post-war years of austerity were over and life was easier. She had a good job, which had allowed her to give her daughter a happy childhood, a happier one than she had had. Angela repaid her by being loving and considerate. She worked hard at school and was expected to do well enough in her exams to get her to Cambridge. Jan would be proud of her if he could see her now. Sometimes she wondered if Angela remembered her *tata*, the man who had given her that rather battered teddy bear which still sat in pride of place on a chair in her bedroom.

One day she would have to tell her about Jan. She ought to have done it sooner, before her mother came to live with them and insisted on telling all and sundry that her daughter's husband had been killed in the war. She ought to have said something to Angela then, but she had only been eight at the time and she wasn't sure she could make her understand. The village had a new housing estate and a lot of incomers from bombed-out London who had settled in the village and had not known her during the war. A few people in the village knew the truth, but they were good friends and saw no reason to bring up the subject.

Angela would want to marry herself one day, though she hoped not too soon, and then it would all have to come out. 'Don't see why,' her mother had said when she mentioned it. 'Let sleeping dogs lie.' And so she prevaricated.

She piled the marked books up neatly and went into the kitchen to help her mother finish preparing the meal, just as Angela came down in jeans and a striped shirt.

'How was it today?' Louise asked her, as they sat down to eat.

'Not bad. We had to write an essay comparing Tennyson with Browning. Thank goodness I'd swotted them up. Only two more to go. The history one is going to be the hardest.' She had chosen to take history, English and mathematics at A level and had a provisional place at Homerton to study modern history. 'Then it's no more school for me.'

'University is still school,' Faith said.

'No, it isn't. It's nothing like school. It's for grown-ups.'

Louise smiled at that, but didn't comment. 'Are you going to take that summer job Aunt Jenny offered you?'

'Perhaps. I want to save up for when we go to Rome.' The school had arranged a visit to Rome in August to see the sights and some of the Olympics. When they came back she and her mother were going on holiday together.

'In my day,' Faith said. 'Young ladies did not go gallivanting about the world on their own.'

'But this isn't your day, Granny,' Angela said. 'We are more liberated. And we aren't going to go alone, are we?'

'What have you planned for the weekend?' Louise asked, quickly changing the subject.

'Nothing, really. Rosemary is going to the hop in Swaffham tomorrow night, but I don't think I'll go. I'll only be playing gooseberry.'

'Why? Can't you go with Nigel?'

'No. I've finished with him, he's a creep.'

'Oh, dear,' Louise said. 'You must have very exacting standards.'

'Is that bad?' she asked.

'No, it isn't. There's plenty of time to find Mr Right. You must see a bit of life first.'

'That's why I want to travel.'

Louise laughed at her daughter's persistence and began clearing the table, collecting everything on a tray. She was carrying it into the kitchen when they heard the front door knocker. 'See who that is,' she called over her shoulder.

Angela went to open the door and found herself staring at the handsomest man she had ever seen. He had crinkly light-brown hair, hazel eyes and an infectious smile. 'Hallo,' he said. 'You must be Angela.' He had a slight American accent.

'Yes, I am, but who are you?'

'You don't remember me? I'm not surprised, it was a long time ago. Is your mother in?' He looked past her to Louise who was coming along the hall towards them. 'Hallo, Miss,' he said, grinning.

'Good Heavens, Tommy Carter. What are you doing here? Why didn't you let us know you were coming? Come in, come in.'

He followed her into the sitting room with Angela bringing up the rear. His name on her mother's lips had stirred a vague memory, but she couldn't put her finger on it. Sometime in the past, this young man had been part of her life.

She sat and listened as Tommy and her mother talked. Her grandmother finished the washing-up and brought in a tray loaded with mugs of coffee and the conversation continued unabated. He told them all about his life in America and what had happened to his mother and Beattie, and his decision to come back to Cottlesham. 'It's changed a bit,' he said. 'But in some ways it's still the same. The school looks exactly as I remember it.'

'That's only at the front,' Louise said. 'It's been extended at the back to make two separate classrooms and we've got cloakrooms and indoor toilets now. Many of the children I teach with the help of Miss Finch are the children of those you went to school with.'

'You're one of Mum's ex-pupils?' Angela queried.

He turned to answer her. 'Yes. I was an evacuee. She was my teacher in Edgware. We came to Cottlesham together at the beginning of the war. We lived at the Pheasant.'

'Oh. You must tell me what it was like. Was Mum very strict?'

'Not really. Soft as butter, though she tried to be stern. Mr

Langford, the headmaster, was the strict one. He had been wounded in the first war and had a peg leg but it didn't stop him using the cane with gusto when he thought it was deserved.' He turned back to Louise. 'What happened to him?'

'He lives with his sister in Dereham,' she answered. 'I haven't seen him for ages.'

Angela had been studying him while he and her mother talked. Sitting in one of the armchairs with his long legs stretched out, he seemed totally at ease. He had a mobile kind of face, the sort that could change from a frown to a grin in a split second. 'I ought to remember you,' she said.

'You were only four when we left,' he said. 'You were a bridesmaid at my mother's wedding – second wedding, I hasten to add.'

'I don't remember that.' Her very earliest memory was of the day the nine-inch black and white television arrived and was installed so that they could watch the Queen's wedding to Prince Philip, only she wasn't the queen then, but Princess Elizabeth.

'I'll show you,' Louise said, going to a drawer in the alcove beside the fireplace and fetching out a photograph album. She turned the pages. 'Look, here's a picture of it.'

Angela must have seen the picture before but not taken much notice of it. The bride and groom were flanked by her two bridesmaids and a very young Tommy, trying to look important. Her mother was standing just behind them. 'I seem to remember there was lots to eat and it was very cold,' she said. 'I recognise Mr and Mrs Wayne and Mr Young and Uncle Stan and Aunt Jenny, but who are all these other people?'

'Friends of the groom,' Louise said, as the smiling face of Jan came into her vision. She had forgotten he had been standing beside her when the picture was taken. It brought an enormous lump to her throat. She looked up and saw Tommy looking at her with a questioning look in his eye and slowly shook her head.

'That's me,' he said, pointing and that's Beattie. She's married now.'

'Are you married?' Angela demanded.

He didn't seem to mind the question, though her grandmother tut-tutted. 'No. I was engaged once, but that didn't work out either, so here I am, thirty years old and fancy-free.'

'Twelve years older than me,' she said.

'Yes. I remember when you were born. Everyone made a great fuss of you.'

'Tell us your plans,' Louise said quickly. The past, so long subdued, had suddenly come up from the depths and was threatening to spill over. 'Are you here to stay?'

'Yes. I must find a job. I'm an aeronautical engineer. And then I have to find somewhere to live. In the meantime I'm staying at the Pheasant.'

'You've seen Stan and Jenny, then?'

'Yes, they don't change, do they? Stan's hair is as thick and white as ever and Jenny doesn't alter – a bit greyer, perhaps, and a bit rounder. You haven't changed, though. I would know you anywhere. As for Angela, I wouldn't have known her if I'd met her in the street. From being a plump little toddler, she has turned into a real beauty.'

Angela felt herself blushing. 'Well, thank you for that, kind sir. I wouldn't have known you either.'

'I'm looking forward to exploring my old haunts and renewing old acquaintances.'

'I'll show you round tomorrow, if you like,' Angela offered. 'Then you can tell me all about what it was like in wartime.'

'Fine, I'd like that. I'll call for you, shall I?'

He left soon after that to go back to the Pheasant, accompanied to the door by Louise. 'I hope I haven't been an embarrassment to you,' he said in a low voice.

'No, of course not. I've loved seeing you again.'

'But Angela doesn't know about Jan?'

'I never seemed to get around to telling her. My mother is a bit strait-laced. She has always insisted I had a husband who died in the war. It was easier to go along with that, especially given my role in the community. There are so many newcomers and they might not understand.'

'I won't say anything.'

'Thank you.'

She watched him go down the garden path, then shut the door and returned to the sitting room. It was empty. She went to the kitchen to find her mother washing up the coffee cups.

She picked up a tea towel. 'Where's Angela?'

'Gone up to her room. She said she had some revision to do.' She paused. 'That young man could spell trouble.'

'How do you mean?'

'He could spill the beans about you-know-who.'

Louise hated the way her mother would never put a name to Jan. 'Why should he? In any case, I think it's about time I told Angela the truth.'

'Then you'd make a liar out of me.'

'You were the one who started the deception, Mum, telling the new parson I was a widow.'

'How was I to know the flower ladies were in the church and listening in? Anyway, it was better for you. You have a position in the community to maintain. If the truth reached the ears of the local education authority, you could lose your job and your house.'

'That's nonsense, Mum. People aren't so judgmental nowadays.'

'They might have been back then.'

Her mother had been living with her, ever since her father's death from a stroke in 1950. He had improved so much under the exercise regime, he had been able to haul himself out of bed and into the wheelchair. He would wheel himself about the flat and follow her mother into the kitchen which, until then, had been her sanctuary. 'He sits there watching me,' she once told Louise. 'I'm sure he hates me.'

'Why?'

'I can walk and he can't.'

He had fallen out of his wheelchair onto the kitchen floor. 'We were having lunch and he tried to reach for a knife,' her mother explained when she arrived after being telephoned. 'I had it in my hand and he grabbed my wrist and made me drop it. I don't know if he was bending to try and pick it up off the floor or whether it was the stroke that made him fall out of the chair. It was only a table knife, not sharp enough to harm him, but he didn't move. I felt his pulse but I knew he'd gone. The doctor came as soon as I rang and signed the death certificate. They've taken him to the mortuary.'

Louise had taken over, arranged the funeral and afterwards persuaded her mother to come and live with her, which was when the deception over her supposed widowhood had begun. But oh, how she wished Mum wouldn't interfere and find fault so much.

'Where do you want to go first?' Angela asked. It was a warm day and she had dressed in a printed cotton dress with a cinched-in waist, round neck and cap sleeves. She knew it showed off her figure and the blue of its background suited her fair complexion.

'Wherever you like,' he said. 'I want to see it all and drink in the nostalgia.'

They strolled up the lane to the middle of the village. She was acutely aware of his tall handsome presence at her side and hoped she would meet some of her friends so that she could show him off. 'What was it like during the war? Mum hardly ever talks about it, and Granny only goes on about the Blitz.'

'The Blitz was pretty awful, but we didn't get any bombs in Cottlesham. A German fighter came over low once and machine-gunned the village. One of the shells went right through your pram. Thank goodness you weren't in it at the time.'

'Tell me more.'

'What do you want to know?'

'Did you know my father?'

'Oh.'

'You did know him, didn't you?'

'Yes.'

'Tell me about him.'

'Don't you know?'

'Not much. Granny always says the past is gone and best forgotten, but I don't think Mum has forgotten.'

'Well, she wouldn't, would she?'

'You know that wedding picture she showed us yesterday? There was an airman standing beside Mum. Was that my father?'

'Maybe.'

'Why are you so cagey? Is there some dreadful secret about him I'm not supposed to know?'

'I don't know. I was only a child at the time, but I don't think so.'

'Come on, Tommy, we all lived together at the Pheasant, you can't not have known what was going on.'

'Why don't you ask your mother?'

'Because I think it would hurt her to think I was dissatisfied with my life.'

'Are you dissatisfied?'

'Not at all. I'm just curious, that's all. I've often wondered why Mum never speaks about my father. I know, or at least, I'm pretty sure, they never married, but what's that matter these days? Was he shot down?'

'I've no idea what happened to him. Can we change the subject?'

'OK.' She wasn't going to get anything else out of him, which was frustrating. His arrival had renewed her curiosity about the man who had fathered her. 'This is the village store, it's run by the Co-op now. It has most things but for anything big you have to go to Swaffham.'

'Do they sell postage stamps? I've a letter to post to my Mom.'

'No, there's a post office on the corner.'

He went in, bought stamps and posted his letter, and then they continued down the lane, past the gates of the Hall. 'They're going to knock that down.' she told him. 'It was costing too much to keep up. I think Sir Edward has gone to live in France. Shall we go back across the common?'

'Yes, it was my favourite spot as a boy, all wild and overgrown. We used to play cowboys and Indians there and have fights between the evacuees and the village boys.'

'I think the council would like to build houses on it, but it's common land and there's been a hue and cry over it. Mum is very active trying to save it.'

The common was rough, with hummocks and dips, the grass uncultivated and the brambles rampant. They walked in silence for a few minutes. She was still thinking of the conversation about her father and wished someone would be more forthcoming about him. Mysteries were all very well in novels, but she didn't like them in real life.

'What are you planning to do when you leave school?' he asked.

'I've got a provisional place at Homerton, depending on my results.'

'What do you want to study?'

'European history.' She paused, then went on, 'Do you like dancing?'

'Yes.'

'There's a hop on in Swaffham tonight. Would you like to take me?'

'Haven't you got a boyfriend to go with?'

'No, I finished with him. He said derogatory things about Mum.'

'Then you did right. I'd have punched his nose if I'd heard him.'

She laughed. 'So, will you come?'

'It's a date.'

Angela found her mother in the sitting room with the inevitable pile of exercise books in front of her. 'Where's Granny?'

'She's gone into Swaffham with Mrs Sadler. They want to find some canvas to renew the hassocks.'

'Good. I want to ask you something.' She went to the drawer, brought out the photograph album and turned its pages to find the picture of the wedding. She laid it on top of the book her mother was marking and pointed. 'Is that man my father?'

Louise looked up at her daughter. 'What has Tommy been saying?'

'Nothing. He was very cagey. You haven't answered my question.'

'Yes, sweetheart, that's your father.'

'Then he couldn't have been killed in the war, could he? The war was over when this was taken. Why did you let me believe he had?'

'It was easier than trying to explain.'

'Is he dead?'

'I don't know.' Louise sighed. 'The last time I saw him was soon after that picture was taken.'

'He abandoned us?'

'No, Angela, abandoned is not the right word.' She shut the album and turned towards her daughter, who had a mulish expression Louise knew only too well. It plainly said she was not going to let the matter drop. 'Sit down and I'll tell you about him. His name was Jan Grabowski . . .'

Angela sank into a chair beside her mother. 'You mean he wasn't English?'

'He was Polish and I loved him very, very much and he loved me and he adored you. He was your beloved *tata* – that's Polish for "daddy".'

'*Tata*,' Angela murmured. 'I remember that word now you say it. But you didn't marry him, did you?'

'No, I didn't. He had a wife in Poland. He didn't know if she was alive or dead until the end of the war, when he learnt she was alive. Of course, he had to go back to her.'

'Of course,' Angela repeated with heavy irony. 'Never mind us.'

'He minded very much, Angela. Leaving you broke his heart, but he had promised his wife he would go back, and besides, he was Catholic, he could not have divorced her.'

'And you haven't heard from him since?'

'No.'

'If you loved him, how could you let him go?'

'I had no choice. I had to do what I thought was right.'

'Do you still think you were right?'

'Yes.'

'I could not have done it. I'd have fought to keep him.'

'Maybe. Times were different then.'

'Do you think he ever thinks of us?'

'If he is alive, I am sure he does.'

'Tell me about him. Am I like him?'

'Yes, you are, and since you have grown up, more so. I see him every day in you. You have inherited his fair hair and blue eyes, but it's not only his looks – it's the way you hold your head, the way you smile, your love of life and your stubbornness when things don't go the way you want them to.'

'Does that make you sad?'

'Sometimes, when I think he hasn't watched you grow up as I have. He would have been proud of you.'

'Is he the reason you never married?'

'No one could take his place, it wouldn't be fair to the man I married.'

'Have you ever thought about trying to trace him?'

'I couldn't come between him and his wife, it would not have been right. In any case, Poland is behind the Iron Curtain. It would have been next to impossible, especially in the early days after the war.'

'But no so bad now, surely? Stalin is dead and the Russians are losing their grip on their satellite states.'

'It's too late now, Angela. There's been too much water under the bridge. We've all changed. The world has changed.' They heard the back door open and close. 'Granny's back.'

'What does she think about all this? She does know, doesn't she?'

'Yes, she knows.' It was said with a sigh. 'She has her own angle on it.'

Angela laughed. 'Yes, I imagine she would have.' She picked up the album and put it away in the drawer, just as Faith came into the room.

'We bought yards and yards of canvas,' she said, dumping a carrier bag on the table. 'I'm going to design some cross stitch for the ladies to embroider.'

'Good,' Louise said. 'I'll get some tea, shall I?'

'Tommy is taking me to the dance tonight,' Angela said. 'Uncle Stan's going to lend him his car.'

'He's way too old for you,' her grandmother said.

'Granny, he is only going to take me to the hop, we aren't planning a steamy love affair.'

'And you are too cheeky for your own good.'

'Mum explained to me about my dad,' Angela told Tommy as they danced. He danced beautifully, not only the old-fashioned waltz, foxtrot and quickstep but swing, bop and rock and roll. When they turned up, Rosemary had stared with her mouth open. Angela had introduced them and, much to Toby's annoyance, Rosemary tried to flirt with him. Tommy bore it with good humour, but otherwise stayed close by Angela's side.

'I'm glad,' he said. 'He was a good man, one of the best, and a brave man too.'

'He didn't die. He went back to Poland, he's probably still alive. I want to try and trace him.'

They couldn't talk and dance at the same time. He stopped and took her hand to lead her to one side where there were some chairs. He sat down and pulled her down beside him. 'Do you think that's a good idea?'

'Yes, I do. I want to find out what happened to him.'

'You might be an embarrassment if he's got a wife and family.'

'I don't intend to embarrass him. I simply want to find him.'

'Do you know how to go about it?'

'No, I don't. I'll have to find out.'

'Are you really determined?'

'Yes.'

'Have you told your mother?'

'No. I don't want to upset her.'

'You'll upset her more if you do it without saying anything.'

'But nothing might come of it.'

'Maybe not, but don't go off half-cock, Angela. Think about it carefully.'

Louise had known Angela would not let the subject of Jan rest and was not at all surprised when she brought it up again on her return from the dance. She had waited up for her, as she always did, filling in the time preparing lessons for Monday morning and watching a report on television of Princess Margaret's wedding to Anthony Armstrong-Jones, which had taken place that afternoon at Westminster Abbey. None of it served to take her mind off Jan. It was almost as if her daughter had brought him to life again, filled her heart, mind and body as he had done so many years before. She found herself listening again to his chatter, his infectious laugh, the feel of his hand holding hers in a firm dry grip, reliving his lovemaking until her body ached. It was a long time to remain celibate. Perhaps she should have married Bill Young, after all. But she couldn't; he was much too nice a man to use as second best.

She heard the back door and voices coming from the kitchen and hastily opened Tracey Johns' maths book. A minute later, Angela came in followed by Tommy. Her daughter was rosy-cheeked and animated. 'Did you have a nice time?' she asked her.

'Yes, smashing. Tommy is a good dancer. Rosemary was green with envy. I've brought him in for coffee. We want to ask you something.'

'Oh.' She put the exercise books in a neat pile. 'I'll make the coffee first, shall I?'

'Good idea.'

Louise left them sitting side by side on the sofa. Tommy looked a little uneasy; it made her wonder just what mischief her daughter was up to. He had obviously been dragged in to back her up in whatever it was. She made the coffee, loaded the mugs on a tray and went back to them. They had been talking in low voices but stopped when she came in. 'Now,' she said, handing them a mug each. 'What is this big ask?'

Chapter Fourteen

'Angela, I am not at all sure about this,' Louise said after hearing her out. She had been half expecting it, but that didn't stop her feeling fearful. What she was fearful of, she did not know. Was it that Angela might fail and this churning in her stomach would all have been for nothing? Or that she might succeed, only to find that the love Jan had once had for her had faded to nothing over the years? Or was it the risk involved in delving into a regime that was only half understood? 'You may be stirring up a hornet's nest.'

'I don't see why. I simply want to know what happened to him.'

'Finding out won't be easy. He might have died. He might have changed his name. He might have left Poland and emigrated.'

'Wouldn't he have come back here to us, if he'd done that?'

'I would like to hope so, but not if he's still married.'

'Then if he's alive, my bet is he's still in Poland. It won't do any harm to ask around, will it?'

'Who are you proposing to ask?'

'The Polish Embassy, the Red Cross, the British Legion, anyone in England who knew him. You surely know someone who might give us a clue.'

'I can't think of anyone. His friends have all dispersed – heaven knows where they are now, or even if he kept in touch with them. His brother emigrated to South Africa.'

'You mean I might have cousins there?'

'I suppose you might. I hadn't thought of it.' She turned to Tommy. 'What do you make of all this, young man?'

'I'm not sure,' he said slowly. 'But what I remember of Jan, he would want to know that he has a daughter he can be proud of. I'm sorry, this must be very distressing for you. And it's all my fault, coming back like I did.'

It *was* distressing in a way. She found herself living again that last parting, the tears and the anguish, the sleepless nights, the way she had followed every bit of news to come out of Poland, wondering if, one day, his name might be mentioned. It never had. Gradually the torment had eased to leave a feeling of emptiness that not even Angela could properly fill. 'No, it's not your fault, Tommy. It was time I told Angela about him. You just jogged me into doing it.'

He laughed. 'And now she's got the bit between her teeth.'

'It would probably have happened anyway.'

'What do you say, Mum?' Angela persisted.

'I don't know. I'll have to think about it.'

'What's to think about?' Angela demanded. 'I only want to make a few enquiries.'

'And then what?'

'It all depends on what turns up.'

'If you do find him, you can't just go barging in. He might not have told his wife about us.'

'I know that. I'm not stupid.'

'If she finds him, they don't have to meet if he doesn't want it,' Tommy put in. 'The usual thing is to use an intermediary. It's been done like that in the States . . .' His voice tailed away.

Louise was tempted, very tempted. If only, oh, if only . . . Would there be any harm in it? In any case, the odds of succeeding were very long indeed, considering all the unrest in the Eastern bloc and the Soviet determination to put it down. She sighed and gathered up the coffee cups. 'It's late and we can't talk about it any more tonight. I'm tired and ready for my bed.'

Angela was smiling as she accompanied Tommy to the door. 'I'll see you tomorrow. She'll give in, see if she doesn't.'

'Do you think I should let Angela do it?' Louise asked Jenny. They had just come out of church and were walking towards the Pheasant. The day was warm and they were wearing printed nylon dresses, light cardigans and sandals. Faith, in what she considered the obligatory suit, hat and gloves, had stayed behind to talk to the parson. Angela was walking ahead of them with Tommy at her side.

'She's eighteen, Lou, you can't really lay down the law, can you? If she's determined, she'll go ahead anyway. It would be better to oversee what she does and make sure she doesn't get into trouble over it.' She chuckled suddenly. 'If she takes the job we've offered her, she won't have much spare time. It's probably only hot air anyway.'

'You are no doubt right. In any case, I can't see her succeeding given the political climate.' Relations between East and West were as bad as ever. Only that week, the Russians had shot down an American aeroplane over Russian air space. They claimed it had been spying, while the Americans had maintained it was only doing weather research and the pilot had simply strayed off course

The row was seriously jeopardising the Big Four summit in Paris.

Jenny turned to look at her friend. 'But there's a part of you that hopes she does, isn't there? Own up.'

Louise laughed, but it was a trifle cracked. 'You know me so well.'

Angela finished her exams and said goodbye to school. While she was waiting for her results she helped out at the Pheasant and in her spare time set about the task of finding her father. But all her enquiries drew a blank. The Red Cross said they would put her request on their books, but finding anyone in Poland was almost impossible. She had the same reply from the Polish Embassy. The man she spoke to on the telephone even went so far as to warn her off.

'I'm not surprised,' her mother told her. 'The embassy people are appointed by the Communist government and would not encourage Polish citizens to have contact with the West. I do hope you haven't made things difficult for Jan.'

'Leave well alone,' her grandmother put in. 'I don't know why you want to stir up the past. What can you achieve? He can't come here, can he?'

'Why not?' Angela demanded.

'He's supposed to be dead.'

'Perhaps, he is,' Louise said quietly. 'Angela, I think you've done enough. Leave it now, will you?'

Angela did not reply. She was disappointed at not making any headway and even more disappointed that her mother wanted her to stop. Frustrated and annoyed with everyone, she slammed out of the house. Other girls had fathers, fathers who had watched them grow up, who had taken them on outings and holidays, who praised them, grumbled at them, who ferried them about in their cars when they wanted to go out, who were there, part of their lives. She had missed all that. Mum had done her best to make up for it, but it wasn't the same. Somewhere, she had a father, somewhere, out there in a world she could only imagine, her *tata* lived, she knew it in her bones.

'I'm home.' Jan put his head round the bedroom door. 'I'll wash and change and then I'll see about supper.'

Rulka smiled but did not speak. Talking was too much of an effort. Poor Jan! He could never have envisaged what his life would be like coming back to Poland. According to the tales he had told her, his life in England had been good, even in wartime. He had never been hungry and there had been a camaraderie, a shared destiny that the end of the war had shattered. Many of his friends who had also returned to Poland had been arrested and imprisoned, some of them shot. With the death of Stalin in 1953 and Nikita Kruschev's vitriolic attack on Stalin at the Soviet Party Congress in 1956, the Soviet hold on the country had eased. A general amnesty at that time had meant the release of some of the prisoners, but they were broken and embittered men and found it almost impossible to find work. Jan was lucky to have his job as a bricklayer.

It was a far cry from his pre-war air force days when life was carefree and fun. How happy he and Rulka had been, looking forward to their life together, planning their family. As it was they would never have children. Near starvation during the German occupation and her ill-treatment in prison meant that she could never become pregnant. Jan had accepted that as he accepted everything with uncomplaining stoicism, but she wondered if he ever wished he could have had a family. He would have made a grand *tata*. Now, all he could do was work and sleep and look after an invalid wife who was no good to him at all.

Clean and in a fresh shirt and light trousers, he came back into the room, sat on the side of the bed and took her hand. 'What would you like to eat, sweetheart?'

'I'm not hungry.'

'But you must eat. Look at you, all skin and bone. You'll never get better if you don't put some flesh on you. Try a little broth.'

She smiled. 'For you, I'll try.'

He went off to the kitchen to heat up the broth he had made before leaving for work that morning. The apartment, on the second floor of a block of flats, was the third one they had lived in since his return, each slightly better than the one before. From the cellar in Jasna Street, they had gone to a tiny one-roomed apartment with a shared kitchen and bathroom, and from there to one that had two rooms and a kitchen. Their present home was spacious by comparison and had the luxury of its own bathroom. It was a far cry from what he had hoped and dreamt of, but they were a great deal better off than many people. He had a job that paid him enough for them to live reasonably well, though nothing like his pre-war standard or what he had earned in the air force.

Sometimes he wondered if he could get a job flying with LOT, the civilian airline, which would have paid considerably more, but to do that he would have to produce credentials and that meant revealing his involvement with the RAF. Rulka had been vehemently against it. 'You will stir up trouble for both of us if you do that,' she had said. 'It's too risky.'

It wasn't only the risk to him she had been thinking of but her involvement with the underground. The prospect of a free and independent Poland obsessed her. She could not give up fighting. She fought bureaucracy, she fought their political masters, she fought dirt and disease, she even fought him. Their renewed life together had been a constant battle of one kind or another. He had only a faint idea of what she had been through in the years they had been apart but he was sure it had been horrendous and had left her scarred, not only physically but mentally. He told himself it was up to him to make her life a little easier and be patient.

She had gone back to work almost immediately on being released from prison and they had soldiered on and in time had achieved a kind of peace with each other. One by one the years had rolled on. The past was a closed book; he did not speak of it. Thoughts of England, Cottlesham, Louise and Angela were buried deep inside him and not allowed to surface.

But in the end the years of privation and cruelty in prison had taken their toll of Rulka and she had started losing weight again. Three months before, while holding her in his arms in bed, feeling her bony fragility, he had found a lump in one of her breasts. She had made light of it, but he had insisted she spoke to Lech about it, who had done some tests and confirmed what they had both dreaded: she had cancer.

He took the bowl of broth and a spoon into the bedroom and put it on a side table so that he could help her sit up, then he fed it to her spoonful by spoonful, until it had all gone. She lay back exhausted. The radiotherapy always left her like that, but they both maintained the fiction that the treatment was doing her good.

'I'm going to sleep now,' she said. 'I'll be better in the morning.'

He tucked the bedclothes round her, made sure she could reach the little bell to summon him if she needed him and left her. He made himself a meal and sat in the kitchen to eat it, then he went into the living room, fetched a box containing his course work and settled at the table to read. In his spare time he was studying to be an architect. Much of Warsaw had been rebuilt, brick by brick, stone by stone, exactly as it had been. The Old Town had re-emerged historically accurate, with its quaint buildings and cobbled streets, and most of the churches had risen again; Communism could not stifle the Poles' commitment to their religion. The ugly concrete apartment blocks built hastily immediately after the war to house the homeless were still an eyesore, but in time they would be replaced and perhaps if he qualified he could make a difference.

He had to believe there were better times to come, or he would not have been able to carry on. He had to believe that Rulka would recover and one day there would be an independent Poland, free of the Soviet shackles. He had taken a leaf from Rulka's book and joined the workers' union, and although it wasn't like a union in the West, independent and able to negotiate freely; it was beavering away clandestinely to that end. He smiled wryly; who would have dreamt, back in those heady days before the war when he had the world at his feet, that he would come to this and be grateful for it? He was grateful he had his health and strength, grateful for a job and a home, grateful and humble for Rulka and her stoical courage.

He told himself that a hundred times a day, but under it all was a deep melancholy for what he had lost. And days like today, when the work he was doing had been especially irksome and the books he was studying palled, and particularly when he had stood in the street and watched a single-seater aeroplane swooping low over the river, its wings glinting in the sun, he yearned for what had been and would never come again, and longed for Louise. He had never written to her. In the beginning he had started several letters but then realised the futility of it and thrown them on the fire.

Did she remember him with fondness? He liked to think she did. But what about Angela? She had only been four when he left, she would hardly remember her *tata*. Had Louise told her about him? Did she know who had fathered her? Or had Louise married and given their daughter a new father? He delved into the box of papers, extracted an envelope and tipped its contents into his palm. A tiny, soft blonde curl lay there. He closed his fist over it and wept.

'Dear Miss Fairhurst, Further to your enquiry about Flight Lieutenant Jan Grabowski, I am afraid we do not know what happened to him after September 1946 when he was discharged from the Air Force. We believe he returned to Poland and though we are sometimes able to help ex-members of the air force in Poland, he is not on our books. We have, however, passed your enquiry on to a member of our association who may be able to help you. His name is Mr Boris Martel. You should hear from him in due course.' The letter was signed by the secretary of the Polish Airman's Association.

It had been Tommy's idea to write to them. 'I believe they give advice and financial help to ex-Polish airman in need,' he had said. 'I think it's only for men still in England, but it's worth a try.'

It was the first half-positive reply Angela had had and she gave a whoop of triumph and tucked it into her jacket pocket intending to show it to Tommy when he came home from work. He had a job at Marshall's aircraft works in Cambridge and commuted every day from the Pheasant while he looked for somewhere permanent to live.

'Don't get so excited,' he warned her that evening. 'It's something and nothing. And how do you know this Boris Martel will even contact you?'

'I don't, but it's a name. I looked it up in the telephone directory. There's only one Boris Martel listed. It's a London number.'

'Angela, you must not ring him, you really must not. Wait for him to get in touch with you if he wants to. Have you shown this to your mother?'

'No. She told me to give up.'

'Then perhaps that's what you should do.'

'Tommy Carter, you are being a stuffy old man.'

He laughed 'So I'm stuffy, am I? Too old and stuffy to take you to the dance on Saturday?'

'No, I didn't mean it. I want to go to the dance. But I can't give up. Don't you understand? It's all about who I am, the genes that made me. Mum says I'm like him. I want to see that for myself.'

'OK, so you tell your mother about that letter and I'll take you.'

'He's too old for her,' Faith said, referring to Tommy Carter's friendship with Angela. 'She's still a child and he's a grown man.' They were talking in the kitchen while they washed up the dinner plates. Angela and Tommy were in the living room; they could hear their low voices and the occasional burst of laughter.

'Mum, she is no longer a child, she is a young woman and I have nothing against Tommy, nothing at all. He used to look out for her when she was a toddler, like a big brother. I've no doubt that's how she sees him now.'

'I don't know what the world is coming to. Am I supposed to stand by and watch my granddaughter make a fool of herself?'

Louise sighed heavily. 'I don't think she will, Mum.'

'I suppose she got her wilfulness from her father.'

'You never met him, Mum.'

'No, nor do I want to. If Angela brings him here, I shall leave.'

'Whatever are you talking about? No one has suggested he should come here, even if Angela were to find him.' It was becoming harder and harder to deal diplomatically with her mother, and though she might dismiss the idea of Jan coming to Cottlesham, there was a corner of her heart and mind that dreamt of it happening. 'The reason he left in the first place is just as valid now as it was then.'

'All the same, I give you due warning.'

Louise laughed. As a threat it was meaningless, but it did show just how far apart they were on some issues. She hung up the tea cloth. 'Let's go back to Angela and Tom, but please don't say anything more about Angela's search for Jan. Leave that to me. She's off to Rome next week, in any case; she might forget all about it.'

'I think she ought to go back to hospital,' Lech said, looking down at Rulka. 'You can't look after her properly here.'

'Yes, I can.' Jan sat on the edge of the bed and took Rulka's hand. 'What do you say, Myszka?'

'I want to stay here.' The voice was barely audible.

'Then you shall.' He turned to Lech. 'Tell me what to do and I'll do it.'

They left Rulka to sleep and returned to the sitting room where Jan poured them both a shot of vodka.

Rulka had come through an operation to remove her breast, but she had not picked up as they had hoped. It was feared the cancer had spread. Jan looked after her devotedly. It was his fault she was like she was; he had left her to fend for herself when he should have been at her side shielding her, preventing her from driving herself so hard in the Home Army. She might then have come through the ordeal of the occupation in good health. His guilt was compounded by his inability to forget his life in that other world, so far from the reality of his present existence, it seemed like a dream. He shook these thoughts from him to listen to what Lech was telling him.

'You do realise, Jan, that it is only palliative care she needs now, don't you?'

'Yes.'

'I'm sorry.'

'You have nothing to be sorry for. You've been a good friend to us. I often wonder if things would have been different if I had stayed in Warsaw in '39.'

'You would almost certainly have been arrested, if not by the Germans then the Russians. It would not have made any difference to Rulka; she would still have done what she felt she had to do. She always used to say she was glad you were safely out of it.' He paused to drain his glass. 'Let me know when you need me.'

'I will.'

He left and Jan went back to Rulka. She was awake and smiled wanly. 'Poor you,' she said.

'Why poor me?'

'You will have to carry on. I'll be out of it. At peace.'

It was no good denying it; she was a nurse and knew exactly what was happening to her. 'Are you worried about it?'

'No. I've had enough, there's no fight left in me. It's time to go. But I worry about you.'

'Don't think about it.'

'Don't grieve, Jan. Don't go about with a long face for me. The Rulka Grabowska you knew died and was buried in 1942. The woman you have been living with since you came back is a wraith. And now she must go too. Give thanks, as I do, for the life we had.'

'Stop talking, Myszka, you'll wear yourself out. Go to sleep.'

She subsided against the pillow, a slight smile on her lips. 'Good night, my love, pleasant dreams.'

He bent to kiss her and watched until she fell asleep. For almost the first time since he had come back, he felt the tug of a love he thought had vanished and could not stem the tears.

She died in his arms in the early hours of the morning. He sat holding her for an hour, unwilling to give her up to death, but in the end he laid her gently on the bed and went down to the hall where there was a communal telephone, and rang Lech.

He attended the funeral in a daze, watched the coffin being lowered, scattered a handful of soil on it and wondered what his life had all been about.

'Dear Miss Fairhurst, your letter to the Polish Airman's Association has been passed to me. I confess I am surprised to hear the Flight Lieutenant had a daughter but I only met him once in 1946 when I returned to England from Poland and brought him news of his wife. As far as I am aware he returned to her. I have not been back to Poland since then, so I cannot vouch for that. I must caution you against interfering, not only because his wife may not know about you, but also because of the political situation. I ask you to think long and hard before pursuing this enquiry. Yours sincerely, Boris Martel.'

'Damn him!' Angela said. 'Damn him, damn him, damn him.' She stuffed the letter back into the envelope and put it in her bag. If he thought she was going to give up, he had better think again. She left to go to work without showing the missive to her mother. All day, while she served the Pheasant's guests, she brooded on it. Boris Martel had been her only lead, she had been banking on his being able to tell her something. She still thought he could if he wanted to. The letter had an address at the top of it; there was nothing for it but to beard him in his den. She'd go on Saturday. All she had to do was persuade Tommy to go with her and not tell her mother.

He was above middle age, tall and thin, with a mass of iron-grey hair. There was a scar down one side of his face which hardly showed when his face was still, but wrinkled when he smiled, which he did now as he showed her into a spacious sitting room and indicated a couple of armchairs. 'Please sit down, Miss Fairhurst, Mr Carter. I must confess I did not expect you to arrive on my doorstep.'

'I wanted to meet you face to face,' she said.

'Why? I explained the position in my letter.'

'And very unsatisfactory it was too. Did you think I would take no for an answer and meekly give up? I have always been led to believe my father was killed in the war and when I found he had not, that he might still be alive, can you blame me for wanting to find him?'

'No, but he has a wife.'

'I am aware of that. It was the only reason he and my mother did not marry. Theirs was a true love story.'

He smiled. 'My dear young lady, you are not the only English child with a Polish father.'

'I don't suppose I am, but that doesn't alter the fact that I want to know if he is alive, to meet him if it's possible, and if not at least let him know that I think of him and wish I could get to know him.'

'I knew his wife well during the war, she was a very brave lady. I should hate to be responsible for causing her a moment's unhappiness.'

'You are assuming he has not told her about me. That might not be the case.'

'If you can give us the smallest clue, we would be very grateful,' Tommy put in.

'And what is your interest in the affair, Mr Carter?'

'I am a long-standing friend of the family and I knew Jan well. I am convinced he would like to know that he can be proud of his daughter. I thought we could work through intermediaries.'

305

Boris paced the floor. 'It is years since I was in Warsaw. Times have changed, are changing . . .' He paused. 'There is a name I could give you, but before I do, I want your assurance you will not make direct contact with Jan. It would be for him to approach you.'

Angela had that stubborn look on her face Tom had become familiar with in the last few months. He smiled at their host. 'You have it,' he said quickly. 'Isn't that so, Angela?'

She nodded; if that was the way it had to be done, so be it.

Boris went to a desk, pulled out a sheet of paper, took the cap off a fountain pen and wrote down a name and address. 'This is where he was in 1946,' he said. 'I cannot guarantee he will still be there.' He handed the paper to Tom. 'Let me know how you get on.'

Stanisław Roman often went to the Church of the Holy Cross to consult Father Karlowicz about funerals, but today's visit had nothing to do with a dead body needing burial. He had received a strange letter that morning. The envelope bore British postage stamps and contained a photograph enclosed in another page of closely written script. The words were in English and all he could make out was the name Jan Grabowski. His first reaction had been to take it to Jan, who knew English, but on reflection he decided to consult the good father first.

He found the priest enjoying a cup of coffee laced with vodka while toasting his toes by a fire in his quarters; at his age he felt the cold in his extremities even in summer. He greeted Stanisław and stood up to pour more coffee and vodka. The two enjoyed a close friendship which had begun during the occupation, when both had been working towards the same end. They had seen the destruction of their beloved city and watched it emerge from the ashes, almost as good as new. Neither liked the regime under which they lived and longed for a free, independent Poland, but the days of militant action had gone. It served no purpose except to bring the Soviet Union down on the perpetrators with brute force. The events in Hungary four years before had taught them that. They had to be more subtle and more patient, but both were convinced it would happen in the end.

But it was not that which occupied Stanisław on this occasion. He sat down and handed the letter to the priest. 'This came today,' he said. 'It's in English. Can you understand it?'

The old man perched a pair of wire-framed spectacles on his nose to read it. It took some time because he was translating as he read aloud and his English was rusty. 'How extraordinary,' he said when he finished. 'I would never have believed it of Jan. He was devoted to Rulka.'

Stanisław picked up the photograph and studied it. It pictured a woman and a young lady, presumably mother and daughter. The elder appeared to be in her early forties. She was slim and dressed in a flowered skirt and a white blouse. Her dark hair curled about her ears and she had a smiling mouth. The younger one was in jeans and shirt with the sleeves rolled up. Her hair was fair and tied back in a ponytail. She was holding a stuffed toy. 'Apparently devoted to an English schoolteacher as well, if this young lady is telling the truth,' he said.

'Don't you think she is?'

'She says Boris Martel gave her my address,' Stanisław said. 'So presumably he believed it. The question is, do we tell Jan? It's only a couple of months since Rulka died.'

'True,' the priest said thoughtfully. 'I have been worried about that young man. He seems lost and bewildered since she died. This might be a way of reviving his spirits. On the other hand, it

307

might send him into even greater gloom. He is unlikely to be given permission to leave the country and I would not recommend the young lady to come here, even if he did want to meet her.'

'You think we should do nothing about it, then?' Stanisław prompted.

'I did not say that. I was simply thinking aloud. I'll go and talk to him, try and find out what's going on in his head, how he feels. If I think he should know about this . . .' – he stopped to consult the letter – 'Angela Fairhurst, then I will give him the letter.'

Jan had returned from his day's work to an empty apartment. Before long someone would suggest that, being a single man, he did not need so many rooms and he would be asked to downgrade to allow a family to take the tenancy. When that happened, he would have lost his last link with Rulka. He had already given her clothes to charity and destroyed all evidence of her involvement with the underground as had been her wish. There was nothing left of her. He felt lost, as if he had found himself in an alien land that did not welcome him. Poland was not the Poland of his boyhood and without Rulka his whole *raison d'être* had collapsed.

He thought about trying to return to England but dismissed the idea as impractical. Even if he could get an exit visa, too many years had passed. Louise might have changed, more than likely had married and had a new family. She might not have told Angela about him. He would be an interloper. And what had he to offer? He had very little money and hardly a decent suit of clothes. It was nothing but a pipe dream.

He had just finished eating a frugal meal when Father Karlowicz arrived. His company was welcome and he greeted him amiably. 'Father, good to see you. I suppose you have come to chide me for not coming to confession.'

'There is that, of course, but it is not why I am here. I have been worried about you.'

'Worried about me? Why?' He went to a cupboard and brought out a bottle of vodka and two glasses and poured them both a drink. Then they sat together at the table.

'You do not seem yourself. It is as if when Rulka died, a little of you died too.'

'Perhaps it did.'

'You are a young man still, your life is before you.' He paused. 'I would help you if I could.'

'I don't think you can.'

'Try me. Tell me about your life in England.'

'England?' Jan queried, astonished. 'What do you want to know?'

'Anything you choose to tell me. You were a young man a long way from home, in constant danger, perhaps lonely, perhaps missing your wife. Did you make friends with your hosts? I have heard the Polish airmen were feted by the populace for what they did in the Battle of Britain. Did you find it so?'

'Yes. I made some good friends.'

'Tell me about them? Was there one in particular?'

Jan was startled. 'Where is all this leading, Father?'

'I wondered if you might like to unburden yourself.'

Jan took a gulp of vodka. 'And you think telling you will help me get over Rulka?'

'So, there is something to tell.'

'Father, stop sparring with me. I am not a fool. You know something, so you might as well come right out with it.'

The priest felt in the roomy pocket of his skirt, took out the letter and laid it on the table in front of Jan.

Jan stared at it. The envelope was addressed to Stanisław

Roman in English lettering and it had English stamps. Slowly he picked it up and extracted a sheet of paper. As he unfolded it, a snapshot fell out. He picked it up. 'Oh, my God, it's Louise.' She had changed very little; still slim and lovely, still with a smile that could light up a room. 'And Angela.' He gave a cracked laugh. 'She is holding Cuddles.'

'You know them?' the priest asked.

'Of course I know them.'

'Then read the letter.'

Jan scanned it, not once, but twice, watched intently by the old man, who took an occasional sip from his glass.

'When did this come?' His voice was so tearful, the question came out as a croak. He had been thinking and wondering about his little family and here was news of them. The best news ever. He had not been forgotten, Louise had not married and his daughter wanted to make his acquaintance. There was a heaven, after all.

'This morning. Stanisław brought it straight to me to translate.'

'So you have read it?'

'Yes. What do you want to do about it?'

'Answer it, of course.'

Jan was hardly aware that the priest had blessed him and left. He continued to sit at the table looking at the picture, studying every feature, and reading the letter over and over again. Then he fetched out writing paper and a pen and began to write. He made several attempts to put into words what he felt, but it was impossible. One after the other he screwed them up and threw them on the fire, watching them curl up, turn brown and burst into flame.

Angela returned from Rome, brown as a berry and full of what she had seen and done, the day before her exam results came through. She had passed with flying colours and could take up her place at Homerton and there was the added bonus that Tommy was living and working in Cambridge. Life was exciting and not even her disappointment over not hearing from Poland could dampen her exuberance. Jenny, who was almost as proud of her as her mother, put on a celebration meal at the Pheasant. She had her first glass of champagne and laughed as the fizz went up her nose. It was a happy time, this moving from childhood to womanhood, from total dependence to making her own decisions. It was unnerving in a way, but on the other hand she couldn't wait to savour it.

Tommy raised his glass to her. 'Here's to your new life and continuing success.'

They all said 'Here, here.' and she basked in their good wishes.

Walking home along the leafy lanes afterwards, she took her mother's arm and laid her head on it. 'Will you miss me when I leave home?' she asked.

'Of course I will, can you doubt it? But you are grown up now. I can't keep you tied to my apron strings. And I will have Granny for company.' She wondered how she and her mother would deal with each other when there was only the two of them in the house. At least Mum might stop finding fault. She was glad she had her job and could retreat behind her books and lesson preparation.

'I wish my father could have been here tonight.'

'So do I. He would have been so proud of you.'

Angela looked up at the clear night sky. 'Those same stars are shining over Poland too, aren't they? We aren't so very far apart.'

'No, looked at it like that, the world is a small place.'

'I thought he might at least have answered my letter.'

'You can't be sure he received it.' In a way Louise hoped that was the case, it was easier to bear than the thought he simply didn't want to have anything to do with her or his daughter. 'Never mind, we'll enjoy our holiday, won't we?'

They were going up to the Lake District to stay in the cottage that she and Jan had used when he was on leave, though it had been extended and modernised to accommodate tourists. She had taken Angela up there the first year after the war and they had roamed over the hills, taken a boat out on the lakes and generally lazed about. Angela had loved it and so they had gone again the following year. It had become an annual pilgrimage, though Angela had never known why it was so special. Louise wondered if this year might be the last time they would do it together.

Ambleside was crowded with tourists, but the cottage was a little way off the beaten track up a steep, winding road. 'Your father used to carry you up here,' Louise said as they toiled up to it, carrying shopping bags of provisions. They had spent two days walking and climbing and on the third decided to go down to the lake and take the passenger ferry to Windermere and do some shopping. 'He carried you everywhere.'

'We came here with him? You never said before.'

'No. It was wartime. When he was on leave we used to come up here to escape everyone.'

She stopped to change hands with the shopping bags. 'I swear this hill gets steeper every year.'

'There's someone standing by our cottage gate. He looks a bit lost.'

The man didn't move, but stood watching them approach. Louise looked up and her heart skipped a beat. It was an hallucination, of course it was. She had just been talking about him, remembering what it had been like years before and her imagination had conjured him up. This man, in sports jacket and beige trousers, was a stranger, he had to be, but oh . . .

'All the same we will do it,' Jan said.

'That's as it should be,' Faith said. 'I've made my own arrangements. I'm going to move into one of the bungalows on the Sadler estate so you can have the place to yourselves.'

'When did you decide to do that?' Louise demanded.

'As soon as I knew Angela was determined to find her father. I knew she wouldn't give up.'

Angela laughed and hugged her grandmother. 'Granny, you are priceless.'

Faith beamed. For once in her life, she had done the right thing. Jan wasn't the ogre she had always imagined him to be, he was charming and considerate and she could see why Louise had fallen for him. But she could not stay under the same roof while they were sharing a bed. Louise might say she considered herself married but she wasn't, was she? They laughed when she suggested he should stay at the Pheasant until the wedding.

'How would that look, Mum?' Louise said. 'My husband comes back after years away and I send him off to sleep somewhere else. Have a heart.'

Faith had no answer to that and was very glad when a bungalow became vacant and she could move.

The wedding took place in Norwich on the last Saturday in September. Stan, Jenny, Angela, Faith and Tommy were the only witnesses. Louise, wearing a suit in pale-blue shantung, could not have been happier. It had been a long, long wait but it was worth it. Jan had always got on well with Stan and Jenny, but it was wonderful to watch him and Angela together. They talked and laughed and teased, just as if they had never been apart.

'You're glad now that I went in search of my *tata*, aren't you?' Angela asked her mother when they were all round the table at

316

the Bell having a celebratory luncheon. 'You would never have got together again if I hadn't.'

Louise reached out and put her hand over Jan's. 'Yes, I'm very, very glad.'

Jan had bought a small car and the week before they had taken Angela to Cambridge and settled her into her accommodation, and afterwards Jan had gone for a job interview. Knowing Marshalls wanted a pilot to ferry wealthy passengers in small private aeroplanes, Tommy had spoken to his boss and Jan had been offered the job. 'I'm going to be flying again,' he had told Louise, whirling her round and round the hotel room they had taken at the University Arms until they were both dizzy and fell onto the bed laughing.

After the wedding breakfast, the guests went home, leaving Jan and Louise to enjoy the rest of the weekend together. They wandered about the town, visited the castle, walked along by the river, stayed in bed late. She couldn't say that the years apart had shrunk to nothing because they were both older and perhaps wiser, but their feelings for each other had not diminished. They were still young, young enough to enjoy each other, to look forward and not backward.

Jan watched her cross the playground and usher her pupils inside, then he set off for Cambridge and his first day in his new job. The misery of the post-war years in a Poland he could not recognise was behind him and the future beckoned. One day, when Poland was truly free, he would take his wife and daughter on a visit. Until then, he was content.

Author's Note

I would like to acknowledge the generous help given to me by Adam Zamoyski, who vetted my spelling of Polish words and set me right about people and events.

Mr Zamoyski is an award-winning historian and author of several books on European and world history, among them *A History of Poland* and *The Forgotten Few: The Polish Air Force in World War II*. He is also a distinguished commentator and reviewer. I am in his debt. Any errors remaining are, of course, my own.

Bibliography

The following are among the many books I used in researching this novel.

Rising '44: The Battle for Warsaw by Norman Davies, Pan Books, 2004

The Forgotten Few: The Polish Air Force in World War II by Adam Zamoyski, Pen & Sword Aviation Books, 2009

For Your Freedom and Ours: The Kościuszkco Squadron by Lynne Olson and Stanley Cloud, Arrow Books, 2004

Story of a Secret State: My Report to the World by Jan Karski, Penguin Classics, 1944

Poland Alone: Britain, SOE and the Collapse of the Polish Resistance 1944 by Jonathan Walker, Spellmount

The Struggle: Biography of a Fighter Pilot by Franciszek Kornicki, published in Poland by Stratus 2008 and in England by Mushroom Model Publications

The Spy Who Loved: The Secrets and Lives of Christine Granville by Clare Mulley, Macmillan, 2013

Spies in the Sky: The Secret Battle for Aerial Intelligence during WWI by Taylor Downing, Little Brown, 2011

RAF Evaders: The Comprehensive Story of Thousands of Escapers and Their Escape Lines; Western Europe, 1940-1945 by Oliver Clutton-Brock, Bounty Books, 2009

A World to Build: Austerity Britain 1945-48 by David Kynaston, Bloomsbury, 2007